outer sunset

A Novel

MARK ERNEST POTHIER

University of Iowa Press, Iowa City

University of Iowa Press, Iowa City 52242
Copyright © 2023 by Mark Ernest Pothier
uipress.uiowa.edu
Printed in the United States of America

Design by Erin Kirk

This book is a work of fiction. Any reference to historical events,
real people, or real locales are used fictitiously.

Printed on acid-free paper

Library of Congress Cataloging–in–Publication Data
Names: Pothier, Mark Ernest, 1959– author.
Title: Outer Sunset: A Novel / by Mark Ernest Pothier.
Description: Iowa City: University of Iowa Press, 2023.
Identifiers: LCCN 2022040049 (print) | LCCN 2022040050 (ebook) |
    ISBN 9781609388836 (paperback) | ISBN 9781609388843 (ebook)
Subjects: LCGFT: Novels.
Classification: LCC PS3616.O8438 O98 2023 (print) | LCC PS3616.O8438
    (ebook) | DDC 813/.6—dc23
LC record available at https://lccn.loc.gov/2022040049
LC ebook record available at https://lccn.loc.gov/2022040050

"Final Soliloquy of the Interior Paramour," copyright © 1951 by
Wallace Stevens; from *The Collected Poems of Wallace Stevens*
by Wallace Stevens. Used by permission of Alfred A. Knopf, an
imprint of the Knopf Doubleday Publishing Group, a division of
Penguin Random House LLC. All rights reserved.

for Kee

part one

CHAPTER 1

Three years ago, once it was clear our kids were gone for good, my wife packed the car with some clothes and things, told me she'd withdrawn half the savings, and, after a farewell that I cannot recall verbatim, she left.

Since that day, I've spent a good deal of my time reading in this back room. I'd drywalled this room, originally the porch, for Jackie. The house felt smaller when the kids were young, and one day she said we needed extra storage for earthquake supplies; there's no basement to speak of, as the entire neighborhood is built on dunes. I was still working then—I used to be a high school English teacher—so I had some spare time one summer, and we never expected the landlord to do anything. For a few years afterward, Jackie made pickles and stored them in the corner where my chair is now. Sometimes that irony amuses me. The room is small, with two windows facing the backyard and a door between them. It turned out it wasn't practical to have two windows in a room that would be used for storing pickles, but you can always pull a shade, whereas seeing outside without a window is another matter entirely. The room doesn't echo emptiness like most of the others, so I spend my time here comfortably enough. One thing can be said for aging and a certain amount of solitude: It helps you accept what you are and are not. One thing I'm not is a carpenter.

Nor am I a gardener. When my daughter, Dorothy, visited so often out of concern just after her mother left, she used to try to coax me back inside whenever she caught me sitting here looking out the windows at the flowers and shrubs her mother had planted years ago. Because Dorothy is the most attentive person I know, I believe she worried that even the least reminder of my wife would crush me. I'm not as tender as all that, nor can you uproot the recollections of more than thirty years so easily. Weeding through memories is a wheat and chaff situation, so I try not to pull up either. Besides, I wasn't just sitting here staring at the yard, which is still quite overgrown; I was also reading the pile of books I'd always said I would read if given the chance. Even now, when I look up to rest my eyes, I'm pleased to see the borders blur as weeds gain control and the roses dry to tangled dead buds. That progress marks the passage of time, and it soothes me whenever I feel bitter—the last thing any self-respecting man my age should allow himself to do after a drink.

Another fact that I'm fairly resigned to is that I am not, and never was, much of a writer. This realization was a bit trickier than with carpentry and gardening. Jackie might chuckle if I were to share that discovery with her now after so many years, but she's gone, and I've learned that the only way to be good company when alone is to be frank with yourself.

It was just after she'd left, and my son, Gerald, had come back to stay with me for the summer. He'd been attending community college and living with his buddies and their pony-sized dogs in a big house in Marin, but he said he needed to pursue some tech training after work, down the peninsula, and that he preferred to spend nights in his old bedroom here, near the beach, rather than commute north through the fog each night. My guess was Dorothy had asked him to spell her a few weeks in watching over me. Either way, he was much quieter than I remembered. Jackie'd always said I was too critical of him, and like so many of her other words that poured back in her absence, I wondered if she hadn't been right in that too, so that summer I tried to stay out of his way.

We fell into an easy routine. When he came home from classes we'd chat a bit over a cocktail in this back room, and then I'd cook. After dinner, he'd go out or watch television in his bedroom, and I'd stay out here. One warm evening the fog didn't begin to roll in until around dusk—rare for us on the coast in San Francisco—and as we sat before dinner, I noticed the rosy glow of the sunset as it reflected off the backs of the stucco houses behind mine. An autumnal light struck a eucalyptus tree outside the dark outline of my house, the crisp shadows making each leaf distinct, like backlit stained glass. I was certain it would last only a moment. I remembered a line of Wallace Stevens's—"Light the first light of evening"—and as it grew darker outside my window, I closed my eyes to recite the entire "Final Soliloquy of the Interior Paramour." It's one of my favorites, although impossible to teach to high school kids. I had memorized the poem when I was young, back when I thought it was the real world, and not the imagined, that held all the delight awaiting me in life. The poem itself was new then. Jackie, to whom I'd once whispered it for the simple enclosing sounds alone, had been young then too.

> *Out of this same light, out of the central mind,*
> *We make a dwelling in the evening air,*
> *In which being there together is enough.*

Oh my, I thought.

I thought I'd always understood those lines, but sitting there that evening a lump grew in my throat. *My life is mostly past and I still have yet to say anything so beautifully.*

Behind me, Gerald heavy-handedly mixed a drink.

I'm not so callow, I told myself, that such a delicate disappointment could make me weep. By having acknowledged it, I expected the lump to go away. But it would not. It was fear, I think. I was instantly and deeply afraid that the solitude I'd garnered all my life would prove to be worth nothing.

So, when my son returned, I stood to embrace him for the first time in years, thinking: *One thing I am, and that I will always be, is a father.*

But, at the same time, I thought: *Jackie would have liked to see this.* We fell away. He handed me my drink; he'd made plans to go out.

Gerald moved back in with his friends, and Dorothy stopped visiting like she used to, so I usually spent this time of day—dusk—out here alone, in my chair. There's a wonderful all-night jazz station, and in the violet light, before I turn on the lamp and draw the shades, an alto sax can sound so sweet it stills my mind. Then I'd close my book, make one of the martinis I'd been relying on, and I'd wait for the moon or the first star or, if it was foggy, for my backyard neighbors to turn on a television. Being alone is usually easy at such times: You can sink so softly into your thoughts that whatever sadness you felt during the day fades into melancholy—which is, I've found, a trustworthy pleasure.

Then I had a date.

Dorothy first introduced me to Carol, one of her work friends, at her thirtieth birthday picnic in Golden Gate Park. It was an unusually big shindig for Dorothy to throw herself, especially with her mother off on vacation somewhere, and she'd looked surprisingly exhausted to me, rushing around filling cups while her own stayed empty, dodging lawn darts and asking everybody questions without saying much herself. As soon as she'd spied me snuggling in by the cooler, she sought out Carol, pulled her by the elbow through the crowd, and planted her in the lawn chair next to mine. She then stood back a second as if composing one of her photos, smiled, and left the two of us alone.

Because, you see: Carol is just a few years younger than I am, and she's single. She's a reader too. She's my height—that is, on the short side—with thick salt-and-pepper curls that, when she's not smoking, she repeatedly tucks behind her ears. Her black-coffee eyes are warm and bright, and what little of her slight body has bowed to age—her shoulders, maybe, or the corners of her smile—has done so with grace. She talked easily, in a way that made me feel as if we'd already met. Of course I had no idea I was being "set up" when I'd accepted Dorothy's party invitation, but I found I wasn't unhappy about it either, and once, after some small talk, I surprised us both by saying as much to Carol, her sudden, sharp laugh made it clear she felt the same. We chatted till twilight and the dousing of the grill. It's strange: When I was young and meeting a girl for the first time, my mouth would be shut and my hands deep in my pockets. It's become simpler, somehow; I still have a few things left to lose, but these days, losing holds more promise than keeping.

Because we'd talked a great deal about our favorite cookbooks but also about how little cooking we'd actually been doing for ourselves, I invited her to the house for dinner sometime. We could walk out for a drink or movie afterward, I suggested. "Let's play it by ear," she said, accepting. After we'd parted, however, and I chose the long walk home alone, across the park, I wondered: Why did I just invite her *out here*? Certainly the world had changed since I was in college, and I knew cooking for a woman on a first date wasn't out of the ordinary, but still: I felt unsettled. For the past three years, the only woman to set foot in this house has been Dorothy. And an assessor.

Anyway, I soon looked forward to the intrusion. Carol would come over, I imagined, and I'd pour us drinks; we'd sit in this back room and she'd talk and new memories would be made to erase all the words I still sometimes hear—a new voice in the window screens, a new laugh sweeping the corners of the ceiling. Perhaps, she'd help in the kitchen; we'd work together at the counter and we'd reclaim that territory too. Perhaps, in time, we'd work our way through the entire house, chasing ghosts. Then I recalled that I didn't even know her last name.

I dusted the house. The chair I occupy out back is in a sad state, so I put a quilt over it. We would avoid the living room, in the front—an overly composed shrine where no one has looked at home since the kids left. Had Jackie, when moving out, packed up a U-Haul instead of the car, I would have pushed out all the resolute furniture she'd corralled in there.

Carol arrived at six sharp, just as she'd said she would, and the novelty of her made the house look twice as dingy. Blinking under the front door light—the fog was already thick—her big eyes gleamed.

She was wearing a necklace of large, colorful beads and a wine-red cardigan over a white cotton blouse. I wasn't prepared for how quickly the living room faded into gray obscurity the moment she entered. I may have whisked her in by the elbow, rushing her through the living and dining rooms, to the kitchen.

I thought she must have felt as uncomfortable as I did, so I offered her a drink. After a moment of standing in the doorway, righting her shoulders against the jamb, she walked over to the oven door, peeked in at the roast, and said coffee would be fine. That was when I remembered I hadn't seen her drink anything but club soda at the picnic, and that I had nothing else to offer her but flat tonic water. When I asked if she minded my having a glass of the wine I'd already opened, she asked if I minded her chain-smoking, and, relieved, we laughed a bit. I put the kettle on. *It's just as well*, I thought. *I have only one wineglass.*

We both relaxed after we sat on the porch, radio on, her sipping her coffee and smoking several cigarettes. She reminded me again of how proud I should be of Dorothy—how creative and dependable she was to work with—and described her concerns about her own son, who is Dorothy's age and lives somewhere in Oregon. She told the story of how she'd moved from New Jersey to Berkeley for college ("to reinvent myself"), where she'd been during the Loma Prieta earthquake, how crowded the Bay Area had become because of the internet, and how she hoped "the Y2K thing" might slow it down. She told me about her career change to become a counselor-in-training, and how she, like me, doesn't own a car. She pointed out a few biographies she recognized in the "to-do" stack of books by my chair. The longer our conversation meandered, the more comfortable I became. She wore wooden bracelets that matched her necklace, and they rattled gently, like branches, each time she drew on her cigarette. Jazz played softly, and the fog blanketed the tatty boxwoods that border my yard, falling from the eaves and over the windows to mimic Carol's curling smoke. In fact, the room was growing woolly with smoke—we had the windows near closed to keep out the chill—but I didn't mind. How long had it been since I'd sat here with someone my age, in the chair next to mine, who wanted to talk to me? As it grew dark outside, I shut off the oven and poured more wine and coffee and we continued to talk with just the light above the kitchen sink reaching us through the doorway as the fog hid my neighbors' windows. Carol's eyes sparked in the shadows. I could have sat like that all night, watching her gaze past the windowsill, her face lit by the glow of her cigarette as her words filled the room. Then she abruptly turned to me and said, almost sharply, "You must be hungry by *now*?"

I shot up, apologized, and asked if she'd like to help in the kitchen.

I'd earlier hoped to ease the awkwardness of a first date by making the salad and sauce together while the roast finished in the oven, but by the time we started, it was so late we did these chores without a word. She ate a few radishes from the bowl. In the refrigerator, a round of cheese I'd meant for an appetizer sat under the light, cold and ignored, and when I pulled it out to offer it to Carol, I found her looking out the window above the sink, drinking a glass of water. She had her back to me. I felt a shiver of surprise: Until last week, I couldn't imagine even the fragrance of any woman but Jackie in this place; I still find her scent on pillowcases in the back of the linen closet, or buried in the folds of the few scarves she'd left behind.

We both felt better once the meal was ready. She said she was sorry for being impatient; she'd eaten little all day. I apologized in return because the roast was overdone, but she said she preferred it that way.

I always take my meals—when they're large enough for a dinner plate—in the kitchen, but I had thought it might be too casual, or too intimate even, for Carol and me to sit at either side of the yellow Formica table. So, even though the dining room now serves as little more than a passageway between the kitchen and living room, and despite my avoidance of the latter, I'd polished the old oak table before she arrived, set down place mats, and put out some flowers I'd clipped from the bushes that overhang my fence. From the kitchen, I could see Carol moving around out there, lighting candles. She switched on the lamp in the corner of the living room and peered deep into the stereo console to turn on the radio. It hadn't been used in years. The speaker crackled as if clearing its throat; a piano came through hesitantly, followed by an upright bass.

She returned to the kitchen with a toothy, reassuring smile, but we didn't say a word. She took her ashtray from the windowsill, emptied it, polished it with a paper towel, and went back out to the table.

She was seated by the time I arrived with the platter. Her smoke had been carried out with the aromas wafting from the kitchen, but that was fine. I've always liked the crisp, bitter smell of exhaled smoke; mingling with the lavender and ocean air that seeps in my windows, it was refreshing somehow. The dining room seemed new.

As she unfolded her napkin, she paused a moment to take in the table, then me, and said, "This is lovely, Jim." Candlelight flickered in her eyes.

"Thank you," I said, surprised at how deeply I meant it.

She was hungry, quiet. It seemed dinnertime was my turn to talk, and, with something like gratitude, I did.

I'm leaving you, Jackie shouted back to me three years ago. *You need to listen to me this time. I'm leaving you now.*

Let me fix you something, I'd said. *Come sit out here with me.* I remember thinking: This is just Jackie going through her change.

I'm not sitting with you anymore, she yelled. *I'm leaving you. I'm starting now.*

In the corner of my eye, I'd caught the leaves of the hedge outside my window fluttering in the afternoon breeze. That hadn't been intentional on my part; it's simply the sort of thing I see.

I don't love you anymore. Jackie's voice receded as she rushed through the rooms. *I can't continue living like this, lonely with you, waiting for something. You say you can't live without me, but it's all in your head. You can. You have been for years. I'm not self-sufficient like you. I can't live alone, up in the air. I'm not blaming you. I don't expect anything more from you than to understand what's happening now: I am taking these things, and coming back for the rest. I took half the savings and one of the cards. The rest is yours. We can talk later if you want. We can meet later, after a while, if there's a need. After a while.*

Then, turning, outside the front door, she said: *I wish I could have told you sooner.*

I've rerun this story so many times these past three years that I don't trust the details. If I'd bothered with formal divorce proceedings, I might now hold a record of facts—quantified losses, measured distances, all nailed down on paper. But the truth is: I can find a way to doubt anything. Even at fifty-eight. I always have.

Perhaps that's why, that night with Carol, I couldn't bring myself to repeat any of the words Jackie had used when she left me. Or maybe, like eating together at our small kitchen table, it might have felt too close. Instead, what I did tell Carol over dinner was the history of how my back room came to be, how little my kids visit now, and how relieved I am to be free to read whatever I want after years of teaching.

Carol gave the impression that she was enrapt. It's a deep pleasure to be listened to so generously. Sometimes she nodded along and laughed, and sometimes she asked questions and her eyes went moist with sympathy, and it became impossible to feel alone. How she managed to eat so quickly throughout all this is beyond me, but it slowly became clear that she'd finished her meal and that, although I'd nearly finished my wine, I'd barely touched my plate.

We again grew quiet, as we had earlier in the kitchen. I put down my fork and emptied my glass.

"I'm afraid we're late for a movie," I said.

She looked away, almost shyly, and reached for her cigarettes. She wasn't the bashful type; it was stirring.

"That's okay," she said. "You're quite a storyteller. How about a walk? On the beach—some fresh air?"

Good idea. I was full. We could walk the mile and a half up to the Cliff House for a nightcap.

I could see Carol wasn't prepared for the cold, wearing just a cardigan, so I rummaged through the front closet and found a scarf and one of the jackets Jackie'd left behind. I'm not sure why it was still there, but I wasn't surprised to find it, nor was I surprised that it was too big for Carol. She wrapped the scarf over her head like a cowl. We turned off the music and stepped outside.

A walk along the beach in the Outer Sunset district on a summer evening is not romantic in the way an outsider might imagine. A strong wind often blows off the Pacific, and when you face west it's always damp and chilly as it rustles the fog inland. The sky is often low; you rarely see stars. The beach is long and undeveloped—just the coastal highway along the shore and, on the other side of it, rows of smallish houses like my own, packed close together on narrow lots. The surf can drown out the traffic noise, even when young people park along the seawall facing the ocean with their radios booming in contest with the waves. Still, even on the darkest night, there's enough ambient light from the city to catch the white crests of falling surf and the wide, moony beach as it stretches down the peninsula. It's a good place, I think; I prefer it to a busy boardwalk. The Cliff House, the only bar in the city that's truly on the coast, caps the northern edge of the beach at Lands End.

Just a few cars were parked facing the ocean that night, some with high beams aimed at the waves. We had to face the northwesterly wind to avoid the headlights we walked past, but there was a broad space farther up the wall where we could stop and listen to the surf. We were quiet.

My hands were in my pockets. Standing on this sandy sidewalk, silent, is something I've done a thousand times before—alone. Perhaps, for that reason, this new silence became uncomfortable for me. I suggested we continue up to the Cliff House, but she said, "Let's go out in the sand?" She held her breath, perhaps against the chill, her blinking eyes watering in the passing lights, as if she were worried I'd actually say no. As another car pulled close to us, we made our way down the steps, to the beach.

The tide was low, and a broad path of sand had been packed by the surf. It was easy to walk on.

Carol stopped to light a cigarette but had a difficult time—the wind thwarted her—so I put my back to the ocean and shielded her face with my hands. When she finally got it lit, she squeezed one of my hands: "Thanks." Her hand was startlingly warm, and I held it longer than either of us expected. It felt like the first acknowledgment that we were still as alone as we had been earlier, sitting in separate corners, chopping on opposite sides of the counter, or talking across the table. She squeezed again and gently withdrew her hand, took the cigarette from her mouth, and tucked her free hand under her arm. It was an easy, insignificant movement, a way to warm her fingers, but it also felt like holding hands then would not have been right, for her. She seemed to have more to say.

We walked in silence for a while. She looked at the water, at her cigarette, at me. Soon she stopped, toed the butt deep into the sand, and, folding her arms, she searched the waves for an opening. Her standing there staring off into the night would have felt melodramatic if the wind hadn't been so strong that she repeatedly had to pull at the scarf to keep her head wrapped. Her gestures, words, silences—everything about her was authentic.

She turned to head back and began to talk about her divorce and how she'd first adjusted to living alone. It became clear, from her well-chosen words, that this wasn't the first time she'd told the story, but it was also clear she needed to tell it again, to me.

I am often carried away by my own thoughts. Sometimes it's the very moment itself that sets off my imagination. This is what happened as Carol spoke. While we walked, stopping now and then at a ghostly wave or a slow-moving crab, she told a story that echoed mine—one I hadn't shared.

After her divorce, when she'd begun living alone again, she'd unwittingly created a new routine of pouring herself a stiff one each night after work and sitting at one end of her living-room couch. Every time she heard a car alarm or someone raise their voice in the street outside her apartment, she'd get up and peer out through a finger's breach in the blinds. "As regular as a zoo animal," she said. Then one day she noticed she'd worn a path in the carpet—a soiled trail with little craters from the cigarette ash she'd dropped.

I didn't say so, but I could easily picture that scene. It reminded me of my own habit in this back room. I drifted into that memory, staring at the ends of the scarf she wore as they snapped behind us in the wind.

She stopped suddenly and turned to me.

"You walk out here often, Jim? Alone at night?"

I fibbed a little. I'm not sure why. "Not too often," I said. "Not at night, usually."

"Oh," she said, nodding enough for me to notice.

She faced the waves and retied the scarf.

"I enjoy talking with you," she said, "and I hope you don't mind my telling you this, but since we're getting acquainted, you should know: I'm an alcoholic. I'm sober, but—I go to meetings. They mean a lot to me. I want to be up front about things now, in case we decide to see more of each other. I don't want to surprise you, I mean. Later on."

I started watching the waves too.

"I respect your honesty," I said.

And I meant that. But as she took that encouragement and went on to describe her group, their meetings, and other people's struggles, all I could feel was me falling away. I'm sure her stories were true, but they floated around me like leaves on a stream, and soon I wondered: *How can she smoke so incessantly?* It sounds petty to admit it, but that's how I felt as we walked in the wind and she spoke, loosening up and sometimes laughing in quick, loud bursts to herself. The headlights of another turning car washed over her face, and in the glare I noticed how her entire countenance had gone slack in telling these stories. Soon I felt the way I always do when watching the sun set on my neighbors' leaves, realizing all I lost when I'd lost my wife—our shared story. That foundation had been laid not so much on the things we said but on the things we both knew we would never say.

Years ago, one unusually warm fall morning after one of the frequent nights Jackie couldn't sleep, I'd come out early to this back room with my coffee and found her in the garden, her braid swaying from her long neck. She was in shorts, barefoot, her slender knees dimpled with pebbles as she weeded a row of radishes. The weeds were still wet with dew and lay limp in the paths between rows, and to one side sat a basket with a few green onions and three perfect, oversize lemons from the tree we'd planted when we first moved here. They glowed from within. I watched, quietly, because I'd so rarely seen her as I had just then, apart, as she was before I began to draw her inside. To speak at such moments means leaving them.

I didn't notice when Carol stopped talking. We were no longer walking, and before I knew what was happening she was lighting another cigarette, this time shielding the flame with her own hand. She squinted, snapped the lighter shut, and stared off down the beach. She'd made it clear this new silence was my fault.

"So," I tried, "I guess you're not up for a quick snort at the Cliff House, are you?"

She laughed—more like a gasp this time—and took a long drag on her cigarette. "I should head back," she said without turning. "It's getting late." She tossed her half-smoked butt into the sand and snuffed it out with her shoe.

"At least let me walk you to your car?" I said.

She turned back to the highway.

"Sure," she said, facing the headlights and knotting the scarf more tightly until I recalled she had no car.

We trudged back through the softer sand.

The streetcar runs west out of the city, straight to Ocean Beach; there it stops for a break, turns around, and heads downtown again. We reached it just as the power came back on in the train. The interior lit up, and it began to hum. Carol had to jog to catch it.

She took off the windbreaker and tossed it back to me as she jumped on, looking smaller in the bright lights and plastic. On the step, she shook and searched her big bag, thanking me for a "nice time" as the hydraulic doors closed and reopened like a reflex. I told her it was my pleasure. She found her transit pass. The doors shut again. As the train lurched forward, she walked back to a window on my side and, turning suddenly, waved an end of the scarf she still wore around her neck, saying something I couldn't hear.

"I'll call!" I shouted, gesturing.

As the streetcar dissolved in the fog, however, I realized I still didn't know her last name, let alone her number.

I once read that Wallace Stevens wrote the same poem over and over again. This is true, I think: Each poem is a love song to his imagination. He spent a lifetime exalting his. I'm just now acknowledging mine. Some of us have no choice but to attend to our imaginations; otherwise, we're enslaved by them, and we live unwittingly until someone shows us it's not the truth that's veiled, but our eyes.

Right after Jackie left, I'd sent letters, left phone messages, bussed by her new apartment—all out of rage, not love. I railed on back then like a drunken teenager, thinking that by sheer force of my anger, despair, or eloquence I could make her feel a way that she had clearly told me she no longer feels. At such times, a small, sharp voice came through. *Save yourself*, it said. At first, I didn't listen. The self-righteousness I'd felt at the injustice I thought I was suffering made my troubles feel far grander than a simple struggle for survival. But, over time, I learned to see that was the only real motivation I had left. It is a sad, little truth.

To save myself from Jackie I brought back every small thing that annoyed me, every demand she'd made, every hateful thing she'd said in anger, especially during those final days, and I gripped them close, as if preparing for one last rebuttal. When I opened a book I imagined her sitting there, closing up sullenly as she sometimes did when I chose a book over her conversation. I imagined her turning coolly from my touch and reaching for her glasses and paperback later those same evenings, in bed. I imagined the mean stare she gave me when she told me I wasn't listening, I wasn't there. In my imagination, I took those moments and amplified them, exaggerating them until she became the opposite of all I knew I'd lost: She became a thoughtless, hysterical bitch. And this has gotten me through a number of nights. Many are the evenings I've raised my glass and said: *You can take her.*

But once you do something like that, it leaves you on shaken ground. Once you've reinvented a woman you love into someone to hate, you're left with the possibility that you might also have invented the woman you loved. If you're to be honest, you have to begin doubting you loved an actual person. You have to think everyone is replaceable. You might have invented the woman who (you thought) loved you, and with whom you'd planned to share these long, dark nights.

I once strained to see only the selfishness in what Jackie did, only the mean side that enabled her to save herself first, but I can't now because I am doing the same thing. Wasn't she the first to view me in one light only? Instead of watching the breeze rustle the hedge, didn't she instead watch me looking out, not seeing her? Wasn't she the first to feel, with the certainty and weight of age, the shell we'd made of our marriage for just what it had become—two windows and a door? I don't think I'm so angry at her any longer for ceasing to love me; it's more because she knew it before I did.

Three years now after she left, I know that the Jackie I miss most no longer exists. I miss the woman I married—not the living person who left. I miss having the chance to sit out here with the wife I once knew and say: *I see what you're showing me—I'm alone now too.* I used to think I could say such things to no one else—that we had a private understanding only she could share. Then she showed me that's not true.

A few nights before Carol's visit, I'd taken down two wineglasses from the kitchen cupboard. They were part of a set we'd received as a wedding gift—Jackie had managed to preserve two of them, all these years. At first I went on mixing a double in the shaker, but once I realized what I was doing and saw the two glasses, I tossed the extra one over my shoulder at the wall behind me. It landed on a throw rug without breaking. I walked over, picked it up, stood over the sink, and pitched it full-on into the drain. It exploded—shards flecked the countertop, stuck in the butter, glittered like drops of water in the sink. And when I turned again, with shaking hands, to pour my martini, I saw drawn on the surface of the toaster a reflection of myself: a gray-haired, red-eyed man venting his rage on old stemware. *Save yourself,* he said.

CHAPTER 2

The morning after Carol's revelation, as I faced off with a dry leftover roast on the counter and an empty wine bottle in the recycling bin, I felt a few regrets over how I'd spent the previous night—getting lit with an engaging but recovering alcoholic whom I'd invited to dinner. But I'd also slept unusually well, and late. When I went to the living room and pulled the drapes wide open for the first time in a while, the sun was high, the sky creamy blue, and I imagined I could hear the waves push each other over beyond the houses facing mine. A breeze from the Pacific ran through the open door, chasing out everything stale.

I noticed a gunmetal and green-glass dining-room set sitting out by the curb: The bungalow that had been recently bought by a young childless couple was already back on the market. They'd moved in just a few years ago, wearing business suits to work each day—something you notice in this neighborhood of teachers, cops, and tradesmen. Their first month in the house, the couple had thrown a loud party, with a boatload of energetic young people in Hawaiian shirts and sandals parking up and down the street. None of my neighbors had been overly friendly to the yuppies, but that night they let the party's music go on longer than usual, perhaps because the kids seemed so happy and hopeful with their tiki torches stuck in the sand out front. That night had been mercilessly cold and wet, and after they were done grilling whatever it was fit people grilled back then, all the fun moved indoors, the curtains closed, and the reggae rose several notches until someone called in a complaint. It's happened to all of us, the same initiation everyone gets out here, where only the most stubborn or thick-skinned people persist in inhabiting the chilly, gray backyards in our neighborhood.

Opening the door to an uncommonly warm, fragrant breeze felt like an extension of Carol's visit—something new. It struck me how infrequently I air out the house, and how often and easily I ignore the front room. My distaste for our old living-room furniture—fat, unevenly faded stuff that squats on a worn carpet, all bought secondhand when we moved here in 1970, when Dorothy was still a baby—is more due to my simple, long-standing dislike of it than to any memory it holds from our past. When I exposed the brocade armchair to a bright, vertical slice of sun, I thought it winced. *Good.* But the light also brought back memories of earlier days, and with surprising clarity.

I had just passed my probationary period then, and secured a school district contract for life: I was guaranteed a teaching job in San Francisco until I retired, died, or committed a violent crime. Of course, at the time I also fantasized about larger ambitions than teaching, but job security had become paramount for us, because Jackie—who had also been teaching (elementary school)—had decided she wanted to have our second baby before she was thirty. By then the three of us had long outgrown the one-bedroom apartment that we had kept since college, on the slope of Russian Hill above Chinatown. Jackie's folks were still on their ranch in Bakersfield, and they were glad to hear we would stay in California—we'd met in college in Ohio, where I'm from—so they helped with the large deposit and cosigned the lease. Back then, the Outer Sunset was one of the few remaining places where a young couple with nothing could afford a rent-controlled, stand-alone house, garage, and yard, with the beach and Golden Gate Park nearby, and we both found the cool and quiet irresistible. It was a great place for kids too—even if they were just about to tear down Playland-at-the-Beach—as long as you knew enough to sidestep the riptides and rough types. It's always felt like home.

Dreams can be insidious things, however, and just like the yuppie couple, we too were swept up in magical thinking our first night here—July 5, 1970. It began with a cinematic sunset and an ocean breeze that rattled the neighbor's eucalyptus behind our then-new home. We were celebrating the Fourth of July late, since we'd been moving and cleaning the whole holiday weekend. Dorothy had already caught the first of what would be many sinus infections from the damp house, along with her first fever, and although that was a worry, she'd passed out on Dimetapp, so Jackie and I had our first barbecue in the backyard, just the two of us. I'd bought a small grill as a housewarming present—that and some hedge trimmers, things we'd never been able to use in our old third-story apartment downtown. We left Dorothy's window ajar, because we'd never been more than a few yards away from her in the past. Neither of us knew what we were doing. I doused the charcoal with so much lighter fluid that the flames licked the eaves of the house, and I had to run the grill out to the center of the yard like an Olympic torch. We pulled our folding chairs close to the fire.

Jackie noticed some neighbors peering through their blinds to watch us—we, the new young people—and as we sat facing the smoke, the wind picked up and we got our first lesson in why no one grills with charcoal out here. Jackie couldn't ignore the spying neighbors—the move had exhausted her. They didn't bother me. *Ignore them*, I'd thought. *The new dog always submits to the first sniff.* But Jackie couldn't relax as we waited for the charcoal to heat, and when she turned her chair around to put her back to the neighbors, the loud scrape of aluminum on cement woke Dorothy. Jackie shot up and stomped inside, despite my offer to go instead.

It took me too long to finish the chicken on the grill, and by the time I was done the fog was vaulting over our roof. Inside, I found Jackie standing in front of this very living-room window, swaying an open-mouthed Dorothy back and forth so rigidly she reminded me of a madwoman clutching her own elbows. I could tell they'd both been crying. Again I offered to hold the baby awhile, but she shook her head—*It's okay, it's okay*—with a surprising sadness, as if she'd just gotten bad news rather than begun life in her new home. I could only wait. As we stood together, gazing out wordlessly at the other homes on our darkening avenue, it struck me that we were the only people with a lit window looking up at the encroaching clouds: No one else had their curtains open or blinds up. Would it be only a matter of time before we too spent our nights closed up inside? Was she feeling that?

By the time my phone rang, the sunlight weighed upon my lap like a fat cat. It was no surprise; I'd already guessed Dorothy would want to talk after Carol's visit. I took the call on the cordless phone she gave me last Christmas—my kids are always up on the latest gadgets.

"You alone, Dad?"

Even before I sat, she answered her own question.

"Wait, what—are you *reading*?"

Usually she chuckles at her little jokes, just to make sure I know she intends to be funny. And when she does, it's infectious. At least to me. Even when she was a baby, she'd occasionally be so tickled by something that her chortling got me giggling myself. Then she'd stop. This morning, however, she wasn't laughing.

"Good morning," I said.

"So?"

"So nice of you to call, Dorothy. I was just telling Carol how little I hear from you kids."

"So you got along?"

"We had a nice time, yes."

"Good."

She didn't ask for more; evidently that was all the information she needed for now. Dorothy can be mercurial, and seems to have too light a grip on things, especially lately. I'd felt that when talking with her the few minutes she could spare at her party. Her focus on surface details has always been a concern—her blinking, the way she cocks her head to change perspectives, how easy it is for a noise or light to distract her even in extreme moments. It's not deliberate, to call attention to herself—as some of her teachers used to claim—but far from it; it was more her ability to take in everything that's happening around her. Jackie used to link Dorothy's reading problems with this part of her too: She had trouble seeing around punctuation to the words.

During a longish pause—which was also unlike her—I heard the shuffling of papers.

"Will you come out and have lunch with me?" I said. "It's unusually warm."

"I got a shoot, down the peninsula."

Dorothy makes her living producing short films for public relations agencies and corporations. Her dream is to make documentaries.

"Then I've got to run back into the city for something," she said. "Man, the *traffic*! Have you *seen* it lately?"

"What's it about?"

"I don't know, but it's *crazy*. It took me *hours*—"

"Your movie?"

"Oh. It's an HR thing. Human resources."

"They called it HR in my day too."

"It's about benefits. Retirement planning," she said. "What's *that* about, right?"

She didn't laugh at that either.

"So what did you two talk about?" she said.

"Grown-up things," I said obligingly. "You might have told me she doesn't drink. I wasn't entirely prepared for that."

She drew a long breath.

"You're saying her being sober was an issue for you?"

"I just said I wasn't prepared."

"What prep would that involve?" she said. I could imagine her shoulder-length hair swaying side to side, like stage curtains shutting after each question, her alternating looks of big-eyed silence and wrinkled-up irritation. She's been that way since adolescence. Once I mentioned it to her—her two modes of being: watchful or wary— and she pushed back by saying she takes after me. Aside from the fact that we're both not so tall, I doubt that's true.

All the same, it was nice to hear her sounding more like herself.

"It's just that, other than coffee and tea, I had nothing to offer her," I said.

"And—?" Again, distracted.

"I recall she drank coffee."

"But what did you *talk* about?"

"Are you okay, Dorothy? You sound short."

"I've got to run. I just wanted to know. I like Carol a lot, and you two have a lot in common. That's not so usual for you. You agree?"

I supposed I did.

Yes, I said.

The paper shuffling stopped.

"Good. Because you need more friends," she said.

"You have no need to worry about me," I said, growing irked myself.

"It's not *you* I'm worried about," she said. "It's me. Honest. You shouldn't expect me to be pushing you around in your dotage."

Oh—ha, ha! At least her word choice was amusing. My kids do have vocabularies, when they choose to use them.

From that point on our call sped toward its end, under her command. For a minute more, she hopped topics like a black bird on hot tar. She did add that she needed me in some footage for the film she was making—specifically that she needed to "shoot some seniors"— and asked if I'd allow her and perhaps a cameraman to film me for a few hours one morning. Just walking around—nothing scripted, I was somehow disappointed to hear. Just me being myself, but muted and on camera. It sounded as close to a visit as I would be offered, and we both knew I had the time, so I said yes.

But I couldn't let her hang up right away. There was something in her voice, when she said I needed friends, that caught me. I needed to hold her a little longer.

When you make a new friend or fall in love, it's you who becomes bigger, not the world—you're connecting more with a world of others who already exist. But when you have a child, the world itself enlarges—you've added someone entirely new to it, and you too now live in a bigger place. It all sounds overly metaphysical, but it's noteworthy to me. Raising kids expands your world like nothing else, or, perhaps, as only another creative act can. You're making more of everyone and everything out there. In the biographies I read, I've often wondered if any writer who'd had a child would say, at the end of their life, that they would have been satisfied with having done their creative work only, if it meant never being a parent.

"One more thing," I said, keeping her on the line.

As I held the phone, I saw one of my homeless neighbors on the sidewalk out front, a skinny man my age who looked like a hirsute version of my dead brother, but in board shorts. He cut a shadow on my window's glare as he pulled his empty cart behind him. He usually tosses me a loose, floppy wave—*Hiya!*—which I always feel obliged to return, even from the kitchen, but today he simply passed by, head down in the sun.

I told her I wanted Carol's number. I knew she'd be pleased to hear me ask.

"Sure!" she said, sounding startled to hear me say it, like I'd dozed off on her.

She gave it to me along with a loose schedule for our "shoot"—we would do it the first day she, her cameraman, and the sun were available—and then she said a hasty goodbye, leaving everything more unsettled in her wake than it had felt before she rang.

The light dappled the carpet at my feet as a herd of dense shadows marked the inrush of midday fog. I knew my noontime demon would arrive at the threshold of 2 p.m., and I also knew that a few hours after that, I could be back in my chair, listening to the radio and sipping something, but for some reason I didn't feel the easy anticipation I always have for that routine. Perhaps it was the minor notes in Dorothy's voice, or how chilly the house was growing from the breeze. That or, more likely, the fact that I still needed to make another call that I wasn't entirely prepared for, to Carol.

I shut the door to gather my thoughts. I sat on the big couch a moment; I wanted to see if it really was as distended and uncomfortable as it always appeared to be each time I passed it. And indeed, it was. *In your "dotage," do you really want to continue paying a good-sized chunk of rent to house this swollen monster? Why not do something about it? Replace the whole lot?* Jackie had already made it clear she didn't want this stuff. I could donate it—they'd haul the whole batch off the sidewalk in one truckload. Maybe I could drag it to the yuppies' pile: I could replace it with something from one of those warehouses in the Mission we used to visit. Maybe there was an old leather club chair somewhere out there, just waiting for my imprint? *That* would be living.

A day trip. Diversion. I would follow the blue skies down to Valencia Street and stare at someone else's used furniture for a while. And I could still beat rush-hour traffic and get home for happy hour.

When I'd first moved to San Francisco in 1964, one thing that excited me about the place was public transit—buses and cable cars that carried you anywhere for fifteen cents. As a lifelong nondriver who loves to daydream—someone who grew up in a small, flat town in central Ohio that was noteworthy only for being the county seat and home to a state-run mental hospital—I'm still happy with how far my token takes me on MUNI. And, living near the end of the line as I do, I can board an empty streetcar and claim one of the few stand-alone seats all the way downtown—a rare luxury. It's like one of those rap songs my son used to play over and over: *Every day is a holiday.*

That morning, however, a young couple caught my attention. Their rough teeth, scraped necks, and matted hair made it clear, even before the stink of moss and smoke, that they lived in the park. Many people do. Sometimes, when I'm undershaven and tucked too cozily into my seat, people look at me warily, as if I too am en route from the dunes.

Whether they were running from family, the law, or were just too far out on some intoxicant to inhabit everyday life, they didn't strike me as stupid. The young woman, whose dark hair lay flat between her shoulders like a beaver's tail, still had a sparkle in her bloodshot eyes, so that when she looked back at me as she swatted their seat for invisible pests, she reminded me a little of my Dorothy. She gave me a tight, puckered-lip smile, as if proud to be watched cleaning her space while her boyfriend hauled the second of their duffel bags up into the car and through the closing doors.

She slapped the sliding window open and dropped into her seat, putting her feet up on a grimy bag as her boyfriend folded himself in next to her. His narrow back arched as he bent down to unzip some pocket compartment. Once the car started he jerked his head back, as if whiplashed, and as he turned to the girl, I saw the bridge of his nose was crowned with a single scab and his eyelashes were sticky over starry eyes.

"What the fuck?" he said. Not without some warmth.

She faced him blankly.

"The window," he said, nodding toward it.

She pointed up at the open window with a fake question in her eyes—*Oh that?*—looking amused.

"It's fucking *cold*," he said.

"But you *stink*," she said flatly, in a tone I might have used to tell them what street we'd just passed.

He cocked his head back again.

"Well—you—you stink too," he said, grinning and leaning in close to her face until she smiled back. "You stink like me."

She laughed out loud, dry creases pulling at the corners of her mouth. She leaned her head on his shoulder. He began sharpening a penknife on the whetstone he'd unpacked. The cold, damp air blew over us all.

I felt like I should do something too. I, well fed and rested, was watching and judging these people, thinking what they ought to do differently, or what I could do to lessen their misery, or whether I should just let them be. Everyone needs more money, of course, and no one wants advice. There was no reason for me to ignore them—she'd made it clear she knew I was watching. For all I knew, she'd opened the window for my sake too.

"I can close that, if you'd like," I said softly, leaning in to be heard.

I tapped the young man, mid-spine.

He jumped clear out of his seat and stood, wavering above me.

"The window," I said, pointing. "It's not bothering me, but I can close it, if you'd like?"

His eyes widened into a feral glare that left me wondering if I too weren't lost.

Growling, he swiveled and slammed the window shut, yanked it open again, and slammed it shut once more. He dropped back into his seat, mute, and resumed working with his tools.

She, in solidarity, tipped her head back to his shoulder. In two stops, she was snoring, in a dream of her own.

I watched the world outside. It was the end of a long-suffering century, and I'd always imagined that, at this point in history, we'd be long past the time when kids like these still flooded the Haight and Castro looking for a home. Jackie and I put a lot of work into teaching our own kids just how far off those sixties myths were—that those runaways they saw on their way to nursery school hadn't come to our small city so much to change the world as to change their own. Personal pain or fear of dying in a war or a nuclear attack brought them here the same way I, on my trek to a used-furniture store, sought escape. I thought, *If someone were sitting behind me watching, I'd probably look like a cliché too*—another lonely old guy riding public transit in off-peak hours, with nothing to do but pass time.

It must be nearing 2 p.m., I thought.

We rolled aboveground, east, for another mile. As we approached Civic Center and began our descent into the tunnel, the car now filled with people, I realized I hadn't ridden all the way downtown for months. I hadn't shopped for furniture in a decade. I rarely buy anything but food on my own. Dorothy drives me for errands on request, and Gerald takes me to Costco, as needed, but otherwise I do my shopping on foot at the little store in the middle of our block or at the Safeway up the beach, with my list and laundry cart. So why this trip today?

Perhaps having Carol see my old upholstery up close the night before had impressed upon me the need for a little low-risk, recreational change. That, or maybe Dorothy's unusually pointed reference to my "dotage"—a term that makes you feel all the worse when it's your own child using it. I'd never before wondered whether I would spend my retirement years without company because I have two kids and they both live reasonably close, but whether *they* might get anxious at that prospect was a new question, to me. I have no real context for understanding what's involved in eldercare aside from my grandmother's having moved in with us after my mother died, when I was little. I'd lost my whole family by college graduation.

As I stepped off BART in the Mission, my sneakers stuck to the platform's caution strips. It took some time for me to get my bearings once up on the street, in the white light. And so much had changed. I was grateful and relieved to find one of the cavernous used-furniture emporiums still in business on Sixteenth and Valencia. Jackie and I used to spend full days exploring this very place, an abandoned garment factory that was now stocked with furnishings from estate sales and closeouts. There are three jam-packed floors, with all the oddest, oldest stuff stored on the top level. The nostalgia kick I got from taking a lift in the room-sized, whitewashed freight elevator was worth the trip alone.

There were so many chairs and sofas that I could find no direct path through them. None of the old stuff looked any better than what I'd hoped to replace. In fact, it rather reminded me of *my* old stuff. Not sure why that surprised me; some part of me must have foreseen that, even before I got on the streetcar.

But, so what? Why not linger? I've already lived most of my life without thinking, for any real length of time, *What's the best possible use for this day?* So I indulged myself: I took my time test-driving armchairs. I wondered how each might transform my room or if, instead, over time, they might only come to remind me of what they'd replaced. It was fun for a while. It pushed aside whatever anxiety I'd picked up from Dorothy, or might have been feeling about seeing someone new.

As I reclined in a stranger's chair, midafternoon encroached with its unfailing gloom. A lone, trapped swallow darted through the rafters overhead and vanished to its nest. I worried about nodding off and being left behind, upstairs in an old furniture store, locked in for the night to wake up with bird shit on my collar. Time to go.

I had hoped to grab a bag of my favorite homemade tortillas on the way home. There was a place I used to know, near the Sixteenth Street station, that I hadn't visited in years—they'd had little kids, who must be grown now—but the shop was gone. In fact, looking around, I no longer recognized anything, anywhere. Not even the dry, bright heat.

The stink and bustle of the intersection left me so dazed that I jogged down the escalator. I was grateful to beat the rush-hour traffic—reasonably assured that, barring some accident on the tracks, I would be back in my fog by four.

Down the tunnel, empty-handed, pleased to beat the mob.

Not a bad epitaph. Or so I thought once home, preparing to hold Happy Court.

As I poured my first martini in three days—larger than usual, to kill the dregs of the old bottle—I was pleased to recall I'd foregone a cocktail the night before: I hadn't touched the gin when Carol visited, even before learning she didn't drink. That's something I'd promised the kids. I'm on medication and shouldn't be drinking much at all. I never really "drank" before, but just after Jackie left I did indulge in a bit of drama, so I've been weaning myself off hard liquor. Around others, at least.

Halfway through my martini, it became clear that this solace was leaving me too. I couldn't escape the day's thoughts. Usually, any threat to my porch party could be pushed aside with little more than a shake of the head. Just the other week, for example, when I found myself pondering whether to pull the shade as one of my new neighbors went about their post-shower business—fully exposed in his own curtainless window—I'd settled the matter with a simple wave. *Hiya, neighbor! I'm no prude either!* But that memory no longer amused me.

Another concern: the fickle fog. It trotted away as quickly as it had come that morning, right after I'd spent my return trip from the downtown sun with my eyes shut, daydreaming about reentering the mist. Given that I'd bought nothing on my trip, I had to wonder if the main reason I went to the Mission in the first place wasn't to heighten the savor of the cold, gray damp of home. The evening's clear sky was unsettling when I'd expected the opposite.

Perhaps I look forward to so little in general to avoid greater disappointment?

The rosy sunset glowed against my neighbors' back sides.

I detected a coil in my chair, a spring I usually overlook until I cross my legs a certain way. That evening, though, it felt more pointed. Either it had finally surfaced through the padding, or I'd been losing weight—Dorothy had mentioned she was worried about this—or I was simply getting flat-out pissed at everything. Not once in the half dozen chairs I'd tried out that afternoon had I considered any as a possible replacement for my old friend on the porch, but now that struck me as strange, because my chair was so much more beat—I saw clearly—than any of them. Or than anything else in the house. That the thing remained functional at all, in fact, was due to the props I used—a quilt and two limp, flat pillows. And although I must have had some unacknowledged emotional attachment to it, and even though the armrests were just right for me—worn to my elbows, even—there were probably one hundred alternate reasons why *this*, rather than all the other pieces I was so intent on losing, should be the first to go. *Why have we not noticed this before?* Or, why had I never thought of switching the chair with its twin on the other side of the room—the chair now used by my kids on their infrequent visits? Or by Carol, the night before? It's the same style—one of a pair. All it lacked was my depression.

Suddenly, the point became such a literal pain in the ass that I shot up with a growl and yanked the old chair from its corner. I quickly switched it with The Other—with "Jackie's chair."

Pandemonium. Dust bunnies fled.

Was the significance of this reversal lost on me? Of course it was not. My heart raced.

Once the skidding stopped, with the two chairs resting in their new positions, I dropped into The Other. But it was *not* more comfortable. *How long have we endured these things?* Nearly thirty years—right after moving in. It had been a joke of ours after we'd given up on our backyard barbecues; they were the markers, the boundary of just how far we'd allow the neighbors and fog to push us back inside. *Here we make our stand.* But the outsiders outnumber us now.

There was an upward pressure in the center of The Other; the fabric drew tightly in odd places under my crotch. It forced me to sit too upright. Had my guests—Jackie, even—been this uncomfortable all these years? Was this why Carol got impatient?

Then it spooked me to see how sunken and lonely my *old* chair looked from that distance, by *her* window—like a once-favored old hound locked out in the rain. I nearly reached out to pat the poor thing. Soon it became so impossible to relax in the new spot that I returned to my old chair, on Jackie's side of the room. And *Lo!*—another fresh perspective, a regained view northeast that my head must have obstructed over the years for anyone sitting on this side. I could see quite a distance past the butt end of our neighbors' homes, down the lot lines. For what felt like the first time, I took in how unfortunately most were painted—one lavender with a glossy peach trim. Another yard had a flat-topped redwood, cut mid-height for reasons yet to be determined. So many things to see from a new angle, and all of so little importance.

A whiff of Carol's smoke escaped a cushion, and the foreignness of it hooked me by the nose. I recalled how easy the hours had felt, talking with her the night before. How her dark eyes had shone whenever I bothered to look in them.

Dorothy is right, I thought. *I will call. Tomorrow. Once I get a few things in the cupboard.*

CHAPTER 3

I was roused too early (for me) by some bully rapping a stick on my bedroom window, saying *Wake up, sleepyhead!* in a singsong voice. Only my son, Gerald, would do such a thing. I had forgotten I'd called him the night before, asking when we might make our next Costco run—my reserves were low. And so he'd come, dutiful and prompt as a soldier, just like he always does.

My son makes a lot of money downtown working on computers. He says he manages a "Help Desk" for one of the "Big Six" accounting firms. The first Christmas after Jackie left, he'd mailed me a photocopy of a picture he and his colleagues made of themselves wearing Santa hats and wrapped together with electrical cables, with Christmas garlands on the wall of computers behind them. "Servers," he calls them. In the photo, one of his crew cradles a stocking stuffed with a Chihuahua donning little foam antlers. I'm not sure why he sent this to me—his first adult Christmas card. The message is some joke about "Checkin' I.T. twice." Clearly it was created for in-house distribution, but, all the same, he'd taped it high on my freezer door, with his work phone number printed in bold marker, where I wouldn't be able to avoid seeing it each morning. He looks at it and chuckles whenever he drops by—which, lately, is only for our Costco trips. He lives in Tam Junction, where he's still the primary leaseholder on a house he's held since community college and doesn't want to lose.

I would never have guessed any child of mine might grow up to be technical, but Gerald and his first computer were love at first sight.

Even as a baby, whenever he saw something he wanted, he'd simply adjust course and roll directly toward it. My brother had a similar quality. Dorothy takes a different, more comprehensive, view of the world. She was the one to struggle her way through four years of Christian Brothers' college, across the Bay—my kids are nominally Catholic, and Dorothy spent a few years at a nearby parochial school until Jackie could get her into the public elementary she taught at—whereas Gerald shot straight into computer work after high school. Without any push from me, Dorothy chose to pursue a bachelor's in liberal arts, whereas Gerald enjoyed a protracted, four-year associate's experience in Marin, where he could ride his mountain bike, surf, and live with buddies across the bridge that neither I nor his mother—who doesn't do freeways—would drive over. So, while Dorothy once, as a fifteen-year-old, dragged me up to the Surf Theatre for a French film, or might now recommend a *Bay Guardian* article to me, Gerald delights in taunting me that he has "zero interest" in the arts, liberal or otherwise. Once he dropped in to slap a splendid, newspaper-wrapped salmon on my counter—*No doubt you can do something with this?!*—but otherwise, since that one summer we shared, he prefers his visits to be prearranged, with an agreed-upon activity or purpose. I'm blaming the computers. His graduation barbecue was the only invitation we'd ever gotten to visit his damp, decked place in the redwoods—The Keep, they call it—and we've been introduced to only one of his girlfriends, when they'd stopped in for the bathroom and ice cubes on their way to Santa Cruz, speaking even less than he usually did on those occasions back then whenever he was (I suspect) stoned.

As I've said, Dorothy showed a great deal of concern for me after Jackie's departure, making almost-daily visits and calls to keep me aloft. Gerald, on the other hand, simply drove up one day with a stout friend, unannounced, and started kicking boxes through the garage to his old bedroom. Although I believe he moved in to give his sister a break, his version was that he wanted to stay in the city for the summer while he completed his training down the peninsula. I can't say I actually welcomed the intrusion. Not at first, anyway. I'm not the sort to feel lonely in an empty house, and even though there are three bedrooms here, Jackie and I had just spent the three previous years getting used to living without him in his. That was something I'd always looked forward to, in fact—that and retirement—and something I thought she would enjoy too, even if she did opt to continue teaching until she turned sixty-two.

Don't get me wrong: I love my children. But I also love having free will, control over the emotional climate of my day, the freedom to direct my own attention and keep my head as clear of chatter as I choose. You gradually let go of those things, unconsciously, when you first have kids. It begins with that wonderful bang—your first baby—then reverberates and amplifies over a few decades. And when, finally, the kids move out and the commotion just as suddenly stops? Well, you're either in for some yearned-for rest or a jarring shock. You can guess which I got, and I can tell you it was not the same experience for Jackie: Everything good that went south inside Jackie began packing up the second Gerald let our front door shut behind him.

Only afterward did I understand a bit of how she might have felt back then, because I was stunned at how wobbly I myself was at summer's end, the afternoon Gerald's stout friend returned and, just as quickly, helped him repack and slide the boxes out front to the same old pickup, in retreat to The Keep. Back to the life he preferred. I'd had no warning that day; he'd been a little quiet, perhaps, more attentive to me over coffee—even gentle, after his fashion—and he'd shown a surprise softness that slowed him down as he walked past with his last box. In deference to me, he ran the vacuum once around his empty room. I remember watching, just outside his door, when he asked if I'd like to sit out back with him for one last beer to say goodbye to summer. I could tell he'd felt uneasy—he'd grown louder, struggling to sound upbeat. He wagged a finger and lectured me about gin and not leaving burners on or the doors open to raccoons at night, trying to be amusing, and then, when he stood and I walked around him to recycle his empty, he pulled me into a bear hug. He was the one to get choked up that time, although, as he held me, I couldn't actually see his face.

I don't know why I hugged my kids so infrequently after they grew up. I must have hugged them often when they were little—how can you not?—but physical affection never came easily to me. Words make a more lasting connection. Jackie used to accuse me of being distant, but my family simply wasn't a touchy bunch, nor were any of our Ohio neighbors growing up, and I don't recall any of them seeming particularly cold or mean because of it. My father was stoic for good reason: He was a half-deaf foreman at the local foundry and a widower by forty-five. Not a hugger. My mother was sickly most of her life, and my older brother Craig, who I loved, enlisted into the army, post-Korea, when I was a sophomore in high school. I once squeezed him tight, outside a car full of buddies who would drive him away to basic training, but even by then he'd become a mere shell of himself, so it felt like holding a stranger. My maternal grandmother, who'd moved in when I was five, after my mother died, would tousle my hair or pat me on the head, and I can still feel her soft, doughy hands on my shoulders as she stood behind me at the piano, with her sweetish, oaky breath falling down, but that's the most touching I can recall from childhood. Life in the Midwest guarantees you ample personal space, and if you grow up in a flat place, you're comfortable with distance. Sometimes hugs can be more alienating than comforting.

Anyway. Gerald had his own key, but he kept tapping on the glass of my bedroom window until I shouted back. He said "they" would wait out front. So he had a friend with him. I appreciated the warning, but still, when I opened the front door to a dark, wet morning, I was taken aback by his big cheek-to-cheek, comrade-like embrace. I felt his course beard and the full height of him. The boots, perhaps. Today's greeting was more than a simple "Good morning." He filled the doorframe so fully it took me a second to see the reason, behind him—a bright-eyed, broad-faced woman who tromped right in and squeezed my hand in both of hers.

With his widest grin he introduced Xenia. She was nearly as tall as he was, also in leather and jeans and boots, with a huge scarf, bright blond hair, pale makeup, and sparkling green eyes that quickly appraised, and approved, everything—first me, then the room. Even as I closed the door behind us she took to the largest chair and looked more at home in it than anyone had in years. She rose just as quickly when Gerald nodded us all back to the kitchen for coffee. He likes to keep things moving.

He frowned—back to her—at my morning mess: the picked-at roast on the table, the knife lying in platter fat, the wineglass on the counter, cloudy with fingerprints. I was glad to have emptied the recycling the night before.

He plunked the knife down in the sink.

"Looks like the yuppie house down the road is on the market," he said. He winced into the spare, bright fridge, searching for milk. Xenia peered in after him with her hand on the small of his back. "Bet they double their money, easy. In less than five years."

I excused myself; I should have set an alarm that morning. Gerald wasn't usually so responsive to my Costco calls that he would show up with less than twelve hours' notice. Typically, I'm prepared for his arrival; I keep a running list on the fridge. A few days ahead, I repurpose the odds and ends of various half meals from the freezer into one big stew or casserole that I'll then work through (and vow not to refreeze) to ensure there's room for new goods.

When I returned, showered and dressed, they still filled the kitchen, flowing easily around each other as they rinsed mugs, sniffed the dishtowels, and refilled the sugar bowl. It was nice to see. Matching keychains jingled from their belts as they stepped down into the back room with their coffee. *I will be safe at Costco with this escort*, I thought. I get oddly agitated before a shopping run—I usually don't sleep well the night before—but I'm happy as a farmer in fall once Costco has been "achieved," as Gerald says. He's my front man in these skirmishes, where even the walk through the bustling parking lot can be a challenge for me.

Xenia was sitting in my spot. Rather than take the remaining—my former—chair, Gerald chose to stand in the doorway.

"What's up with the chairs?" he said, smirking but also seeming truly surprised at the switch I'd made. "Should we be worried?"

Xenia beamed as if she got his joke, but her face was too honest—
it was obviously lost on her. Gerald gulped coffee, and we followed
his lead.

It was soon clear that Xenia's English was very rough. She'd emi-
grated from Odesa little more than a year before. She and Gerald had
met at work; she'd come in through a nonprofit agency. She smiled
widely when he explained how they were trying to hire her full time
at his firm. Immigration legalities, I assumed. Xenia wasn't shy about
retelling the story of her entry into the country, but even after she'd
finished I still wasn't sure if she'd come in with family, as a student, or
even with a boyfriend, and it felt inappropriate to press for more personal details. Clearly she was happy to be in San Francisco, and particularly out west in the avenues, where the Russian Orthodox and
Jewish communities have been growing for decades. Most Russians
live north of the park, rather than on my side in the Sunset, but when
Xenia made a sweeping gesture with her hand to take in my window
and the view out back, one sensed it was the whole city—no, the
entire country—that was "very beautiful, very good." As the burden
of conversation increasingly fell to her—I'd put my energy into com-
prehension—Gerald relaxed more, pressing his shoulder into the
side of the doorjamb with his empty mug tipped out. Xenia needed
to talk, it seemed, and her energy revived my interrupted morning. I
had the hunch that the grandiosity of Costco, which typically makes
me tense, might actually suit her.

"You read books!" she declared, splaying her hand atop my "to-do"
stack, and then pressing it hard to her heart with something like a
sweet grimace. "*I* love books—to read books."

Gerald beamed down at me with a wide-eyed expression that said:
Wow, Dad, hear that? His favorite joke is to tell me he can't read. Since
college, I haven't seen him crack the spine of anything but a fish or
one of his buddies.

Truth is, I am amused by this, grudgingly. I respect that he, after just
one summer of night training, can bring in a paycheck equal to what I
drew down fifteen years into teaching. His interest in this stuff is passionate and full bore. He's told me he plans to leave the accounting

firm soon and strike out on his own. "Interactive media" is heating up, he says. I question why people should need to have their interactions mediated at all, by anything, but he pretends not to hear. Whenever I encourage him to think twice about leaving Arthur Andersen before he's fully vested in the retirement plan, he says: "Why plan to live?" Somehow I love him all the more for it. I had few career choices in my day, particularly as a secret wannabe writer. Back then, someone like me could become a teacher, a librarian, or a lonely, raving, impoverished, romantic drunk in some dark place. Or—as I now imagine Gerald saying—*You could write, send work out, get it published, see if it lives, and if you learn you're not good enough, suck it up and move on to your next gig.* I would counter that my brief attempts at writing after college taught me that *that* plan can still lead to the dark place. Had he been in my shoes—if he'd had any sincere love for words or literature along with a pressing need to pay off a mortgage-sized college loan—I imagine he might change his tune. But money no longer has the same properties it did in my day, and it comes faster now the younger you are. By the time we'd reached his twenty-six years, Jackie and I were already married with a baby on the way. True: It *is* a much rougher economy now. He's often talking about watching his back and surviving the annual round of layoffs due to "reengineering," with even the editorial department shrinking regularly. *They killed another 1.5 editors this quarter!* Whereas in I.T., he says, they can't even find the temps they need. They "grew" by three people last quarter, he says. Or perhaps that was two-point-five people. I can't recall.

But more than his ability to talk tough like some dude with a Harley out back on blocks, or to meet all these girls—he has never lacked company—it's his unspoken acceptance of his own will that I admire. It's not the money that matters to him, but rather being passionately engaged and unburdened by inner conflict. Lucky for him, no one understands his work well enough to supervise him. Which, as I think of it now, actually *is* similar to writing.

Gerald nudged my seat with his boot, smiling. "Books, Dad. Xenia reads *books.* That's why I asked her along—so you have someone to talk to."

She tipped her head, looking affectionately at him from under her brow—*Funny Gerald!*—and it tickled him. Clearly, she meant a lot to him.

"Excuse me," I said, coming to and turning to her. "Who do *you* read?"

"I read Russian only. And Ukrainian." She blushed, but just for an instant. "My English is not good. You know this." Huge smile, for me. "In English, I read textbooks. Computer books. Sometimes newspaper."

"But in your native language?" I prompted. "You should be able to get any book you want out here in the avenues—yes?"

I myself blushed. Decades of teaching English to immigrant kids and I still can't stop pulling out this jackass syntax of mine whenever I first meet them.

"Yes, *yes*," she said, waving and clearing the air between us. It felt like we were old friends. "I love to read great masters." She looked to Gerald for confirmation, but he was already nodding. "Dostoyevsky. Gogol."

Her expression again eagerly sought acknowledgment that I understood, but before I could ask after Gogol—*before Tolstoy?*—she spoke.

"And—I read saints."

I looked to Gerald, puzzled, but he nosed me back to her.

"The life of saints," she said, working for clarity. "It is maybe Orthodox thing. It is prayer—church—they are friends. Here, now."

"Here, in this room?" I couldn't help it.

"Yes, this—" she scanned the room. "All places. Like icons." Her hair fell out from behind her ears as she turned to fumble with a big zipper on her jacket. She pulled out a little, well-loved paperback. The spine was stapled, the purple cover worn to white at the corners. The cover had a poor, gray photo of an intense-looking, bearded old cleric. The title was in Cyrillic or something like it—a mystery to me.

Gerald, unmoved, had clearly seen it before. He left to rinse his mug.

"*This* man . . ." She pointed at the photo with her bitten, maroon-painted fingernail. "He is Orthodox saint. He is *here*."

"She means here in San Francisco," Gerald said from the kitchen. "The big church on Geary. That's Saint John. His remains are under glass. Incorrupt."

"You've seen him?" I said.

"I have."

After thirty years of living within a mile or two of that gorgeous Russian cathedral, I still had not stepped inside. They have a reputation for being guarded around outsiders. The bronze doors out front must be fourteen feet high. But suddenly it became easy for me to picture Gerald bounding up the steps as if it were his local library, right behind Xenia.

"We'll take you," he said, flashing his watch from the doorway. "Some other day."

Xenia nodded assent at both points—Yes, yes—and shot up. When she grabbed her mug from my stack of books, she put her own little booklet down on top, faceup in its place, bringing her fingertips to her lips and tapping the robed man's wan portrait as if bidding him farewell.

"You read this," Xenia said. "I take it next time. I hope you like it and we go see Saint John with you."

And before I knew it, they were heading out the front door, zipping and snapping up with their sharp, booted steps sending tremors through the floorboards as I followed.

Our transition from the sacred to the profane—to Costco—was made more than comfortable by the lordly seats of Gerald's large, four-wheel drive. The trip started with a seven-mile cruise down the Great Highway, south along the beach, with the Pacific to our right. I rode shotgun. It was a gray day, and as I sat warm and dry with my young guardians, high above the waves that we could easily outrun, I felt a certain exhilaration. Nothing but mist on the windows obstructed the horizon. Gerald always indulges me and plays an old Brubeck album I'm fond of, the classic quartet at Oberlin. I believe it's the only jazz he keeps in his tank, but we hear it every time. We make this trip every other month or so, and after a few years it's become a routine that means much more to me. A family tradition. For an indulgent half hour, his vehicle is not merely a conveyance, but a chariot of dreams. Ride it when you can.

In the rearview I saw Xenia behind me, also watching the waves. Her pale skin was pocked in the gray light and her green eyes were wet and wide with sky. She gazed out with almost tearful awe. I tried to imagine the other oceans she'd seen.

"Has Dorothy called you lately?" Gerald said.

He had to stop for a light; driving over the shallow drifts of sand that rim the highway, Gerald can usually modulate his speed to avoid braking at the intermittent lights where surfers cross, but sometimes his timing's off. I told him about Dorothy's plans to come out and make a movie. He seemed inordinately pleased to hear that news, but then got serious again.

"You know Mom's in Italy?" he said.

I did *not* know. Jackie on a plane? Across the ocean? *Glad to have missed that,* I thought. But then the old bile began to rise, and the only trick I've learned for keeping that down is to say: *Good for her!* She'd always wanted to travel, after all. Though for someone who always shut her eyes in the BART tunnel, just stepping foot through an airline gate must have felt like being in a feature film.

"I can't see your mother in Europe," I lied.

"Her last postcard was Pisa," he said. "She sounded pretty breezy. Like, *Ciao!* She's buying a scarf every place they visit. Living her dream. You know."

I did indeed know how easy it was to conjure up picaresque images of Jackie.

"*They?*" I said.

"Yes—her and Mr. Adrakian. They're on a group tour."

"Is that her doctor?" I felt the urge to poke at him. He gets sensitive whenever I manage to trip him up, so I like to try.

"Her boyfriend. You didn't know?"

I did not.

"You call him that—*Mister?*" I said.

"His name is Dick." Gerald lowered his voice. "I can't call any guy Dick to his face anymore. I tried to play dumb and call him Richard when we first met, but I still couldn't keep a straight face. I didn't want to set Mom off."

He sensed my surprise at the fact that she was already half a couple who traveled together.

"He's pretty mellow," he said, with effort. "They're compatible."

He began to lay it on thick, worried perhaps that this news about his mother might bring our day down. *He's not like you: He's laconic, no sense of humor. Tall.* He told me Dick was a retired almond farmer and amateur winemaker from Lodi; they'd met at a gourmet cooking course through UC Berkeley Extension. She'd always wanted to take courses like that. Evidently she too was working posthaste on her own to-do list. That should not have surprised me, given how she'd gone into overdrive after menopause and the void left after our kids moved out. She'd started waking up earlier, staying later at work, inflating her old bike for evening rides, going out for drinks with fellow teachers on Fridays. That we didn't have the *same* to-do lists had been an obvious challenge in our late marriage, although I probably could have managed to travel overseas—to England, at least—if they gave me the right pill.

Good for her!

Still, it was touching that Gerald wanted to soften the news for me, perhaps because he'd witnessed my you-can-have-her days too closely, as well as all the baby steps I needed to take after that.

A pit bull, just visible above the hood of the vehicle, leaped high on its chain, towing its ragged, bent owner through the crosswalk.

"I met someone too, the other night," I said.

I felt Xenia's eyes on me, but Gerald looked straight ahead, smiling impatiently out the windshield.

"Well—I guess I'm glad your mother's finally doing her thing," I added. "She and Mr. Johnson."

He tooted the horn twice.

In no time we were walking into the shockingly bright, end-times emporium that is Costco. Gerald usually has a short list for himself, and I'll indulge him a few minutes by pretending to be interested in the new electronics that are displayed just inside the door—computers not much larger than Big Chief tablets, brick-sized cameras, new stuff I would never look at otherwise. This also gives me a chance to acculturate to the garish warehouse after our relaxing car ride, because once inside the place, I'm weak. I can get overwhelmed, clutching my list in that churning sea of carts pushed by people who are much more direct and less courteous than I. Gerald generally stands sentry over my cart; he serves as my second set of taller, sharper eyes as I work down my list of needs, which always includes large bags of coffee, lasagnas I store in the freezer, and gin. I can get a magnum of my go-to brand for half of what I'd pay at the Safeway up the beach while also avoiding the potential indignity of trundling home with too many bottles rattling in my wire cart. Oddly enough, even though Gerald knows I'm phasing that out, I can still see his grip on my Costco cart tighten when I stand my bottle up inside it; he looks away or beyond, even when I clang the bottle on the side as a joke. I wouldn't do that if I thought he were truly embarrassed—he's not the shame-filled sort.

"We are here to *achieve the objective*," he repeats each time we go, with the "objective" being a quick and painless purchase of all items on our lists. For fun, he'd even begun setting a timer on his watch and recording the minutes on a little card he keeps strapped inside the visor of his car, to see if we can beat previous performances. I don't enjoy that.

Xenia adapted in seconds. This was her first time, and when we and dozens of other hunter-gatherers queued outside the door with our carts—"queue" being an optimist's term here—she stood on tiptoe to see over the heads in front. Once inside, by the electronics, she hung back for a moment, her arms limp at her side, surveying the scene—the factory ceiling, the towering overstock, the white-hot fever of wholesale consumption. Gerald forced a tight smile at each of her delays—it's the same look he gives me whenever I dawdle—but she insisted on rifling through the heaps of folded clothing, which he and I ordinarily bypass, as if she were in a summery, open-air market. She hoisted a magnum of champagne to read the French on the label. She sighed at the islands of seafood and tasted every sample.

I typically stop to catch my breath at the far end of the store, in the refrigerated room that's as big as my living room, with floor-to-ceiling shelves of the freshest produce—crates of asparagus and green beans. There, again, I stumbled upon Xenia. Or perhaps she'd followed me, at a distance. She stood in a sort of reverie gripping a three-pound pallet of muddy-looking chanterelles, lifting it up to her nose and shaking it in both hands. She lingered, feeling the weight, until a grabby shopper nearly knocked it from her hands while reaching past her for a different box.

"Welcome to the land of plenty," I said from behind.

When she turned to me, her eyes weren't happy, as I'd expected. Rather, she looked hurt, almost angry.

"I could laugh; I could cry," she said, plunking the box back down on the stack. She shook her head. "Too much. They go bad. You need less too much."

I realized then: I liked Xenia.

Gerald always made our trips around midday to beat traffic, and he'd justify the extended break from work by picking up a few items for the office. That day he'd bought power strips and two cases of some energy mix they drink all day. As usual, we were back home by two—too late for lunch and too early to think about dinner. He and Xenia helped carry in my booty, except—as usual—the box with the gin, which he let me haul in by myself. It's his unsubtle way of telling me he's still watching me and waiting. The only real power I have in the face of that—aside from remembering he's the kid and I'm the father, and that he has no say in how I choose to live as long as I remain independent—is to pretend I don't notice. Dealing with his wariness was trickier in the early days of my abandonment, when I had indeed been drinking too much, for show, out of self-pity—I admit that now—but since he's moved out and I've gotten into a rhythm that sustains me, it amuses me to pretend I don't understand him whenever he gives me the stink eye. All I see in that annoyed, jaw-jutting stare is a disappointed forbearance. And that's a look I endured my entire childhood.

My brother, Craig, wore that look beneath his smile. Even before I'd grown old enough to be conscious of it, it was there in his middle school pictures—in his high school yearbook it's more pronounced. He was hazel-eyed, sandy-haired, and freckled, with a cleft chin and small, straight teeth that, when he smiled (rarely in public) looked like he was gritting them. When he was unhappy, his jaw muscles flexed like he'd chewed too much gum for too long. I looked up to him. Everyone did. He wasn't the best student, but he was our school's fastest runner, the star of the school musical, and also the only kid who dared do hand-stands atop the grain silo or jog down the roofs of freight trains—parked or crawling through town—when no one else was looking but me. In our town, he was a hero. But even though he always protected me, he'd give me that angry, frustrated look often, for seemingly no reason.

I'd begun serving as an altar boy with Craig in fourth grade, right after my grandmother died. My father insisted we do this—going to Mass and eating were the two remaining things we three did together as a family. My father would watch us up there with a fierce attention; it meant something deep to him. And I liked the drama of the Mass—the ritual movements, the incense and robes. I loved ringing the bells as loudly as I could in the quiet church, an honor my brother shared with no one else. Craig taught me everything. He was the one who told me you never want to be alone with Father Stephen.

That couldn't be avoided, of course; there were only two other altar boys, and Craig was often sick or away for his games. As he suggested, I tried to arrive as late as possible on any day I knew I'd be serving alone, robing up and lighting candles in a last-minute rush. Father Stephen had seemed as benign a man as you could imagine—a gray nonentity at worst. It was hard to believe that someone with such a rubbery face and a chanting voice that sounded like a snore could hurt anyone. He never scolded or even looked at me when we vested and prepared for Mass, and if I arrived late, he'd raise his eyebrows briefly, but the expression in his aqueous eyes was not one I could read. If he wanted me to attend to something—light a censer, fetch the chalice—he'd simply nod toward it, or point, and I was proud that I knew what to do.

I'd insisted on serving the Saturday night Mass the week following my first, and worst, seizure. I'd fallen backward and hit my head on the porch, biting my tongue so hard that I had to have three stitches, and because no one could say why it occurred or if it would again, I felt very down. My father, brother, and I had kept it private, hoping it was an isolated incident. Because I wanted to prove that there was nothing wrong with me, it was a relief to return to the altar that week at the same scheduled hour, to pull on my usual cassock, light the same lights, and recite the same words, falling in line with Father Stephen. And it worked: It seemed as if nothing had changed, except for the fact that summer had arrived—the only time of the year when, for a few weeks, the setting sun fell between the buckeyes outside the sacristy at just the right angle to flood the leaded windows with golden light.

Father Stephen had pulled his wooden chair into that light and was reviewing his homily notes when I arrived, alone. I rushed to the closet and was fumbling with the buttons on the collar of my cassock when he looked up and caught my reflection in the mirror.

"My dear boy!" he cried, in real alarm.

Like a robed judge, he remained sitting and motioned with his short, outstretched arm for me to come to him and let him see my wound. My lower lip was bruised and swollen. I stood before him and bowed a little, embarrassed. He took my chin in his hand.

I blushed at this attention—as I've said, we're not a touchy family—but his fingers were as warm as my grandmother's. The white, wiry shrub of his brow rose as I stammered through an explanation—a confession—of what had happened to me. He seemed pained at hearing me, his wet eyes searching and then avoiding mine. The sunlight behind him was too strong, triggering one of my middle school migraines. He closed his eyes in what appeared to be prayer.

For a lengthening moment we remained still. The light amplified the tufts of hair sprouting from his ears and refracted off the scruff on his green vestment. He became pitiable to me—I felt sad being near him. My headache's flash spot spread quickly, pulsing from the corner of my eye, but what little of his face I could focus on seemed to be crying. With a rustle of fabric, I heard and then felt his hands drop to my shoulders. He patted them, as if to slowly put out a small fire.

I recall the man with no affection, but to this day I believe that's all he'd intended to do.

The sacristy door shut behind me.

"I'm late," Craig shouted too loud, creaking open the cedar wardrobe.

Father Stephen's arms withdrew slowly into the folds of his robes, where he pulled out a handkerchief to blot his eyes and wipe his brow. I remained standing, limp and speechless, momentarily half blinded by my headache. I was stunned by the noise of Craig's rushing, and how fast and mechanically Father rose to walk past me.

As we served Mass I felt disembodied, light-headed from the scent of warm, freshly cut grass wafting in through the open windows and the aspirin I'd swallowed. My mind's eye rose to a spot high inside my forehead, and soon, as the pain dulled and thinned there, everything outside spiked with clarity and grew distant.

I stared out at my father, in front, at the end of his pew. I saw the half-moons of perspiration beneath each arm of his shirt. The steel fan he stood by was too tall for its oscillations to reach him, but he would never change seats. A green ribbon tied to the grill trilled off toward him, away from me, in a blur.

Craig's movements were surreal, precise like a timepiece. He never once looked at me or the priest—who, as usual, never looked back at us—but I knew what expression he wore.

At the consecration, Father Stephen held the bread and wine aloft over his damp, shining head, but when he knelt to kiss the altar, he fell to his knees. He planted his face full, hard, on the stone.

Craig waited. He nodded for me to ring the bells.

Father didn't rise. He gripped the sides of the table above him, heaving to catch his breath. His palms slipped on a corner of the altar cloth; the chalice tottered.

Craig ran to him. From behind, he grabbed the old man under each armpit, pulling him to his feet. They staggered together like clowns while the parishioners gasped and watched over their unfolding hands, but before anyone else could get past the railing to help, Craig had him back in his chair, head down, panting. I heard whirling fans and whispers. When Father Stephen finally stood, shaking, to wave dismissively and have us carry on, Craig put his own hand up— *Wait!*—and everyone obeyed.

After a good, long silence, Father Stephen breathed deeply and spoke. We abbreviated the Mass. I continued to linger in the wrong place and miss my cues, and each time I looked to Craig for direction, he glared back with that same sharp stare he'd given me in the sacristy. *Wake up!* it seemed to say.

After my son and his girlfriend dropped me off at home that afternoon, it was Gerald's, rather than Craig's, disappointment I felt watching me in the kitchen as I left the gin out for my Costco Achievement Martini. My frozen goods were safely stowed, and the plastic-wrapped cans could wait awhile on the table. If Gerald had real concerns about my overindulging, I thought, he should accept my invitation to stay for dinner—he and Xenia. Then he could keep an eye on me. But work trumps all with Gerald, even my hospitality. They left quickly.

One day, you turn around and see you're no longer a kid: You're not unsure of much, and nothing's pushing you back. You suddenly realize that you're the strongest one standing in the room, but for that reason it's now your turn to hold things up. You're in charge. Craig seemed to have been born knowing that. Perhaps that was to steel him for a short future. And it now would appear that my son's noticing things he might not be so keen on overseeing either. If that's so, in his case I truly hope that scowl is just an inherited look, and not any sort of augury.

The day's fog had grown so fat it was dripping from the eaves. I took my cocktail—only the second of the week—and hit the porch. Regardless of whether he would ever want to join me out here again, I toasted Gerald—to his health, his strength, his wheels, his new love, and to manning his place in the world: Mine.

CHAPTER 4

My doorbell needs help. It's been busted for years and emits more of a sizzling, short-circuit sound than any sort of greeting. I don't know why Dorothy still uses it—she has her own key—but she tore me from a dull, cloying dream when she rang the next morning. Repeatedly.

By the time I'd girded myself and walked out of my bedroom, she'd let herself in and was busy in the kitchen, her hands on her hips and her Giants cap on under the buzzing tube lights. She had her back to me and appeared to be surveying the spoils of my night as the damning sunshine spotlit the countertop. The room was more than bright enough without the overhead light, and as she turned toward me, I saw her quick, birdlike eyes flutter behind her sunglasses, which she hadn't yet removed. She seemed worried, which in turn made me feel sheepish, then impatient at feeling sheepish in my own kitchen. Then again, first things first: Coffee.

With an exaggerated sigh she picked up my phone from where it lay facedown on the Formica table. I'd left it out of the cradle again, and it had no charge.

"I tried calling you last night," she said. "Many times."

A motorcycle ripped by out front, like a monster roaring. She must have left the front door open. Morning had never been Dorothy's best time.

"The cameraman comes in fifteen minutes," she said. "*His* time is valuable."

Her little teeth showed—more to inhale than smile—and she sounded shakier than I felt.

"We need this morning sun," she said.

I promised to get ready as fast as I could. On my way to shower I pointed her to Mr. Coffee, but she first went back to my room to lay out clothes for the day's shoot.

By the time I returned she'd slowed down a bit, sitting on the porch in the sun with her steaming cup of tea. Her fingers looked thin and bluish on the white mug, and the straight-cut hair that stuck out from under her cap looked dirty. I worried she might be over-dieting again—something we used to watch when she was younger—and I tried not to stare as I entered the room, but we know each other too well. As soon as she caught me furtively examining her, she diverted my attention, wagging her long finger between the switched chairs.

"What is all *this*?" she said with a little grin. At last.

"Oh, we have big projects of our own too," I said, hoping for more smile. "What's that bit Gerald always repeats, from work? 'Change or die'?"

Her smile fell. She hopped up to appraise my hair. She refolded my collar and had me tuck in my shirt. She asked me to go back and shave—that made sense—but when she also pointed out that my nose and ears needed trimming, I insisted on sitting a moment to finish my coffee before taking anything sharp to my face.

Again the doorbell buzzed in its shirking way, and Dorothy sprinted out to it. Even if I hadn't known her cameraman was coming, I could have guessed, from all the apologies she gave the man out front, that he was someone doing her a big favor. He didn't get past the doormat—instead she called back to fetch me, and in a minute the three of us were outside, trudging toward the beach.

Dorothy caught her breath and introduced us on the way. Brad was a squat, woolly, quiet man who carried large packs of gear over both shoulders with the strength and dutiful acceptance of a mule. Dorothy's shiny new camera—the one I'd seen her use at her birthday picnic, for stills—hung heavily from her neck alongside her light meter. In each fist she carried a case with one of her large, silver-lined umbrellas. It felt like we were embarking on a voyage. I felt proud to know a little about her gear, and I was even more pleased to see her energy start to pick up. She loved her work—something I've always admired about her. But she wouldn't let me carry anything.

"We've got to hurry for this light," she said. "But don't get all red and sweaty, Dad. Look good."

Finally, after scampering across the Great Highway and down a parting of the dunes, she eased up a bit. It was a hopeful morning, with an open, milky-blue sky that would lighten anyone's mood. Even the gulls that followed us were laughing. We slowed our pace and joined the few other people who jogged past us along the smooth beach with dogs or boards or their shoes in their hands. Dorothy and Brad put their palms to their brows to scope settings, their teeth gleaming. The slanting morning sun cast long shadows and flashed from the foamy tips of waves as the Pacific batted roll after roll of tangled, sparkling lace upon the shore.

To the south, a white Beach Patrol truck with two red rescue boards stopped, facing the surf. Brad nodded us away from that. He returned to climb a dune behind us. Dorothy and I followed.

First they wanted to film me high on a dune, watching the passing waves with Mount Tamalpais and the coastline in the background. The Miwoks saw the silhouette of a sleeping woman in that mountain's shape. We could see all the way past it to Point Reyes and the bright sand cliffs where Sir Francis Drake first discovered them for himself. Looking out, I began to guess what story Dorothy thought this scene might tell—the lone elder, standing at the edge of everything, holding a hand to his wizened visage as he gazes out in wonder at what might lie beyond that last horizon. Either that or he's watching the currents drag out some overly cocky surfer, as they do each year.

It took a great deal of fuss for them to set things up—to take light readings, readjust reflectors, and set up additional lights to wash out the shadows. It made me understand Dorothy's earlier anxiety about time, so I did my best to help by being responsive to her direction.

She hummed a little as she tried to put some shape in my hair. She plucked at my eyebrow and rubbed something on my nose to mute the shine while Brad kept shooting stills.

Suddenly, Brad waved her back, she ran to his side, and they both began taking pictures. I turned toward them once, to see what more they wanted, and they yelled—*No, stay!*—redirecting my gaze to the ocean. I felt a tad self-conscious as some strangers passed by, but then Dorothy plodded back to rearrange my collar. She held me gently by the shoulders and repositioned me.

"Stare out," she said, pointing west. She walked backward, away from but still facing me.

Brad moved in and aimed his camera from beneath my chin.

"Search the horizon," she said a second later. Her voice grew softer; it was difficult to hear her over the waves.

"Turn south. Squint. More."

"Dude looks like Redford," Brad muttered, ostensibly to her.

"Doesn't work with him," she replied.

"No—serious," he said from behind his lens.

She continued, "Now—slowly—turn to me."

I was relieved to turn and face her again. She stood still, holding her hand up to keep me back, in place. She looked small and lovely in the sunny breeze; to me, she looked more like the actor on-scene than I felt.

Brad lowered his camera, and our attention scattered.

I hoped we might be done. Dorothy dabbed a tissue at her eyes, checked her watch, then drank from the stainless steel bottle she wore dangling from a carabiner. Brad, after studying the shoreline, pulled out one of those cellular phones everyone talks at on the bus. He shook it in frustration, and then held it close again, reading something on the little black screen. Dorothy pulled hers out and began pressing her thumbs on it as if to ascertain that it was indeed made of a durable material.

I may one day be the last man alive in this city without the requisite nomad gear. Leave me behind.

Dorothy pointed into the dunes.

There came Carol, descending uncertainly over the shifting sands like a boozy spinster in heels. She looked up from her feet just long enough to wave a small pastry bag with one hand while she pressed a ragged sun hat to her head with the other. I gasped as she nearly fell. It was a relief to see her—an ally senior, a friend. Even in shades and a big hat, and with the sun so bright, it was odd how easily I'd have recognized her on my own, despite that distance and how dark and cold it had been when we were last here.

It was a happy surprise to me, seeing her join us, but obviously they'd been expecting her all along. I then recalled how Carol, over dinner—just three days ago?—had mentioned Dorothy's film, but I'd thought nothing of it at the time. Dorothy must have driven Carol out from her place and dropped her off to fetch provisions at the Java Beach Café before rousing me. It was uplifting to see her so eager to join us—she whooped a little down the small, sandy avalanche she'd caused—but when I moved to go help her, Dorothy made it clear this was no time for fun: Carol was late, I was to stay neat, and Brad was already reassembling gear so fast you'd think we were under attack.

Dorothy grabbed the bag from Carol and dragged her over to me.

"Sorry—got lost," Carol said in the shuffle. "Wrong dune."

She and I were to be costars, evidently. Dorothy pointed the camera at her from a few angles, almost like a threat of punishment, and then held her meter under the rim of Carol's hat as Carol smiled and struggled to say a quick "Good morning!" to me. I was flattered by her winking, as if it were some accomplishment of mine that she should continue to be friendly to me, and in that instant I remembered having delayed calling her back the other day out of worry that I'd offended her. I felt I should apologize, but how could I say it? *Sorry I made a wisecrack about your hard-won sobriety after inviting you out to watch me drink wine?*

Dorothy gave us no time for small talk. Carol tried to retie the ribbon of her hat, but Dorothy whisked it away from her, roughly, and we both stared in alarm.

She explained that we were rushing because the tide was rising, and fast. They wanted to use the surf-flattened sand, and the beach would fill up with people the longer we waited: It would stay empty and quiet just a little longer. Carol apologized profusely.

We watched in silence as Dorothy replanted a tripod and Brad switched lenses. It seemed pointless to start a conversation when some new direction might be shouted at us at any second, without warning. Carol tried to light a cigarette, bowing her head against the wind and clicking her lighter even more dramatically than she had the other night. I decided she's one of those people who look more at ease, more themselves, out of bright light. One teetotaler I used to know, a fellow teacher who'd go out to lunch with me now and then on Fridays, always said he was more comfortable with others when they drank. I tried to help Carol by cupping my hands for her again, but I was too slow: Dorothy shouted *Carol!*—and she stubbed it quickly.

The morning had been plotted, in detail. Carol and I were to walk the edge of the water, with the surf erasing our footprints, as they shot us from behind. Dorothy had us move slowly. Carol was to dangle her sandals at her side in one hand. My tatty sneakers and socks had been taken from me, and my jeans cuffed.

Each time we got about one hundred feet away from them, Dorothy and Brad called us back to do it again, just a little differently.

The first take we kept our hands in our pockets, with our elbows occasionally touching, so that we appeared to be in deep, but shared, thought.

Then we were told to stop and look out at the surf and sky. We stepped closer to the water until it lapped at our ankles. We did this once without a word, toweled off our feet quickly, and did it again.

Finally, for the last shot, Dorothy ran up and showed us how she wanted us to hold hands and walk into the wind. She had us stroll a bit, a dozen paces out, saying and doing little, and then turn to take a long, fond look into each other's eyes. Fade to black.

I imagine both of us knew this direction would come sooner or later, so the most awkward thing about doing the scene for me was taking it seriously enough to keep a straight face. First take, we walked away from Dorothy and Brad too fast, and they both shouted for us to come back and start over. Then, this time slower, we made it nearly all the way out when Carol yelped and leaped off a burrowing hermit crab she'd stepped on. That was good—it loosened everyone up a bit, and Carol, who couldn't help but be a little unnatural on camera, had been trying too hard to please Dorothy. For our next take, we were allowed to talk to each other but were told to keep our facial expressions and gestures "big." It was the first chance I had to look her straight in the eye that morning, and when I did, I was reassured that the clouds I'd seen earlier had vanished.

We stopped on cue and turned to each other.

"I planned to call," I said. "But I planned too long."

She smiled as she took my hands in hers.

Since we were in profile, I hammed it up a little by furrowing my brow and peering into her eyes to give her a dramatic, searching look, as if to say: *Where, Martha, would we be without that annuity thing?*

That was partly for Dorothy's amusement and Brad's camera, and partly in the hope that Carol might pardon me. And she did.

"I host next," she said. "Okay?" She squeezed our hands between us, perhaps a little too naturally for the camera. Carol is very genuine. Earlier, when she'd watched a passing dog with too much interest, Dorothy had immediately cut the scene in obvious frustration. But this time we were allowed to carry on, and when I accepted her dinner invitation with a knowing nod, she too nodded grandly, pointing her chin over my shoulder, nudging our attention to the far horizon. So it would appear Carol can act too.

Together we turned, shielding our brows to redirect our calm, self-satisfied watch over the Great Riptide of Unfunded Retirement. She put her arm in mine and pulled me closer, pressing her cheek to my shoulder even though the camera would never see it. It felt as if we'd worked together before.

Dorothy tried to shout—*That's a wrap!*—but she'd gone hoarse, her voice taken by the wind. As Brad mobilized to strike the set, she dropped heavily to sit in the sand, warily watching the waves.

I didn't need to remind Dorothy that in return for my being in her production she'd promised to stick around afterward, for lunch. Brad had repacked his satchels in minutes and was running up the dunes like a dog chugging upriver when Carol called out to him to bum a ride. I'd invited her to stay and join us, but she got cloudy on me once again, saying she needed to rush back into town. I almost didn't believe her. When she said "I'll call tonight," I knew she would do better than I had. She ran to give Dorothy a kiss on the top of her cap and said a farewell that made Dorothy grab her hand and squeeze hard. Then she tottered off after Brad, across the shifting sand.

Dorothy stayed sitting until she'd fed all her pastry to the shameless gulls. This time she let me help lug her gear back to the Jeep. When she told me she preferred to take *me* out to lunch, it sounded scripted. And when she took my elbow and tugged me away from the house and down the sidewalk, and I felt her grip as weak as a child's, I knew she'd planned this time together too—that our lunch would be something more than payback for my performance.

"You know Carol and I are getting together again?" I said, hoping to get her talking and make her feel better.

She smiled from behind her shades—that news pleased her—and then returned to staring into the few storefronts we passed on Judah Street. She peered in each window as if she were a tourist in her old neighborhood, or worried about her looks. Her footsteps were quick but tentative, and I let her set the pace until we realized we'd walked past the half dozen places that serve lunch.

I stopped her.

"Are you okay?" I said.

She entwined her arm in mine, squeezing as if to shush me and pull me out of the path of an oncoming stroller. In that tighter grip I'd begun to get my answer.

We turned back to the Vietnamese noodle restaurant that used to be our family's favorite. We hadn't been there together in years.

I led us to a table deep inside, away from the windows, hoping she might remove her shades and show herself at last. Suspended on the wall above us were three huge lacquered panels with a pastoral scene—something I must have seen dozens of times. Dorothy settled in, methodically repacking her glasses and touching her cellular phone to shut it off.

Finally, she folded her hands and looked up.

"I've been having stomach trouble. I was taking tons of antacids. So I decided it was doctor time. Yesterday they had me do an ultrasound." She distractedly pressed her hand to her belly, below the table. "They found a growth on my pancreas. I never even knew where that was. It's connected to your liver."

I nodded like a fool. Remembering how she'd told me, on our last call, that she was going in for tests—that helped delimit my growing panic at her words. It anchored what she'd said to a real spot in time that was *past*—an already happier past. Her eyes looked flat, as if she were lost in the dark but growing accustomed to it.

"We scheduled the earliest PET scan they have. This Friday."

"It's serious, then?" I said. "Pancreas growths are bad, right?"

It sounded ridiculous as soon as it came out. Even she grinned as she looked down, shaking her head in disbelief. She took off her cap and pressed her hands to her temples, smoothing her hair back like a bathing cap—an old tic of hers, something she does when she gets tense.

"It's a tumor." She took a sour-looking sip of water. She watched beyond my shoulder as someone exited the restaurant and the refracted bar of daylight passed over her face. "They're sure of *that*. So it's not good news. A scan will help see how big it is, and where. And how aggressive it is."

Aggressive? They use *that* word—like it has a will of its own? Like something with bared teeth rushing at the baby I bathed when she was just a little handful? Dorothy had been cute as a field mouse. I'll never forget the marvel of watching her blossom, like a whole summer's unfolding in a field of wildflowers—a miracle that's defined "growth" for me ever since. Until this moment.

I felt queasy. It was a struggle to look her in the eye.

She pressed her chin up on her fist with the same controlled, hard expression she'd worn earlier that morning at my door. She looked like she might laugh, cry, or shout. I wondered if she were amused, even—that's how much bitterness was welling up inside me at hearing her deliver this news, and so coldly.

"Really, Dad? You're going to do the word thing *now*?"

I didn't know I'd spoken aloud.

"I'm so sorry, Dorothy. So, so sorry."

She sipped her water again, her eyes never leaving mine.

"It's just not good news. There's a biopsy scheduled soon after the scan. We will know more next week. It might mean surgery right away. Almost definitely chemo."

She would not want to see me tearing up. I had to look away.

How absurd they were—these enormous, heavy panels hanging over our lunch. *Should these oxen really be standing up to their necks in a rice paddy? Would little kids really ride cattle to fly kites?* It must irritate Dorothy too—I imagined—to see this shiny fantasy looming above our heads. But she kept still, watching me, giving me the time I needed to take in all she was saying.

I've spent many hours pondering death, all of them wasted, because you can't win: Death will come, and you will go. But despite that I've still allowed myself the comfort of believing that if you go with your eyes open, dragging along a little glory, love, or courage in your wagon as you cross the line—*that* might help. But what if you aren't given even enough time to gather *that*? What possible solace can any parent even pretend to hold out to their dying child?

"Dad—stop?"

She was still staring. Her eyes grew wide as inkwells. She again flattened her hair behind her ears, and, for what felt like the millionth time, looked exasperated to feel it not stay in place—just as it never had.

She let her hands drop.

"We just don't *know* yet, okay?"

"But you're telling me you might have cancer."

She scanned the room, but nothing good was coming.

"Sweetheart?" I said.

"Please," she said.

"What can I do?"

"Just hang on. Take care of yourself. Keep your phone charged. Answer your calls." Her fingertips tapped mine, on my empty glass. "Just don't go *off* again."

It wasn't entirely clear how she meant this, but I agreed to everything. Her hand was clammy. I took a big, deep breath, as if I were once again teaching her how to hold hers underwater.

"I can't deal with you if you do that anymore," she said. "I can't worry about you right now."

"Please do not," I said.

"Just let me call the shots for a while."

"Like this morning," I tried.

"Yes—like that," she said, shaking her head, but with a tight grin. "And now we'll change the subject."

A sizzling fire pot descended between us.

I was famished. Dorothy ate a little too. The last table soon cleared and we had the place to ourselves. She did most of the talking, with an ease I hadn't heard in her all day, and for which I was also grateful.

Dorothy spelled out a few more things for me, during lunch.

She became friends with Carol a year ago when working at one of the firms she contracts with, on a film project. Carol was the in-house copyeditor, and she said she'd seen the writing on the wall—that the value business placed on copyediting and proofreading would plummet as the world regressed to audiovisual communication. However, Carol needed to keep her job long enough to finish her master's in counseling—her AA experience got her interested in this—so she'd "proactively" volunteered to be involved with the HR film project, and so, by working with Dorothy, she made herself a "value-added" employee. Dorothy said Carol's the easiest person to talk to; they got to know each other well over the year and, based on Dorothy's stories, Carol said I sounded like someone she'd like to meet. So our picnic introduction had indeed been no accident—although Dorothy wouldn't say why she'd never before thought of matching us herself.

Dorothy also said that right after yesterday's ultrasound, she and Carol had walked by the chemo clinic to take a "desensitizing" peek. It's a good preview of what she may eventually go through, she said. That's how she is: Jump in feetfirst, look at everything. She didn't say, however, if said desensitizing had actually been achieved.

"Does Jackie know?"

Her eyes widened as she shook her head.

"Gerald told me about Italy," I said.

"Mom hasn't called in a month."

That was a relief. Poor Jackie would be a mess when she found out.

"She went for the full summer. I don't want to call her back early," Dorothy said. "You, Carol, and Gerald—we'll keep it just us for now, okay?"

Carol had already offered to accompany her to whatever appointments and treatments she needed. It was unsettling to realize I now shared such a big secret with a woman I'd only just met. What was even harder to imagine was Dorothy alone, stepping further from family into these circles of near strangers. When I pictured that, she grew smaller, more vulnerable. I should have guessed yesterday that Gerald knew.

"Carol's like a mother to you," I said, too quickly.

"No, she isn't," she said, straining to smile. "But if you two hit it off, I'm good with that."

She worries so much about everyone else that she leaves little care for herself. When Jackie first left me, nothing in Dorothy's childhood had prepared me for the regularity of her calls and visits, the surprise take-out, and all the feelings she started sharing when we sat alone together. That was when she first opened up with me and criticized some of her mother's choices—the melodrama, the weight she'd put on. Dorothy said Jackie once griped about me for so long on one phone call that she'd hung up on her. I know she loves her mother—even though they fought a lot throughout Dorothy's high school years—and if she really did feel the need to ask Jackie to stop trashing me, I'm sure it was just as much out of care for her mother's dignity as to save any high image she has of me. Still, what surprised me more than Dorothy's compulsion to tell me these things was, in the next breath, her immediate apology for "oversharing" (her word)—as if she'd been a burden.

I'll never know my parents as intimately as my kids have been forced, by divorce, to become acquainted with theirs. I regret many things they've seen and heard. No wonder Dorothy reached out to strangers first when she herself, with her tumor, became her own biggest problem.

After lunch we walked back to her Jeep. She was dry-eyed and calm. We said our regular goodbye-things like we always do, offering no room for the new intruder in our lives. It was reassuring to make simple comments about the fog and plot our next visit. She said the shoot had gone well; she was pleased and she'd seen a few things on camera that she'd like to work more with. Could we schedule another shoot? *Of course.*

But at the car, when we hugged goodbye, as we occasionally do, I couldn't help but hold her longer than usual, closer and tighter. I felt her harden. These things happen sometimes in an instant: You go from caring to desperate clinging for fear of what you'll say next, once it's over and you're separate—what new distance you might see.

She beeped her car open before I let go. To my surprise, she faced me with the same wary look I'd grown familiar with back in the early days of my divorce: *Don't go far*, it said.

CHAPTER 5

William Blake once wrote that "the road of excess leads to the palace of wisdom." Of course, those words have been misquoted to excess since then. But they've always struck me as true, despite being an inversion of the pop wisdom of my thirties: That you don't know what you've got till it's gone. Blake instead reminds me that you don't know what you've got till you've had too much.

We may be there, I thought that evening after hearing Dorothy's news. *Maybe I don't need any more time to myself.*

I had been sleeping more and more, but you can always chalk that up to age.

I had been eating less, but that was because it felt so fruitless to cook for myself each night, so that, most days, food was merely fuel. In the beginning, I used to go through the motions, setting my place at the table, timing the meal prep with *All Things Considered* for that ersatz conversation—talking back at the news—but when it was over, sitting in the middle of the empty kitchen, the noises of suppers past would return to me, and I'd see the wife and kids that used to make them, and then I'd fold in and simply wallow. You learn to indulge yourself as you would a guest. I guess because I still believed I was *choosing* to wallow, it was safe. But I'd also discovered that the trouble it takes to launder and fold a napkin and light a candle isn't worth the thin comfort it brings while you work through another stew-o'-the-week. I always spent the better part of those meals in anticipation of getting back to my porch chair.

And—I might have begun drinking to excess again. That can creep up slowly. I had yet to quit the martinis, as I'd promised Dorothy, and with my condition I'm to limit myself to a little wine or beer at most, with food, but after Jackie left I'd regularly ignored that, sometimes skipping my seizure meds a day here and there to make room for things. I confess: I courted shame and pain; I wanted to suffer and look ugly and hurt in front of everyone. But I can never dodge self-reflection for long.

Then what does an excess of solitude look like?

I remember my grandmother, who, though she lived with us, spent most of her free time in the large pantry off the kitchen that was hers alone. I'd catch her sitting sometimes, upright and quiet in the rocker by her window, as she worked her way through one of her precious slices of Schweitzer cheese, which she took in tiny bits from a saucer she held on a pillow in her lap. If she didn't notice me in the doorway, she'd slowly chew and swallow every morsel, her jaw quivering, as if savoring each molecule of flavor. She'd sit for half hours like that, staring past our fence at the surrounding cornfields, her powdered nose dilating at the lilacs in the spring breeze, and then she'd rise, rinse her plate under the faucet, and resume whatever chore she'd been performing as if it were all one ritual. It was wrong of me to consider her lonely during her final days, however: She lived with three more people than I do now.

Thinking along those lines that night, I ignored the urge to have a second drink and get morose about Dorothy's illness. That self-indulgence would just sicken me as well. She needed better from me.

The next morning I called Gerald first, even though he never picks up at work. I lied in my voice mail and said the Costco cashier had double-charged me for each bag of coffee. *Must be those new laser-scammers!* I told him I'd already spent ten minutes on the phone with Costco leadership, and that they'd insisted we show up in person with my receipt to fill out some paperwork for a refund. And besides, I'm not the card-carrying member—he is. Technology errors drive Gerald around the bend. My story guaranteed a callback.

I called Carol next. There was no reason to put that off anymore. She answered on the first ring, as if she'd been sitting there waiting.

"I was just about to dial," she said. The word "dial" had a cozy sound, when she used it.

I tried chatting about the shoot the day before, leaving her room to bring up the Big Topic first, should she choose. I remembered her saying, that first night, how she disliked telephone conversations. Still, she sounded surprisingly at home on the other end of the line, with a little more New Jersey in her voice than I'd noticed before.

She was enthusiastic about the film. In fact, she seemed to feel some stake in it—part ownership. She joked that Dorothy had initially come up with the idea of involving me because I work cheap and I'm always available—living on set, if you will, as I do. She said that my being relatively lean—"which is not so common for your demographic"—also worked well on camera. That and my thick head of hair.

How ridiculous it would be, at my age, to get swept up so easily by such flattery. I thought she must be teasing.

"That's thick *gray* hair," I said.

"It's *there*, is my main point," she said. "Feel good about that. Half our kids' friends are bald already."

She said it was important that all audiences be able to identify with me on both sides of the story we're presenting. "You look active enough to be sympathetic to everyone. We want people our age to see you and want to be like you, and start planning their retirements. And the young people should think: Hey, when I'm in *my* sunset years, I want to get my ducks all lined up like this dude."

Dude? Carol was in a jolly mood.

"I'm surprised you wouldn't worry instead that the young people might panic at the idea of having to one day push someone like me around in a wheelchair."

That stopped her. Me too—I didn't know what to say after that.

"You're very lucky, Jim," she said.

"I am. In some things."

"I mean it. You've got your health. Your pension. A nice place to live by the beach. You've got hobbies too, I guess—your books."

She slowed. The list sounded like something with which she'd hoped to comfort herself more than me.

"The books are real," I said. "No guesswork involved there."

"Two lovely kids," she said, slowing.

We both went quiet.

Finally, she said, "She told you, didn't she?"

I was nodding to myself before I could say it out loud: *About the tumor?* That's one hard word to utter without thinking too much beforehand. It overwhelms everything around it.

"Jim, I don't know how to—I'm *so* sorry." The sudden fall of her voice was very moving. "I—I don't know you well enough yet to say all the things I feel like saying right now."

I needed a moment myself, to respond.

"That's just why I called," I said, and then accepted her dinner invitation.

That was enough. We set a date for the next evening—Friday night. The urgency was understood. I told her I looked forward to talking more in person. And after another, longer, somehow moist silence on her part that I could not find a word to fill, we said goodbye and rushed off the phone.

Gerald got through as soon as I hung up. It sounded like he was pacing a noisy floor somewhere. He mumbled in frustration as I rebuffed every alternative he suggested to his driving out to the house. Soon he gave up, agreeing to come immediately after work; he even promised to try to get out early so we might beat the commute traffic down the peninsula.

It was dishonest of me to force him into coming, but what else could I do? We needed to talk. I could feed him a warm dinner. I was sure that if I'd told him over the phone that I knew Dorothy's news, he'd put off seeing me for days—during which a lot could happen. And any real engagement with him *on* the phone is impossible, especially at work. Talking openly about Dorothy over supper would be a relief for him too.

I thawed a lasagna—his favorite—and got it in the oven before he arrived, just before 5 p.m., huffy but as punctual as ever. I pressured him to sit for an after-work beer before we "took off," but he remained standing, pushing his back to the doorjamb and tapping his foot loudly until he noticed the oven was on. He peered inside, shook his head, and softened.

"Did you *lie* to me again, Dad?" he said, hunching over the open door for a whiff. I will never grow used to how tall he's grown.

He inhaled deeply and let his shoulders drop a bit as he stood to face me.

"Dorothy told you, didn't she?" he said.

I nodded.

"Well, you're a lousy liar," he said, his eyes already, briefly, misty.

He accepted a beer and headed for the porch—just like in the old days. I hadn't had him here alone, for an evening, in nearly a year.

"I'm glad you're not angry," I said.

He tried to grin. He told me that Dorothy had already emailed him, saying to expect my call. It made sense that she'd prepare him like that—he hates surprises. And, he said, he'd already planned to be out in the neighborhood anyway, since X (as he calls her) was at the cathedral that night.

"But it's Thursday," I said.

"She rehearses for choir," he said. "They do a lot of singing."

I marveled that Gerald was already so serious about this choir girl to go to such trouble. But then I also realized he must have been out here pretty frequently in the past few months, within two miles of home, without ever once stopping in to see me.

"Maybe we can hear her sing sometime?" I said.

"Not from here," he said. "You'll need to actually step inside the church."

He turned away as I mixed what I considered to be my last real drink. He can sometimes make you feel like you need to fight for his attention. My father had *my* full attention any time he was in the same room with me, as infrequently as that was.

When I sat, Gerald waved his beer between our switched-around chairs, as if he hadn't just mentioned that change the other day. Or to see if I'd forgotten.

"I see *you've* been busy," he said.

I raised my glass. "To old times."

He tipped his chin—*Yeah*—as if he'd just remembered why he'd come. He sat and stretched his legs. The toe of one boot touched the back door.

"Okay," he said. "How much did Dorothy tell you?"

"They're sure it's a tumor. On her pancreas," I said. "She's got a scan tomorrow. Only Carol knows." The mention of Carol didn't surprise him; he must have met or heard of her already too.

"She also said your mother doesn't know yet."

He remained quiet.

"I think she told me everything," I said.

"She didn't tell you what the recovery stats are yet?"

"No," I said.

"Me neither."

"I think they need the scan and biopsy before they know that," I said.

"Yeah, well—with a growth on your liver or whatever—there's zero chance it'll be good news," he said. "But she hasn't been in touch with me about that either."

I began feeling guilty for having tricked him into talking.

"Have you tried to reach your mother?"

"I haven't heard from Mom in a month," he said. He plowed his nail-bitten fingers through his hair. "Perhaps, if you people would allow me to teach you how to *email*—"

"My understanding is that one must first be willing to use a personal computer before sending electronic mail."

Pulling on the worn Luddite-Dad mantle was no relief, however. It couldn't cover our shared dread for Dorothy.

"I don't think any of us should track Mom down yet," he said. "Not until there's good reason—like they're sure about surgery, or they discover more bad stuff. I told Dorothy we should just let Mom do her Mom Things overseas for a while."

"With Dick," I said.

"You've *got* to stop that, Dad," he said, smiling at last. "You know I'm a jerk, and you'll get me in trouble. I already have this bad daydream where one day, when X meets the fam, she calls him *Deek* to his face with her great accent—I'll totally lose it."

"So it's that serious?" I said.

"Me and X?"

"No," I said, although that struck too. "I mean, sure, you two—but your mother?"

Clearly, I still needed to digest the fact that Jackie had a new beau. That, and the fact that I was the last to know.

"Well—*Yes* to X," he said, giving me a thumbs-up, even blushing a little, bringing back the private, emotional boy he'd always been. "*She is great.*"

Nothing in his tone showed that he sought my agreement, and that confirmed the sincerity of his feelings for her all the more.

"But," he said, "as long as Dick is in the picture, it is probable that one day X and he will need to be introduced, correct?"

A light popped on in my neighbor's back window.

Gerald shook his head to change topics, forcing the gravitas back into his face.

"Did Dorothy say anything else?" he said.

"No."

I waited.

He looked down.

"So you *do* know what she's most worried about right now?"

"No."

"You," he said.

I readjusted myself in my seat. *Worried about me why?*

"Because of last time—when Mom left? How bad you got?"

He leaned forward and put his empty down by his booted foot. He folded his hands in his lap. Every trace of mirth slipped off his face; he hadn't visited just to make jokes on the porch with me, or even to get some refund from Costco. This was the conversation he'd stayed for. And in truth, it wasn't a conversation I wanted to have with him just then, if ever. Yes—back then I did let all my balls drop, as I've admitted; I did drink to excess, consciously. And I still think that was somewhat excusable—at least for a while—given the shock. But I've never defended it to anyone afterward. Sometimes you need to flail a bit to see around the corners of your situation, and I willfully did so, but no one was ever invited to watch. It's nothing I would like to witness in others; that's why I did it alone. And I *do* take care of myself now—more deliberately and effectively, I sometimes think, than my kids look after themselves.

Gerald watched in silence, like he half expected me to ask: *And just how badly did I behave after your mother walked out on me one afternoon, son?* So I simply stared back and waited. Because, had I ever given my own father the imperious look Gerald was giving me just then, he'd have swatted my face off without looking to take aim.

Perhaps Gerald could read my thoughts at that moment, because he warmed up a little.

"Okay—Dorothy didn't say exactly *those* words," he said. "But it's true, you know: She really worries about you. So be good. Okay?"

That "Okay?" irked me. He wasn't really asking anything. Jackie and I had never demanded much in the way of formal respect from our kids—nothing beyond everyday common courtesy. Back in the seventies and eighties, and especially in the Bay Area, it would have been pointless to even hope for such a thing. But after Jackie left, I do remember feeling the floor going soft under me each time I faced off with the kids alone. Whenever you expose yourself as all-too-human before those who owe you respect, you lose some of it, irretrievably. After a divorce, if you try to enlist your kids' sympathy to listen to "your side," and I highly recommend *not* doing that, you give them the false impression that they're your peers, and that they understand more than they ever could—that your decades of additional life experience, which includes raising them from seed, isn't of value enough to tilt the scales forever. Even more worrisome is the possibility that your self-exposure might encourage them, later on, to take parenting even more lightly themselves.

I remember how Dorothy's interactions began to feel overly familiar, particularly in the first weeks after her mother left. Dorothy's increasingly outspoken concerns that I was wallowing in lonesomeness and sitting in the dark too long started to feel like an intrusion. Nagging. It simply was not her business. But if she dropped in and caught me napping or grumpy or unwashed or less than perfectly sober, she'd pay even more attention to me, and try even harder to sound cheery herself. It saddens me now to recall how she'd phone me every evening, and, because I had so little to report back, she'd tell me about her day, and I'd drift off, bored, in the details. She'd had a boyfriend for a while, and soon after Jackie left, they had begun having problems of their own; she'd replay their quarrels verbatim along with her analysis of what was wrong between them, and then go off on the differences between men and women in general, as if this were a fascination we shared, or as if she'd already been through enough battles herself for us to swap and savor war stories. I tried to be indulgent; I knew she was doing this for me, and I almost said as much—*You don't need to worry about me, sweetheart!*—but she craved that constant contact. She backed off a bit during Gerald's summer here, and after he'd returned to his place, I tried to keep my territory secure by not answering the phone each time she made her evening call. Slowly I nudged some order and scale back into our reduced-family system to ensure we didn't atomize entirely. And I still feel sure that was what she needed. Three years ago, anyway.

So I really didn't like Gerald's stare. I pretended not to notice. When my kitchen timer rang, I quietly rose to serve.

But Gerald stood and followed me into the kitchen. When I opened the oven, he opened the cupboard. When I opened the fridge to hand him another beer, he passed on it—he pushed it back at me with his palm, in fact—and poured himself a full glass of water, which he half finished standing by the counter. He poured me one and placed it smartly on the table next to my setting. I guessed this meant: *We are drinking water.* His mounting irritation was clear, even if his reasoning wasn't. So I had a decision to make: I could insist on having a glass of wine with dinner, as is my wont, and thus piss him off further for whatever reason he was choosing to be pissed off—something unpleasant for both of us—or I could do the generous thing and wait.

I chose the latter. He never stays long, anyway.

He pulled out a third plate.

"I invited X," he said over the running faucet. "Hope that's okay."

"Whatever you want, Gerald."

That irked him too. He turned.

"You remember the emergency room—correct?"

It took a second for me to realize we were still on his first topic: The Way I'd Been. That first winter after Jackie left, I'd taken a spill in the kitchen and on the way down knocked my head on the corner of the counter. I'd let everything go back then, and probably slipped on something. But head wounds leave an ugly amount of blood.

"You're referring to when your mother ran away?" I said. "Of course I do."

"You *do* remember?" he said.

"The hospital bills?" I said back, trying to smirk.

He waited.

"That I'd hit my head? Passed out?" I said. "That I still have the scar?" I began feeling the back of my head for it, to part my hair and show him.

"You were in the ICU for *two days*," he said with that look. "They even tested to see if you had the *DTs*."

He watched as if I were acronym-illiterate. I faced him squarely.

"I am aware of my own medical history."

The water trembled in the glass he gripped against his chest.

"Dorothy even made appointments to visit nursing homes for you."

I struggled to remain calm. He'd never told me that before. I do not like secrets.

"You know, it's most likely I just had a seizure," I said.

"So *what*?!"

"Look *here*, son." I'd begun to shout.

He stood taller and lowered his voice.

"What I'm saying is: That was really, *really* hard on Dorothy. That was *scary*, Dad. She found you in a pool of blood. You'd pissed yourself, you kept staring out, and all she could do was wait to see if you'd come back. *For sure* what Mom did sucked—one hundred percent—but you were not much more fun yourself, believe me."

I'm ashamed to say I wanted to smack the glass out of his hand.

"I have never done anything to intentionally hurt you *or* your sister," I said. "*Or* your mother. *Nothing.* You know that."

My eyes smarted, but I couldn't forget the fact that, for me, tears are rarely more than a self-pitying embarrassment.

"Never, Gerald. *Correct?*"

He pressed his lower back against the counter and exhaled.

"I know—okay, I know," he said. "I'm just saying Dorothy was in there with you every single hour, and for days afterward. She was there when they strapped your head square in the stretcher and when they shot you up like an animal. I was not. That was rough. On her."

"Well, I am sorry. Sounds like I was well attended to by pros. Maybe she shouldn't have hung around so much. I guess it's kind she chose to stay."

I addressed myself to the oven, but Gerald wouldn't move away from the counter. His knees knocked back and forth.

"You remember calling the ward nurse a 'festering barnacle'?" he said.

I refused to look up. He stepped aside.

"Are you sure that wasn't 'carbuncle'?" I said.

I dropped my potholder near his foot—intentionally or not, I cannot say—and waited for him to pick it up.

"Okay," he said, handing it to me. "I made up that one."

I stood and looked him in the face, and the poor fool thought he could grin us back to everyday life again. But behind that, in his big wet eyes, I found suffering, and I was more stung by that, and by imagining what terror must have been in Dorothy's face that day she found me, than by any of these other details he was retelling from my past. His voice had risen to a pleading I hadn't heard from him since he was a little boy, and when I set the bubbling casserole on the table, he watched me closely, alert, like a good dog who'd been trained to quietly stand guard, but who couldn't help but prick up his quivering ears in alarm at the slightest noise: *Something's wrong! Someone's coming!*

Above all, I was shaken to my core by the sudden, real possibility that I could one day lose the respect of my only son, who was telling me just then that the possibility of losing his only sister was hurting him even more. What if, one day, she left us, and he no longer cared?

"I bring all this up for one reason," he said with effort. "From now on, we've *all* got to be about Dorothy. Serious."

He was right. I reached up and patted his shoulder.

"Don't worry," I said. And I meant it. "I'm not going anywhere."

We let the lasagna cool, and as we both relaxed, he unburdened himself a little. Dorothy had told him about her symptoms from the very beginning, so he'd been struggling to keep it all to himself. Again, I was proud to see how close my kids were. I couldn't help but sense her presence from her side of the kitchen table, where the two of them as juice-lipped kids ate their Cheerios every morning. Gerald seemed to feel her presence too, even looking over to her spot once at the mention of her name.

"You know she has no health insurance?" he said.

Shit. I'd never given it a second thought after they graduated college. Our kids grew up in a family where, if you got sick, you simply went to the doctor. As city employees, we'd never thought twice about medical coverage.

He launched into describing the worst-case scenarios. He said Dorothy had blown most of her small savings on tests; the hospital took credit cards up front, but she would max hers out soon. Unless she applied for more. Her Jeep was still fairly new—she always needed a good-sized vehicle for her equipment—but she hadn't paid even half of it off yet; she'd probably need to sell it and spend down her assets, if such existed, before qualifying for Medi-Cal. "She needs to be poor," he explained unnecessarily. There were some soft services she could access for free, some support Carol was trying to hook her up with, including a trial program she'd discovered at UCSF. He also said Dorothy was considering letting go of her rent-controlled apartment—"Which is *suicide* in this market"—as it would be a stretch for her alone, since Viktor was moving out.

"Dorothy and Viktor have been living together?"

"Yup," Gerald said.

He also said bankruptcy might be an option, down the road.

At that, I had to put up my hand. I could take in most of what he was saying, but at the word "bankruptcy"—a concept I've never fathomed any deeper than is necessary to play Monopoly—he'd reached a point past which I'd be only pretending to follow him, and he would see that in my eyes. We'd already spent too many nights before like that, at the very same table, with me nodding as he described his technical work in "granular" detail. I had to be honest: I could take in no more.

"I'll do everything I can," I said, to make him stop.

He nodded. He knew that was true.

"If this is as big as they're afraid it might be," he said, "or even if it's a tumor that hasn't spread to her liver yet, her chemo treatments are probably going to start soon, and it'll be thousands of dollars. Tens of thousands."

"Whatever she needs," I said. "Tell me what to do."

I heard the second hand of the wall clock scratch against its plastic crystal as he froze and stared.

"I don't *know* what to do, Dad," he said. "That's what I'm saying."

The doorbell sputtered, and he jumped up to answer.

It was comforting to feel the kitchen floor rumble gently again as Xenia stepped inside, kissing Gerald audibly at the front door—her jacket crinkling warmly, like a saddle—before they both stomped back to me. Again, they were dressed alike. I suppose that's easy when all you wear is black. It was nice to get a kiss of my own from her on each cheek, after first meeting just two days ago, and to see her happily accept a wineglass. Gerald took one too, now, and relaxed.

We shut off the tube lights, lit candles, and ate together.

It took my breath away to see Xenia sitting so comfortably in Jackie's place. She and Gerald ate and drank and talked with gusto. They opened a second bottle of wine (I kept to one glass), and as she swept us up with a syntax that bordered on the absurd—"I am looking forward for this beautiful food!"—I felt like I was rewatching an old, well-loved movie.

Xenia also reminded me of someone I'd nearly forgotten, from my teaching years—a story that would have been inappropriate, that night, to share with the two of them.

I'd kicked off the first school year after Jackie's departure by impetuously announcing to staff and students alike that it would be my last: I would take the early option and retire at year's end. I figured I'd be virtually free of professional responsibility during that final stretch, knowing that in nine months I'd be done teaching forever, and so could focus my emotional energy on nursing my private wounds. I moved temporarily into Gerald's room, relegating my and Jackie's former bedroom to storage. I might have hoped she'd return and find a mess. I'd also deepened my back-porch routine by then, resulting, that winter, in my fall in the kitchen, the hospital stay, and the other troubles Gerald had just brought up. However, despite all that, I was still able to manage a full teaching load and make it to fifty-five, ending my career for what I'd dreamed to be an easier, long-postponed, well-earned retirement full of "literary activity."

The cherry atop all of this: I'd finally got a senior honors class, after nearly thirty years in public schools. If you're a certain type of teacher—which, that year, I was—you can walk through senior honors with your eyes shut. I taught at Lincoln High, just a dozen blocks from home—to which I could also walk with my eyes shut. I enjoyed the exercise, trudging uphill each day to assume my post at my gray steel desk before classes that averaged thirty-eight kids. The room was sometimes so overpacked we were grateful to absentees: It left us more air to share.

Those were *not* halcyon days for Lincoln High either, nor for the district overall. San Francisco has never been overgenerous in educating its kids. Even after the eighties, when Mayor Feinstein was accused of "Manhattanizing" the city by building more empty office towers in downtown's sludge, our city's per-pupil funding remained among the lowest in the nation. Still is, last I heard. Jackie and I and our colleagues had always tried our best to make the system work for kids, but it wasn't until she'd left that I'd allowed myself to truly see how shabby our facilities were, and to experience how distracting hardship can be. We had fixtureless bathrooms and holes in our windows; I'd stop midlecture to find myself momentarily blinded by gaps in the torn shades that half covered our window grid in patches, while my kids moved desks every ten minutes to keep their papers out of the glaring squares of sun.

All this to say that my final year of teaching was no idyll, for anyone. I don't recall much of it; I'd let down all illusions, knowing we were all at the end of our respective school careers, and I saw every day the finish line of a race in which I'd already not come in first. I even indulged in some role-playing—wearing a sports jacket each day, using a fountain pen, lecturing gravely from my desk over folded hands. I'd also managed to eschew the personal computer that some corporation had been trying to insinuate into our classrooms, and instead hauled in an old bookstand for the corner of my desk, where I placed the same moldy, unabridged dictionary I'd used my entire career. (I raffled it off for free our last day, and even then it was left behind in someone's locker.) The bookstand spun like a lazy Susan, and the dictionary was usually open to my students, who were forced to use it almost as a penance. I would require the student to pronounce their word aloud, tell the class how it functioned as a part of speech, explain its etymology, and use it in a sentence. A few students loved being called to use the dictionary, but my abiding memory is that most kids shunned it, and instead asked only the sorts of questions that led to a discussion of our feelings.

Anyway. There was a noodle house down across the tracks where a colleague and I would repair on Fridays for lunch and a quick beer during our prep hour. Thus fortified, I'd teach my honors class the last period of the afternoon. For teens, this is the longest hour of the week, a time of torpor—a torture to us all—and even though I never got much love from that late Friday class, I expected even less, and the best I could hope was to keep most of them entertained. The few stoners were willing to join my game, addressing me as

Captain—we'd watched *Dead Poets Society* together in class, over two Fridays—and doing their best (often successfully) to launch me off on some subject on which they knew I'd all too happily sail. Clever, lazy, buzzed kids. Once I caught them wagering on who could get me talking the longest. That stopped when one day I confused them by threatening to place a bet myself.

This was just over three years ago, in 1996, just before Hong Kong's return to China and after the USSR's post-glasnost collapse, and because San Francisco is such a small city and so densely packed, our public schools instantly felt like they'd been flooded with a fresh influx of Russians and Chinese. Of the former, Pavel was my sharpest and best-loved student. He loudly and repeatedly announced that he was descended from Vladimir the Great. None of us knew what such a one-thousand-plus-year lineage meant, nor how to prove it, but looking at him, it was possible to believe. He was tall and narrow with hair like rough-cut hay and a gray-gem glint in his overactive eyes. His constant smile gave him a vulpine look, and he sometimes grew so animated that he seemed to be speaking in tongues, putting on characters and entertaining his classmates nonstop in the back of the room, where he sat with his buzzed clique. His family had been in the States less than three years, and although his spoken English was quite good, it had taken some very aggressive bullying on his father's part for him to get a slot on the honors track because, along with being one of my brightest kids, he was one of my worst students. His handwriting was as much graphic art as anything else, and he rarely completed a test before the bell because he could not stop talking, even if only to himself.

At first I'd moved him to a desk up front and center, and yet, before I even noticed it happening, he'd slowly receded back, one desk every few weeks, bartering with and cajoling classmates until, lo and behold, there he was again, back in his former corner of power, where he'd started. Perhaps I'd unconsciously displaced him with new offenders up front, to face The Book, and I'd lost track over time of where Pavel was from week to week; or perhaps I'd willingly let him get away with these shenanigans out of respect for his doggedness, or because I'd grown fond of him and the diversion he created for us all, or because he, for some reason, had grown fond of me. It had never been my intention to impress my students in any way by wearing a sports coat and carrying a leather book bag that year—it was just a costume to cover the nothingness I'd felt, a mask of faux pride in my work—and I think Pavel, somehow ingeniously, understood and responded to that better than anyone. My classroom was a gray sea of faces that year, and Pavel's was a whitecap amid the small waves. By mid-April, just before my fall, I'd come to look forward to seeing him shoot up from the back of my last class each Friday to belabor some absurd point that would still manage to touch upon the entire week's discussion.

"My Captain!" he cried out one such day. "Today I read that the great poet Wallace Stevens was a *lush*!"

His eyes popped with false indignation. Some kids laughed; others looked altogether baffled.

"You were *reading*, Master Pavel? I am impressed," I said, playing our game. "But what is a 'lush.' Where did you see this?"

"In Florida. He was drunk."

"You were in Florida?"

"He was. I was here. In class. He was drunk."

"Wallace Stevens was a high-level insurance executive in Hartford, Connecticut," I said. He smiled to hear me capitalize on the teaching moment he'd created. "But it is true that he vacationed in Key West. So perhaps you read about what he did while he was on his spring break. He was very good at his day job. He was known as 'The Dean of Surety.'"

"But Captain, he tried to fight with *Hemingway*! He was fifty—he was an old man! And Hemingway—he was young and strong. He would beat him. He must be super drunk!"

Everyone relaxed into it. Pavel stood tall with his wet, wild smile. I myself had just enjoyed a Tsingtao with lunch at the Kingdom of Dumpling. A cool, briny fog spit through the shattered panes, ruffling the remaining window shades with a sound like distant sails taking wind. Ah, school days.

"Captain?! Would *you*," he said, "if *you* got drunk—would *you* put up your fist to fight a strong young man? Even if *you* were famous poet?"

"Who is drunker?" I said. "The young man or me—the Dean of Surety?"

"I bet you are more drunk."

There was more good-natured tittering around the room. But also, all eyes were on us.

"Well—tell me first, Master Pavel: What does 'surety' mean?"

Hmmm. He held his chin for effect. "'Surety' means 'to be sure'?" The dramatic lift of his voice, and eyebrows, at his own question also showed me he was now engaged.

"Want to bet on that?" I said. "Are *you* sure enough to bet *me*?"

And while I said that, and just as I had so many times during the year, I leaned forward from my desk to rap my forefinger on the great dictionary that lay open on the corner of my desk, screwing up my eyes like a bony old schoolmaster and jutting out my chin with just enough challenge to get a few hoots—*Ooooh, game on!*—daring Pavel to take it to The Book.

He loved this. Without hesitation, he strode up and bowed before the dictionary. Whenever Pavel bent forward, he looked as if he were hinged at the waist, neck straight. Perhaps he really did have some noble, inbred blood. The class watched him breathlessly, his fingers riffling through the big pages like a sprinter kicking up dust, until he stopped and slid his finger back down the page, peering closer.

"S-U-R-E-T-Y?" he asked.

"You tell us," I said.

"Yes—that is how to spell the word. And I am correct again. It means 'to be sure.' 'Guarantee.'"

"There are other meanings too—yes?"

He slammed the book shut, surprising us with its woody thud.

"Yes. But this is all the meaning I need now."

"Okay," I said. "So if *you*, just now, were a leader in the field of surety—because that's what they meant, by calling him 'The Dean'—you would have known whether or not you were right about the definition you'd given me, and you would have bet and won—right?"

His eyes glittered as if he'd just risen up from underwater.

"*Dah*, Captain!" he said.

"And if *I* were a surety expert, in the question you just asked me, I too would be sure of the odds for whether or not *I* could beat the young man, and I could make a safe bet on that basis—right?"

It had become too complex for anyone to laugh. Impatience flashed across Pavel's face as he became aware that he might be losing the floor. His knee knocked back and forth.

"He was drunk on spring break," he blurted out. "The Dean of Surety was what he did for work. When he didn't work, he was drunk."

He stared at me. He looked hurt.

"You smell like beer, Captain."

I wasn't shocked by this, but it silenced me. It seemed to have silenced the entire room too, for an instant.

"And you, Pavel, will see me after class." I waved him away even as he began his unsteady, slow-jog return back to his seat, slapping high fives down the long row of desks.

And now, at last, I recall why this memory would come so strongly to me the day after my daughter told me she was sick.

I had no intention of keeping Pavel too long after the rest of the class bolted out at the pealing bell. After all, I too was looking forward to my weekend, which would soon begin with an easy walk downhill, toward the Pacific and my porch. There was little to gain in disciplining Pavel now—on a Friday, within weeks of graduation, and at the whipping-tail end of my career. However, there had been something in his eyes and voice that day, in saying what he had about me before the stunned class, that worried me. It was out of character for him to so overtly make me—or anyone else—the butt of his joke.

He came back after a trip to his locker, and as he approached my desk in the vacant classroom, the wincing pain in his eyes, which I'd first seen earlier that day, returned. I recognized it: He reminded me of my brother. Why, I can't say, but he did. I could also smell liquor on him, and in his face, his usual wryness had gone soggy.

I carefully capped my pen, folded my hands on the blotter, and sat back—another week's work done.

"Pavel, you realize you're not getting a passing grade in this class?"

He clenched his jaw and nodded.

"And you know you must pass this class to graduate?"

No need to nod again, so he waited.

"Have *you* been drinking?" I said.

He nodded so vigorously, it stunned me.

"You could be kicked out of school for that, you know—so close to graduation?" I said. "*Why* are you drinking in school?"

He widened his stance.

"Why does any man drink?" he said. He took a deep breath and his nostrils flared.

"Why do *you* drink? Why does my father drink?" His eyebrows arched like a clown's. "I will tell you: We drink to be happy!"

He smirked, amused by his self-caricature and, no doubt, by my smiling at him.

"And are you happy?" I said.

"I was. Before."

"Good," I said. "And you're unhappy now because you regret having made fun of your favorite teacher in front of all his students—right?"

"No," he said. "I am not happy *now* because—I am not drinking!"

His smile this time did not work: I waited.

"Okay. I am not happy because—my friends are gone home. It is Friday and time to go." All guile drained from his eyes. "And I am not happy at home. Just like you."

"How do you know that?" I said.

"Because you tell us on Monday."

I do?

"You say how happy you are to be here with us and with all the great books we will read. And when you read your Monday poem, you sound happy. You look happy."

I used to begin each week by reciting a poem I knew the kids could get with little effort. For example, although my man The Dean was someone I dared not try aloud until the end of the school year, my kids always understood Dickinson or Frost or Angelou if I read with any feeling. Then, having thus reset the bar at a certain height for the week, students took turns on the remaining mornings reciting something they loved, explaining what the words meant. They experienced how reading aloud to others is so different from reading alone to oneself.

As I watched his shoulders sink, I recalled how Pavel had once stood tall and wide-legged before the class to recite "The Tiger" by William Blake. It was on one of our coldest, wettest afternoons. We'd all put on layers to keep out the chill, and he had worn a woolen trench coat. As soon as he'd begun—*Tiger! Tiger! burning bright*—I had to smile. He *would* choose such simple lines. With his back to me, chest out as he shouted the poem from memory to his speechless classmates, the expressions I saw on most faces showed an awe that bordered on fear. No funny personas for Pavel *that* day—just his clarion voice, with each straight line piercing our gray room with its martial cadence. No one dared move for seconds afterward, but when he dropped forward in that deep bow of his, the class stomped and clapped and hooted for a very long time, until he slowly rose.

I also recalled how, the Monday following his performance, I'd chosen "The Lamb" for contrast, and how moved I was to see him listen, sitting as quietly and crumpled as I'd ever seen him, with his eyes so heart-heavy they finally shut. *My brother.* No one else felt that poem as deeply as Pavel had that day.

I guess I've forgotten how much I loved teaching.

"You tell us on Monday you are glad to be here," he said again.

He'd caught me off guard, but I had to agree.

"You're right," I said. "I am happy to be here, teaching you."

"And you are not happy at home?" he said.

"That is my business."

"I ask only because you ask me," he said. "I feel that is fair."

I nodded.

I could have asked him not to drink, but that would have been hypocritical of me, we both knew it, and I would have lost whatever pedagogical power I still had over what he might be able to learn.

Instead, I reminded him of the classroom discussion norms we'd all signed off on at the beginning of the year—how we would not make fun of any individual, and how we'd always respect others' feelings. He nodded along.

I knew he was true to his word, and that I'd made my point, so I dismissed him.

But he remained.

"Captain, why are you retiring?"

He took a step closer.

"Are you *sick*?"

"No. I have family business to attend to." I had no other answer to share back then. "But I'm not sick. Thank you for your concern."

He looked only partially relieved.

"I am glad hearing this," he said. "My father—*he* is sick with cancer, but he will work as long as he can because working makes him strong. He says this."

I told him I was very, very sorry his father was sick.

He nodded, his eyes bulging as he continued—no time for my sympathy.

"He is happy when he works. He is happy when he drinks and eats. And he is happy with me. This is what he says. Every day. So I think you should not stop working, Captain. You are a good teacher. And you like to teach, correct?"

He shifted from foot to foot, focusing in turn on me, my desk, out the window, then staring away as I watched him become overwhelmed by the heartbreaking gloom that was growing around us.

What could I say? I knew his mother had died, years ago. She'd been a chemist in Chernobyl. I knew he'd been raised by his babushka and his father—an ashen, angular man who, the one time I visited to discuss Pavel's truancies and possible nongraduation, had left a rifle leaning nose up in the corner of the entryway. I know nothing about firearms, and I couldn't tell if the thing was loaded or a museum piece, but it sure looked ready for action to me, and that kept my visit short and down to business. It was clear the man shared my concern for his son—painfully so—and while his arm barred the advance of his mother, who'd trundled out wearing an apron over her blue nursing scrubs to invite me in for a bite, I had no doubt that the very last thing he'd ever do was inflict more suffering upon his highly excitable son. In fact, my guess was that things were quite the opposite—that Pavel could probably get away with literal murder and still be safely hidden, at home, by his father.

But when Pavel told me the man was sick, and that continuing to run his washer/dryer repair service was one of his three remaining pleasures in life, even my clammy heart unclenched.

I stood up from my desk and offered Pavel a firm, final gentleman's handshake.

"I give you my word, Pavel. I will continue to teach as long as it takes to get you a diploma."

The light flared back in his eyes.

"*So!*" he said, beaming. "I can *still* pay you compliment and get what I want! This is good!"

And then the young fool flashed me a silver flask he had hidden deep in his pocket, as if to proffer me a toast. I swatted him away and shooed him out the door, laughing for the first time in weeks.

That's where Xenia's and Gerald's laughter brought me, by the end of that evening's loud dinner. Seeing them both so happy and young, with Dorothy's pain so close at hand, firmed up a resolve in me to start a new chapter. The choice on the table was simple: You can straighten up and be who your kids need now, or you can lose them like you lost your wife.

Gerald's pager beeped. They rose to leave as abruptly as they'd come, with another kiss from Xenia and hugs from both. Gerald gripped me tight in parting and looked more directly into my face than he had in months. He'd come to deliver his difficult message, and he'd successfully achieved that delivery. I was glad to have helped him. I needed to.

CHAPTER 6

It seemed like I'd shared a long evening with my son and his girl-friend, but in truth they had stayed little more than an hour after Xenia joined us. When they left, they took all the light with them. What remained of the night, in their wake, grew darker with each ticking minute. It threatened to become endless, and I couldn't endure it much longer than it took me to do the dishes.

Out back, on the porch, I turned Saint John facedown.

I filled a tumbler with gin, then poured the remainder of my new bottle down the drain. It would be the last evening I spent drinking alone on the porch; I planned to bid my interior paramour good-bye. The thought that I'd been slowly poisoning my liver by drinking while taking seizure meds made Dorothy's plight, and my response, all the more pitiful. *My daughter might get sicker,* I thought, *but I can still choose whether or not I do.* One final night of self-directed misery, then. And after that, everything will be about Dorothy.

I lost my dinner just before midnight. After cleaning the toilet, I felt compelled to scour the entire house. Of course that cannot be done in a single night, but the idea did force me to my hands and knees again, which felt appropriate as I crawled through some improvised prayers. Whether those whimpers were for myself—regret, self-pity—or more purely for my Dorothy, promising to do whatever I could and begging for the strength to never let go of either of my kids, I can't really say.

By the time I heard birds scratching outside and the gray dawn dripping, I had resolved to invite Dorothy to move back home. The idea popped into my head like a root baring itself aboveground. It was the generous, fatherly thing to offer—even if I hadn't already begun wishing, desperately, for her return. Just imagining her back here, talking with me, made me shudder with hope.

I peered behind the door of Dorothy's old room. It smelled of mold, as does most everything in this damp place when left to itself for too long. The yellowed gloom seeping in from the drawn window shade silhouetted all the boxes and odd stuff inside them. Although Jackie was the sort to maintain her grown kids' rooms like shrines to the past, we still managed, somehow, to bury those memories beneath a new layer of clutter. Some used, unfolded bedding had been tossed into the corner after one of our bad nights; folding beach chairs leaned against Dorothy's old bike, which threatened to stumble over its kickstand. Dorothy's gapped beaded curtain still hung over the window, the sequins she'd glued to her ceiling still sparkled when I switched on the overhead light, and I knew her closet was still full of the floppy, too-big clothes in which she once used to hide herself. I dared not go there. I pushed back the palpitations I'd stirred up all night and sat on the floor to breathe and think—as Gerald would have thought—about what to do next. How best to achieve it. And from that perspective, life was quite simple: *You make your decision, shove the old stuff into another room, open the shades, wash the windows, paint the walls, and get Dorothy back in here as soon as you can. If she's amenable.*

I collapsed and slept till midafternoon.

I awoke when Dorothy called: The PET scan confirmed with certainty that the tumor was growing on her pancreas, but not whether it had spread to her liver. If it had spread, surgery might do more harm than good. There was still a biopsy to be done by another specialist to determine what specific type of cancer this was and what her best treatment options would be. Her five-year prognosis would be forecast then. What was certain was that she'd start some sort of chemo the following week to see if it might shrink before they "went in." They said it was no one's fault "we" hadn't caught this earlier: It's nearly impossible to do so, because the symptoms don't really show until things have progressed this far. "We" included Dorothy and those closest to her. Bile rose in my throat when I realized that I hadn't seen her more than twice all summer, and even then she'd been wearing caps and shades and hoodies, so that I could no longer call up an image of what her eyes had looked like, or whether she'd been losing weight. The ugly, false coyness of cancer.

"Are you all right?" she said softly, sounding like a kid again.

How could she ask after me so sincerely like that? I felt disgraced again, and strained to sound upbeat.

"Will you move back in with me, Dorothy?"

She was quiet. I worried the words sounded too rehearsed and desperate, since they were. Or that I sounded as sick as I felt.

"Have you really thought this through?" she finally said.

She sounded tentative, vulnerable. And realizing how reassured I was to hear that weakness compounded my shame at having let her come so close to death, alone, without ever noticing any change in her.

"Please?" I said.

I no longer heard her breathing, so I talked faster to fill the space. I told her how Gerald had described her housing and financial situation. I told her I'd repaint her room. She could choose the color. I would stay out of her way. Trying to think like her, I told her how much easier it would be *for me* to have her here—I wouldn't have to bus out to the hospital when she needed me nearby. *If* she did. I explained how easy it would be for her to keep an eye *on me* here, if she were indeed worried about my "dropping out"—which I promised to never, ever do again. I even told her I was seeing Carol that evening—a fact I'd just remembered myself—and warmly described all the time there would be for the three of us to hang out together, in the days ahead, if she lived here. And how she could invite other friends, anytime. Fun. We could walk up to the cathedral with Gerald to hear Xenia sing whenever we wanted. We could walk on the beach in the early mornings when we couldn't sleep. I would eat better if she were here, and promised to prepare whatever she needed, whenever she wanted.

I never once insinuated that it might be "like old times," because I was no longer sure what those times had actually felt like for her. But it was easy for me to make it sound like she'd be doing me a favor by moving back home because, as I started daydreaming aloud about the future—more than I'd daydreamed about anything real for months, beyond shopping runs—I realized that, in truth, she *would* be helping me. Her entire presence in my life has been an unearned, life-expanding gift. I got wistful imagining how wonderful it would be to have another chance at everyday life together. If she came back.

I held the receiver out a bit, as if she could somehow feel the benefit of that extra space I was struggling to give her. But she instead must have heard how shaken I was, because she began to sniffle.

"It's a very sweet idea, Dad," she said.

"It's my deepest hope. I mean it."

"I know."

"I won't drink," I said. Hearing the words, I knew I wasn't lying: *We can do this.* But still I worried she might think me impulsive and untrustworthy. "At least not gin. A beer or glass of wine at most. And I'll get regular with my Dilantin again. You have my word. I'll never do anything to make you worry. I won't drop out on you again."

She paused.

"That's not—"

"I'd already decided to do that, Dorothy, before you called. Whether you come home or not. So, no pressure."

That didn't sound right.

"Please just come home," I said.

"You don't need to make the promises," she said.

"They're promises to me. Really."

She stayed quiet.

"I *do* need to do some work," she said, a little louder. "On my own stuff, I mean. As much as I can. It's so hard for me to work over here—it doesn't feel good anymore—you should see all the gear piled in my room. It's like I'm sleeping with it."

"There's space here. Set up anything you like. Work around the clock. No schedule, no chores. You get a staffed, all-night kitchen. Like an artist's residency." Maybe I could somehow make her a dependent again so she could get on my health plan.

"There might be . . . if this gets bad . . ." she began. She breathed in hiccups, but her voice grew steadily stronger. "I might need medical equipment, like a special bed, down the road. I don't really know what this will look like yet."

The receiver shook in my fist.

"There's so much room, sweetheart. And lots of time," I said. "Oh, how I wish it were me."

That too may have sounded manipulative, as if I thought I could force her to move back just to make me feel better, but I'd already hoped for that very thing so many times the night before that it just came out.

"Please let me do this with you," I said. "Stay as long as you want, and move out anytime. Once you're better."

She blew her nose.

"I'm still sort of in shock about everything right now," she said. "Can we test-drive a week or two, maybe?"

Yes, yes, yes. I went hollow with gratitude. And when she added "Thank you," I laughed out loud, thanking her in return.

She needed to go for another call. But before hanging up, she wanted to forewarn me: She was getting in touch with her mother. The time had come to share the bad news with her, and she wanted to let the first blow hit Jackie overseas, where we wouldn't need to witness it in person. Dorothy had already reached out to Dick's office, to see what contact information they might have for him, because she hadn't received anything but a postcard from her mother all month. So, she said, Jackie would probably be trying to reach me. Any hour now.

Dorothy promised to call back and work out the details. She asked me to tell Gerald about the scan, and also to let Carol know about the extent of the tumor when I saw her.

"I'm the first person you've told, then?"

"Yes," she said.

I was ashamed to have asked, and embarrassed to feel so pleased at hearing it.

I postponed my call to Gerald. I felt too shaky, anyway. It's always been harder to share bad news with him than anyone else—I often feel as if I'm letting him down.

I looked forward to the distraction of Carol that evening. I managed a fitful nap, showered, and even ironed a shirt, but I still dozed on the streetcar in. I was slapped by sunlight as I rode the escalator up to Powell Street, coming face-to-face with a tap dancer hustling tourists waiting a cable car, and had to step aside into some shade for a moment just to catch my breath. I'd been looking forward to the walk to Carol's, through Union Square and up Nob Hill, but I had to take it slow.

Carol lived just two blocks from where Jackie and I first rented in the city, where we'd spent our first two years with Dorothy. It's a little nest of peace and quiet above where the Broadway Tunnel spills into North Beach and Chinatown—where, with all the crosstown traffic diverted underground, the blocks of old apartments on top are sleepy due to the steep hills, narrow streets, and lurching cable cars. The little alleys and trees invite walking, and it's where Dorothy took her first steps. The mailman used to know her by name; the bald Italian brothers who ran the store with wooden coolers always stocked her favorite strained carrots; and the old Chinese lady who lived below us, who'd initially avoided our eyes, always waved half a block in advance once Dorothy had entered our world.

Back when we were young, we'd never felt gloomy or alone—we always knew when our neighbors were watching television or cooking on the other side of our kitchen wall, or struggling to park in the alley outside. They knew how we lived too. I remember one afternoon being drawn to the fire escape by the sound of flapping wings in the air shaft, and seeing a woman squatting down below and sawing a hen's bent neck with a cleaver over a bowl to collect the blood; she flashed me a big, crooked smile because she knew me—the jumpy white guy who was always walking somewhere. It was home.

We'd found our first apartment simply by walking around and calling the numbers taped to windows, then signing a lease that same afternoon with our plumber-landlord who spoke no English. It used to be a thrill to walk down to the Financial District each day, to the temp jobs we held while earning our credentials—like living in a movie—and although I'd never really been a big fan, there was still some leftover glamour to living close to all those beatnik haunts just blocks away in North Beach. I'd always felt like I was *somewhere*.

Old city blocks are thick with ghosts from previous lives, and while I made my way up to Carol's that night, I was comforted to be stepping back into that richness—to feel that our lives, too, were now part of the backstory of each place I passed. *Here* was where we'd strolled with Dorothy for the first time, pushing her through a hilltop intersection, blankets flapping in the wind as Jackie cried in panic when cars didn't stop fast enough for her. *There* was the small playlot where we'd spent whole days barefoot in the sandbox, chatting with friends while we watched what the babies put in their mouths. I used to think that the bigger the daydreamer you were in your youth, the greater your capacity for nostalgia in old age—the larger the surrender value of your annuity, if you will. My slow walk to Carol's confirmed that.

I had to refer several times to the address I'd scribbled down, but I still managed to arrive on time. Hers was a big golden apartment building at the peak of Broadway, with sidewalk views of the Golden Gate and Headlands in the distance. Peering through the beveled glass of the front door, I saw a mirrored lobby with a wall of mailboxes; junk mail and newspapers carpeted the marble floor. I found and buzzed her apartment number, and was surprised to see her instantly step out from behind a door on the side of the lobby—the building manager's apartment.

She greeted me with a nervous smile, moving so quickly I worried I'd come late. She grabbed my sack of clanking bottles and tugged me in by my sleeve, as if embarrassed to be seen with me in the lobby.

We passed down the dark, narrow hall of her railroad flat. The kitchen was midway down and had a white enamel stove, painted cupboards that touched the ceiling, and potted plants in the windows to the alley. Nothing was on the stove. When she opened the bag I'd given her, she breathed a little easier at seeing it was sparkling cider. And then we finally caught each other's confusion: I thought she'd been planning to cook for us.

"I like your place," I said. It was all I could think to say.

"I wish it were mine," she said. "I'm house-sitting for a friend. He's overseas."

It dawned on me then that this apartment did not, in fact, match the place she'd described on our first date—this didn't have the floor plan of the place she'd been in her sad drunk days, where she'd peered through a slit in the drapes at the street and burned little craters in the carpet on her path to her chair. I was somehow a little disappointed; feeling as sickly as I still did would have been easier against a darker backdrop. Besides, I still had some bad news to deliver. I'd pictured doing that over a table, in the comforting context of a kitchen. She may have seen that in my eyes as I made to sit on a tall stool by the window.

"No—wait," she said, waving me up as if shooing a fly. "I'm taking you out."

I stood. She pushed the bottles into the fridge. *For later.* She reached back to pull her hair free of its elastic, grabbed a red beret from a hook, and checked her face in the cupboard glass.

"We need to hurry," she said. "I got the only reservation they had. You know Des Alpes? Did you know it's closing?"

Des Alpes was a family-style Basque restaurant down the hill, in North Beach. It had been there forever. We used to roll Dorothy down there for a special treat, to get out of the apartment. I felt sticky, remembering how she used to gum up her french fries and smear the checkered tablecloth. But no one there ever cared.

"They lost their lease?" I guessed.

She shrugged. She inspected her open pack of cigarettes, tapping and counting the filter of each with her fingernail. There were just a few left.

"I'm trying to quit again," she said.

"That's good," I said, "because—"

She looked up—*No, wait!*—and again led me by the sleeve until we were outside, bopping toward the top of Russian Hill.

She kept half a step ahead of me, walking fast in her capris. Within minutes we reached the stair-top landing that faces Telegraph Hill and Coit Tower, in spotlights—right out of *Vertigo.* The lights of Broadway clubs and downtown offices already blinked in the early twilight down below.

Carol stopped at the concrete balustrade that overlooks a patch of grass above the tree-lined Vallejo Street steps. It's a place Jackie and I used to sit to take in the view while Dorothy toddled about, pulling up dandelions and chasing bugs. It was also a little out of Carol's way, I thought, if we were indeed rushing to keep a reservation.

She quickly sat on one end of the balustrade. A younger couple was busy at the other end, the girl sitting with her legs wrapped around her beau's hips as they kissed and their Shih Tzu shat by the boxwoods.

Carol swung her legs around to face the city view. She kicked her feet in the air in front of her. Then, as quickly as she could, she lit a cigarette, sucking it like a surfacing diver taking in air.

"I can't smoke in the apartment," she explained after a deep second drag. "It's tough. Good for me, you know, but—I hate quitting. And yet look at me: I seem to be quitting all the time." She smiled.

She squinted at me as she took another drag. For the first time, I saw the light catch a big diamond on her finger.

She saw me notice, and switched her smoking hand to hold the ring up even closer, under my nose. She fluttered her fingers before my eyes, smiling. Relaxing, finally.

"Sometimes I wear this—" she said.

"I can see."

"—when I want to hide a little."

"Not my business."

"But you *looked*, Jim," she said, winking. "Your face—that worry! How flattering!"

Her fake bashfulness made me smile too.

"To be honest, I was more worried I might have simply overlooked it," I said. "You told me you were divorced."

"No. I told you I was 'unmarried.' We split up for good, years ago."

She studied me more closely now, and her wry expression faded a little with concern.

"It's my grandmother's. I'm sorry, but I don't usually bother telling people we never got married—too much trouble. It's easier to say divorced than 'no-longer-partnered,' right? He was a good guy, but the wrong guy. He's moved back to L.A. We shared some good years. And our son. Now you know it all."

That was as much as I'd learned about her ex in the entirety of our first date, but it was good to have a second chance. The skyline and distant traffic noise seemed to coax out what remained of her New Jersey accent, and it was a pleasure to hear that too. Someone new. I was glad she felt talkative because I had no idea what to say next, or how to start, or whether I'd caught my breath enough to share my bad news.

Carol turned to the view and smoked her butt down to the filter.

She patted the concrete next to her without looking back.

"Want to sit?"

Gratefully, I slumped down beside her.

"So . . ." she finally said. "I'm guessing you heard from Dorothy?"

"She told you?" I said.

"No. But I knew she was getting the scan today. I figured she might call her dad first."

"It's a pancreatic tumor," I said.

She flinched.

"Has it spread?"

"It may be inoperable."

She searched my eyes, and as her hope soured, she turned back to the darkening skyline.

"That's the worst case," I said. "But I tend to plan for worst cases."

Out came the cigarettes again. She exhaled a long plume of smoke—angrily, almost—far across the grass. Reaching over to take my hand, she squeezed it so tight my knuckles cracked. That little bit of pain felt good.

"*Shit*," she whispered to her kicking feet, shaking her head. "*Shit, shit.*" She squeezed my hand each time she said it, until I broke a bit.

The couple downwind stood, cradled their pooch, and left us alone.

"I asked her to move in with me," I said. "Back home. She said she would."

"Then I'm sure she will," said Carol. Out of the corner of my eye, I saw her dab her eyes with a tissue. "That Dorothy—she's true that way."

I nodded.

She flapped her purse shut.

"Let's go eat," she said.

It was easier to talk as we walked, having gotten the worst out of the way. Carol admitted that she was ashamed for not having noticed Dorothy's fatigue and all the weight she'd been losing. She'd simply thought Dorothy had been working too hard. That made me feel better.

I told Carol the promise I'd made to forego my martinis for a while. That amused her, for some reason. She surprised me by telling me to take it easy; the weeks ahead would be rough, she said, and I should approach the few changes I have control over as gently as possible. That was a relief to hear, as I'd already been reminiscing about the house red they used to pull from a wooden keg at Des Alpes, and how nice it would be to have just one, with dinner.

In return, I encouraged Carol to come out to the house anytime she wanted, to be with Dorothy and me. That pleased her.

A leafy canopy covered us as we strolled down blocks of stone steps to the busy sidewalks of North Beach. As we talked, the cool violet evening fell, just as it always does. The neon signs buzzed, Chinatown aquariums bubbled up in windows, and the sugared air of bakeries and cafés perfumed our passage, forcing us to be attentive. For the first time all day, I had an appetite.

Next to a round, half-curtained window on Broadway, the plank door to Des Alpes opened into a warm cavern of hominess, with little bent-wood chairs at the few dozen small, red-and-white-checkered tables. And just as I'd remembered, they do *not* take reservations, but nevertheless, as soon as Carol stepped in, a chapped-cheek old man with an apron knotted high above his gut bustled up to her with a quick nod and led us directly to the table he'd saved. He pushed in her seat and dropped a prix fixe menu before her. It was a comfort to see how little it had changed: Dinner begins with a thin pea soup—a house specialty—then a choice between three entrées, shoe-string frites, salad, a scoop of spumoni, and coffee. It's the only place I've ever eaten sweetbreads; they're tender in a tasty, light sauce. I hadn't had them in years.

Our table was in a little arched recess of a wall. Seeing Carol tucked in so snugly reminded me of how Jackie always stood out in the place, with her elbows just on the corners of the table, struggling to keep the stroller out of the path of all the diners. But she'd loved it there too.

Carol and I ordered immediately. There was nothing more to say about Dorothy's condition, and there'd be plenty of that later. We both knew Dorothy would prefer we spend the night talking about something else. So we sipped our water and started again.

Carol's ring sparkled in the candlelight. I told her how I'd taken my own wedding band off the day Jackie walked out. In fact, I'm still not certain where it is.

"So your divorce *is* final?" she said.

What? I was surprised this was even a question. Jackie had already carted away everything she wanted. Neither of us ever fought for anything more from the other. If there were any more divorcing to be done, that would be Jackie's mess; she could deal with it.

Carol's eyebrows arched nonetheless.

"But your house?" she said. "Did you buy her out?"

"It's not ours," I said. "Rent-controlled for nearly thirty years." The original owner moved to Denver long ago, and that's where I mail the check. I never complain about anything. So everyone's happy. In fact, I sometimes send two months' rent all at once, just to save the stamp and the trouble of remembering.

She looked stunned.

"Aren't you afraid you'll lose it?"

Her worry felt a bit out of scale.

"To what—a quake? A tsunami? It's built on sand. It's rotting. You can reach under the siding by the gutter spout and grab a chunk of fudgy support beam in your fist. Who would buy that? Gerald says the house *lost* value in the 1987 crash. The lease is probably the most solid thing about it."

She shook her head and forced a brave smile.

"Well, here in *this* neighborhood," she said, "rents have doubled in just twelve months. Hasn't Gerald explained the dot-com thing to you?"

I did *not* know all this, having had no reason to look into the rental market in decades, but her panic threatened to make me jittery too, so I nodded along just to calm her. In truth, I intend to stay in my home till I drop, at which time they may mail the deposit to my kids after rolling me out. I'd never worried about losing the lease—not since the kids grew up, anyway. The Outer Sunset was still unpopular with most people—that's one of the boons of being so far out in the fog—so I've always felt natural disaster was more of a threat than greed or other "market forces." In addition, our stucco out front had taken on some gothic scars during the Loma Prieta quake, and I've deliberately not touched them up. The back porch was never truly level, even when we'd first moved in, and it too seems to tip a bit more each year. That, or I'm imagining it. But if something happened and I were ever kicked out, I could probably get by with a smaller place. I don't need three bedrooms. I rarely go out front.

"I'm serious, Jim," Carol said, calling me back. "It's not the same city anymore. Things are changing. People too. Maybe forever."

I pushed my wine aside to save half for my entrée.

"Like the place I'm in," she said. "The guy I'm house-sitting for is already a subletter himself. He's a nurse. We met when I was interning—my smoking buddy. We always ran into each other in the stairwell. You know that board and care on Pine, near the hospital?"

She could see I didn't.

"It's where they put you when you can't take care of yourself any longer and you need medical assistance. He and I shared patients. We had this ninety-year-old lady who lived her entire life on a ranch till she fell off her horse. She broke her hip and wasn't recovering well. Then her son—a realtor here in the city—was so busy he couldn't be bothered to drive back and forth each weekend to check in on her, so he moved her down against her will."

Could be worse, I thought.

"She already hated being bedridden," Carol said. "But to be stuck with a roommate, in a city, with all this street noise? It took it out of her, and then the painkillers tipped her canoe. She came down with pneumonia, lying in bed all day, and then *that* got worse. She never said much to anyone, but she was always frank with me, and I saw it, the very day she decided: *That's it.* Chuck, the nurse, says there are signs—you can tell when someone's getting ready to go by the look in their eye. It's not simple acceptance—because not everyone can make their peace—but it's more like an acknowledgment of this thing they can no longer avoid. It's like: Whatever they're looking at seems to be farther away now. They look at you, but they're seeing more than you; they can't turn away, and they have to square themselves with that, or let go.

"Chuck also says that over the course of a day or two they stop moving their toes."

Why someone with Carol's emotional intelligence would choose that moment to launch into this topic was a question I would ask later. At the time, I thought perhaps this was what people who wanted to be counselors talked about—this is how they Follow Their Bliss. Sad to say, I'd found the AA stories equally trying our first night, but then I'd had the added excuse of being caught off guard. I liked Carol, however, and I also knew how grateful I was to be sitting with her, so I had no choice but to participate, or stop her.

"The motionless toes would be a dead giveaway to me," I said.

She laughed quickly, then continued.

"So, one day this tough old lady starts looking around differently at everything, as if her room were getting bigger, and—even though she'd already stopped talking to us by then—one morning, when I opened her curtains, her eyes popped open, and she sneered outside at the tree like there was someone there and she wanted to say: 'Really? You want me? *This*? Go for it.'"

I have been around dead people, but not anyone on their way out. There have been times when I've actually regretted not having been bedside for the passing of someone I loved, just for the sense of conclusion and wholeness I imagine you must get when you go through that together. There was a growing but cold comfort in Carol's ability to discuss this so matter-of-factly, and for a moment I wondered if she might be doing it for me intentionally—because Dorothy's news, and the stridency with which she'd startled me in talking about her brand-new diagnosis, had already slapped me awake to how inexperienced I really may prove to be—helpless right when she needs me most.

So I swerved a little. I told Carol how Jackie and I had taken the kids camping only twice, with some teacher friends with kids of their own. We'd packed the bags and pillows and swim toys and rode five hours in the back of a hot van to spend a week at a camp the city runs in the Sierras. And although there certainly were some fun times, in the end, the overriding memory was of utter exhaustion—we got no sleep; we ate gritty food; we were welted with bug bites; and the kids were sugared-up, hot, and cranky every hour. On our return, we even applauded the fog as we crossed the Bay Bridge. But after the first trip, we must have somehow forgotten all that discomfort and remembered only the good parts, because the next July there we were, loading the van to do it all again. We'd somehow become nostalgic for the smoky campfires, the snail-paced mini-hikes. Maybe we'd hoped the kids were more mature, or we had a better plan that year, but once we'd zipped up the tent screen for another night on a hissing air bed, it was the same thing all over again, and even more frustrating because this time we knew what each of the sleepless nights to come would bring.

"So," I told Carol, "I do think I understand what your old friend might have been trying to say. We probably all come to a point in life where we ask: *Is this still worth it? If we do this one more time, will the pleasure be enough to make us forget the struggle?* One day you probably stop, look around, think again, and then, if you're old and tired enough and there's no realistic hope for improvement, you finally answer: *No*."

Carol looked shocked. She shook her head adamantly.

We were getting to know each other better.

"Why *live*, then?" She rapped the air with her soup spoon. "You don't just *stop* when it's not fun. You do something *different*. And I think there is *every* good reason to sit around a campfire with your kids. Or your grandkids, for that matter. Can you imagine that—grandkids?"

Next question, please.

"You just learn how to do it *better* next time, is what I'm saying." She pushed on. "Maybe you don't need to sleep in a tent anymore. Unless you like that—I mean, I sure don't—but maybe you shell out the bucks for a cabin instead?"

"I'm not saying I'm there *yet*," I said. "But you wanted to understand your old lady friend, and I'm saying that perhaps she, after living for ninety years and falling off her horse and surviving a hip replacement with painkillers and pneumonia and a roommate, maybe she felt as if, you know, when she said, 'Go for it'—"

"She didn't actually say *those* words, 'Go for it,'" Carol said.

I take things more literally when I'm tired.

"But you said you saw that in her eyes?"

"Not like *that*," she said, leaning in. "It was more a taunting thing, like, 'C'mon, I can take you. Bring it.'"

"And not like, 'Okay—I'm done: Flip me over'?"

"Right," she said, although she stared uncertainly.

"So what's the difference?" I said.

"What's the *difference*?"

At the next table, a big, mouth-breathing man raised his eyebrows and fork above the steaming plate set before him but waited to take his first bite as he listened to us.

Carol leaned closer over the table.

"This old lady would never have said 'I'm done,' like you just said. That would be like giving up—like she had no other choice."

"Wasn't she?" I said. "Did she?"

She pushed back in her chair. She glanced at my wineglass, then back at me, and then, thankfully, she found something in my face that seemed to reassure her. The calmness returned to her voice.

"Okay. I may agree with you," she said, "but we're splitting hairs. In the end, sure, most people *do* lose control and, yes, most people *don't* have much choice about when they're going to die, but if you're lucky you can still choose how you make that descent. You can choose to accept it or to keep fighting it. You can say, 'I understand,' or you can say, 'Is that all there is?'"

"Even if your toes don't move?" I said. "And you can't say the words?"

"Yes, Jim. Sometimes words are implied."

Our plates arrived, and she addressed her entrée—baked sole with lemon—with abandon. It was so delicious she went quiet. Ditto my sheep glands.

When we resumed talking, however, the remainder of our conversation kept hammering on the same bell:

Her: Since you plan for worst-case scenarios, then: What expectations did you have for your marriage? What did you prepare for there?

Me: Certainly not abandonment. If I'd ever once even half expected she'd leave me, I'm not sure I'd have gone to all the trouble.

Her: I don't believe you.

Me: If you knew, up front and for certain, that the relationship you were in would one day kick you off the wrong side and leave you hurt forever, would *you* do it?

Her: Would you instead sign a contract saying you'd live and work together until the kids are grown, but then go your separate ways? Is that better? Because that's how young people do it now. I read some research that there's barely a one-in-two chance of making a marriage last these days. You and I are proof. But I can tell you: Yes, I *would* still do it. Those statistics just make it courageous. More romantic.

Me: Agreed.

Her: Really? Because the way you're talking, it's as if the real question were whether or not it's worth the trouble to live life, knowing you'll one day die. And you should also know you're probably going to suffer on the way out too. That doesn't sound like a question to me.

Me: People have to live.

Her: Marrying for love is a *good* thing, Jim.

Me: I'm saying a good thing is better the longer it lasts. That's true for both love *and* life. And so a guaranteed bad marriage would be better the shorter it is. Same for painful days. It's a quality-versus-quantity equation.

[Coming out, that felt like a Gerald statement, and not entirely my own. Carol's fed-up expression confirmed it.]

Her: So what if it is?

Me: So, at the end of her days, your boring-care lady was simply choosing quality over duration.

Her: She was ninety years old. She'd already proven she wanted quantity. And it's "board and care."

Me: But you're saying she had a right to choose when she was "done" too? Regardless of whom that hurt? You're saying, in marriage, someone can just decide: "Oh, well, had enough of *that*"?

Her: Look—we agree: People gotta live. They live for what they value. Some people take money over love, some want glory over money, or some, love over life. All good things, in their way, right? My old lady friend saw one choice left: She could talk back, or close her eyes again and wait. I give her points for chutzpah. I always will.

Carol tapped her hand to her heart, then lifted her chin as a misty pride beamed from her eyes at the memory of that moment. I myself had lost sight of which side I was arguing on, but I raised my empty wineglass to toast them both. And when the waiter came up to refill it, I did not accept.

Carol insisted on paying for dinner. I thanked her for the nicest meal anyone had given me in years. I couldn't tell her how exhausted I was.

We stepped outside. The night had grown wetter, and the traffic sloppy and loud, so we stood facing it awhile on the sidewalk, getting acclimated to the change. Then Carol retied her scarf and put a new tilt on her beret.

She tugged on my arm gently.

"Come with me," she said. "I've got another surprise for you."

We walked downhill a few blocks, wordless in the evening crowds. She turned us down Columbus, and stopped in front of City Lights. It startled me, how familiar the old storefront looked. It's still an exciting place. They still display new copies of *Howl* and *A Coney Island of the Mind* in the plate glass windows, just like the very first time I'd come.

"I haven't been *here* in years."

"Why not?" Carol said.

I couldn't answer.

"Well—you ready?—Ferlinghetti's reading!" she said. Her face lit up like a kid looking forward to Santa. "*Tonight*. It wasn't advertised—a word-of-mouth thing—almost private. The cashier told me, last week."

In the glass, the crowd passing around us made our moment feel cinematic.

"You know he's the city's poet laureate this year?" she said.

I didn't know that either. That we even had one.

"He first saw San Francisco in the navy," she said after waiting a moment more. "He fell in love with the city on shore leave and never forgot it. He came back in fifty-one. Then he never left."

I stared at his book.

Carol waited, cocking her head like a dove, watching me from a growing distance.

I'd first seen San Francisco the day I moved here. I'd come with Jackie in 1964, after graduation, when we were twenty-two. I had no immediate family left: Craig had just died my senior year of college, and my father had had his stroke the year before that, and the farm had gone to the state to cover the outstanding bills. I don't repeat this to enlist sympathy—and I didn't recall any of this for Carol—nor are these facts my excuse for not wanting to sit and listen to someone recite words I'd rather read myself.

Jackie and I had moved here to establish state residency for me, so we could earn our teaching credentials tuition-free at San Francisco State. This was a few years before the Summer of Love, with the beatniks still at large in North Beach, just blocks from our first apartment. City life was new for her too—she was fleeing her parents' inland ranch, where she'd always stuck out like a red gladiola—but neither of us fit in so easily here either. When the first Be-In happened in 1967, when it was so warm in January that people ran around naked in the park, Jackie and I had been in our small apartment's kitchen drafting lesson plans. That was no judgment on our part, really; we were morally aligned with all the movements, but if I'd been eligible for a draft card, I'd have burned it quietly at home, and Jackie always wore a bra because it irritated her nipples to go without. And we'd watched warily as the hordes of lost kids migrated into the city, becoming first a nuisance, then a danger to themselves and others. But we weren't real, full-on squares. Education is a right too, after all. Teaching is civic action.

But when Dorothy was born in 1969, we had no way of knowing that the drugs and gangs we had to deal with in our schools would one day get better. It was another reason we'd moved to Ocean Beach the next year: to get away. Lots of families did that. Several of our neighbors were cops or teachers when we first arrived, and there was a vital church every ten blocks. We thought we'd be safe.

Dorothy's adolescence was spectacular, however, and she and Jackie were already at each other's throats by the end of fifth grade. I had no background for understanding her teen-girl outrages, not beyond Jackie's stories of her own coming-of-age, so when our doe-eyed little girl muttered her first "fuck" over breakfast, and dressed slatternly, and one night pushed a thumbtack into her earlobe "for fun," we were too quick to blame San Francisco's counterculture. Dorothy had been such a quiet, sweet-faced girl up until then that we were too slow to pick up on all the rage in her music. Gerald would pretend to laugh along during her dinnertime scenes and then retreat to his room to act out with action figures, but Dorothy insisted that we—her mother, in particular—witness her every struggle, close-up, at full volume. If she couldn't get Jackie to scream at least once a day, she'd stay out late until she got it on the phone. Jackie did her damnedest to pretend Dorothy wasn't wearing her down, but Jackie's too thin-skinned, and even then Dorothy could smell falsehood like a shark gets blood. It was sometimes hard to watch.

One morning when Dorothy was in high school, Jackie'd made up some pretext for mucking around in Dorothy's backpack and found a small wooden pipe and a baggie of pot. We'd always been clear about marijuana in our house—it was forbidden—and I regularly told the kids pot makes you tear off your clothes and dance around like a slow, amateur mime. But being native San Franciscans, they just listened with a small, skeptical smile.

That morning Jackie said nothing to her; she simply replaced the baggie with the sandwich I'd made. That was a mistake, though, since Dorothy, who even then was great at noticing details, would immediately suspect her mother. Jackie's next mistake was to get so distraught that she took the entire day off to stay home and stew about the situation, lying in wait for Dorothy's return, especially since Dorothy was sure to sense an ambush and stay out late.

When I'd come home after school that afternoon—Gerald was at karate—I found Jackie in her running shorts, sitting cross-legged on the couch with her favorite pewter mug half full of Chablis, staring out the front window with an unusually liquid, childlike gaze. The baggie lay open on the table.

"That pot is Dorothy's." She spoke slowly. "I don't think I'm high. But I tried."

It was 1984. Jackie and I were in our early forties. Even we would remark, on occasion, on how straight we'd somehow remained, relative to our peers. So this was something new.

I stood still. Jackie could sometimes make her speaking voice sound as rich as Sarah Vaughan's—surprising for a tall, thin, white lady—and this was one of those times. I wanted to hear more of it. She seemed to want that too—to be heard.

"Maybe you didn't smoke *enough*?" I suggested.

She stared at me in crinkled-eye disbelief—sort of playful, sort of lost.

"I smoked it out in the back," she said. "That's why it's not too stinky in here."

"I've read that there's a saturation level," I said. "A threshold you need to go past, before you really feel it?"

"But, Jim, I smoked a *whole bowl*!"

"Okay," I agreed. *That should do it, I guess.*

"What I want—I want Dorothy to come home and find her mother *totally* stoned," she said. Her eyebrows twisted. "I mean, *wasted*. I want her to know what it's like to come home to a not-so-nice mother like mine. To an unhappy home."

Her eyes shrank and darkened, briefly.

"I want her *to be afraid*."

"Afraid?"

She sipped more wine, nodding some bad memory to the side.

"Yes," she said. "Dorothy's fearless, you know?"

That's a good thing, right?

She straightened up but then, as if in afterthought, re-slumped.

"Someday something's gonna happen to her," she said. "If she, I don't *know*, if—"

If she's not constantly watching out for bad surprises?

The idea was too jarring. In my youth, crises seemed to come as regularly as seasons. Common stuff. Not an experience I'd wish on our kids, despite our growing need for disciplinary tools.

But Jackie—obviously high—just nodded. Her eyes slowly followed her fingertips as they planted the mug on the table with a loud clunk. She folded her hands in her lap, gazed a moment at them, then back up to me. She still looked young. I saw, anew, where Dorothy got that look we'd been seeing—it was the glittery stare Jackie got when she was watching her life from the outside and hadn't yet found reason enough to stay put. I rarely saw that look on a weekday afternoon. It made the moment stark and wrong-feeling, like a Christmas tree blinking in a summer window. I wanted to pull her back through it, to me.

"Isn't that what keeps *us* together?" she said, nodding her own agreement even as she spoke. "Fear of *someday*?"

"Fear of *what* someday?"

Her eyes blurred. "When she looks at me," she said, softer. "It's like—"

She blinked her wet eyes quickly, but they wouldn't fully clear.

I rose.

"Jackie, it's okay to be afraid your kids are growing up."

By the way she wilted again, with a sadness washing her face, I could tell I'd guessed right.

"I have regrets too, sometimes," I told her. "But no, I don't feel afraid."

She stirred up so much in me.

"Well," she said weakly, letting go, "I don't know if I ever really thought about all this. Not till today. And now it seems like that's all I can do: Sit here and think. I'm tired of work. I don't like getting old. So many things I never think about."

I glanced again at the baggie. This wasn't an everyday conversation, but something in her voice made these sound like her everyday thoughts.

"Left alone," she added, misting up again. "I'm afraid of *that*."

I heard that ache in her. I felt it too.

She searched, up into my face, for a lifeline.

I stared and leaned in, hoping she could find it.

She stood, I reached, and she gripped my hand and followed me down the hall. We pushed into bed with a haste we hadn't made in years. Her eyes stayed open like a twilit sky until I caught a shiver of the things she'd been trying to share, and I was released when she quietly, calmly closed them.

I don't recall what we did with that stash of Dorothy's. Jackie may have kept it to try with her Friday after-work friends. I do remember, however, forcing Dorothy to go to North Beach with me the following week—my Father's Day request. I told her the biggest stories I could about our college days, making it sound as if her parents had sailed around the world and done it all, rather than simply studied and taught and paid rent in a small, yeasty city they'd always found so very beautiful. But Dorothy surprised me: She bought it all. She smiled and seemed to be happy to sip a cappuccino with her old man. And when we went into City Lights that day and I saw her pick out a few good books—and when, in the months ahead, I caught her reading more and more—I grew proud, and reassured, to watch her teenage rage mature because it could never again be inarticulate.

"So—don't you think that's a romantic story?" Carol said, louder. "Opening a bookstore because you fall in love with some place?"

She'd turned to face me, her shoulders pressed back against the glass, and was tapping my elbow to get my attention.

"Of course it is," I said.

"Good," she said. She sounded relieved. This meant something to her.

"It's a good story," I said. "But live readings—they're just not my thing."

Disappointment seeped into her face.

"He's not going to be around forever, you know," she said.

"I hear *that*," I said. "Honest. Maybe it's the whole beatnik scene. They always seemed more like performers to me—pretending to be down and out when it was really their choice."

She let go of my arm. Had she any cigarettes left, the butt would have dropped from her open mouth.

"You sound so sure about that," she said.

"I wish I weren't. Lots of writers seem like that—poseurs, once you get to know them."

She looked around my face, then behind me, as if searching for something.

"Give me one example?" she said.

"Never mind," I said, reaching past her to pull open the door. "Come on—let's go in."

It wouldn't open. It had been sealed to make the display we stood in front of.

Carol, too, didn't budge.

"I'm not walking out in the middle of a reading by Lawrence Ferlinghetti," she said, emphasizing every single syllable of his name. "He was a writer way before he signed up for World War II, and after he walked around the blast zone at Nagasaki, he swore he'd be a pacifist forever. Then he lived his life for poetry. Doesn't sound fake to me."

She was folding up again, impatient, like she had our first night together. I was grateful and reassured to know I hadn't yet said anything stupid or too personal out of drunkenness. This was simple, sober, everyday unsociability and regret.

"I guess I thought you'd be a fan," she said.

"I didn't mean to upset you."

"It's not me I'm worried about, believe me."

The foot traffic that passed us, into the shop, had thickened.

"I'm just curious," she said, calmer, sincerely. "Who *do* you read— that's still alive? Would you go downstairs if they found some way to warm up Wallace Stevens?"

I didn't recall having mentioned Stevens to her before.

"Stevens called readings 'ghastly,'" I said. "He rarely did them. He never made recordings—or, that is, not until he was close to death."

"You know for sure he said that? *Ghastly*?"

"It's a great word," I said. "I get it. I can't listen well in public either. I can't really hear a poem in a crowd of strangers. I see the words they're saying, or I read the spines of the books behind them, or I daydream about what car they drove in or what they just ate. Even in college—I always fell asleep in lectures. Every lecture but my own."

She didn't find that funny.

"There is one recording of him reading," I said. "I played it for my class once, and I regretted it. Out loud, he's slow and grave. He sounds unnatural. The kids laughed at him—I lost them. But now I think I understand."

She checked her watch.

"It's not personal, Carol. And I'm not a snob."

She flapped her bag open, grabbed some gum, and shut the bag again.

Beyond her, up Columbus at the Condor Club, the cycling neon letters lit in rhythm with the dancer's legs. A line of pedestrians stepped to the beat, crossing Broadway.

Carol walked uphill at a normal pace just ahead of me, to the intersection. At the light, I offered to take her out for coffee and dessert across the street, but she reminded me that we'd already had both. Our evening was over. I was most to blame. I regretted that too. For the first time all night I considered my transit options for getting home.

The walk back up Russian Hill was too steep for small talk. Halfway, a near-empty cable car clacked around the corner, heading up Mason with its gassy headlamp projecting a horn of light into the fog. It was likely to be the last one running that night. When I suggested I grab it, Carol made no protest.

I reached out to thank her. She gave me a little kiss on the cheek, a pat on the back, and a push up the step.

The bell rang and the brake released. I lurched backward into the small, lit cabin. As fast as I could, I found a seat to wave goodbye, but I could no longer see Carol, or much of anything else beyond my reflection in the glass.

I got sleepy once underground. But I wasn't overly sad. My daughter would be home soon.

part two

CHAPTER 7

What threatened to be a somber occasion—Dorothy moving home to fight cancer—might have felt less disquieting if it hadn't happened so brightly and fast. Less than one week after our call, she drove over early, opened the windows, set up her boombox, and lit incense. It was her light-hearted everydayness that most unmoored me. For someone so young, she seemed awfully comfortable with death peeking down the hall. It must have been my own indeliberate belief that one day we'd each simply decline, painlessly and gradually—that I would slow, stoop, then stop, with my kids doing the same decades after I'd gone, so I'd never see—and that, despite my own family history, there'd be time for us to acquire the gravitas appropriate to each stage. Why? In the eighties, when AIDS ravaged our town like a gruesome plague, we'd lost some of our best teachers—including my Kingdom of Dumpling buddy's partner—in what seemed like a matter of days. Again and again we'd brush off our dark suits on short notice to show up for another makeshift ceremony and go numb at the brutal waste of men in their prime—some of our most creative, caring colleagues. I'd be dumbstruck by the emotional courage, the valiant wit—it's a strength that's hard to name—of the mourners whose eulogies managed to wrest every last trace of pleasure and humor that could be found in memory, pushing it out to live beyond us all. Their stories filled the air with a charge that threw you back into the arms of those you love, to live more gratefully. They showed me for the first time how a memorial really could be a "celebration of life"—a phrase that had always sounded hideously inapt for an occasion meant to package death. Until then, my experience had been: Death is the thing that tries to break your wings and gradually leave you alone. You can't ignore it, even in thought. No reason to party.

To be diagnosed with a life-threatening condition and, even worse, to be given a highly educated guess about how long it should take to run its course: What does that feel like? We all will die and we all know it, but even the most clearheaded are capable of living with that fact only by putting it aside. Who can last through even one day of utter, self-emptying grief? We either lie to ourselves about the ubiquity of death or we blind ourselves to it by turning to duties and pastimes till they're all we see. The philosophers say keeping death in mind makes you live more consciously, but I don't see how you can actually do both at the same time—not unless you consider sitting around stewing about death "living." (I may have, on occasion.) But to live—as I imagined Dorothy might be living—with most everyone and everything around you being attentive to your possibly accelerated end? And with whatever plans you make (or should be making) becoming increasingly constrained by episodic, mounting pain? Well, that must make you more philosophical by the hour. Or bitter.

This is an overlong way of saying that I didn't expect Dorothy to arrive, run into my arms, and spend each day with me looking at photos and talking about her legacy between bouts of shared tears, but I also did not expect her to be so unflappably commonsensical about it all either. For example, when she parked her Jeep halfway off the street, straddling the curb with her bumper denting a shrub next door, at first I (inwardly) applauded her ballsy move: *Why not? Why should she care any longer about parking tickets or pissing off the neighbors?* But after we carried in all her heavy monitors and steel shelving, I realized her bad parking was simply practical: It's the easiest way to unload the car. Or when she gave me a quick, everyday peck on the cheek: At first I thought she was holding back to avoid a flood of reunion tears, in case we might break down right there on the sidewalk, but it was soon clear she needed to unload quickly because Viktor was waiting to help reload, back at the apartment. And later, when she rushed around her room uncoiling cables and testing floorboard outlets, I assumed she was under duress due to the new, higher value she placed on her time: *She must race the clock now.* But she'd simply wanted to get her workspace up and running as soon as possible. When she caught me watching, she smiled and reported, happily, that our home was well grounded. Noncrisis averted.

Finally she stopped. She stood in the middle of her room with her small fists pressed to her hips. She looked flushed beneath her cap, eyes bloodshot, but as she surveyed the room, she seemed pleased at our progress.

In no time at all, her gear, with all its meters and switches and dials, along with the shelves of videotapes and boxes, had transformed the place into something resembling an intelligence bunker. I'd tried hard before she moved in to convert the room to adult use; I switched out her old goth bedspread and any pictures that might remind us of childhood, as this was to be the beginning of a different chapter in our lives together and not some nostalgia trip. At the same time, there was good reason to make it more homey and warm, so I'd cut a few roses from next door's overhangs and pulled a floor lamp in from the living room, but now that my home had been requisitioned, my little touches faded into irrelevance.

I wanted her to sit and catch her breath. To slow down.

"You moved all this equipment here just for a trial run?" I said.

Her twin bed now looked as out of place as a couch in a car showroom—which, I then recalled, was something I actually *had* seen recently, downtown.

She smiled. "Can you believe all this stuff was in my walk-in closet?"

And now all this stuff is in your childhood bedroom?

"It'll be great working with no distractions," she said. "Out here, in the fog."

"But you *will* sleep here too—right? You're staying?" I said. After all, I'd invited *her* to move back, not this chattel.

She focused on me.

"Looks like it, huh?" she said reassuringly. "Sure I will. Don't worry—I'm leaving my furniture behind. Mom might use my old bed, if she needs to stay in the city overnight for some reason this month. After that, Viktor can burn it for all I care."

She didn't even wince, saying that out loud.

I turned away, for the kitchen, but she flicked a switch on her machines and said, "Wait," with a tug in her voice.

Here we go, I thought. *She's ready to cry now.* But when I turned back to her, she faced one of her gray monitors where, on the shelf, little lights and meters twitched to life.

"Come look at this," she said, tapping the round screen.

She popped a big cassette tape in and played back a slow, muted scene in black and white. I had to stand close behind her to see the profile of an older man gazing across the waves of Ocean Beach like a sage. It took time to see: That man was me.

"See," she said, growing excited. "You've *got* it."

"What do I got?"

"The camera *likes* you. Some people just look better on camera. And it looks like you are one of them. Shorter people, mostly."

I admit it was difficult to recognize myself—the clip looked so artful.

"Shorter people, you say?"

She kept staring at the screen.

"I don't know how I've overlooked you all these years," she said, smiling.

"Well, I guess it's time for us to take stock, isn't it?"

I regretted that immediately, but she didn't flinch. It's always been easy for her to be blunt with me. I suppose after you've seen someone wet their pants while bleeding on the kitchen floor, you feel you can let your own guard down a bit. Nonetheless, I wanted to be less tone-deaf in the future. I no longer lived alone.

I pointed back at the screen.

"Kind of like Lloyd Bridges in *Sea Hunt*, huh?" I said.

She nodded blankly, without looking up. Clearly, she had no idea what I was talking about.

As we continued watching, the scene replayed—or rather we re-enacted it—this time with the camera zooming in from the same spot down the shore to get a close-up of my face in profile. The way the shadows stretched behind me indicated that this shot had been taken while I'd faced east, away from the water and into the morning sun. But the closer she got, the more it looked like I was instead gazing out past the waves, at the horizon, into a sunset. It was easy for her to flip the image, and to darken or brighten and slow or quicken it somehow, at will.

It looked like fun—my daughter's work.

"So—we need more of *that*," she said, pointing. "More tape. If you're willing."

"For the human resources film? Don't you have a deadline?"

Her hand slid from my arm and fell to her lap, where it gripped at nothing.

"That's done," she said. "I'm taking a—sabbatical. This one will be for me. *My* project."

I understand completely.

"It'll be easier than this last shoot. Promise," she said, nodding back toward the screen. "Just let me follow you around with the camera whenever I want, okay?"

"Sure. If my agent's cool with it."

A flash of horizontal static introduced a new clip in which Carol and I walk away from the camera. Carol, who I'd always thought of as somewhat shorter than me, wasn't really—not by much. Or, rather, I was not much taller. Regardless, we didn't look entirely like ourselves, sauntering like that with sunlight flaring between us. We looked better—more intentional, defined. Less gray, somehow.

"The camera likes Carol too?" I said.

"Not sure," Dorothy said without turning. "Keep watching."

On-screen, Carol and I stopped to face each other. The tape was muted, but in my head I could still hear Dorothy's direction from just days before: *Stop. Turn. Come together.*

Our pretend, dramatic-looking on-screen chatter ceased just as the camera began to close in on us. We faced each other, volume muted. Reflected sunshine glittered and flashed behind us, silhouetting our faces.

Dorothy turned a dial to slow the motion.

"Watch right here," she said, pointing to Carol's lips, which parted slowly to reveal—in sharp, dark profile—her two front teeth. They looked too big for an instant, despite the slow motion, then they disappeared just as quickly when she puckered for a kiss, at which point Dorothy graciously shut the thing down.

When she'd reached for the knob I noticed, for the first time, the yellowed spot where some needle had punctured the inside of her arm. She hadn't even begun chemo yet. She saw me look as she pulled back and the screen darkened.

"Is there pain, Dorothy?"

I'd surprised us both by asking.

"Like—in the world?" she said. She grinned, impossibly, but only briefly.

"Sorry," I said.

"Just little waves so far," she said. "You can never guess if a stronger one's coming, or when. But I've got pills, if I need." She grew quiet. "That's between us for now, okay? Not Mom. Not yet."

"You talked with her?"

"We found their hotel. In Bologna."

Jackie in Italy was still as unimaginable to me as Dorothy in chemo.

"It was hard for her," she said. "For a while she kept talking like I just had the flu, and then you could hear it seep in slowly: She got louder and started sounding like she was going to swim home, move in with me, and start making soup. Tomorrow."

Dorothy had always been comfortable making jokes about herself—about being short, flat-chested, or pudgy when she was young, any quality she would have preferred not to deal with—but I hadn't heard her make cracks at her mother's expense for some time. We were entering a new era.

"You know your mother can't make a decent soup," I said.

"Yeah, and she can't move in with me if I've already moved out."

I could only nod. She rolled her sleeves down.

"Leave the bed in the corner, okay?" she said. "We can rearrange everything after the last load. Gerald's going to help. I'll be right back."

"Whatever you say," I said. But when I remembered that I hadn't yet called Gerald—as she'd asked me to, and as I'd promised—my shakiness returned. Here we are, I thought, her first day home, and already I'm hankering for a martini and some means of banishing all cancer-talk to the front room. Dorothy's at-home convalescence would need to take over more of each day for weeks, for months. I wanted that, of course. With all my heart. But I needed to remind myself that, beginning tonight, I would never again know for sure when I was free to sit peacefully alone with my thoughts in my chair.

She stopped in the doorway, a small silhouette toward which I turned.

"I know it's weird to say, Dad, but—in a way—I'm looking forward to this."

Her voice brightened my gloom so much that I felt grateful, and guilty.

When Dorothy ran out for the remainder of her belongings, I sat out back. I could think of nothing else to do but wait for what would happen next.

My anticipation of Jackie's return from the Continent was complex. A small part of me would be glad to no longer be a single parent facing all this. Another part wanted to manage this alone. Her return trip could take a few days. Either way, she'd end up at the front door soon enough.

That prospect got me out of my chair.

The night before, I'd taped a short to-do list on the fridge. I peeled that off to read, holding it tightly, like it was my ticket to a better place:

1. Clean/paint room (D choose color?)
2. Research: C treatments
3. Research: Cooking for chemo
4. Research: Pension/dependent
5. Tell Gerald

It was already too late for me to complete my first action item, so I was mightily relieved (and unsurprised) to see that the next three bullets required a trip to the library.

I take at least one good walk every day, but that late afternoon I sprinted like a horse out of the gate. I jogged north through Golden Gate Park, speeding around the sheltered, dripping path that contours a small lake—a couple with a stroller veered away from me— and then looped around the polo field and uphill to the Anza Branch Library as if someone were waiting for me there with a stopwatch and prize. Which, in a way, was true: Once I spelled out my caregiver needs to the gray-eyed, crew-cut circulation clerk, she swiftly led me to a shelf that held everything I'd asked for, and then some.

Perhaps no one but I would be surprised to learn that an entire "industry" has been built up around the process of living with, battling, and surviving cancer, with subindustries for every affected body part, type of caregiver, and treatment option. It was as if my librarian had prepared the collection for me in advance. She even allowed us to bypass the computer station on our way to the stacks, without a second glance. In silence, she shied away from my gushing gratitude to face the books.

My grandmother had always kept a family medical guide handy in the kitchen. It was an encyclopedia in which you could find instructions on how to deal with everything from bed-wetting to sucking chest wounds—a thick, dark-covered tome. Only the most hard-to-describe items were illustrated, and all of those were line drawings. In contrast, the new books I was shown on our library shelves were so richly illustrated and colorful they almost made me look forward to rolling up my sleeves and engaging in the new cure economy. I scanned the titles on each spine as my librarian pulled out selections for me that were not only on-topic but seemed to be written to address my specific needs—like *The Caregiver's Guide to Cancer* and so on. I piled them on the table next to me, but after she left, I rolled a stool over to browse all the others that had caught my eye.

One of those books was called *What to Expect When You're Expecting*. I imagined Emily Dickinson tacking *the Unexpected* onto the end of that title. The homey, heartwarming pictures brought me back to our baby days, so I began to read it, for relief. It's sobering, how much more hopeful labor and delivery medicine is than oncology. The entire book was so folksy and do-it-yourselfy that I half expected to find blueprints for air castles and pine-bough cradles alongside the baby food recipes.

In one chapter, a series of Da Vinci–esque diagrams of the various orientations a baby might take in the womb stopped me short. It was one such position that had taken my mother from me when I was five, when she died from complications due to a late-term miscarriage. I would have had a little sister, as well as my mother, otherwise. She'd had two miscarriages in the four years between me and my brother, and for that reason her pregnancy with me was anxiety-riddled, with a lot of bed rest, and ended in a caesarean. But what, after me, would have been her next baby, her fifth pregnancy, had its heart stop beating sometime in the fifth month. My mother had grown very heavy by then—she had been bedridden for several weeks, that round—and her blood pressure was extremely high, but what most likely stilled the fetus was the umbilical cord having wrapped tighter and tighter around its neck. I saw that all too clearly in the eerily beautiful drawings, where a baby with huge closed eyes fit one amphibious little hand under the cord encircling its neck—its lifeblood, and its ever-present threat. How benign and simple it all looked, in the book. I wondered how horrifying such an image might have been, back then, to my mother. Perhaps not as bad as what she imagined.

I have very few memories of her—far more of my grandmother—but the few moments I recall vividly are from the final, tense weeks of that pregnancy, because she was always in bed, usually awake, and I was still home. The affection we shared involved me standing on my tiptoes by her bed; she would lean over to the side and press me close as I grabbed as much arm or neck as I could, but in the end, when she lay in our living room—we'd moved a hospital bed in, to prop her up—she could just hold my hand or pat my face. Even before that pregnancy she'd been melancholic, often going to bed midday with migraines and the lights off. (I have only one picture of her smiling, in sunglasses, under the shade of an elm at a picnic.) Then one day the ambulance took her to the hospital to "have my new baby sister." I was never brought to visit. She never returned. And when she "went to heaven," I never saw the closed coffin in which she'd flown up there, nor heard the prayers or songs that accompanied her. That was my father's decision—to have me go home after the wake. It would have been too hard for him to have me near the actual interment. I didn't even see her gravestone until months later, with Craig, who one day declared that we needed to see where Grandma—who herself had begun aging fast—would be buried when *she* died. We biked there; I was incredulous, seeing my mother's name, and my last name, freshly chiseled into stone. Craig said we would all end up in that dirt—including me, if I stood there long enough. I remember bolting away, screaming all the way home as he sped after me, moaning like a throat-cut ghost, chasing but never quite catching me. He'd frightened me so thoroughly that I never went back into the cemetery alone until I was a teen. Which, I imagine, had been his aim all along.

In my open library book, the blank eyes of the homunculus seemed to watch me in lifeless silence. I looked away, out the brined window. A steel clock ticked rhythm on the wall. Ordinarily hours passed more comfortably and slowly in a library than anywhere else, for me. But now it seemed that time was up.

Who am I really helping, sitting on a rolling step stool by the radiator, reading picture books?

I decided I could allow myself to check out just one pregnancy book along with the others about cancer because I knew where my attention would turn first, once home, if I had too many options. The circulation clerk date-stamped them all, then held the stack out for me in both hands as if it were a newborn in a basket.

I spun around to leave as a black-jacketed woman strode up to the desk: It was Xenia. Without a word, she dropped her heap of books and movies on the counter behind me with a *thud* and grabbed me by my forearms, squeezing hard, almost shaking me as she gazed warmly into my eyes. In the bright overhead light, focusing on her shining face felt like discerning features on the sun, but her surprise at seeing me there was a delight. I felt an urge to turn and explain our relationship to the clerk.

"Good to *see* you!" she said, beaming. But then, just as fast, she scowled a little and bit her lip. That meant: *I heard about Dorothy.*

"You wait," she said, giving me a quick wave as she turned to give her card to the clerk. She packed her books and videocassettes into a big messenger bag.

When we stepped out into the fog, she said: "We pray for you and Dorothy. For family."

"Thank you," I said, but she continued searching my face, as if expecting me to report on some immediate benefit we'd received from this.

"What brings you here?" I said.

"No work." She shrugged her shoulders, palms lifting up in the air. "I am only temporary, so—"

"I mean, this neighborhood?"

"I live here." She pointed somewhere east, down Geary—toward Little Russia. "My uncle."

She rolled her eyes as she explained that the situation was less than optimal—living with extended family in a three-bedroom flat—but just as quickly she dismissed that cloud with another shrug. I noted how she'd waited till we were out in the cold wind to chat in earnest, and I worried that she might think I was prying into her immigration status. I would have felt bad if she had, because already I felt more at home with X than any other friend of Gerald's.

"I didn't know you lived so close by," I said. I may have assumed she spent most of her time at The Keep.

"Many Russians live here," she said. "You know this. How is Dorothy?"

Her brow furrowed; her concern ran deep.

I couldn't guess how much Gerald knew or had shared. And I still hadn't called to tell him the worst.

"She is very sick," I said.

She shook her head and looked down. As she kicked the stone step, a small bit of chain jingled on her boot.

"What can you do?" she said.

Hell if I know.

"That's what these are for," I said, pointing to the books under my arm. "Caregiving manuals."

She leaned in to look at a cover. *Yes*, she nodded.

"We can only wait and learn more," I said.

"To wait is hard," she said.

For a moment, she looked down the hill, over the roofs of houses, toward the ocean. The blowing mist made her hair clump. She kept kicking the step with her toe.

She nodded down the street.

"You need ride?"

I'm not sure if I even said *Yes* before following her downhill, into the wind, to the passenger side of an old, dented Mercedes sedan.

"My uncle," she explained, prying open the door. "We make one stop first, Jim."

Okay, X, I nodded. *Sure.*

It should not have surprised me, after the little talk she'd given me on Costco day, but within minutes we were parked in front of the enormous, onion-domed Holy Virgin Cathedral, Joy of All Who Sorrow. Xenia hunched over to pull a disabled-parking placard from under her seat—*My aunt*, she said—and toss it up on the dashboard. She looked up at me as if worried because I hadn't yet unlocked my door.

"This helps," she said, nodding to the cathedral. "Then we drive home."

I followed as she marched up the broad steps to four tall, heavy bronze doors. With both hands she pulled one open and nodded me inside.

The closing door sealed us into a quiet, dark narthex. It took time to adjust. Incense lingered like memories in the cool air, and behind a large oak counter, a bearded old man with a ponytail stood guard over stacks of small icons, prayer ropes, booklets, and candles. A wall and doors of tinted glass separated us from the shadowy nave of the cathedral. As I stared inside, my eyes found lit candles thickly clustered in stands before the many icons. It looked as if the deep, gilded space had no floor or ceiling. An enormous, chained chandelier hung in the middle, unlit, with its polished brass reflecting colors from the stained glass.

The gray-faced man tipped his head to Xenia—they recognized each other—and he held two candles out for her as she dropped a few coins in a slotted wooden box. I began to fumble for my wallet, but she grabbed my arm and pulled me toward the doors. The attendant stepped out from behind his counter as Xenia and I turned to enter, but not once did he look at me: I was the foreigner here, and as I saw Xenia gently adjust a kerchief over her stiff, damp hair, I grew embarrassed of my fluorescent windbreaker. Nevertheless, the man held the thick glass door for both of us, giving her a dignified nod of welcome.

Perhaps it was my mood that made the dense sweetness inside so overwhelming, but it touched my core. I followed Xenia for two or three steps, and then stopped. The place felt far richer than the world outside. My heart beat faster. There were soaring lines with columns of stained glass lifting my eyes in every direction I turned, and the air was so densely fragrant from roses and incense I felt like I was floating. The nearest feeling I have to compare it to is the sudden swoon I'd felt the rainy morning I'd first seen Jackie at my door—the first and only time I ever fell in love.

Xenia strode over the parquet floor and ornate, scarlet carpet runners on her heavy heels. She crossed herself and bowed low before one golden icon, lightly touching the floor with her fingertips between each show of reverence. I'd never seen this gesture before, and even for a lapsed, old-school Catholic like me, it was an exotic way of genuflecting—so very foreign it deepened the space between us even more. My attention swept past her to the wide-eyed, gilded faces that watched from above each cluster of candles and flowers, and up into the vast frescoed arch of Mary. Her arms were outspread as if she would gather and protect us.

I could not see all the way up into the central dome from where I stood, so I stepped in deeper. My tennis shoes squeaked and echoed on the waxed floor. I bumped into Xenia's back, but she just grabbed my arm again to guide me. We stopped several yards before the closed front of the iconostasis, and she pointed to where my eyes had already been drawn—up the frescoed sides of the dome to the apex, where an enormous image of Christ, at least twenty feet wide, looked down upon us. There was nothing sentimental in the expression, and yet Xenia felt compelled to wait a moment, to watch, and then to whisper: *He sees us.* I could only nod.

She then led me to the shrine at our right, by the east side of the nave.

"Saint John," she explained. "*Vladika* helps."

I did not know we were approaching a glass-covered coffin until we were but ten feet from its side, and she again released me to draw nearer, standing alone before it and crossing herself. She dropped to her knees to press her forehead to the carpet. Each time she lifted her face, I heard the catch of her breath, the wrinkling of her leather jacket, and the slight whispering of her consonants as she crossed and sighed before again dropping to her knees. She kissed the glass top of the coffin; lovingly, she touched its edge with her fingertips and lingered a moment, her eyes searching inside and then shutting.

I felt like an imposter as she made these prostrations. I held back.

When she arose, she bowed again, crossed herself, and turned to light one of the candles she'd bought, placing it upright in the sand-filled tray of a brass stand. She lit one only, and once done she looked out for me, as if I'd backed far away. A faint but impatient grimace passed over her face as she held the second candle out to me like a talk show host proffers a mic to her guest, and looked to me as if to say: *Well?*

I stepped up, closer to her and the small, supine saint. In an instant I saw his rich silk robes embellished with gold, the bishop's miter, the embroidered cloth covering his face—and quickly I averted my eyes, turning to Xenia.

She stood immobile behind me.

I took the candle from her, dumbstruck, but stepped back to whisper:

"I'm not sure what to do?"

Then do what I do, her look said. *Pray.* She said it as simply as another might say: *Speak. Walk.* Or it's possible she hadn't spoken at all, and that I'd imagined it.

"I haven't been in church for years," I said.

She scowled again: *So?* Quickly, grabbing my hand, she held the candle with me, lit it at the oil lamp, and stuck it upright in the sand, by hers. She pointed up to the large icon, which I'd already recognized from the little book she'd left as an image of Saint John of Shanghai and San Francisco. In his hands he carried a tiny replica of the very cathedral in which we now stood. She dropped my hand to again cross herself and kiss the icon, over his folded hands, gazing up at his face before closing her eyes.

It was my cue to do something for myself. I felt it would be bald mimicry for me to do more than simply nod in honest respect. But then I realized it wasn't hypocrisy I was most concerned about, but embarrassing myself. *Saving face.* That's a selfish, lonely need. *Saving Dorothy*—that was what I should be more concerned about. That there was within me at that moment an implied choice I needed to make between the two, real or not, somehow knocked the will right out of me.

Xenia walked around me toward the door. Without looking back I followed in her wake, at a respectful, unhurried pace, to her uncle's car.

She waited and watched as I belted myself in.

"Thank you," I said.

"Why 'Thank you'?" she said. She didn't move. She looked bigger behind the wheel, watching me.

"You prayed for Dorothy's health," I said.

Her eyebrows arched high, incredulous. In that light, it wasn't flattering.

"You want something, you ask," she said. "You pray."

Slowly, she unzipped her jacket pocket and pulled out the keys. But again, she stopped.

"Saint John, you know—he saves hundreds of people," she said. "You see all those little papers—those papers are prayers of people who ask for good health, or job, or house, or children, or marriage. Worse problems too." She tapped her heart with her free hand, then pointed out. "He builds this church. And before that, he saves people from communists to Shanghai and to Philippines so they make home in United States. He talked to the president! This little man who speaks no English! And he has orphans from China. The home for orphans is here, on Fifteenth Avenue. You go see it. When I need help in Odesa—so much help—I ask him to bring me here, and look—now *I* visit *him!*" She stared out the misted windshield, at the steps, squeezing the keys in her fist.

"I pray for Dorothy," she said. "I pray for you too—for Gerald and for you."

"Thank you," I said again.

She searched my eyes but didn't seem to find what she was looking for.

She turned the key in the ignition, knocked on the wipers, and stamped her boot to the clutch. With the most perfunctory of glances over her shoulder, out the rearview, we shot backward, reversing across a lane of oncoming boulevard traffic on blind faith.

"You two," she said, shaking her head before looking out to turn. "He is like you."

In silence, she drove me and my books home.

Dorothy returned that evening with Gerald, his truck, and the remainder of her belongings. It was reassuring to see the two of them here together, for the first time in over a year, and in surprisingly good spirits. He moved quickly, whistling loudly. After sliding a few cartons of Chinese food and a six-pack across the kitchen table to me, he jogged back out to unload Dorothy's books, music, clothes, and sundries—more things you wouldn't expect her to move unless she'd made up her mind to stay for good. I was deeply happy for that confirmation.

She unpacked a box at the table—her favorite mug, some special teas. She gave me a blue enameled, cast-iron Dutch oven—which, Gerald said, "practically screamed *Dad!*"—but she'd left most of her kitchen equipment behind. Her eyes were rimmed with fatigue as she arranged a half dozen new prescription bottles before her on the table. Then, with the saddest expression I'd seen on her all day, she told me Viktor was keeping their cat. Her allergies were a challenge to her immune system, and no one needed more challenges.

So it felt final: She *would* be living and sleeping here. This was home again.

Gerald stomped back into the house, buoyed with the achievement of having emptied his truck, and began pushing everything where Dorothy wanted. He found it hard to slow down. Once he'd noticed all her medications, he seemed to find it difficult to look at either of us. Nor would he sit. Had I not known better, I might have thought the two of them had just fought in the car. He popped open a beer, shook his cellular phone impatiently, then suddenly ran downstairs to rummage for something in the garage with such urgency that we heard him through the floor.

It had become dark outside, and Dorothy looked pale under the light. Neither of us touched the take-out: The dyspeptic hiccups that escaped Dorothy as she sipped her lukewarm tea made it clear she had no appetite. Distracted, she slowly slid her chair back under the table and drifted out to her room. I followed.

She pushed her heap of clothes to one side and sat on the edge of her bed. Slowly, she surveyed the cluttered, crowded space of her room. One hand lay palm-up in her lap, as if waiting for the other to put the mug aside and wring it.

"Should I leave you for a nap?" I said.

No. She shook her head, looking up.

"More tea?"

"Some cold water might be good," she said. She put her mug aside and stood as if to fetch it herself.

"No, no—let me," I said, grateful to know what to do. Gerald hadn't let me help either.

"It's okay," she said. "It feels good to keep moving."

I sank in frustration.

"Dad, don't worry," she said. "There'll be plenty of that later. Save yourself."

A popular phrase, that, in my world. She must have sensed how startled and worried I was at hearing it come from her, because she quickly explained.

"Save yourself for *me*," she said. "But maybe you're right—about the nap."

She leaned against a stack of mismatched pillows as Gerald stomped back up into her room. He'd dragged in her old longboard, still waxed, from the garage. It sprinkled sand onto the floor as he knocked the doorjamb coming in. Immediately he too grew quiet when he noticed me pulling Dorothy's quilt up to her chin. He stood the surfboard in a corner where it leaned like a dare, just as it had years ago, behind the Christmas tree, opposite his. He grabbed her half-empty mug from the floor, nesting it in both hands a moment to give her a nod, then trod back out to the kitchen without a word.

"Tomorrow afternoon," she said to me, "I have a biopsy appointment. So maybe we can shoot a little on the way in—okay?"

I would do anything.

"Sorry I forgot to tell you that—" she said.

"Please rest."

"I think I will," she said. She was still nodding as I kissed her forehead.

She closed her eyes too tightly, the way she used to when she was little, pretending to fall asleep, but I left anyway.

Gerald was leaning over the kitchen sink, wolfing down noodles from the box. He didn't look up.

"You know Mom's coming back tomorrow?" he said. And another surprise: She was flying, coming into Oakland at noon. He'd taken the day off work to pick her up, but he would only drive her home to her place in the East Bay. He didn't think Jackie should come out to see Dorothy until she'd had some rest herself.

I was proud he'd thought of all that.

"Dorothy really needs to pace herself," he said, finally composed enough to turn and point his fork at me. "You might want to keep an eye on her. No overscheduling."

So he too had noticed she was in visible decline.

"You're talking to *me*, Pack-It-In-Jim?" I said.

He tried to grin and chew at the same time, but chewing won.

"This deeply sucks, Dad," he said, scraping down into the carton and blinking hard.

I couldn't have said it better.

CHAPTER 8

The next morning, despite my love of routine, I was relieved to find Dorothy ensconced in the back room with her mug of tea and camera in hand, panning the backyard like a hunter. Without knowing it, she'd taken my old chair, in its new position. Perhaps in doing so she'd assumed I could never be forced out of my former corner. Obviously it would take us a bit of time to establish new patterns, now that our second life together had begun in earnest. When I innocently suggested she might be more comfortable on the other side, in the less worn chair, she slowly tilted the camera back up at me, to some point between my eyes. The camera was compact, just bigger than a fat paperback—not nearly as large as what you'd imagine necessary for any serious work. I could see how its handy size would allow her to keep it at the ready in the weeks ahead. I even hoped to learn to use it myself.

All the same, being forced to stare down a lens first thing in the morning, before you've made coffee or even eye contact, does make you feel displaced. She too still looked tired from yesterday. For the first time in weeks, she had her baseball cap off, and it was surprising to see how stringy her hair had become, especially given that her chemo wouldn't start until after the biopsy. She had pulled out one of her old surf shop T-shirts, a hoodie, some loose, resurrected jeans, and her Chuck Taylor high-tops—her old high school uniform. That was a comfort to see, despite her camera's shiny black eye.

I said "Good morning," but the lens just hummed and slid closer, zooming in on my face.

"That'll do," I told it.

Obediently, Dorothy removed the camera from her face. She held it sideways in her fist, studied it as if seeing it for the first time, and pushed a little button. It beeped in reply. She grinned up at me.

All this change must be awkward for her too, I told myself.

The windows rattled with bursts of wet summer fog, the type that burns off by noon and leaves the air clean.

She picked up the saddle-stitched biography of Saint John from the top of my "to-do" stack and held the cover up to my face.

"Who's this severe-looking dude?" she said.

I was glad I'd hidden my medical research books in my bedroom, out of sight.

"That's X's book," I said. "From her church on Geary."

In calling her that, I was flaunting my familiarity with Gerald's life. I guess it still smarted a bit that Dorothy had never told me about Viktor.

She thumbed through a few pages.

"What do you think of Xenia?" she said, not looking up.

"She's a refreshing change," I said. It sounded surprising—how much I meant it.

She stopped skimming and held a picture up close to her eyes.

"You know she's divorced, right?" she said.

I did not, but said, "Who isn't these days?"

"She's also a good six or seven years older than Gerald."

I didn't know that either. Xenia wore her jeans and jacket tight like a younger woman. And from my perspective, thirty-three isn't exactly what I'd call "older." It was Xenia's straightforward manner and enthusiasm that most gave me the impression that she was closer to Gerald's age. That, and how impatient she'd gotten with me the other day.

"Do you know anything more about her life, before she came here?" I said.

Dorothy shook her head.

"Well, they seem close," I said. "Well matched."

She gave me a quick look—*Really?*—before holding the booklet up to my face, to inspect. She'd splayed it open to a grainy black-and-white photo of the shrine I'd visited just yesterday. It was a picture of the sepulcher, with the body of Saint John Maximovitch just visible inside.

"Did you see *this*?" she said, her voice dropping as she pointed to the picture.

"X took me to him, yes," I said.

"That's his *body* under the glass?" she said, turning the page back to her, to gape.

I nodded.

"So you actually went into the church to see—him?" She looked a little shaken, and not due merely to my having stepped inside a church, Russian or otherwise.

"He's a saint," I said. "His remains are incorrupt."

I watched her closely as she scrutinized the poor photo.

"X wanted to pray for you," I added.

"She did?" She blinked. "And did *you*?"

"I'm not Orthodox."

"I doubt that matters to him."

Gently, she closed the little book and stood it up so the cover faced her, on the windowsill of what, that morning, was becoming Her Side of the back room. Her fingers trembled as she did this.

"Please," she said, "next time, just go for it. I can use all the help I can get."

Our "shoot" that morning felt more like an excuse to cruise along the Golden Gate than anything else. Dorothy always acts freer and louder when she drives her Jeep with the cap off. We hugged the city's northern shore, past the red-tiled mansions of Sea Cliff and then higher, into the Presidio, atop the green serpentine cliffs, toward the bridge. She pulled over at one of our old haunts, the World War II–era battery that once hid big guns to protect the Bay from enemy attack, and that, a few decades later, had become one of our kids' favorite playgrounds: Dorothy and Gerald used to love scrambling over the concrete cliff-side bunkers and tunnels. The grand view of the ocean and headlands is dazzling, and disarming; it was always a wonder to me how any soldier would have been able to take their eyes off the glittering Pacific long enough to take aim.

Near the bridge, Dorothy stopped the Jeep again in a scuffing of gravel. She shot me standing on a bluff, gazing down at the thinning fog that rhythmically ebbs and flows beneath the span, between the towers. She directed me to shield my brow with my hand, pivot, and walk away, at a funereal pace, through some Monterey pines toward the shimmering city. Dorothy said the trimmed, elegant trees reminded her of a postcard Jackie'd just sent from Rome. That was distracting.

After filming this scene three times, Dorothy showed me how to take shots of my own. For practice, I made her repeat the action she'd just given me, and it was oddly fascinating to watch her through the lens. As she turned and walked away from me, she shrank to looking so small and lonely that it made me anxious, as if I were watching my little girl stumble, alone, deep into the woods. I asked her to stop and stare back into the camera as I moved toward her, trying not to bounce, focusing on her face, but when I got close enough, she grabbed it back and showed me how to use the zoom instead.

The camera reminded me of something we teachers used in our professional development workshops—a knotted piece of wood we called "the Talking Stick." When it was your turn to hold the Stick, you got everyone's undivided attention. Of course, the camera is different in that you're not actually the one who's talking when you hold it, but you *do* call the shots—you're the one controlling the moment, pulling it outside the shared present to package it into your own, entirely separate narrative of the now.

The more I used her camera, the more I respected it. I always used to think movies were simple recordings of the material facts of life, whereas other media could create fully imagined worlds. But I learned that's not so. Movies may be the most powerful way to create an entirely new experience, because when you make a movie, you directly engage and control more senses: You manage what others see and hear, how fast or slow, when, from what perspective, how close—all at once. Add a soundtrack and a narrator, and you can even make people feel and think the way you want them to. The more I shot, the more alert I became to everyday surfaces—sounds and light and movements—and the more I saw how filming can override whatever thought and mood I'd originally brought to them. I saw and heard things with an uncluttered rawness: Dorothy's few freckles, the breeze riffling her bangs, her delicate, still-girlish profile—even, when I zoomed in, the two bridge towers reflected in her sunglasses. And you're safely hidden behind a camera; through it, you're pushing your focus on the world, while that world remains at a manageable distance, undisturbed. No need to speak, even. I felt I understood Dorothy better.

We sat awhile on a bench above the bridge, facing north—a view so picture-perfect it made everything else unreal. I zoomed in and out of the lanes of traffic. Dorothy hunched up in the chill, then sidled closer to me to watch the small screen too.

"You like it, don't you?" she said.

I put the camera down. Even my hands looked more real, just by holding it.

"Well—I definitely prefer making movies to being in them," I said.

Her eyes were runny and sleepy as the sun cleared to the east.

"I know what you mean."

She looked back out at the bridge.

"Want to try driving today too?" she said.

My brother, Craig, once owned a big, beat-up De Soto, baby-blue and chrome, and sometimes he took me cruising outside town where the state roads cross in grids above flat miles of corn. One hot August day, probably just to get me out of the house and away from our mourning father, he drove me down the freight tracks—literally straddled the rails, trundling over the ties, through the fields. He'd wired a stolen drive-in speaker to his radio that he usually clipped inside his window, but that afternoon it lay dead silent, bouncing on the seat between us so we could hear the thumping tires and listen for trains. Even though the wheels squealed and shimmied on the sides of the steel tracks, the only way to make the ride halfway smooth over the gaps between ties was to keep up a decent speed. So we did. I was terrified the axles might snap, or the tires would fly off, but the sky was empty and the sun was glinting, sharp, in Craig's eyes: He was excited.

I was scared but also willing, because it was during his reckless moments that he treated me most like a friend. There was never the need to talk. I've since wondered: Why would you do things like this with your sixth-grade brother when you're a sophomore in high school? Why not with friends your own age? In public, he was loud and gregarious, surrounded by admirers he always seemed to be performing for—his classmates and ball team, his Dairy Queen coworkers, his parade of short-term girlfriends. But the only time I saw him comfortable being quiet was when he was alone with me.

That late-summer day, after clonking down a quarter mile of track, he stopped on a rusted bridge that crossed a coffee-brown creek. The tires squealed into a jarring stop, between ties. He cut the engine, and that old car shuddered dead like a bucket dropping down a well: It amplified the emptiness around it.

Craig jumped out. As I watched, he walked to the front of the car and dropped out of sight. I shot out, frightened. He was kneeling in front of the grill with his ear pressed to a rail. The veins throbbed at his temple as he caressed the blue polished steel with the fingertips and palms of both of his hands, his forearms taut like he might lift into a handstand at any second.

"We're going in," he said.

He tore away from me, running down the dusty slope to the bank of the turgid creek. Before I'd even peeled my socks off, he was loping naked through the muddy current, up to his waist. He was taller then than I am now, with square shoulders but a chest so concave it looked like he'd taken a cannonball to the sternum. I was chubby and slow. I could never run as fast or go in as deep as Craig could, but I always went out farther for him than I would anyone else, and by the time I was tiptoeing toward him on the slimy stones and silt, he was already frisking midstream like a beaver in spring.

He hooted. He called me out.

I watched him sink beneath the dull, thick water, surrounded by eddies that bubbled and glittered above his head. The horizon tipped and dropped with him, in my eyes. Even then I knew I'd one day lose him.

He popped up like an otter, next to me. He pulled his hand out, palm to my face: It pulsed and glistened with blood.

Crocs, Jimmy! Snakes!

I yelped and flailed to get away.

He howled, loping past me in slow motion to bound up the bank before I could get either of my feet free of the muck.

He froze, a profile against the corn: *What's that?* he whispered.

I stopped breathing.

Listen, Jimmy—Listen!

He grabbed his clothes in his wet, red fist.

Whistles! Trains!

He scrambled to the bridge, kicking up new dust.

I'd heard it—I thought. I scurried, dragging most of my clothes.

He yanked open the door. He shoved me in, past the stick shift, all the way to the steering wheel. He made a visor of his dripping hand, jerked his head north and south, up and down the tracks, and tossed his bloody keys at me.

Drive, Jimmy! I'm cut. You gotta!

He clambered in. Slammed the door.

Everything shook but my two hands on the wheel. I couldn't ask *Why?* I could never say no to him.

I turned the key in the ignition. It wouldn't start. I did it again, and again, squeezing the key till my white fingers went numb.

Do it!

I stomped on both pedals. I slapped and shook the steering wheel. I kicked the dashboard till I was crying like a baby.

And then Craig broke. There was no train. He roared with laughter, heaving into a coughing fit. I, watching him, began to sob, then pant, and, finally, I did my best to smile through my tears, too relieved to stay mad.

As he twisted his T-shirt around his hand, grisly with blood from the gash he'd gotten underwater, his eyes sparkled like cheap class rings. I stared. He didn't look once at the blood drying thick on his leather upholstery, his speaker, his knee. His voice dropped as he told me, step by step, how to clutch and shift and accelerate, as if driving around bare-assed was what we would now do each day.

Once I got the car in gear, I stopped sniffling. And, soon enough, I found driving easy: The car steered itself down the rails like an amusement park ride. I couldn't have turned left or right even if I'd wanted to—not without help from Craig. And that was a very good thing, because as we reentered the canopy of corn and he grabbed the wheel hard to jump us off the tracks, my chest tightened, the air went milky, and I crashed forward into my second seizure—the confirmation, the one the doctors were waiting for before prescribing me a lifetime of medication.

I'd never told Dorothy that story before, but none of it seemed to surprise her as I recalled it for her then, by the bridge. She patted my hand once and kept quiet until the bench grew too chilly for us. She checked her watch, and then closed her eyes. We were late for her appointment.

She drove past what had once been the Presidio's army airstrip. When I asked why they were dismantling the hangars and outbuildings, she said it was to reconstruct a beach. That was news to me—a massive project—so I suggested we take some "before" shots. She told me not to bother: It wouldn't be finished for five years. She drove faster.

She gunned the Jeep straight up a forty-five-degree incline to Pacific Heights. I swear our front tires lost contact with the street. I rode shotgun, camera in hand and aimed at the clouds. She said nothing.

Soon the daylight changed, with skinny shadows peeking around each object just after noon and drawing the world into deepening relief. I could see it behind Dorothy's shades: How red-eyed and harried she looked leaning in to scan the next hill, playing the emergency brake against the clutch, as if looking for a hidden way out. She lost her patience with cross traffic and flinched, dramatically, in the direct sunlight that hit us between buildings. I couldn't engage her with small talk. She didn't want her water bottle. When she finally pulled over to a curb and yanked her phone from her hoodie, her grimace confirmed my suspicion: She too was anxious about Jackie's return.

She dropped the phone in her lap and let out a long, slow breath.

"Gerald left a voice mail," she said. "Mom's delayed."

She looked ahead, watching the tail of traffic wind past us.

"Mom doesn't know the scan results yet," she said, turning to me. "I don't want her rushing over the bridge right off the plane—there's nothing she can do, and she'll probably be exhausted after flying. Gerald said he'll give me a heads-up when he knows anything. Poor Gerald."

She looked down at her silent phone and said: "He blew a whole day of PTO for this too."

It surprised me again, that selflessness—how I'd never noticed it before in my own daughter.

We sped down the dark spiral of the hospital parking garage. She seemed to know her way well around the hospital too, depositing me in a comfortable lounge to wait out her biopsy. I had a floor-to-ceiling view of Pacific Heights and the Bay beyond. It was an unusually wide view for me to have all to myself, but it couldn't distract me from imagining Dorothy lying flat on a table just a few thin walls away. Already I missed sitting with her on our bench by the bridge. Or on our porch at home.

Flapping, molting pigeons scrambled for position at the edge of the plate glass.

The phone Dorothy left with me began to buzz and blink to life. It took me a moment to figure out what to do. Gerald wasn't surprised to hear me answer; he must have known Dorothy's schedule too.

"Well, we know she's landed in the States," he said in a huff. Botched schedules made him short-tempered. "But she totally missed her connection. I stayed and watched everyone get off the later flight. Tell Dorothy I'll wait."

It was absurd to feel this news as relief, but I did.

The phone vibrated again just seconds after he'd hung up. It wasn't his number. I immediately pictured Jackie sitting on her bags in a phone booth. I held the phone out at arm's length until the irritating buzzing stopped. Then, like ghost-writing behind a mirror, a little arrow appeared on the gray screen—*Play Message*—so I pushed the lit button it most resembled. In the recording, the chaos of an airport was repeatedly pushed back by a loud voice I hadn't heard in a very long time.

"Hello?!" she shouted. "Dotty, I'm stuck in Newark. I'm coming as fast as—Gerald said you're already in the *hospital*!"—she choked on the word—"and I can't find a flight. Hang on, Dotty—I love you!"

Her voice broke as the recording ended. I tried to replay it but somehow erased it instead.

Dorothy meandered out an hour later. Her arms hung limp, and she spoke slowly. She said she'd fallen asleep, so they let her rest awhile. I relayed the gist of her mother's message and apologized for having deleted it—an honest mistake. She didn't care. In the car, after a little self-talk I couldn't quite hear, she drove us up and out of the garage. She pushed her shades back on, repositioned the bill of her Giants cap, and took us home.

For supper, she managed a small bowl of soup. She was in bed before six o'clock. If left uninterrupted, she might have slept through the whole night.

Just after 2 a.m. I was reading when I heard a frantic rapping on the front door, and the jingling and scraping of keys. I'd forgotten I had changed the locks during my Save Yourself days.

I rushed out and opened the door. Jackie was hunched over the doorknob in deep shadow, flabbergasted to see the door pull away with her keys still in the lock. She straightened, breathing in short bursts, and wobbled to a standstill before we faced each other.

I had never once imagined what this moment might be like. A sourness fell with her breath, reminding me how terrified she was of flying, and how far she'd traveled over the past two days. She stared over me and beyond, as if she might run inside, past me, crying. She looked out of context, as if she'd outrun herself. She was tanner and drier than ever, and without glasses her crepey eyelids beat wildly to keep open her blue-brown eyes—tinted contacts. She'd stopped braiding her hair too—it was loose, as she'd worn it only twice before, when pregnant—and she'd dyed it an auburn color that glistened at points in the street-lit drizzle. I was shocked by how much a stranger she looked, standing there at our door, so much so that it was easier than I would have expected to remain quiet and stand steady. Despite that, my heart was racing.

Even though I've spent months pushing every image of Jackie as far away from me as possible, a part of me had still harbored the tiny hope that she and I might go soft and fall crying into each other's arms over our daughter's condition. Instead I could not move. I had no idea what to say, and that had always been the thing I did, whenever she or we were overwhelmed: I put the words on it to fill in the blanks with something we could use and repeat or refine later. But not that night; not at my door. All I could understand was the pinching pain in her eyes as she too fought everything back into a twisted, half-frightened, half-angry expression that said: *Why didn't you tell me sooner?*

I tried first: "How was your flight?"

She gasped, then rolled her eyes and puffed out air as she looked down to shudder her stuck key out of the doorknob.

"We didn't expect you here tonight," I said.

She stared again behind me as she fumbled to get her keys back into her purse.

"Where's Dorothy?" she whispered.

The sound of her round, wind-worn voice weakened me for a moment. I wasn't ready to let her back in yet.

"Gerald said she was *here*," she said. "That she's out of the hospital. But that's all he'd say."

She stood on tiptoe, teetering to look over my shoulder and into the house. She pulled her cardigan tight around her shoulders, nervously fingering the top button. She'd put on weight; I noticed a new crease low on her neck, beneath a new silver necklace.

"Jim?" she pleaded.

"She's in bed."

"*Oh!*" she swooned and put her hand to the doorjamb. It alarmed me; I thought she might fall off the step. "She's bedridden *already*? Oh, why did you *wait*? Why didn't she tell *me*?" She clutched her big bag to her ribs to steady herself as she leaned forward.

Then her eyes popped with tears: Dorothy was walking down the hall, slowly, in her bathrobe. With a cry, Jackie barged in and ran to her, scooping her in her arms and releasing her just as quickly, as if Dorothy were a fragile thing she'd just crushed. She squeezed her again and held her close, then shut her eyes, swayed, pressed her lips to the top of Dorothy's mussed hair, and began to sob.

Dorothy slowly wriggled free enough to wrap her arms fully around her mother's back. How small and bitten her fingers looked. As she submitted and dug deeper into the damp knit of Jackie's sweater, her birdlike eyes peered back at me, briefly, as if to make sure I remained standing nearby.

I brought in the shopping bag Jackie had left on the step and locked us all inside. Dorothy gave me a quick nod over her mother's shoulder—*I'm okay*—so I left them alone. I had filled the coffee machine earlier; it's the same one we've had for years, sitting in the same spot on the counter we'd assigned it the day we brought it home. On my way back to the porch, I flicked the switch. They could serve themselves.

Jackie had also been wearing a cardigan the first time I ever opened a door to her. That one had been coral-colored. I remembered her, in autumn, leaning her face in toward mine from the brick campus sidewalk with the wet yellow maples lighting the clouds behind her. She didn't wear a sweater like the sorority girls did back then, caped over their shoulders with just the top button done, but rather she buttoned it all the way up to her neck, with her long, thin arms sticking out of the sleeves, by her sides. Her black braid fell down her front, over one of the bright silk scarves she's always liked. She wore big tortoiseshell glasses, and that morning she'd stuck a black-eyed Susan behind one ear. Jackie never did fit in Ohio—that was one of the first things I noticed, along with her big laugh—but to me, that difference, when I first saw it, was a thing I loved about her. We were freshmen: Everything was genuine and new. Her hair had been dampened with drizzle that morning too, because, being from California where it never rains until October (I later learned), Jackie had yet to buy herself an umbrella. She'd always dressed warmer than our weather in college, and she never minded getting wet.

She'd come to my dorm to walk with me to the refectory before calculus. The day before our prof had paired all of us up with study buddies, and after my complete weakness in that subject was made obvious to our classmates, she'd quickly volunteered to be mine. The only private conversation we'd had before then was to confirm our assignments, so I was unprepared for the moment when she stood smiling at me from the stone portico of my dorm, when everything else collapsed behind her loud "Good morning!," coaxing all the other sounds around us—the breeze slipping through wet leaves, the doves cooing in the eaves, my pulse drumming in my ears—to fall into her rhythm. I don't believe anyone else on campus ever got to see that smile, just as I hadn't until that morning: Usually she peered over the rim of her glasses, without lifting her face, whenever someone gave her unwanted attention. Which happened frequently. Given her height, others felt she was looking down on them. But she had a big bloom of a smile that, in no time at all, became my welcome to the wider world—even that morning, in the front door of my dorm. And, lucky for me, my umbrella was big enough for two.

As Jackie and I got to know each other, it felt as if we'd been reunited after a lifetime forced apart. We began meeting for breakfast each morning before class, and then for every meal. There's a feeling of "home" that we all carry around within us—you know where it is when you find it—and that's right where Jackie and I met, together, from the very beginning.

How could she abandon that? I can now understand the parts of me that someone might want to leave behind, but why would you decide to walk away from your *home* just as your darker, later years begin to catch up with you—right when you need shelter most? When we were first learning to love each other, she used to laugh so heartily, her shoulders shaking, and a relief would fall over her that washed over me too. She'd grown up in the dry foothills of the Sierras, and at college she was living outside that hot sun for the first time in her life, so seeing her soften day by day and grow cozy in our leafy little college town was like watching a parched field soak up rain. We'd both grown up with blank, wide spaces and seen our share of ten-mile stares, but whenever she looked into mine, I felt like we'd been together a long, long time, and always would be. Everything was fresh with Jackie. She found surprise everywhere. I must have mistakenly imagined I'd given her that.

I heard muffled voices inside the house—Jackie's, mostly—so I remained on the porch. Outside, in the dark yard, a flickering streetlight reached out for me from above my neighbors' homes.

I was startled by the familiar, gentle tremble of Jackie's weight in the kitchen behind me as she turned on lights and opened cupboards. She'd always been heavy on her heels. Dorothy shuffled, in slippers, to sit opposite me, and as she passed her mother, Jackie turned to stand in the doorway, a silhouette in the light. She looked taken aback at the oddity of seeing Dorothy sitting in her own, former spot. She dragged a kitchen chair out on two legs and sat facing us, between the windows with her back to the door, her knees parted like she was in the saddle.

We looked at each other blankly, without a word spoken. I was sure Jackie, despite being so exhausted, wouldn't be able to sit still much longer than it took to frame a thought, so I waited.

Dorothy turned my lamp on to show me the brightly colored wallet she was holding. It was from Italy, a gift from Jackie. In her fingertips, she turned it for us under the light, trying to distract her mother from whatever wave was building in her.

Jackie looked down and swallowed, frowning with regret or worry, as if she'd chosen the wrong color, wrong gift, or wrong occasion. Then she lurched forward to shake Dorothy by the knee, as if she herself had a sudden need for support. Her coffee sloshed into the lap of her long denim skirt.

"Well—at least we're all together *now*," she said, trying to sound as if their private conversation out front hadn't been interrupted by Dorothy's walking out on it. "But why did you wait?" She sounded hurt. She glanced at me, as if I'd been responsible for her not having been summoned earlier.

Dorothy held her water glass tightly in front of her with both hands.

"We didn't know," she said. She was still sleepy. "We were waiting for tests. I wanted you to enjoy your trip."

Jackie's eyes widened in the shadows, searching Dorothy's, then mine.

"But you all *knew*?" Jackie said. "You knew I'd come home right away—that I'd want to be with you—right?"

"There's nothing anyone can do," Dorothy said.

We both froze, hearing that.

"I didn't know myself till last week," I said, to ease things.

Jackie shook her head in disbelief.

"Nothing?" she said, turning to Dorothy. "*Really?*"

Dorothy uncurled and pushed a foot out to the floor, as if to calm the boards. I'd never once thought to question why she'd kept her diagnosis private until she knew for certain. That made sense. I couldn't take offense at it. *How wise she's become*, I thought. *How well she must know us both, and herself, to manage this moment calmly.*

I rose to get a mug.

Jackie snapped, "You're leaving *again*?"

By reflex, I stopped in my tracks. Exactly who had been leaving whom would not be an appropriate topic for discussion just then. Even in the poor light, I could see her face reddening as she sat, staring back and forth between us, her knees jittering.

At her mother's tone, Dorothy turned away to a dark window. She'd finished her glass of water. I felt she wanted to go back to bed, but Jackie looked like she would spring up and push us both down if either of us stirred.

"Listen, Jackie," I said. "I'm going to the kitchen to pour myself some coffee. Then I'll come back."

I took the empty glass Dorothy held out to me.

"But we *are* going to do this *together*?" Jackie said.

"I'm not sure I understand what you're saying," I said.

"Dorothy told me she wants to live *here* now? With you?"

I left for the kitchen.

"Yes," said Dorothy behind me. "I'm staying here as long as I need." Her voice left no room for argument.

Even at the sink I could hear Jackie's breathing.

"But—what I said, out front—you can move in *with me*?"

"I want to be home, Mom. I've got work to do. And you need to teach this fall. You really should. Dad's got no schedule."

"Maybe," Jackie said, "I should try to move back to the city too—to be closer?"

"No," Dorothy said.

"When do I see you, then?"

Dorothy looked out for me to return.

"Visit anytime," I said. "Any time Dorothy says."

Jackie pressed a crumpled tissue to her quivering lips. Her lipstick had wiped thin.

"I want to take care of you, Dotty," she said. "That's all."

"We will," I said.

"It's going to be okay," Dorothy said firmly. Her voice barely rose above a whisper. "I'm doing fine. All I need right now is a little room. I'm going to give you the keys to my apartment—I'm paid through the month. Use it if you need. Dad's good with my coming and going here, and that's what I want to do. We're all going to need to wing this for a while."

I did not recall the "coming and going" part but nodded in full agreement nonetheless, trying to soothe Jackie enough for her to hear how reasonable our daughter was being.

"Just stay busy, Mom—okay? Do not take the semester off. You should teach. I want you to. This could be a long ride: There's no reason for us to go and get all bunged up just yet. Just wait. I don't need the intensity right now. I need to save energy."

147

At hearing that, Jackie shuddered. She looked ready to pull Dorothy into her arms again, to hug and rock it all away, but with visible restraint she held her own elbows instead. She looked up at me from under her brow, let out a big sigh, and then looked outside. Understanding gently smoothed the anxiety out from her, and then the room. She bowed forward in her seat, resigned. Calm is such a rare thing to find in Jackie, something I've always treasured—after finding the lost path on a hike, talking past midnight over dinner, at the end of some surprising tenderness or quarrel. Until three years ago, I'd always thought we would come to rest like that together in the end, after all our youthful edges had worn down. Now, however, seeing Jackie deflate like that somehow made me feel weaker myself.

Slowly, she eased her focus back to us, shaking herself upright. Dorothy waited a moment to make sure she could trust it.

"Okay," Jackie said in a hoarse whisper, nodding. "Okay, okay."

Dorothy stood and drew a key ring from her sagging bathrobe pocket. She'd come prepared. She pressed it into her mother's limp hand. Then, with the toe of her slipper, she nudged the shopping bag of gifts aside, to a corner of the room.

"Let's open the rest of these together later—okay?" Dorothy said. "I'll call. Promise."

Jackie's eyes twitched at being told good night, but again she nodded and accepted it. She put her hands to her knees, which creaked as she stood.

Dorothy gave her a hug and a kiss on the cheek, then me, and left. Down the hall, we heard her close her door gently but surely.

Head hanging, Jackie searched the floor at her feet before realizing her purse still drooped from her shoulder. She held her wrist to her face to inspect her watch. The last streetcar had gone hours ago.

I very nearly offered her the couch for the night, just then. Instead, once I realized she was rummaging in her bag for a cellular phone of her own, I gathered our cups and went back to the sink.

She followed. She stood behind me under the kitchen light, and I saw her reflection in the dark window, bent over her phone.

"It's late," I said without turning back.

She looked up a moment, then pressed more buttons.

"Where's Dick?"

"Home," she said.

That word caught.

"Did Gerald drive you?"

"He said he couldn't." She addressed the back of my head as I began rinsing everything, again, under the faucet. "He's got work tomorrow, so he dropped me at home. He told me not to come. I cabbed. And now I'm cabbing back."

That must be a fifty-dollar fare, easy, to the East Bay. *Not my problem to solve,* I reminded myself.

"You could stay at Dorothy's—her keys?"

"It's been weeks since I've slept in my own bed," she said.

I had no idea of what her bed might look like now, but images came to mind. I must have reacted somehow—perhaps shaken my head over the sink—because I saw her look back down at her phone, as if she too were sorry she'd just said that.

Even in the window's reflection, her gray roots showed.

I grabbed an extra set of house keys from the bowl on the fridge.

"Visit any time," I told her. "I mean it. Just give Dorothy a call first. I can take a walk on the beach or something."

She looked down at the keys, then patted my hand in genuine thanks as she took them. Another wave of distress passed over her face as she closed her phone and her gaze went long again to stare about the table, the countertops, the sink and fridge, as if she were inspecting the place for change. Or as if she were thinking: *Did I really walk around this kitchen every day for thirty years?*

Yes, I thought, watching her. *All four of us did.*

"Just let Dorothy call the shots now," I said. "Let that happen."

Quickly, she clutched the keys to her heart, in her fist.

"Let that *happen*?"

"Yes," I said. "It's best."

"What do you mean, 'best'?"

She gaped at me, lost and hurt, as if worried I might push some additional advantage I'd gained at having made up our daughter's sickbed first.

Down the hall, Dorothy slammed the bathroom door decisively. We fell back to whispers.

"This is *not* my fault, Jim."

"What—the cancer?"

"All of this—our family—this place."

"What are you saying?"

"You can't *blame* me for this."

"No one's talking about faults," I said. "Look, Dorothy needed a place. You were gone. I never left. She came back." I shrugged my shoulders. "Material facts. No blame."

Dorothy needed to sleep. We were tired too.

"What she needs is out of our hands," I said. "For now."

She winced at my saying, "For now."

"I'm just saying—I have a right to be here too," she said, continuing to look strange. "My name's on that lease."

I searched her face for her meaning. It was getting too late.

She shifted, pocketed the keys, and nodded, *Thanks*, sincerely, but in a way that also meant *Goodbye*. Then she wrapped her scarf tightly around her head and walked out.

She left the door open as she waited a few minutes more.

I held back, rewiping the kitchen countertops until I could hear her corky soles sticking on the wet, sandy sidewalk, and then a cab door close.

CHAPTER 9

The worst news came the first week Dorothy moved back—news that she shared with Carol and me only: Her doctors would not recommend surgery. Not immediately. Her cancer wasn't as aggressive as feared, but because the tumor still wasn't as clearly defined as they'd hoped, the possible, unknown risks of surgery at that point outweighed the hoped-for benefits. They would first try a chemo regimen to shrink the growth, after which they might "go in" to remove it, perhaps with some of the "surrounding tissue"—a portion of her liver—if that were affected. They told her that with chemo she might experience a dramatic improvement in how she felt, or the opposite. Wait and see. She had a wide array of pain relief to try if she chose, but nonetheless, if the tumor were not isolated and she did indeed have Stage III rather than Stage II pancreatic cancer, the books I read gave her unspeakably bad odds for surviving beyond five years. Dorothy herself never uttered that gruesome figure, though she also must have heard it. I refused to give it any substance whatsoever by saying the numbers out loud.

Thus began our new life. Right after Jackie's reintroduction, the days Dorothy and I spent together became minor variations of a simple routine. She had daytime appointments to which Carol or I might accompany her, and then she planned a little outing every other day around that schedule. Any filming was informal—she toted the camera everywhere—with me taking more and more shots on my own. I liked to capture simple scenes at home, like the changing slant of morning light through wet leaves. The camera brought us closer together.

Most mornings, Dorothy would join me with her tea for an hour on the back porch. She'd then work in her room on her unscheduled days, and most nights she'd come back out to sit quietly with me again as the sun set. Just like Gerald used to, the summer he'd returned home. Those were my favorite times. Still, to be honest, and selfish, I sometimes did find it exhausting to share so much of my day with someone. Not that both kids aren't excellent company—I wouldn't have preferred to spend my time with anyone else—but in each instance I'd lost my solitude so suddenly I felt put out, unmoored. I had known with Gerald that it would last a summer only, but in the case of Dorothy, anticipating a return of my alone time became dreadful the more I imagined the circumstances under which she might actually leave me one day. Examine your hopes; I did, this time, and it taught me to hold them high and loose, and to be patient, with her and myself, as a result.

Nearly all of the time Carol and I spent together was with Dorothy. In the few unplanned moments we did find ourselves alone—in waiting rooms, passing in the house—we spoke easily about everyday things like sleep schedules and meds and meals, with a familiarity that would have been awkward under other circumstances. It was tacitly understood: We were all about Dorothy, for the time being. At least until we all understood better what more we needed from each other.

Jackie called Dorothy daily. They'd sometimes go to a movie, or shopping, or to a rare weekend or evening appointment. My own infrequent interactions with Jackie were down to business and by phone. For Dorothy's convenience, I regularly encouraged Jackie to come spend time with her at the house, promising to leave the two of them, but she always got cagey about coming out. Transit was an issue; she was already BARTing in each day from the East Bay for work, and it could take up to an additional hour for MUNI to get her all the way to the beach from downtown—so that even the one night she'd chosen to sleep at Dorothy's old place, it was still a long day for her. She accepted my invitation only once, on a sunny Saturday, when Dick drove her out. I ran up to the library before they arrived, and the three of them took a picnic to the beach. He'd left the unctuous scent of his aftershave in the back room—it permeated half the house, actually—where I imagine he sat while Jackie packed everyone sandwiches. Can't say I wasn't glad to have missed that, or his watching Jackie fuss around Dorothy. That the ups and downs Jackie must be experiencing were now someone else's challenge—Dick's—was a welcome relief, and I was almost grateful to him for it, because this truly was the worst crisis she and I had ever faced together. This cancer was the first time either kid ever made us truly afraid.

Jackie's pregnancy with Dorothy had been utterly uncomplicated. And yet, back then, she'd still, unintentionally, managed to make it a neighborhood event. We'd lived a few blocks above Chinatown, where Carol is now and near where I used to teach. Even if Jackie hadn't been so tall and striking, she would have stood out simply by dint of our being the only young white couple in an apartment building full of Asian immigrants. Few of our neighbors spoke much English, and although we were on greeting-level familiarity with everyone because we all walked the same sidewalks, any communication beyond "Hello" involved a lot of gesturing.

An old lady named Mah lived beneath us. She walked down the steep hill to Chinatown daily to shop with her pink plastic bags. One day, soon after the baby began to show, Jackie bumped into Mah on the landing and stood, wide-legged, swaying back with her hands rounding her abdomen, patting and smiling to give Mah the big clue: *We're expecting!* She beamed to let Mah take in what we'd been up to. And Mah broke into such wild, gold-toothed laughter it was embarrassing. After all, there were already plenty of babies and kids on the block, but we'd never paid too much attention to them beyond giving little smiles and waves as we walked past. Children were a big part of what we loved about that neighborhood, but having a first baby of our own made us realize how small a role we'd been playing in anyone else's life up till then. Looking at us, Mah was clearly tickled by something, and seeing her giggly hiccups made me wonder, for the first time, if we ourselves weren't more a point of local color to others on the block. I'm still not sure if Jackie ever got that.

The summer Dorothy arrived, every day was bright. When you've got a newborn, the world reveals its inner glow. I've heard people say it's angels protecting you. We'd both felt that, with Dorothy. Sometimes I even thought I saw it. And while that light lasted, Jackie too seemed to bloom. She felt safe in our little nest, I think. For the first few weeks, there was no outside world beyond the three of us, and no shadows.

Dorothy was perfect, with a fuzzy, round head, dark beady eyes, and a precociously sly, curly smile that she wore throughout her day except when faced with one thing: excitement. This made it difficult for her and her mother to get along sometimes, especially in their first months together, when Jackie suffered strong postpartum blues. She took everything too personally. Our one-bedroom apartment soon felt over-cozy. It's not the addition of a seven-pound baby that squeezes you, but all that gear, the seamless days, the brand-new chores, and the slow-building awareness of just how fragile living flesh truly is. That first week, I'd put a chalkboard schedule up to help us both enjoy a few guilt-free minutes—so we'd each know when we were officially on or off duty—but Jackie could never keep to it. She was always "on." And after a few weeks, when all the angels split, we were left all alone to our stinky devices.

Jackie wouldn't allow herself to do anything unless it involved Dorothy, even though we'd timed her birth so I could be home on summer break to help out the first few months. Jackie couldn't sleep. She seemed to be balding at her forehead. Even when it was my as-signed chore she cleaned obsessively, but in a scattered way—the bathroom grout still molded, and food still hid in the forks in the drying rack. I thought: If it were me, this would be a sign I needed some time off. So I projected that onto Jackie one day and lied to her that I'd thrown out my back and couldn't walk easily: *Would you please go do the food shopping for us, and leave Dorothy behind?* It had been nearly four weeks since she'd given birth, and this would be the first time she'd left the house alone.

Our old supermarket was just eight blocks away, but Jackie still took a half hour to dress and gear up for the trip. She insisted on strapping Dorothy into her bouncy seat before leaving, and even then walked backward out the door as I approached to gently close it after her.

It was peaceful once she'd left. Dorothy made big eyes for me and grew happy in the new quiet. She went down for a nap in five minutes; I'd always been able to do that by putting her bouncy seat up on the kitchen counter—too high and unstable for Jackie's comfort—and babbling to her while I cooked. Noonday sun used to sneak through our alley window, and that pleased Dorothy: She'd slowly blink and drop her head sideways to snore. She's always been easy company.

That afternoon I'd hoped Jackie would take her time—go get a doughnut or do some window-shopping—but instead she'd rushed home in far less time than it takes to trudge uphill weighed down with two full sacks. She pushed in the door sideways, sweaty and carrying barely half the items she'd printed in big letters on her shopping list. She was also leaking through her smock. She ran back to the kitchen to find Dorothy, and even though the sight of her must have been some relief, she whisked her up from her curled sleep to press her to her squirting breast, which made Dorothy shriek awake in shock. Jackie too was shaking and near tears, but when she finally calmed down enough to tell me why, it made no sense to me: She said she'd been dragging her laundry cart down the sticky aisles, feeling moist and fat while all the rangy locals looked her over, when panic hit her like a truck: *The whole reason I'm here is not with me: No one knows I just had a baby girl.*

Dorothy used her time consciously but casually after moving back home. She often joined me, unexpectedly, at the table, out back, or to putter in the yard. Sometimes we'd walk to the beach or, in the early days, go out for lunch—her easiest meal of the day. I saw the relief letting down in her eyes each time we had a simple, appointment-free day ahead of us. I remained on my best behavior, and at dinner kept to one glass of wine at most. Carol showed no surprise at this, which in turn surprised me, until I recalled I'd never really been a heavy drinker, predivorce. I can count on one hand every hangover I've ever had. I bet "drinking" was a handy, romantic excuse to drape over my struggles. So that's another thing I learned during those initial days with Dorothy—that, just as I've often been told, I really am lucky.

We lived a few weeks like that, trying to minimize the bumps as Dorothy's condition hit some of the expected, negative milestones— the thinning hair, the nausea. I was first to see how the time she spent with her mother took an ever-greater toll on her. I say that without any gloating—I'm not jealous of Jackie's time with our daughter— but I was in a better position than anyone to track the rhythm of Dorothy's fatigue, even better than Dorothy herself. For example, Jackie's idea of spending a day in Santa Cruz with Dorothy and Gerald "for old time's sake" was odd nostalgia, since the only time our kids got down to the Boardwalk was with friends or on school trips that neither Jackie nor I, as teachers ourselves, could chaperone: It was nothing we ever did as a family. But Dorothy chose to indulge her mother's dreams, for a change. I wondered why she was so unable to be as frank with her mother as she was with me. Gerald quickly begged off that trip, leaving Dorothy to drive her mother alone, an hour and a half each way, and when she got home that evening she was sick and red from sun. She spent the next day in bed with tea and the curtains drawn, but she never complained to her mother about it, nor would she let me. I'm sure that without the regular, day-to-day access to her that I enjoy, I wouldn't know how to act or plan a nice day for Dorothy either, but it was still surprising to see how tone-deaf Jackie could be to her ups and downs.

Another unsettling indicator that things were getting harder for Dorothy was the changing tenor of the joyrides she'd plan for just the two of us. What had, at first, felt like random tourist excursions became deliberate trips down memory lane. One day she decided we must revisit the Old Main Library, one of our childhood haunts. When Dorothy was little, before Gerald was born, she and I used to read there together, sitting on a stone bench inside the arcaded marble stairwell. It was our favorite place. She used to love the way the words bounced, if I faced the wall, and ricocheted under the arched ceiling as if I were speaking from the bench on the other side of the stairs; she used to twist around, grabbing the balustrade to watch them fly—as if she could see the words. She's always insisted she could. But it was not until we were strapping ourselves into the Jeep to drive downtown that she remembered the Old Main, damaged in the Loma Prieta quake, had been half demolished. With a little moan of disappointment, she got out of the car and spent the rest of the day in her room.

That evening, hoping to make her feel better, I dug out our copy of *From the Mixed-Up Files of Mrs. Basil E. Frankweiler*, one of her old favorites. When she was in third grade, she'd threatened to take Gerald and run away to hide overnight in the Old Main, just like the kids in the book do at the Met. I've been saving our copy in a box in the garage for grandchildren. But when I offered it to her that night over dinner, she held it at arm's length to read the title, and her face went blank. She had no energy for it. I realized I'd pulled out the kids' book for me, not her—a selfish impulse I vowed to avoid in the future. I buried the book in my stack.

After a few weeks of stumbling like this in the unknown, Dorothy's doctor reported that her chemo was working notably well. The tumor seemed to have stopped growing. We'd been told this might happen—The Unexpected—but we'd never openly hoped it would. In addition to that good news, she noticed she felt more energetic the day following a treatment, once all the discomfort passed, and even better if she took steroids. Knowing this enabled her to plan around treatments to make the best of her energy.

On the evening of one such day, I was sitting out back with my radio—enjoying one of the first quiet evenings I'd had to myself in a while—when I heard her keys jingle and scrape out front. She walked more heavily than usual, flicking the lights on and then off in each room she passed through.

She stood in the porch entry, facing me as she pressed her hands to the doorframe like a skydiver bracing for a jump.

"Everything under control out there?" she said. She wore mascara and had a little color on her cheeks—which was surprising because, aside from a ghoulish phase in middle school, she rarely wore makeup. She had a curious glint in her eyes.

Stepping back to drop a boutique shopping bag on the counter, she shrugged a backpack of equipment onto the kitchen table and grabbed her camera.

She dropped heavily into her chair.

"Do I smell *pot* on you, Dorothy?"

She smiled and nodded: *Yup.*

"Did you ever notice that about yourself?" she said coyly. "How much you go nose-first at things—like you *smell* before you *see*?"

I wasn't sure this observation was true, nor profound, but it was more amusing than what I'd been reading, so I sat up and waited.

"Mom and I went on a date," she said.

When she looked up, her eyes were red, with sallow crescents underneath, which the cosmetics barely hid. Still she sparkled, somehow.

"Mom wanted to take me to The Spinnaker. She's been talking about it forever. And since I've been feeling so *good* lately, I figured it's time. And she was right: It *was* awesome."

On the fridge we still have a postcard of this restaurant, built on a pier in Sausalito, with a picture-perfect view of the San Francisco skyline that hasn't changed much since the 1960s.

"The city looked *so* pretty. I got great shots—I mean, you'd have to try hard *not* to on a night like this."

"Were you able to eat?"

"A little clam chowder—Manhattan-style." (Dairy had fallen off her "good" list.) "Sourdough. A sip of wine. Got half a crab cake down. I'm stuffed."

I truly regretted missing that. It would have been heartwarming to see her eat a full meal, on linen, in a roomful of happy people.

"So—how come *we* never went there?" she said. It sounded like she'd planned the question before sitting.

"Because driving the bridge is too much for your mother."

I couldn't recall Jackie ever expressing any desire to cross the bridge with the kids for a meal. I used to think Jackie was being dramatic, refusing to drive on freeways, but after years of riding with her, I applaud the decision. We both used to joke that the thoroughfares of the world were safer without either of us on them.

"I know *that*," Dorothy said, unfazed. "But couldn't you have driven? On your meds? If you'd actually taken them regularly, I mean?"

"I suppose I could have," I said. "I chose not to."

"It's just—you never talk about why."

"There're lots of things we don't talk about, Dorothy."

She didn't argue. Instead, she patted her camera. "Can I?"

"*May* I," I said. "But, no. I'm happy to talk about whatever you want, but please: Don't shoot."

With an exaggerated shrug of her shoulders—*Oh, well!*—she gently put the camera down on the windowsill and dropped the subject. She pushed herself back out of her chair as if disembarking a canoe, and on her way to the kitchen gave me a peck on the forehead. Her lips felt feverishly hot. She began to worry me.

When I wrenched around to watch in the kitchen, she was standing over the sink, rinsing a brightly colored goblet she'd unwrapped from the bag.

"*Look* at this!" she said, holding it up in one hand like a torch. "It's hand-blown. From Venice. Can you believe Mom brought this back in her luggage, on the plane? She wouldn't let Dick ship it for her."

With one frail hand on her hip and her big tropical shirt flapping at her elbows, she rotated the glass in the overhead light. It was as gaudy as neon. Her obvious delight in it made me happy.

"What do you have to drink?" she said.

"The wet bar in my bedroom is well stocked," I said, then waited to see how long it would take her to get a joke. And it did take a moment. Then I directed her to a beer Gerald had left behind. I'd stick to my decaf coffee, I said; I'd dutifully taken my pill with dinner.

Carefully, she poured the beer into her goblet and returned to sit across from me. Her eyes were small and wet in the shadows. She held her glass out for me to admire, catching the light from the kitchen, then took a sip and grimaced. She'd forgotten she didn't like beer.

"Nice glass, though," she said, setting it on the sill.

I agreed.

"We talked most about you," she said. "At least Mom did. I was surprised to hear her go down memory lane. But it was all good. Otherwise, you know, the whole night would have all been about—" She pointed her finger at her guts and made an uncomfortable face. "That's one thing about getting sick—everyone starts acting better around you."

"Dorothy—"

"Oh, you know what I mean." She pushed her hair back, as usual, but now seemed to enjoy how it sprang forward again. She pulled her knees to her chest and stared at me until I stopped scowling. "I know *you* know what I mean," she said. "Right?"

I had to agree. I nodded.

"You know she still loves you?" she said, unflinching.

"I don't see any good reason for us to be talking about—"

"But it's important to *me*. *That's* your good reason. You're my parents and I like knowing you care for each other. Even if it's from a distance."

My heart beat faster.

"So," I said, "you just sat down with your mother, smoked a joint, and she launched into how much she still loves me?"

"No, not exactly. Mom just started saying things she wanted to tell me—now that I'm older. But then it did all sort of tumble out of her, that one little truth. Kind of against her will. You know, she's really sorry about how she left."

The kitchen light faltered as the fridge turned on.

Obviously, I didn't know what to do with this talk of hers, but I'd been indulging her for weeks. She would direct conversation toward her topics unless I actually became visibly upset; I played along. She hadn't looked this comfortable—this *at home*—since she'd first moved in.

"You didn't ask her personal questions like you always ask me?" I said.

"I didn't expect it. I mean, I went as a sort of duty-date. I can't really get excited about restaurants lately. I want to keep everything positive, and I'm not so generous with Mom sometimes. Carol noticed that, when I was on the phone once: She said the more Mom talks, the harder I don't."

Perhaps she'd inherited that dynamic. Gerald, when faced with his mother's enthusiasms, always seems to jump on the train with her without a look back, but Dorothy can be outright sullen when it suits her.

"And you filmed your mother through all this?"

"Some," she said coyly.

"Can I see?"

"*May* I," she said. "Later."

"Then will you please tell me what else she said?"

"Oh, so you *are* interested?" She jumped up again to dump her beer down the drain and fill the kettle. When she returned, she wrapped herself in the quilt, pulled her feet up, and recounted her dinner with Jackie.

First off: She'd just gotten the medical marijuana card that week. Evidently Carol knows all about *that* too, and she guided her through the dispensary the other day. *So* that's *what they do when I'm not in the back seat*, I thought. Dorothy teased me for my innocence, listing the names of all the potheads she and Gerald used to hang out with when they lived under our roof. I had to laugh. Dorothy said she'd never really liked getting high, but was finding it helped her appetite. "Mom's *way* down with it," however. Jackie had "overshared" that night and confessed that she and Dick enjoyed catching a buzz now and then. I felt nothing at hearing this news, but when Dorothy said Carol "doesn't party," I was surprised at my relief—at how realigned my allegiances had already grown.

Dorothy first drove Jackie to the bluffs above the Golden Gate, in the Marin Headlands. They found a bench all to themselves on a hill overlooking the north tower, and there they sat, undisturbed, until the setting sun reflected off windows in the Oakland Hills like flecks of mica and the commuter traffic blurred across the bridge like strings of red and white lights. The city "effervesced," she said. They smoked, they laughed, Jackie cried, and they huddled together until the thin evening fog tickled the underbelly of the bridge. I could imagine it: the humbling Bay view, the rush of cars and wind, and how uninhibited Jackie must have felt out there, able to stretch and carry on at full volume with her baby to herself. Dorothy said they'd had such a good time on the bench—and had stayed so long—that dinner sort of fizzled by comparison, aside from a fit of giggles Jackie had trouble fighting when they first sat down. Dorothy said she hadn't eaten so much in weeks, even if she did put most on her mother's plate.

It warmed my heart to imagine them high on a hill, but even more to realize that our daughter thought to orchestrate such a moment for her mother—who so desperately needed it—when she herself was so sick. It's easy to wonder at your baby's first steps or words, but when you discover your kids doing something more compassionate or altruistic than you, it's a stunner. As Dorothy recalled their evening, I flushed with respect, and affection, for them both. I truly wished I'd been there.

It was later in the dinner when Jackie slowed and told her about "our other big fight." It's something I'd forgotten about, in a way: the great teacher's strike in 1979. As a result of school underfunding due to Prop 13, the city laid off 1,200 teachers, so we—3,600 of us—went on strike until they were rehired. Most of them, anyway. We struck for six weeks without pay, and it stressed every relationship we had—with our neighbors, with our colleagues, and especially within our home. Jackie was on the fence at first; her ailing father and mother gained a great deal of security from Prop 13, which cut and capped their property taxes as their ranch was failing and the land surrounding them was being assessed and sold at a premium. Jackie, being the mathematician, always managed our finances, and back then she told me daily how fast we were falling into debt.

I was thirty-seven then, a young father, and swept up, for the first and only time in my life, in political fervor. I got such a righteous kick of pride on the picket lines, I wrote an op-ed that was passionate enough for the *Chron* to publish it, and then Herb Caen picked up one of my lines: *We won't teach where we can't live!* I'd never published anything before, and my head spun at hearing my words become a slogan for thousands of dedicated colleagues with whom I stood. It was overwhelming: For that season, whenever I saw my words on placards, or heard them chanted on the lines or quoted by union reps at massive meetings or on TV news, I was bigger than myself; I became someone stronger and sure. Each time I marched—once with nine-year-old Dorothy on my shoulders, waving her UESF banner and chanting with hundreds of others—I knew exactly who I wanted to be—who I was. A great photo of Dorothy and me ran in the paper—I got a print for her, and it'd always been one of her prized possessions, sitting in a frame above her desk until she took it to college. In it, she's riding on my shoulders, shouting with me on the line, and I look—according to what Dorothy learned that evening over dinner—happier and more alive than Jackie had ever seen me.

Before then, I had harbored a fanciful ambition to write. I say "fanciful" because I never acted on it after college, aside from a few finely wrought letters to editors or friends, or the occasional stab at poetry for the inside of a greeting card. I've always been more passionate about reading biographies than high literature—I'm still the only person I know who's read Boswell's life of Johnson. (Abridged.) In biographies, I've always found qualities in great writers that I not only emulate but felt, in all humility, I understood. At the same time, I've always taken pride in having successfully avoided the tragic excesses and sloppy lives of most of them, even if that were more due to my job security and the limits of my constitution than any virtue I possess. Whatever the case, it wasn't until that letter was published that I'd ever felt any power in my own words. I'd found my voice, if you will. It made everything matter more.

That was not an exhilaration Jackie shared. She grew impatient with the strike. Whether she admits it or not, she has a streak of cowboy justice in her, and to me she'd accuse colleagues of grandstanding and whining, being incapable of such strong convictions if they didn't already have the spare money to stand on in the first place. Each week she lost a little more sympathy for the union, until one day—alongside dozens of others—she crossed the line and taught her class. And, from then on, we could never discuss the issue again. Her decision won her a career full of passive, unofficial blacklisting—getting lesser school assignments, bypassed for the best schedules and perks, and ignored or never forgiven by many fellow teachers. If it hadn't been for my being the public face of our family in the strike, we'd probably never have gotten our kids into the middle and high school slots we wanted.

Every student's learning was delayed that year. Over time, seeing how roughly Jackie was being treated struck me as unfair too. My own distaste for politics, on any scale, grew. I participated less in the union the louder others with ambitions became. And, in the late eighties, once it became eminently clear to any thinking person that the demand for another older white man to step up to the podium was in decline, I stepped back into being the former self my family and I knew best.

But now, hearing that those were the days when I was most attractive to my ex-wife—a time when we as individuals were living lives as separate as we ever have, until recently? That was difficult to see around.

"Did your mother explain this?" I said. "Why she liked me best when we'd disagreed most? There might be a few clues there for me, about our current situation."

She grinned tentatively, to see if we should continue in this vein. She loved talking like this with me. But she'd hooked me too.

"You know how it is," she said. "When you see someone happy doing what they really want to do. It just feels like everything's—right."

"That's how you look to me, Dorothy—when you work on your movies: You come alive."

She focused on her toes, and her hair hid her face, but I think she was pleased to hear this. On the radio, Billy Eckstine's melancholy "I Want to Talk about You" played.

"Did you tell your mother about your film project?"

She shook her head.

"Why not?"

"Later," she said, looking up. "I don't like to talk much about work before I've actually done it."

"Because by talking about it you stop feeling the need to do it?"

She looked puzzled.

"I'm just sharing that possibility," I said.

She pulled her wrap tighter.

"Talking about it just wastes time," she said.

We both knew what she meant.

"I don't mean to sound morbid." She looked out the dark window. "I'm just super aware now of how valuable it is—time. And it's easy to focus. I never had the chance to totally shut down everything else and act like *nothing* was more important than what I'm doing."

"Fighting cancer?"

She shook her head again.

"What could be more important than that?" I asked.

"I mean work," she said. "I never allowed myself to *make* it as important as I've always said it is. You do this contract gig and that public service announcement and you feel like you're achieving something, but—" she swallowed. "You know, Mom got pretty emotional, especially on the way home, and she asked me, like it was *the* most important question: What if you never have kids? And hearing her say that just cut everything loose in me, like: That is really *not* my primary concern right now."

She sounded steady enough—more sober—but there was also something in her voice that didn't sit well. It was beginning to sound like one of the conversations she'd had with me after her mother left—something too facile had crept into her voice, as if she were more world-weary than she should be. You can never be your parents' peer within the natural order of things. And if it were true that

I'd never talked about wanting to be a writer with her or with any-one beyond my ex-wife and a few lunch companions, it was because that struck me as a possibly pompous and even fashionable ambition to talk about—just as, regrettably, my daughter's disappointment over her thwarted filmmaking threatened to sound just then. *Really Dorothy? Of all the things you might never have a chance to do, the one you'd miss most is making a movie?*

But as I saw her blink in the dark—shrinking, with her empty hand lying open, for something, in her lap—a surge of pity rose in me, and I realized: *She's* the one facing mortality up close, not me, even if I did see my family die before I'd reached her age. Either she was seeking my reassurance now about the choices she'd made, or she wanted my express admiration for them, or, more likely, she just wanted to hear a few loving words from her father. Should I tell her it might be more a daydream of celebrity that she's afraid of losing? Or is there really something she's spent her short adult life aching to say, perfectly and beautifully, that matters more to her than anything else? And was this my fault—had I introduced her, without knowing it, to so little of what's beautiful in the world that she's found nothing more to live for than make-believe?

She'd never really "dated" in high school. She rarely brought class-mates home. It had always sounded like she ran around with a mixed pack of friends who made her happy. I'd assumed she was simply being private about her relationships, although I now couldn't recall anyone other than a prom date and Viktor, whom I'd never met. The few college friends of hers we saw at graduation dressed the same, boys and girls, in flannel shirts and patchy jeans and frayed outer-wear, and all their music was just as angry-sounding as her punk rock in middle school. She'd always liked being alone. And I'd never had any experience talking with girls about love or sex, outside the bro-chures we handed out at school, so Jackie'd dealt with that. Or so I'd thought.

Dorothy pulled up tighter in her chair.

"*All* I'm worried about now is wasting time. Make sense?"

I nodded. *Of course.*

"I was surprised to hear from Gerald that you and Viktor were living together," I said. "But *that* was a definite commitment, wasn't it? A real life choice?"

"I thought you knew?" Her bloodshot eyes widened. "Did Gerald also tell you he cheated on me?"

Viktor left you, Dorothy?

"I came home one day and he was in our bed with some twit from the gym."

The way she tossed that scene out, so glibly, made it sound too melodramatic a betrayal to be real. And the way she stared at me: It felt as if she'd wanted me to be shocked. I'd already spent so many months thinking about how my own abandonment would make a bad movie—I had no room for hers.

"I'm sorry you had to go through that," I said.

"Oh, it wasn't meant to be." She sat back, trying to smirk. "I knew the day I moved in that things weren't working. Whenever something's wrong for Viktor, he runs to the gym, and he'd been working out *a lot*, right from the beginning. But we see what we want to see, right? Part of me was actually relieved when I caught him. Like, now I know. Thankfully his uncle sounds cool about our breaking the lease—he owns the building—big Chinese family."

Viktor's Chinese?

Imagining that this story might count as the love of her life made her world feel insipid to me, like afternoon TV—something unpleasant I didn't want to take in but couldn't turn from when it was in front of me.

"Even I didn't know how little it all meant, until I moved out. For four months we'd been stuck together, living in the same place, but then the day he helped me move out I realized: I still like him. Not to live with—but as a friend. How could I have wasted so much time being pissed off?"

She gazed into her mug, and her hair hid her face.

"This is feeling weird now—talking like this," she said. "Sorry."

I was sorry too.

Outside, a raccoon deftly pried the siding from the corner of my neighbor's shed, flattening its fat back to slink underneath as we watched.

"Have you thought about what you'd do if you lost this place, Dad?"

"Don't worry," I said, as reassuring as I could.

"No—really," she said.

"You'll always have a home here," I said. "I already know—Gerald told me you're uninsured. We can make you my dependent, if it comes to that. I've been reading up on this. If you make no income—"

"I've already billed more this year than all of last year," she said, interrupting. "It's been a good year for me—the dot-com boom."

A good year?

"But can't we write off all your medical expenses and whatnot?" I tried. "And then, once you're bankrupt, you can stay here and be my dependent again—we can get you on my health plan?"

"I don't think it's that easy," she said, wagging her head to shake off the topic.

It was nearing midnight. She slowly stood and grabbed her camera from the sill, holding it up to her eyes like it was a kitten.

"You know," she said. "You're pretty cagey. I guess I'd hoped, after my long night with Mom and all the stuff she told me, that you might tell me your side of things. But, once again, I end up doing almost all the talking."

She meant it. She really looked frustrated at how little I'd said. How could I explain that I might have felt happier before she'd come home and told me all this?

"What do you want to hear, Dorothy?"

She held back but stared, almost pleading, into my eyes.

"Maybe why you loved Mom? If you've stopped? Why?"

On cue, a sudden breeze made the boxwoods shiver. One of my neighbors shut their window and drew the curtains.

"Before your mother," I said, "there was a lot of death in my life. It was unclear, even in college, how capable I'd be of standing on my own, in the future. Your mother was bright, colorful, and warm, and she swept all that away—not just by who she was, but because she found something good in me she wanted. Being with her, and feeling and seeing alongside her, brought meaning back to everything. But later, when she no longer felt the same way, all that meaning left too. Of course I can still see what's wonderful in her. God knows I've tried to ignore or wish it away, but I'd be lying if I said I've been successful. So, sure: I still care for your mother. Even if who she thinks she loved no longer exists, for her."

Oversharing, perhaps, but she'd asked. She looked impossibly grateful to hear it, in fact, nodding gravely, but her eyes had gone brittle with exhaustion. Her look said: *Thanks—that's good for now.*

She rewrapped her quilt to free a hand and, with it, pushed a little red button on the side of her camera until it beeped.

For some reason, I was once again left wondering if I'd provided the right words.

CHAPTER 10

There was a scene next morning at the Safeway.

Minutes after Dorothy had left me the night before, I heard her snoring gently from down the hall. Once again, that simple sound was more a worry than a comfort—the way hearing your baby's heartbeat makes you go weak at the sheer tentativeness of it. So I did not sleep well and, at dawn, I went shopping.

I enjoy little trips to our old Safeway, where I know the staff by name. It faces Ocean Beach, whose wet winds corrode the big lit letters of its sign and brine the carts so heavily they're hosed down each week. Gulls and dune dwellers usually scavenge in the parking lot, but on a sunny day, like that morning, the supermarket has a boardwalk feel.

Because it was early and the store near empty, the canned music was turned up loud, but despite that din, deep in the back of the store I heard a grocery cart slamming behind the steel door of the restroom. Locked behind the door, I heard an older man curse and then moan, as if he were summoning the dark powers themselves. A cart smacked the back of the door three times, then stopped. The hair on the back of my neck stood on end. I knew from experience it was dank inside, with fixtures and grout marred by spray paint, hacking, and fire. I jogged up front to fetch the guard, trying to recall if there were any ceiling pipes from which a tormented man might hang.

I recognized the young woman on security that day. Her professional cool had already impressed me once in the past, when she had to escort a drunk through the automatic doors: He'd goaded her, putting his arms around her to feign being pushed, but she'd stuck to her script and calmly told him, over and over, to step back until he was out the door. It was never clear if she carried a weapon, but she comported herself as if she did.

She recognized me too, and jogged back with me to the restroom. It was quiet.

She rapped hard on the door, staying off an arm's length: "Hello?"

We heard one quick, limp kick of the cart against the door. That could have been anger, something accidental, a desperate plea—could have meant anything.

She knocked again. "You all right in there? Need some assistance?"

No response.

"We need to open up, okay?" she shouted at the door, pushing me aside with one arm and pulling at her key ring with the other. "Hear me?"

Dead silence.

The balding night manager walked up to join us, standing just behind the guard, who tried several keys. We heard nothing as the lock turned.

She rolled her eyes back to us—*You ready?*—and pried the door ajar with the toe of her boot. An unholy stench rolled out at us. The guard cocked her head, shaking it away as she wedged her foot more firmly inside and said: "We're gonna come in now."

She pushed the door until it hit metal.

A shopping cart lay wedged on its side between the door and the toilet, like a barricade. Draped over the cart were the grime-slicked effects of a man who hugged his leathery knees up tight to his guts. His upper torso and head were hidden from view by the little fort he'd made of his cart, but his midriff was pale and scabrous, his naked feet mahogany-colored from sun, and his soles waxen white. On the floor, against the wall by the fouled bowl, stood a dimpled quart of Dr. Pepper and a full bag of cheese puffs. We heard a gentle, grating snore come from within the rag-covered cart. Only his ribs moved, barely.

The guard held the door open with one arm—she'd done her job—as the manager nudged the cart to rouse the man. "Mister?" he said. With the toe of his shoe, the manager flipped aside the T-shirt draped over the cart, exposing a face.

I gasped: It was my "neighbor," the guy who always waves to me out front. He'd shaved, but I still knew him without his gray beard. His nicked cheeks and chin were pink as a boy's; his sunburned brow gave his closed eyes a bandit's mask. The manager too was touched at seeing his fragile face, and he bent over to tap the man's shoulder with a gentleness that stung me, since I'd never even shaken his hand. We'd never talked beyond a salute. The longer I stared, the more impossible it was to see this ribby body as the gap-toothed guy who cheerfully gathered my empties to redeem each recycling day. All I could see was Craig, my dead brother.

It was impossible to watch or ignore this small, curled-up man, but only the medics could do anything now. I stepped away, backing up slowly past the fish counter's ice buckets and bumping into an end-cap display of jug wine. I dropped my bananas and walked home quickly, empty-handed, to check on Dorothy.

I'd promised Dorothy to participate with her in a counseling program at the hospital. It would help us make the best use our time, she said. Who wouldn't benefit from that? She'd also invited Carol—who'd set this up, I later learned—to join us, at least for the initial sessions. What about your mother? I wondered. She said Dick was already paying for Jackie's shrink.

I was not looking forward to this. At work, I'd long ago learned to keep a distance from the behaviorists; the few I dealt with seemed more adept at managing their cushy schedules than at helping the troubled kids we teachers stood in front of each day. You don't need a well-paid professional to tell you a kid in the Sunnydale projects who sleeps in the tub at night to avoid bullets suffers "toxic levels of stress." On the other hand, I too had no reason to get cocky, since my own career had also proven me more or less ineffective at fixing many kids' problems. Nor, I realized, did I have a right to feel aloof at never having sought counseling myself, although I've never had any complaint I couldn't see or talk around. But since I'd promised Dorothy I would join her and her counselor, I did.

So that Friday morning we picked up an underslept Carol—she'd kept us waiting ten minutes on the sidewalk while she finished dressing—and then drove to the hospital in silence. We rode the elevator up, watching our toes and nodding in unison at each stranger that stepped in or out. It was clear from the moment we walked into the office that each of us felt we'd been forced there, for different reasons.

The room was small and bland, with a computer and a kidney-shaped desk banked into a corner by the huge window. We found three hard chairs in a close semicircle facing the counselor. Sharon—I read her diploma as we waited for her to look at us; it was the only frame on any of the beige walls—was a marriage and family therapist. She must have heard us squeeze through the door, but it took her a moment to turn nonetheless. When she did, suddenly motioning us to our seats, she watched us with a dull smile as if we'd all been coming together for decades for tea and bridge—even though she couldn't have been much older than twenty-five herself. She had a webby shawl around her shoulders, mousy hair, close-together eyes, and a whitened smile.

It was disturbing to hear Sharon snap her clipboard and immediately launch into questions. Her voice squeaked like a kid's.

As we exchanged names, she faced Carol.

"I understand you're not an actual member of the family?" she said.

"Carol's a close friend," Dorothy said. "She'll be on my team, all the way."

Good for you, I thought. *You tell her what's what, Dorothy.*

"Great," said Sharon. "And you're studying to be an MFT yourself?"

"Social worker," Carol said. She still looked crumpled and tired, and for some reason that irritated me too.

"She's almost done with her MSW," said Dorothy. Carol gave her a surprised, kind glance.

"Great!" said Sharon.

The pale office would have felt suffocating if not for the tinted plate glass behind her, with its view of Pacific Heights. The marbled light in the wide sky made Dorothy appear frailer than she had in any of the other medical contexts I'd seen her in so far. Her voice sounded determined, like she was trying to reach us from far away. But even if you were a stranger, or this were a movie you watched without knowing anyone's role or history, Dorothy's would be the voice you heard; her dark eyes, like wet stones, would be the ones you'd watch because she was the only one who seemed solid, albeit diminished, in that moment.

"We know each other well," Dorothy said. She glanced warily at Carol, who was trying, unhappily, not to fidget. Dorothy smiled and rested her small hand on Carol's denim shoulder, and Carol leaned quickly toward her, squeezing her eyes tight as a presage of the sadness to come. But when she straightened, clenching her jaw back in control, I saw how Carol too could get a strong grip on her feelings. I grew proud of them both.

"We're old friends," Carol said, now clear as a bell. "We got to know each other in Al-Anon."

I rearranged myself in my seat. *Dorothy has a drinking problem too?* Surely, she didn't hesitate to dump her beer the other night. I shouldn't have been so worried at hearing this, but still, it caught me short.

"I've been sober six years," Carol added. Her eyes grew stony.

Had she looked at me, I was prepared to nod along.

"And you—?" Sharon said, swiveling eerily to face me as if she'd heard my thoughts. She shot me the same pro smile, with a bit less tooth, although it's possible I was imagining that because of how sensitive I'd become with each passing second.

"You're Dorothy's father?"

"I am," I said, biting my lip and straining to quiet my interior. There was too much else I wanted to say—*Duh!* for starters—but we all just wanted to get this done.

"The resemblance *is* strong," Sharon said, with another smile at Dorothy, like they were old girlfriends. "The eyes," she said, smiling and pointing to her own as she turned to the women.

I looked at Dorothy—one has to look somewhere—but her pretty, dark brown eyes (mine are blue) stared back in our shared discomfort.

I waited a moment more to be certain it was still my turn.

"Just so you know," I finally said, "I asked Dorothy to move back home with me. We've got a nice space set up for her. She comes and goes as she pleases. I cook whatever she wants, or needs—I'm researching that. Maybe you have some materials about diet we can take home with us. Later I'll do everything I can to help her get better—but I'm still taking direction, if you will."

That was more than I'd said to any stranger in weeks, but under Sharon's affectless, leveling gaze, it still sounded inadequate. She waited, as if expecting more.

"I've also been a drinker of sorts, at a few spots in my life," I blurted, "including the past few years, since my divorce. But Dorothy's condition—her move home was the first occasion I've had to question whether it was ever a problem for anyone. And, well—if that's been so," I turned to Dorothy, whose eyes widened and jaw dropped as she watched, "then I regret it. Honest. So I never have more than one glass of wine now, with dinner, is what I'm saying. I made that promise to Dorothy before she accepted my offer to move in. About having no more martinis. So—"

Dorothy gaped at me full-on, as if witnessing a puppy get hit by a car. I didn't understand.

"Dad, we're not—"

She stopped herself and quickly turned to Sharon.

"It's true: Dad's been great. I have no worries about housing or home care."

Carol too leaned in with a professional, confirming nod.

Sharon turned away to recheck her computer.

"And you and your mother are meeting separately—is that right?"

Dorothy nodded.

I found that odd.

"And Gerald?" I said. "Is your brother going to come in with your mother, or will he join us later, or—"

"Great!" Sharon said, wheeling like a pull toy away from her monitor. "So, Carol, you'll probably find some of this familiar from your coursework. But let's review together why we're here and what's next, and then all of *you* can do the talking."

We were part of a cancer-support pilot program Carol had discovered and suggested to Dorothy. Sharon would become Dorothy's care coordinator, her point person for everything from chemo and specialist appointments to counseling and financial advice. And, should they one day be needed, to hospice resources. We four might meet together every week, or biweekly, or even more infrequently, depending on Dorothy's final diagnosis and, above all, on her wishes and condition. Sharon's unit had already learned that introducing patients and their caregivers to "larger multiclient support groups" was often counterproductive—that care became "too diluted" to effectively meet everyone's individual needs. (I imagined in-fighting, people duking it out for a finite number of pills and wheelchairs and the fattest chemo lounges, with the short-timers pulling rank.) What had also proven most effective, Sharon said, was to start out with individuals and one or two of their loved ones, just as we were today, to gauge where the patient "was at" and what resources might support them best. We could create and "tweak" a needs-specific, personalized care plan from there.

Sharon pressed over her desk to deliver this boilerplate speech to us. It was strange to hear how the world had changed—that medicine was now a "managed process" to be "optimized" for the most "positive outcomes." And yet I found some comfort, unexpectedly, in this language. Perhaps it's best that we reimagine caring for the sick and dying as an impersonal business, a series of transactions. What did we do in the old days? We probably went faster, and with less talk or help.

I had been told that after my mother went into a coma, during her final labor, she'd lain in her hospital bed no more than three hours. She passed without any pain, in the "twilight," while my father and grandmother sat by her side, holding her hands. My brother and I were back home listening to *Lone Ranger* on the radio.

My grandmother went four years later, in the kitchen, first falling and striking her forehead on the enameled sink before crumpling back in a heap to a worn spot of the linoleum. Craig found her, after coming home from high school, with a sticky, black pool beneath her head and her eyes squinting at the ceiling—eyes that, he told me, he pinched closed himself. There was no pain in her expression, but she wasn't smiling either—instead, her teeth were bared from the weight of her cheeks tugging back her lips. Craig repeated this detail several times, as I'd insisted on hearing it, and then he demonstrated. I had come home just as they were wheeling her out on a gurney, covered. I ran into the kitchen and saw that black hole to hell right in the middle of the floor, before Craig, who was talking to the policeman, had any chance to see me and order me back out to the porch. And for days afterward I kept a wary eye on him. I was afraid he too might leave me, since he'd seen Grandma dead but could still talk about it so easily, rocking next to me on the porch swing—in a seat which, right up until that very afternoon, had always been Grandma's.

My father passed away in his sleep from an embolism. I'd just entered college, and Craig had already been discharged from the army—he was in the local hospital—so my father had been living alone at home. By then he'd been retired and had little business outside the house beyond visiting Craig—which he did, dutifully, each week. After the collected mail piled up in our box, he was discovered by the mailman, in bed, with his hands on his chest.

Whether Craig's electrocution had been accidental or something he'd planned is a question I still don't want answered. I'd just turned nineteen, a college sophomore, when he died. He'd been in the hospital nearly two years, after less than two in the army, where they'd given him a personality disorder discharge. He'd been diagnosed with some bogus-sounding psychological disability after a violent incident on leave, in which he'd been struck on the head with a trench shovel. *In a fight*, the army officials repeatedly reported. Once, over lunch, my former dumpling buddy cast some doubt on that, repeating rumors he'd heard about the raw hazing that naive, sensitive young men sometimes suffered in the military, in silence—stories he'd been told by his partner. Those are theories I've tried hard, and unsuccessfully, to push away from me all these years when trying to understand my brother—who himself had never told me a story I could completely trust.

Craig's suffering was acute. He'd grown unrecognizable in a very short time: His crew cut showed his monstrous scar, he'd lost weight, and his eyes moved like machinery. I would sit with him in his ward for up to an hour, but every indication was that the visits no longer mattered to him. He stopped talking. I was still legally too young to have any say in his treatment, even after my father'd died and I was the only kin Craig had within three hundred miles, but they reassured me each month that they were diligently trying to get his medication levels properly calibrated; I'd go in and the ward attendant would review his chart, showing me ratings for diet, exercise, and social interactions, and I had no choice but to accept what they said. Of course, Craig never scored high there on geniality—as if my intrepid, shining brother could ever give a rat's fuck about playing Ping-Pong in that hole—but eventually he put me on the outside too. And he *always* fought the pills. In the end, it took two men to force him to swallow. On my last visit, when I sat on the stone steps out front to compose myself before going in, one of his ward-mates stood in a hedge to whisper what a thrill it'd been to see Craig spit a pill twelve feet, shot like a bullet straight out the caged window, before the ward staff noticed. I admit: That made me proud. It fooled me into thinking he still had fight left in him. I planned to do the same, one day, if it ever came to that. But he was never a warrior; he'd never seen combat, and there was no real war when he'd enlisted. Veterans Affairs claimed it was testament enough to Craig's strength that he'd survived the head wound at all. To me, the greater marvel was that such a brilliant young man—who'd taught me nearly all I know about joy, courage, duty, and how to talk around darkness—could have been lured by movies and magazines and billboards into a world where he would never fit, only to be shipped back, flattened, in months. He'd wanted to be an immortal hero, but only one type was ever advertised in our small world, outside Christ himself.

A lie can win over the long haul only when we cease to doubt. That's why I'll always believe it's just as likely my brother died in a botched electroshock treatment as the pathetic story they'd tried to sell me: that he'd punctured an embedded power cord with a pilfered fork. What *is* certain is that I was never able to make him feel better, about anything, ever.

Remembering all that, and seeing my sweet Dorothy at my side—blinking beneath her Giants cap, growing timid in Sharon's room—I knew where to focus today.

"Any questions before we begin?" Sharon said, wagging her pen before me.

"No thank you, Sharon!"

"Great," she said, recrossing her legs.

A pair of pigeons dropped into view behind her, as if to impress upon us that the scene outside was indeed live, and this was really happening.

"Now. Dorothy has asked me to be direct. She's told me we all understand there's a worst-case chance she may have Stage III pancreatic cancer, and that the prognosis for that, on a strictly data-based level, can sound pretty stark." She frowned to reinforce the seriousness. "The current survival rate past five years is just over five percent."

Dorothy nodded in tight-lipped assent. She and Carol seemed to have discussed this already. Although I had read that same figure, I had never heard it spoken. I'd always known this was bad, and I'd willed myself to think the worst I was capable of ever since she first told me, but I still wasn't ready for public, group agreement about real probabilities. I didn't want expression of my own pain to make things feel worse for Dorothy, so I held my hand over my mouth.

"Just needed to put that out there," Sharon said. "So now, since Carol's prepped you about our program"—she nodded in the appropriate direction—"and most of the practical matters we teammates will face together have been—"

"*Teammates?*" I said. I couldn't hold back.

"Yes," Sharon said, "that's what we call—"

"I understand *that*," I said. "But doesn't the term make it sound like we're playing ball? A little incongruent with the reality we're facing here, don't you think?"

Dorothy shook her head but, thankfully, she also looked a little amused. Maybe she thought I was trying to be funny—acting out some Dad role to distract and comfort her. Which, should she require it, I would be very pleased to do. Or, better yet, maybe she agreed with me, and she was glad to hear someone else say it out loud. It emboldened me.

"You're giving her these unfair, shitty *odds*," I said. "Maybe, instead, a gambling analogy—?"

Sharon wheeled a few inches back from me to address us all.

"Okay—Jim reminds us of one important point. This is *your* story, Dorothy. Of course, it's up to *you* how we talk, what we name things. There is *always* hope. We're also making huge advances in cancer treatment every day. And many people believe in miracles."

"So you're saying it'll take a miracle for Dorothy to win this?"

"Dad, it's okay," Dorothy said, smiling as she blotted her eyes. "It's *okay*."

"There is *nothing* okay about this."

Carol clenched her jaw and turned, tired, to the window to search for—nothing. I must have lost control of my volume.

Dorothy tugged at my sleeve, as if I needed to be led, and redirected me to Sharon.

"Let's just do this," she said softly.

Sharon, mouth open, clicked her pen into her chin. "But please *do* take a moment to pick a different name for this group—for us—if you need."

She fake-scanned her chart to grant us that moment.

Care Crew? Cancer Corps? The very team concept itself, when, in the worst-case scenario, one of the players was ninety-five percent likely to be forced to throw in the towel, was the most bullshit part of it all.

I felt Carol's stare.

"Jim?" she said. Her stern eyes led mine up the wall, to the steel clock. "Is this truly important?"

Somewhat, I thought. If it's the way we'll be talking to each other as we nurse Dorothy through cancer, it is. And if it's what you and I will still be known as, should we lose.

But I was using our time selfishly. I said I was sorry, and I promised to be a better Whoever.

Sharon started up again. The next few weeks of Dorothy's care plan had already been penciled in around her projected chemo cycles. Carol and I instantly agreed to take substantive roles in helping with those appointments. Next, in order to "wring the most out of all the days we've been given," Sharon suggested we take a few minutes to talk about what "everyday" might look like.

I was uncomfortable with how quickly I'd begun disliking this counselor who was, in fact, trying to waltz us across some very scary terrain.

"So, Dorothy," she said, "not to repeat conversations you may have had with others, but please—try something with me? It may sound a little harsh at first, but we all already know how strong you are. And just like a muscle, it's good for us to exercise that strength every day." She paused, and her eyes swept Carol and me in. "And I should tell you two that Dorothy and I have already chatted by phone privately, beforehand, and she's reassured me she doesn't want us to coddle her. But we can always stop and turn in another direction, any time. It's her call.

"So, having laid that groundwork, are we ready to forge ahead?"

Perhaps you mean "take the field"?

"Shoot," Dorothy said.

"Great!" Sharon shook her little fist in the air: *Onward!* "Dorothy— pretend we were just told today by your oncologist there'd been a mistake in your prognosis, and that rather than the far better odds you still truly have, you were instead told you had only three months. Pretend that's certain. How would your plans change? What would you do with those remaining three months?"

Dorothy contracted into her seat. She wasn't visibly upset by Sharon's question—not initially—but she shrank the longer she thought it over.

You really *can* hear clocks tick in silence like that, when you're holding your breath.

"If my timeline were *shortened*? I don't think I'd change much else. I've already done that—made most of the changes I wanted—those I could."

"Please share that with us?" Sharon said.

Dorothy straightened up as if being quizzed by a teacher—not an uncommon childhood experience, for her.

"Sure. First, I finally cleared out of my apartment. Let that go. Even if we do get that miracle you mention, I don't want to go back to that place anymore. It was pretty cathartic, actually, saying goodbye to all that extra stuff. It was always more my boyfriend's, anyway. His family owns it. So it's not like I was sticking him with the rent. And I slipped out of my job pretty smoothly. I was able to give a week's notice before chemo started. I'm not permanent, anyway—at work—so if I'd stayed longer, things would have gotten weird once everyone figured out something was wrong. I want to keep my Jeep. Dad doesn't drive and my mother can't do freeways. My brother and I will sign the title over to him, whenever I decide. Or if the bank comes for it. And I'm already all moved back in with Dad now. So everything's set."

It was chilling to hear how matter-of-factly she narrated the re-packaging of her life—how quickly she'd done it. And how small it sounded.

"So 'everything's set' for what?" Sharon said.

"I don't know. Just 'set.' I mean, I don't need to worry about anything much now. Even the cat's taken care of."

"You kept your cat?" Sharon said.

"No, my ex-boyfriend—"

"Let me push a little here," Sharon said, interrupting. "Remember, we're just pretending you have only three months. You're saying you've used those precious remaining days to get 'everything set'—for what?"

Sharon looked down quickly to sip water and avoid our eyes as we watched her.

"We can stop this exercise at any time," she continued, "but it might help us explore a little more about how you want to *live*—what you might like *to do* for yourself. To someone else, all the things you've just mentioned might sound like arrangements to make before you *go*—a list of things you thought you needed to take care of because you won't be around to deal with them later. Hypothetically. So why not play a moment more and think instead of what you might *enjoy* doing with those three months?"

On the other side of Dorothy, Carol rearranged herself in her seat. She gave Dorothy a subtle chin-up gesture that suggested she herself had considered the very same question, and that she too wanted to hear a good answer.

But Dorothy turned away from her. She looked down at her hands. She said nothing.

I fought the urge to jump in and help her: *Your project! You said you'd always wanted to make a long movie of your own, and now you are doing it!*

Dorothy spoke haltingly, like a kid confessing recess crimes.

"Well, I do enjoy having no schedule," she said. "Or not much of one, at least. I can see whoever I want. I can work whenever I feel like it, day or night—"

"You said you quit . . ." Sharon said.

"No, I mean my own project—a film. I've got all my equipment set up at the house. A darkroom, even. I can work without getting in Viktor's way, anytime, day or night, and for as long as I want. I never had that freedom before—to just let my mind roll out and do creative work."

"Not in college?" I blurted out.

Sharon lifted a fingertip to me: *Wait.*

"Oh, you know, that wasn't my major," Dorothy said. "There were always deadlines and tests. And I always had trouble keeping up with the reading. Remember?"

I sometimes forget what a slow reader she'd been. A "student with learning differences" is how they would label her nowadays. We'd never put pressure on her to excel as a student, but she'd always pushed herself. Hearing her now, at thirty, say that she'd never had a chance to pursue her life's passion freely? That hurt a little. If it were true, then I was responsible, in part. I would be guilty for never having noticed or taught by example.

"That was *my* fault," she said, as if hearing me. "I guess I could have made it a priority over, say, the Jeep. I just didn't know better; I just thought you could have it all whenever you decide you want it. So, in a sick way, it's nice to have that clarity now. That urgency. Because if you ignore the tumor, I have this weird freedom all of a sudden, right? *That's* a surprise. I'm way deeper into my movie now than I've ever been able to go with anything else before. It's like I can just shut the door and lose myself in this—this totally new world."

Sharon did not mask her approval.

"What's so 'new' about it?" she said.

"All my other films have been work. Or assignments. And they've been collaborations. They were always scripted or directed and edited with other people. But this movie has a life of its own. Maybe it's just an escape for me, but some days it feels way more real and important to me than anything outside. Every part of me comes into play, and time falls away, or reverbs. So—if I had only three months left? I'm pretty sure I would still clear my desk for *this*."

That made perfect sense to me. I beamed with pride at Dorothy. Carol was rolling a pencil between her fingers—she needed a smoke—but she seemed pleased too.

"Anything else?" Sharon said after waiting what she must have felt was an appropriate amount of time. "This project would be enough? Okay, let's start there: What could we three 'helpers'—for lack of another term—how can we ensure you're able to make that happen?"

"You?" Dorothy stared at Sharon. She looked like she'd just stepped back from a ledge.

"Yes, the three of us," Sharon said. "It sounds like Jim's giving you space, meals, and a certain insulation so you can work as you please. And your friend Carol too. What more can we do?"

Dorothy blushed suddenly.

"Of course I'd also want to spend quality time with everybody," she said. She looked guilty, put on the spot. "But maybe we're already doing that too—no need to amp that up if time gets short. I'm going to do something more with Gerald. He's really busy, but he always answers my calls. It's just hard to know . . ."

Her voice dropped suddenly, as the starkness of it all became clear to us again.

"Anyone from your past you'd like to check in with?" Sharon said. "Old friends or family? Places you'd like to see? Memories to revisit?"

Dorothy shook her head so slowly I could tell she was only pretending to think hard about this now. She looked ready to move on to the next fake question.

"No. We've been good on that. Dad's a big help."

And here, as she pulled up, she gave me the kindest look—her eyes were full of warmer thanks than I could have ever deserved. It would have been hard to bear if Carol too hadn't caught my eye and given me another little chin-up and nod, as if to say: *It's true, Jim. You're doing it.*

I was suddenly grateful to be there with them.

"He and I have been driving down memory lane," Dorothy said, speaking louder over the catch in her voice. "You know, here and there. We're doing things we used to do together. Carol too." Her breath caught, and she reached to tug our hands, squeezing them into her lap. "I know you're here," she said.

Carol shut her eyes tight at Dorothy's touch. It wasn't often, in those early days, that I'd ever allowed myself to feel, in my guts, the real possibility of Dorothy's one day being gone, but in that instant it hit me doubly hard, because I understood then I also had been assuming Carol would always be around too.

Everything went runny and out of focus while the three of us cleared our throats and looked around for safe places to stare. Carol took a slow, deep breath to drive back her need for a cigarette. Dorothy squeezed her hand again, pulling it up to her chest, and blinked back at me apologetically, as if I would be bothered if she cried—something she rarely did, and only when in physical pain.

In unison, we turned to Sharon, who smiled back.

"Great," she said quietly. "So it really sounds as if you may be 'all set' after all. You have the home you need and the support you want. You're making your own decisions. And you are loved. Let's formally acknowledge that. The cancer can *never* take those things away from you."

Dorothy nodded gratefully, clutching our bloodless fingers even tighter in hers. There was a brief silence, during which any reasonable person might question whether Sharon was entirely correct in making such a bold assertion.

I finally spoke. "And—you still have *a lot* more than three months." That needed to be said.

Dorothy smiled at last, nodding.

"There is one thing, a little request I might make," she said slowly, as if she'd asked for *anything* yet. "I was thinking how nice it would be to have a big family dinner, together. Before the chemo gets much harder."

"Anytime," I said.

"Maybe all of us?" she said. "I was thinking, Carol, and Xenia, and Dick too? And sooner than later?"

"Whenever you want," I said.

I could not yet imagine all of us at one table, but I meant it. Carol's face showed no emotion, but she was sure to go along with it.

Sharon waited to make sure it would be settled that simply. For a moment, she looked as if she expected an invitation herself.

"And from me," she said, looking back at her clipboard, "do you feel you have access to everything you need here right now? You know all you need to about this disease, your condition, and your treatment options? How to reach me anytime?"

Dorothy nodded emphatically.

Sharon marked something with her pen. We all waited.

"Thank you!" Sharon looked up, smiling, but again grew serious. "Now, since we've still got a little more time left to explore, let's shift gears—if you're amenable."

We nodded, relieved to move on. Her metaphors were as bland as the walls.

"Again: These exercises are created to help us do the best we can for you, Dorothy," she said. "Next question is for your father."

Shoot! I thought.

"Okay, Jim—pretend you just heard the make-believe news we gave Dorothy earlier. How might *you* choose to live out those three months, at home?"

My immediate thought was that Dorothy must have been prepping me for this moment, just the other night, when we were talking about writing. Once again, I was amazed and grateful she could show so much caring toward others in the middle of her own ordeal.

"Would you believe I'd just been thinking about that very thing?" I gave Dorothy a wink, which she didn't catch. "So this may sound rehearsed, but—if you'd just told me I had only three months to live, I'd continue—"

"Sorry, Jim—no." Sharon smiled wryly, like I'd intended to pull her leg. "What would you do if you'd just learned *Dorothy* had three months? Not you."

I flushed with embarrassment. It was an honest mistake, but such a ridiculously selfish one that I had trouble walking clear of it.

Dorothy came to my rescue.

"I asked Dad that the other night: When were you really happiest? We were hanging out and I was just wondering what his perspective would be, after kids and a career and marriage—if he missed something." She patted my arm. "Don't be embarrassed, Dad. That was my fault."

"*Nothing* here is your fault, sweetheart," I said, feeling limp. "I did that the other night too, when you'd asked: My first thought was about myself. As usual."

I couldn't look anyone in the eye. Behind Sharon, one of the club-footed pigeons that had been doddering along the thin ledge struck the glass with its beak and sloppily flapped about to claw for purchase.

"It's okay, Jim," Sharon said in a caring tone that sounded like Dorothy's but was at odds with her own sharp eyes. "It's natural to feel selfish, when we face these issues. After all, we're primarily responsible for ourselves, aren't we? When you think of a baby: Its first interface with the world is to open its mouth for air and food? We all have needs to fill. Part of growing up is learning how to do just that."

Dorothy barely cried when she was born, even after they'd stuck the suction tube down her throat to clear the fluids. She'd been slow to nurse too—almost uninterested. She'd spent her first hour with her little black eyes wide open, seeming to stare everywhere without judgment or desire. Patient, but ready.

Sharon glanced up at the clock before she continued.

"Or I can use another analogy, if you'd like. When you land too hard in an airplane, and those yellow air masks come down, you need to put your own on first before you can help those near you with theirs, right?"

I had to stop her there for my sake, if not Dorothy's.

"If I'd just learned Dorothy had three months left, I'd continue living as we already do. That's why I asked her to come home. I want to be there all day for whatever she needs. I stopped with the martinis—I already said that, I know. And I'm willing to let her mother come visit whenever she wants—we're divorced—"

"Separated," Dorothy added quickly.

"—and Dorothy can work any time and come and go and—"

"Thank you," Sharon said, stopping me short with an upturned palm. Evidently I wasn't kicking straight for the goal. *Be efficient, then, and tell me what* you *most want to hear*, I thought.

And she did.

"We've covered all the ways you're supporting Dorothy," she said. "But in our remaining five minutes: Say you just found out *today*— after Dorothy's moved home and you've both settled into routines— that there's a new urgency. What more do you want to do for her?"

"What do *I* want to do? This is getting creepy." I felt flustered. "This isn't real, is it—this three-month business?"

"No, but it's a good question, isn't it?" she said. "How it sharpens things? Is there anything else you would want to say or do with Dorothy?"

"Beyond what we're already saying and doing?"

"Something special you'd like to share?"

"It's *share* now?"

Carol twitched, and then spoke up.

"They already spend as much time together as they can," she said. "More than any father-daughter pair I know."

I felt rushed by the ticking clock, and put off at hearing Carol chime in too. This was *our* family, after all.

I turned to Dorothy.

"You know I love you, don't you?"

Yes, yes, I do, she nodded, sitting back almost fearfully, like a kid in a witness box straining to answer correctly, watching for cues. It was the complete opposite of how I'd hoped she would feel.

"And you *know* I want to spend *every minute* we can together—if that's what you want too?"

Dorothy continued nodding, blinking.

Sharon leaned in to whisper.

"I'm asking how *you* want to spend those hours, Jim."

"Oh, for *Christ's sake*, I want her to *live*! That's all. I want all this pain to *go away*! You need me to say that again? And again? I want Dorothy to fight back and stick around to be one hundred and then I want to die in *her* arms. I mean that: *I* should be the first to go. I want her to outlive me by decades. Can we make-believe *that* for three months?"

My voice must have risen to a shout, because I heard the echo before I shut up. Even the dull-eyed pigeons froze.

Sharon stared at Dorothy. I grew unsure which one of them I'd been addressing. Dorothy was receding slowly, behind her eyes. I knew that look. She shook her head and spoke softly to me.

"We can't pretend this isn't happening, Dad."

"But why aren't you *fighting* it!?" I cried. "Why are you *giving in*?"

She looked at me with the same tell-me-what-you-want-to-hear look I'd seen in my own eyes, reflected in mirrors and windows and sunglasses for weeks.

"Is that what you want?" she said.

"What?"

"Is that what *you* want? For me to pretend I can simply save myself?"

She looked out at me from the distance you would put between yourself and an approaching stranger.

"You want me to put a spin on this and pretend I can cure myself?" she said. "All the shit that may come—that's *already here*—just push it back and redirect it?"

"You could hope for a miracle?" I said.

She cocked her head back, agitated, watching my words hover in the air between us.

"Do you?" she said.

I could not feel more trapped.

"Do *you* hope for a miracle?" she said again. Her nostrils flared.

I could not say no. For a moment, no one spoke.

I turned from Dorothy to Carol, but she watched the window.

I faced Sharon. *What should we do now?* She too looked unfazed, but to judge from her expression—*I can wait*—we were making suitable progress.

Carol surprised me by speaking first.

"Dorothy's asking a real question—"

I stiffened.

"Okay, I do," I said, looking down. "Yes."

"And so you believe," Dorothy said, "that if I put all of my energy into 'fighting' this it'll make a miracle happen?"

"Yes, Dorothy. That is my unexamined hope."

"And what if I *can't*?" she said, tight-lipped and shuddering. "I'm doing *everything* I can, I swear, but it can't be all cancer, all the time. We'll all be together. We'll have a big dinner with everyone. I'll make a movie. But if a miracle is going to happen in the next three months—or three years—I don't really think anything I can do will force it one way or another. We just do our best. You've got to accept that."

When I could finally look back into her brimming eyes, it felt like we'd both been peeled, slowly, layer by layer, with our dry, transparent skins pulled away to leave us clean but raw. From that time on, it would be impossible for her and me to ever again look deep into each other's eyes and not sense that groaning pressure behind them—that thin-doored closet packed tight with tears and loosely latched.

When Dorothy was a firm little baby, her wide eyes were like those black eight-ball oracles you jiggle and watch until an answer presses up from the depths. I used to do that: Ask her a question, give her a gentle shake, peer into her pupils, and wait until she kicked a toe or pointed—she always took her time—and stared back from across the light-years, curling her lips in a wry smile till I pulled her closer. *Should we have noodles, peas, or mush-mush for lunch? Want to play pigeon at the fountain, or go to the sandbox today?* Lately, she most often locked eyes with me in pain. She'd been trying to hide that, but now I understood: She hurts, and I simply can't help. Not enough. No matter how much of your child's suffering you try to take on, the worst day is when you learn you can only go so far. It uncovers the boundary that was established the day she was born. You're separating.

Something ding-donged in Sharon's world. With a little squeak, she faced her computer, scanned the greenish screen with her finger, tapped the glass, and suggested a date one week out. For a sickening instant, I panicked that that was the only meeting we had left to schedule.

Dorothy and Carol had already walked out by the time I thought to stand and offer Sharon my hand. I grabbed a bunch of brochures instead, and followed.

CHAPTER 11

Sharon's bleak thought exercise left me very shaky, with its let's-pretend, accelerated deadline for Dorothy. Even if Dorothy had opted in beforehand, and even though Carol, as a counselor-in-training, was ideal support in that situation, you'd still think such a grim little game would be risky for even the sturdiest of people. The whole scenario felt like a setup. I'd never been in denial about Dorothy's condition, and it was not Pollyannaish of me to think she should be fighting, but still, sitting in that pale office playacting her three-month decline was a good deal darker than any "support" I'd expected to be called upon to provide.

Now, however, that three-month scenario, real or not, would bring an unsettling urgency to the days ahead. Even though I'd confessed in the end to hoping for a miracle, it was clear that nothing I was actually doing confirmed that hope—certainly not my silence in the car afterward, nor the cheesy hospice service brochures I clutched to my chest as we sped away from the clinic.

I rode without saying a word in the windy back of Dorothy's open Jeep. In the rearview mirror, I caught angular glimpses of her face, and she appeared to be in a good mood, something beyond relieved that we'd finished the meeting. She talked and even chuckled with Carol about things I couldn't hear over the rushing air. When it became clear she was driving west to drop me off first, I shouted to her to let me out at a bus stop on Geary instead. I needed the walk. And besides, I thought, this would make her life a little easier—less driving to do on one of her few "remaining" afternoons.

I jumped out at a busy intersection. When she yelled out—*See you tonight!*—I couldn't look back: She would have seen how desperately I needed to hear her say that very thing.

I walked a very fast mile to one of the Irish pubs that still existed in the Inner Richmond, a place where I used to drink and pretend to watch Giants games after work with an old colleague who's since died. The bar was empty—odd even for a weekday at noon—and as I sipped my stout, getting a headache from the insipid pop videos that blared incessantly from a dingy television, it dawned on me that this place too was yet another betrayal of my recently professed hope. *Who's got time for a pint when your little girl's got three months?* My old, red-eyed self mocked me in the mirror: Once again, I was a living cliché, huddled alone over a smudgy glass with the white sunshine pushing through the open door behind me. I endured that image for only as long as it took to walk away in disgust.

I strode another fast two miles west, to Lands End. There I noticed the day's perfect weather for the first time. I leaned far over the parapet above the Cliff House to watch the ribbons of waves unravel up Ocean Beach—a mocking, living postcard of sunny California. They nauseated me. I was sickened by the truths about Dorothy's condition that I'd just pretended to digest so easily in public, and at my utter inability to do or think anything more helpful about them. I couldn't even cry. I just panted and felt numb and enraged by her disease, as if it were something I could yell at or kick.

She was right: How *was* she supposed to fight harder? What more could I hope she would do? She wasn't asking much of us. All she wanted from me was that I take my meds and talk out loud.

And cook dinner for everyone.

That I could do.

It was midafternoon before I got home. I must have hoped that, by delaying my return, Dorothy might be back in the house before me, but it was still empty.

I called Gerald at work. As expected, he didn't answer at first, so I left a voice message. *Thanksgiving in August.* I'd do a turkey with all the trimmings—Dorothy's favorite. And even though I've never been east of Pittsburgh, let alone out to Plymouth Rock, as a midwesterner I still command more authority over a Thanksgiving turkey out here than any native Californian could pretend to, including my kids. This was also a great chance to have Xenia meet the family, I told him. I gave him a date. *Call if you feel you have any conflicts.* My new counselor voice.

I did not want to talk to Jackie next, nor did I know her cellular number, but I had committed to making this happen, so I rummaged through the kitchen drawers. Thankfully, Gerald called back right away.

"No crisis," I said, in case my calling him at work had alarmed him. "Dorothy's fine—we were just at the doctor's."

"I know. She texted."

Already? One day I will catch up with these kids I taught to walk.

"So did she mention her big shindig?" I said, trying to sound light. *Don't worry; be happy.* "Can you come this Saturday?"

Gerald's delay was palpable, even over the phone. I could see him push his hair back, sucking air through pursed lips.

"Sooo—*I* might be able to," he said slowly. He cleared his throat. "Not so sure about X, though."

"This is Dorothy's request. She wants everyone: you, X, your mother, the boyfriend—"

"Dick too? Really?" He sounded alarmed. "You sure you're up for this?"

"She wants it. I'll do it."

I heard beeps and office chatter behind him. I waited.

"I'm just not sure X is a good idea," he said. "She can be pretty intense."

"I'm fond of her. Sit her next to me."

"It's different with you."

"Has she met your mother?"

"Not really." He was trying to apply the brakes gently. "By which I guess I'm saying: No, she has not."

"Now's the hour."

"I just don't know." It sounded like he'd turned his back to the office, with his hand cupping the mouthpiece. I'd forgotten he and X worked together. "She and I might not be so long term."

I recalled how gracefully he and Xenia moved around my kitchen, complementing each other like ballroom dancers. You can't fake that. I don't meddle in my kids' lives, but I'd been happy to see Gerald find himself such a close match, even if she were a slightly older divorcée from Odesa.

"May I ask what's wrong?" I said.

It sounded like he went deeper into the office, to a quiet place. I pictured him skulking away in his boots and flannel shirt, cloudy-browed and hunched around his goofy phone. *Thank God I'll always have my son*, I suddenly thought, just long enough to shudder at the ugliness of it—a thought that itself was also a hope only, and not a certainty.

"You do know X is sort of religious?" he finally said, sotto voce.

"She led me into the cathedral," I said. "Several times she prostrated herself before the incorrupt relics of a saint under glass. She prayed, audibly. I got it."

I had to poke at Gerald's earnestness; it was such a relief after a day of clinical newspeak.

He got excited. "She took *you* to Saint John too?" he said.

"She did," I said. "I'm surprised she didn't mention it to you. In fact, I even wondered if you'd both secretly planned that—to convert me, maybe."

"Wow," he said. It was unclear which thought surprised him most.

"Are you worried," I said, "that X might disapprove of your mother's shacking up with Dick?"

"You know Mom's still got her own place, right?"

I didn't know that.

"Or is it the divorce, then?" I said.

"You and Mom got divorced?"

I felt us getting lost.

"You think we're still married?" I said.

"I mean—you finally, legally, did it?"

"I don't think I could feel any more divorced from your mother right now than I already do."

"It's more than a *feeling* you get, Dad. It's a formal thing. It's real: There's documentation."

"I haven't seen any of that."

He waited.

"I was referring to *X's* divorce," I finally said.

He didn't know I knew.

"Look," he said, sounding frustrated. He'd never liked surprises. "I'm at work."

"Dorothy told me about it," I said. "But I don't think it should be an issue for Xenia *or* for you or anyone else that she's older and divorced. Not in *our* family, it shouldn't."

"She and her ex divorced when he was in prison," he said impatiently. "And he's not in there for doing nice things either—nothing political or righteous or whatever. But you can ask her all about that yourself."

"I shall. How about the following Saturday?"

"I work."

"That Sunday?"

He delayed.

"Right after church?" I pressed.

"Okay."

"Thank you," I said.

"You know," he said with a huff, "it seems just a little bit weird to me that Dorothy's running around blabbing my business when she's so tight-lipped about her own."

He stopped short at that, as if suddenly ashamed to be voicing any criticism of his sick sister. But somehow, to me, that little dig was reassuring to hear. It rooted us back in our everyday feelings.

"You okay, Gerald?"

"It's just—" He stopped shuffling around to struggle with his words. "She *never* calls me, Dad. I don't want to bother her because she *always* sounds *so cheery*, when I know for a fact she must be wiped out—she even talks slower now—so I just stand by and wait till she lets down her guard and needs something. But she hardly ever does. And each day that passes—you know—"

"I know," I said.

How little would I see of Dorothy, or hear from her, if I hadn't coaxed her back into living with me?

"Just keep calling her anyway," I said. "She'll get back. I bet she's the one who doesn't want to bring your day down. And you—come here any time. Just be prepared to keep it short if she needs. She worries about you too, Gerald. That's the only reason she told me about Xenia."

He said nothing.

"She worries more about us than she does herself," I said.

Silence surrounded us.

"She's always been like that," he said. "I never used to believe her."

"See you a week from Sunday," I said. "Bring X, whatever you drink, and a new photo of both of you for my fridge."

We said goodbye, and quickly hung up.

Almost immediately, I wanted to call him back. I wanted to be kinder to him, to confess that the best hope I myself held for his sister's full recovery was a conscious effort, an act of will, but one we must make nonetheless. I wanted to tell him that once recently when hugging her I thought I could feel her ribs, as if the very stuff of her was softening like overripe fruit that bruises under the lightest pressure. I wanted to tell him—or Carol, or even Jackie—that just before this latest round of chemo, I'd dreamed she was evanescing, and that no amount of pot smoke or dumplings would put weight back on her, or keep her hair from going weedy. But I also wanted to share how her condition could still change like the day's weather, and that even yesterday she'd woken up humming. I should have reassured him I was doing everything I could think of—and that he was too.

I should have invited him here more regularly. If he'd come for a visit, he would be happy to see how loose everyday life was getting at home—how our being frank about everything kept Dorothy and me from wasting any precious time. I should have told him how free she felt to belch or barf without an "Excuse me," and how I could now give up on knotted shoelaces or window blinds, spit out a quick curse, and walk away while she laughed at me. He would enjoy the rude names we'd created for one foul-breathed nurse or the ringing phone whose calls we dodged—how we'd stopped punctuating our days with pointless courtesies. Gerald and I had never gotten that comfortable with each other the summer he'd been home. I hadn't allowed it. *Let's revisit that later.*

And her project—did he know about that? I envied how immersed she was in it, the satisfaction it gave her. The time she spent working alone quietly had an ennobling effect on her. Little events like our back-porch coffees, walks to the dunes, or the occasional matinee up at the Balboa—those too were everyday things you'd need to be here for, present, in order to enjoy and draw hope from them. I sometimes felt guiltily selfish that he couldn't join us, despite knowing the time might one day come when just deciding how best to mitigate the day's pain would be our full agenda, rather than where to drive the Jeep. Or that one day I might again be opening her window, stripping the bed, tossing the sippy cups, and relocking the door. For the moment, however, I alone was the one enjoying most of Dorothy's good times. I would remember to include him in more of those too.

What I also regretted, however, was not having asked him to invite his mother. Jackie and I hadn't said much more than "Hello" or "Goodbye" at the door over the past few weeks. I had to do more, and better, now.

The only number I had was her classroom phone, but her voice greeting there listed a cellular number. She answered that on the second ring.

"Jim?"

I was stunned she knew it was me, at first, until I realized my number must show on the little screen. Of course she would recognize her old phone number at the home she'd lived in for nearly thirty years.

"Don't panic," I said. "Dorothy's fine. It's—"

"I know, I know. She's here—with me."

I pressed the phone hard to my ear. I heard some professional chatter in the back, including Dorothy's voice.

"Of course." I pretended to understand; I wanted to get this over with. "You're with that counselor, right?"

She'd already slapped her palm to the receiver, or stuffed her finger into the pinhole that sucks voices into those little phones. "It's your father!" I heard her say, muted, out to the room. Everyone there hushed, or was muffled.

She neglected to answer my question.

"Dorothy's probably told you, then," I said. "Can you come to dinner, a week from Sunday? With your beau?"

"Oh!" Jackie said, sounding almost frightened. She resmothered her phone.

Dorothy should be doing these invitations, I thought.

"Sharon knows all about it," I added.

"Sharon?"

She sounded unusually lost, even for Jackie.

After more off-phone mumbling, she said: "Okay—Dotty says that's good."

"Of course it's good," I said. "It's her request."

"Next Sunday, I mean. The date."

"I'm roasting a turkey."

"He's roasting a turkey," she announced back to the others.

In the background, I heard Dorothy exhorting her mother from across the room.

"Jim," Jackie finally said, reluctantly. "There are some papers. For the—divorce."

Aha! All the mature, selfless resolve I'd pumped up to make this call deflated like a stinking flat tire. My gorge rose. How could *this* be an appropriate time to talk about divorce? And why should she be discussing it with Dorothy, or that Sharon, now? Were she and Dick getting married? I'd have thought they fancied themselves more the bohemian bon vivants than the sort who would race to the legal altar a second time, at their age. But bully for them. It'll all make for less confusion at the dinner table. I'm all about definition.

I kept quiet and clung to higher ground, if only for the slight distance that it afforded me.

"It's probably time we make—it—final," she said.

She sounded just a wee bit like our teammate counselor.

"Probably is," I said.

The only thing more ridiculous than the trouble she seemed to have in uttering the D-word on the phone was that she might worry I'd cry about it. After having several weeks to square myself with the idea of Dick, did she think I might be jealous? And if I were—who cares? I'll probably always be jealous of any man who gets Jackie's attention for more than a few jokes. But why explore that now?

"We're working on the papers right now," she said.

Who are *we?* She sounded as if she didn't fully trust "we" herself.

She used to grade student papers on the very kitchen table I then sat gripping. She used to sit with her elbows pressed into the Formica and her braid in her left hand, tugging and twirling it as if she could yank all the kids' messy thinking right out of her head. That memory made me ache for the past, and that ache slapped me back to attention, into the call, in seconds.

"I got a lawyer. Through the employee assistance program," she said gingerly. "We need to talk about it Sunday—"

"The *dinner* is next Sunday."

"When we—"

"Not *then*, Jackie. It's a special dinner. Just send your papers over with Dorothy next week. I'll sign them and ship them back."

Her breathing picked up.

"It's more complicated than that."

She should not be discussing all this in front of our daughter. Not unless she too were somehow complicit in the whole process. I would interrogate Dorothy later, alone, once she'd come home.

"You'll probably want to talk to a lawyer too," Jackie said.

"I assure you: I do not."

Her earring clicked nervously against her phone.

"I'll just use your guy," I added.

"That wouldn't be good."

"Why not?" I said.

The sky darkened.

"Jackie—what are you *doing*?"

"I'm just trying to make this *easier*." Her voice rose, quivering. It sounded like she'd stood up from her seat. "For everyone. That's *all* I'm doing."

"By taking the house from us?" I said. "Is *that* what Dorothy has been trying to tell me?"

"Dotty!" she shouted, away from the phone, as if she'd caught our baby sticking knives in the outlet. Her alarm made me regret saying that. That and how shaken she sounded. Truth is, I could never bear to see her suffer either.

"That's *not true*, Jim! There are real problems here! I've run through all my money. I don't want to explain how that happened, but—you understand? I need to let go of my apartment, even. They say the best thing for me is to file for bankruptcy—and I don't want any of that hurting Dorothy—or you, honest—not in *any* way, but it's going to take some lawyers to deal with this. It's a goddamn horrible mess."

I quickly knew how low I'd sunk in striking that blow, especially with Dorothy somewhere in that room. But now it was too late: As the phone was drawn farther away from her face, I heard her suck her breath up a little ladder, and then, as if diving, she tumbled into her tears. It meant little at that point for me to say I was sorry, but I did. I'd forgotten, until I heard her cry, how probably no other person could feel Dorothy's cancer more acutely than her mother.

"Sometimes—you treat me like I'm some sort of monster," she said, collapsing. "Both of you. You do! I never understand it."

I remember how hard it had been for her when we closed the doors to each of the kids' rooms for the last time, after they'd moved out. For her a chapter had ended, irrevocably. For weeks she wouldn't even touch the knob of either of the rooms. She wouldn't vacuum Gerald's room downstairs behind the garage; she just kicked his sandals and skateboard under the bed, left the *Star Wars* poster curling off the wall, and kept everything else at the ready in case he one day decided to return and need her again. I'd once found her napping in there, lying on his bed by the window where the sun's blocked out by a shrub. Gerald's is the darkest and most airless room in the place, so I'd never understood, until recently, why she would go back in there: She always threw her heart into the middle of things, even when that thing was absence. I too had missed both kids, very much, but never in the same elbow-clutching, eye-squinting, silent roving way Jackie had fallen into back then. Whenever I'd asked her how things were going, she went quiet and blamed it on menopause, and even though that change gave her prickly rashes and hot feet and no rest for years, I was wrong to believe—or to hope—that that had been cause enough for her lonesomeness. It went deeper. It was something I can feel now too. Because whenever I sit out in the quiet now and listen for Dorothy flip-flopping in discomfort on her old bed down the hall, or hear her padding to the toilet to retch once more, I know how much even those sad noises comfort *me* now, and how much I crave and need even that evidence of her everyday presence.

I didn't want to make Jackie cry. I didn't want to join her either. Whatever Dorothy had hoped to accomplish in her meeting with her mother and the lawyer and whoever else might be there, my call was no doubt postponing their progress, and probably on someone else's meter. And on one of Dorothy's days.

This time, I was first to say: "Forgive me. I've got to go."

Jackie sniffled.

"We'll be there, Jim," she said, and hung up.

Dorothy wouldn't return for hours, and I couldn't be alone any longer. I grabbed my jacket, ran out, and caught the streetcar just as it powered up to head downtown. I would invite Carol in person.

It was early sunset by the time I made it across town to buzz Carol's door. She entered the lobby wearing sweats, her hair was tied up on top of her head, and her half-moon spectacles rode low on her nose. She'd removed the makeup she wore earlier to the counseling session. She appeared comfortably familiar to me as she shuffled up to the door in her slippers, looking surprised and then anxious to see me standing outside the glass, so late and unannounced, and so soon after our session that afternoon.

It was a relief to be welcomed inside. I was glad I'd come. I was also happy to see that Carol too could not have been in the meeting with Dorothy and Jackie and the lawyers. So the entire world was not working against me.

I tried to give her a quick kiss on the cheek—that's how we'd parted last time I visited—but she absentmindedly dodged it as she pulled me inside. We passed her kitchen, which smelled like burned coffee. The table, counter, and stools were covered with shaggy stacks of paper. The radio played gently—classical music. She was working, she said, and couldn't move these piles and clean up without creating more work for herself later. She seemed rushed. She led me back to the end of the flat, to a living room as wide as the apartment, with watery old-glass windows that looked out into the top of a Japanese red maple that must have been planted decades ago, between the buildings. A low floodlight and the golden squares of the neighbors' places lit its delicate leaves, filling the room with a lush, rosy glow.

Carol pointed me to a spot on the couch, facing out, and clicked on an amber-shaded lamp behind me. Without a word she gave me a close, apprising look over the top of her glasses and, once satisfied, waved me down to sit as she ran back to the kitchen.

I had an urge, but no energy, to scan the bookshelves. I turned the lamp back off to rest my eyes and gaze out into the tree. I nearly fell asleep.

After a while, Carol returned with two mugs. She placed one on the nearby stand before sitting opposite me on the couch. The telltale scent of smoke announced that she'd just finished a cigarette in the alley, while waiting for the kettle.

She let her slippers drop and crossed her ankles beneath her.

"So," she said. "You again."

She winked, but still seemed a little on edge. She wasn't the vain sort who cared overmuch about being caught unprepared for visitors, but I noticed she had just combed her hair out, in the kitchen. I hoped she knew me well enough to not think I'd dropped in to make a play for pity nooky, even though that scenario—along with a binge in North Beach—had flipped through my mind on my march up Nob Hill, to her door. On the other hand, it was clear I had no reason to travel all the way across town just to invite her back out for dinner.

Yes, I nodded back. *Me. Again.*

We sipped our tea. The silence became a presence—she'd turned off her kitchen radio—and she reached behind the couch to switch the lamp back on.

"What are you working on?" I said.

She looked surprised, but pleased, to be asked.

"You ran over here to ask me this?" she said.

"It's one place to start."

"Some kid's master's thesis," she said, looking into her mug. "It's in rough shape—needs a hell of a lot more developmental editing than they told me. But then, usually they don't pay someone like me to step in unless there is a mess to clean up. So I'm not complaining."

I nodded to hide the fact that I didn't fully understand her.

"Is it interesting?" I said.

"Developmental editing?"

"The thesis."

"Depends on your point of view."

"What's yours?"

She gave me another wrinkled smile. But she looked harried. Patient, and harried. She wouldn't have rushed straight home to work after the morning we'd just had without some deadline looming. I slowly got that. *I should have called. I won't stay long.*

"Look," I said, "I know you're busy—"

She nodded, but kindly.

"I do need a break," she said. "A little one, anyway."

"Me too. I needed to get out of the house."

Her face showed no expression.

"I wanted to ask you to dinner, a week from Sunday?" I said.

"The Dorothy thing?"

"Yup."

"Of course," she said. In her ringed eyes, I saw yet another care added.

"Let me help?" she said.

"You already have." Which was true, but sounded awkward then. "I mean, I'd be grateful for your help next week, anytime you want. Or after, even."

She stared blankly.

"You've been truly kind, Carol. To both of us."

She looked outside.

"Dorothy's a very special person," she said slowly. "I won't overstate the obvious, but she means a lot to me. She's one of the few young people I know who gives me hope. She reminds me of a friend I had a long time ago, when I was a kid."

"A friend who died?"

Awkward. She went rigid.

"I'm sorry," I said. "Losing people has been a common theme for me lately."

She stared.

"And why do you say that?" she said, sitting up.

I didn't dare bring Dorothy's possible prognosis back up—*that* statistic filled every room—but I did remind her of the stories we'd told recently about our spouses who'd run off, or her old lady friend at the home, and the morbid game we'd just played with Sharon. However, as Carol recoiled quietly back into her end of the couch, it became clear to me that wasn't enough for her to understand—or even to pretend to understand—what I was talking about. Then I realized: Of course she didn't know the stories of my family, stories that I'd been replaying more often lately, to myself, than I ever had in all my life. Carol couldn't know those stories until I told them *to her*.

So I began. I told her about my grandmother, my mother, my father, my brother—all of them, with every sad, concrete detail I could remember. And, as always, Carol listened calmly, with a deep compassion. Again, it was surprising—a thrill, in truth—to be listened to so closely, and without interruption. It was so generous of her, and with each passing recollection, I let down more: I fell back, outside myself. I can't recall ever feeling so at ease in front of anyone else, not even my ex-wife, and in the end I was the one left silent, staring, and waiting for her, as if she should be the one to wrap things up.

She looked out at the tree and waited a moment. She still had stacks of papers to order, waiting for her in the other room—even *I* felt them, once I realized how long I'd been talking—but when she turned to me, tired, she also looked willing and able to listen a little longer, if that were necessary.

"So—thanks for asking," I finally said.

She reached out for me along the back of the sofa and took my hand in hers. She gave it a squeeze.

Outside, another window shade lit up. We both turned.

"You know," she said quietly, "since last time you were here, I read up a bit on your man Wallace Stevens. I wanted to know—I guess I wanted to be prepared, in case I ever try to take you out somewhere again—"

"Hope you do," I said.

She squeezed my hand again but let go, settling back into her corner.

"What I'm still wondering is," she said, "why do you like him so much?"

I had to think a moment.

"I guess I admire that he was able to write poetry like his while working a full-time job his whole life," I said. "That he didn't publish a book until he was nearly fifty. And I know how it feels to outlive your parents and siblings, like he did."

She nodded along. She'd read all that too, evidently.

But then she said: "Did you ever see anything about him being something of a racist? And a chauvinist? Antisemite too, if you ask me. Probably unconscious—but still."

That dumbfounded me. Even after the "culture wars" had dominated curriculum discussions in our school district, I'd never paid much attention to the politics of any dead author, from any background. Why bother? You don't need a paid historian to tell you what Stevens might think of teaching Ebonics in high school, nor should anyone with a real reason for living lose sleep guessing about it. My own limited engagement with poetry has been precious and pure, but it's also a luxury available to anyone with a library card and a public school, and my pleasure has never been taken at someone else's expense nor been contingent upon my respect for any writer's personal beliefs. I like a few of Stevens's poems very much, and for very simple reasons. In me, they connect like raindrops merging on a window, and they accomplish this same, gentle, exact effect each time I read them—I can't explain why. I might have read something of what Carol was talking about, years ago, but knowing how he spoke to or about those around him cannot change one word of what he's written. A good poem makes a moment mean more. Politics, on the other hand, like other ephemera, never fail to lose me. Politics are something you live through, unless you're one of the few to whom fortune has granted some agency for changing them—something no metaphysical poet will ever possess. Not in this world, anyway.

I struggled to return. I cared for Carol—very much, I realized—and this clearly mattered to her. I could exaggerate a little. I could agree it was maybe less than courageous of Stevens to encage himself in a corporate job just to maintain the staid, bourgeois level of comfort and security he felt he needed to keep his demons at bay. And perhaps it was odd of me to be impressed that he'd married his hometown sweetheart young, and to have kept those vows, staying with her till death regardless of how dry that marriage had become, or even that they'd lived their lives without ever driving a car. I could also tell Carol: He most impressed me because I've never been able to write a poem that could survive typing—because I stopped before I even began, years ago. Maybe his words gave me a sweet place to hide in now and then, a little room to daydream on a bigger scale, at a higher pitch. Or they used to. But that was something I could not yet find a way to say, out loud.

Carol was waiting for an answer.

"Yes," I said. "I might have caught a whiff of that. I also read about his friend Marianne Moore being accused of racism."

It was a peevish thing to say. Carol, ever gracious, ignored it.

"I doubt he noticed it in himself," she said. "Few people like him were that aware back then."

"Where did you read all this?"

"In one of Chuck's books." She nodded back to the wall of shelves. "Stevens's daughter published his journals when he died. She threw a lot of stuff out there. For her own reasons, I guess."

"I might have read that one. His *private* journals, right?"

"Yes," she said. "Where he wrote candidly."

"Candidly to himself," I said.

She nodded.

"But," I said, "can't someone manage to be 'something' of all those things you mention and still write a perfect poem?"

"I wouldn't know."

"Or, since you've gone that far in," I said, "did you also find where he says imagination is like light: It transforms everything it touches but 'remains undiminished, imparting nothing of itself'? Or that a good poem resolves the tension between sentimentality and seeing things as they truly are?"

Her face fell softly to one side. She blushed a little. Her lips parted to show those teeth that the camera doesn't like, but that anyone who loved her would miss, as hers, if she ever became vain and tried to "fix" them.

"No," she said gently. "But it does sound nice."

"Have *you* read his poetry?" It was not an accusation.

"I tried," she said, shaking her head. "Some. I'm not sure I get it, to be honest. They all seem self-referential. To me."

"Me too, sometimes," I confessed. "But I like the sound even more."

"And *not* the sound of *him* reading them," she said, recalling our earlier night.

"Yes," I said. "A lot of the time it's the shape and the sound of the words themselves that make the meaning. Does that make sense?"

Yes, she nodded. Which meant more, at that moment, than I could begin to take in.

"But earlier," she said. "You asked for my point of view? I think he was flat-out depressed."

No argument there. Another reason I like him.

She watched me kindly over the lip of her mug until she saw no offense was taken.

"But even if all you say is true," I said, "I can still go on reading his poems, right?"

"Of course you may," she said. "All by your little atrabilious self."

She smiled at last, having finally stumped me. She patted my hand.

"Look," she said. "If I don't get going on this job tonight, you won't see me at all next week. So you've got to go now. But I wanted to tell you one last thing, about earlier today—to make sure you understand why Dorothy came to my Al-Anon meeting. She was working on a film. That's the only reason—we were working together, and I invited her to my group. Her coming back a few times afterward had nothing to do with you. *Maybe* her mother—but that's her story to tell. So don't beat yourself up so much in front of Sharon. That's not why we're there."

I was so grateful to hear it I couldn't speak.

"But I've also got to tell you this," she said, slowly sitting upright. "It was pretty rough in there, hearing you two. It's like you both need to be the last true-blue scouts on the face of the earth. Like you've got to tell God's whole truth or you're just worthless—there's no in between. That's got to stop too. Does *that* make sense?"

I kept listening.

"No one can be pure all the time," she said. "No one. In college, I had a prof—and this is the only English prof you'll ever hear *me* quote—who used to say Hamlet had the conscience of a saint but the heart of an action hero, and he couldn't connect the two. Do you kill an uncle to avenge your father's murder? Can you stop loving your mother when she's sleeping with your uncle? I was worried about Dorothy even before this. She has *never* let herself get away with half of the stuff she overlooks in everybody else, and it ties her up in knots all the time. I want to shake her—tell her everybody's two-faced sometimes. Even Mother Theresa has a front and back side. Like Sharon: Sure she's making good money, but she's also caring for people. Big deal. Does that mean she should stop? Or she's a bad person?"

Her eyes grew fierce.

"Or look at me—I'm a sober drunk. Or you, maybe: You're a man who needs a lot of solitude, but who still feels he's got to run around apologizing to the world to justify some time alone. Think about it. Maybe you just feel safer someplace where the only person you can lose is you?"

I held my breath.

"But, Jim—*your daughter*," she said, choking up now as she turned, sharply, to the window. "Your daughter is a good, sweet girl with this fucking *ugliness* growing in her. Un-*fair*. It is *so hard* to hold all that together. *So* hard. But it's true—this is *really happening*. And we've got to see *all* of that, *for her*, or else we're already leaving big parts of her behind."

Shaken, I reached out. She let me hold her tightly. We rested there a long while. When we parted, she took my hand and my empty mug, and led us both down the hall before she kissed me goodnight, just outside the door.

part three

CHAPTER 12

Dorothy tried exactly once to call it "the Last Supper," but that was too dark even for me. I told her so and, with an unnerving cheerfulness, she just as quickly waved the idea away. For similar reasons, I asked that we postpone all talk of lawyers and divorce. We would "stay in the present."

After all the invitations had been accepted, however, there wasn't much planning to keep my mind occupied. Over the years, I'd created a little notebook of recipes with a timetable and shopping lists I use each Thanksgiving. We've always had a traditional turkey meal, even when Jackie and I were younger without kids or extended family nearby. My grandmother had always done up the holidays, using her old china from the cabinet—cream-colored stuff, with coin-gold rims and a brittle sound—to serve ham dinners at Easter and prime rib for Christmas. It's the only heirloom I ever shipped to California. It suited Dorothy's meal, so I pulled it out. A plain brunch with daisies wouldn't seem appropriate. Not for this scene.

That Monday, waving the familiar gravy-stained to-do list at Dorothy, I told her we would go all out. *Wax table. Polish silver. Iron linen.* I pointed to where I'd written *Turkey Apron* at the bottom, in big letters—another family tradition—so she could see. She loved that apron.

"You haven't done all this since Mom," she said, looking happier than she'd been in weeks. Mischievous, even. "If you make the cornbread stuffing, I won't even need to fire up the bong!"

She watched to make sure I knew she was joking. That wasn't always clear to me, with all the changes in her.

She spent her week working hard in her room, on her project. My guess was she wanted to have something ready to show the family. And the week's classic summer weather was perfect for staying inside: overcast skies, a thick morning mist that burned off after noon as the denser stuff unspooled like cotton batting over the horizon, with swelling winds sweeping it ashore like a movie effect. The fog buffered us, and it made indoors feel even warmer as the aromas of our favorite meal pervaded the house: the ginger and lemon of cranberry relish, the clove and cinnamon we would bake into squash pies. Bell's Seasoning would eventually dust every corner with parsley, sage, rosemary, and thyme, and soon the skunky ghosts of Dorothy's medicinal smoke and the leftover funk of my bachelor days were swept aside. Everything felt comfy and cozy for the first part of that week, with the exception of a small quake seven miles offshore, on the San Andreas Fault—a common hiccup just bad enough to put a new worry line in our stucco outside. Looked at from the proper perspective, it was no more than a friendly reminder to take nothing for granted.

I am not an exceptional cook, and I've seen enough of the local foodie scene to know how short anything I do falls from the "California cuisine" that's recently put us on the map. I prefer more humble and trustworthy home fare—the noodles and burritos and pirozhki that have kept us happy out here for so long. I am happiest when cooking, however, and that's why I'd been so glad Carol had consented to come for dinner our first evening together: It's easier for me to be with and talk to someone in a kitchen than anywhere else I know. Unfortunately, despite every effort to get her editing under control, she couldn't make it out to help that week for more than two afternoons.

I relied on Dorothy for a ride once, that Tuesday, to hunt around town for a frozen turkey, which was out of season, with time enough to thaw. The other shopping trips—for fresh herbs, a non-Safeway pinot, or the blue squashes from the Civic Center farmers' market that I like to use for pies—those were trips I did on foot or by bus, because Dorothy needed to stay home and work. In fact, she was so committed to working she allowed us all to play hooky and postpone Sharon that week. After all, the three of us were already acting on our Three-Month Plans, more or less, so why waste time talking with her about it? It pleased me to see how confident Dorothy was at dropping a professional counseling session from her list of "last wishes"— even if they were pretend ones.

Jackie had left behind a tablecloth and napkins we'd received as a wedding gift, and on Wednesday, when Carol first came to help, she handwashed and line-dried all of it. She folded them gently into a drawer with sprigs of lavender—something her mother had taught her, she said, although they'd used old, dried roses back then; no one grew lavender when she was a kid in Paterson. Both afternoons she turned on the old console radio to her classical station and went to work. I saw her smoke—sneakily, out back—only once. She washed the fog-brined windows inside and out, polishing the panes with newspaper while I trimmed our surviving shrub into an intentional-looking shape. On Thursday, from the place she was subletting, she brought over a set of wineglasses and a case of old tarnished silverware, in a velvet-lined box, and she spent an hour buffing it bright with paste and chamois. An absurd chandelier droops over our dining-room table—it's always looked out of scale—but she managed to restore its (and our) dignity with a dozen softer, berry-shaped bulbs. She too seemed to lose herself in the busywork, and we took only one break alone together, walking out to the beach one day after we'd noticed, by the lack of light and noise from under her door, that Dorothy was napping again.

Carol didn't return to help after that; she had too much work to finish. She also said she didn't want to "privilege" herself over Xenia and Dick and imbalance things by appearing to be more established than they were in our family. That felt like an overly fussy concern to me, but I'd acquired a deep trust for Carol's read on people by then, particularly in her understanding of Dorothy's wishes and needs, so I acted like I agreed. In truth, I hadn't given Xenia or Dick much thought all week, but Carol's concern made me feel as if, perhaps, I should start.

I hit a wall on Friday morning. I'd laid a drop cloth over half the dining room and pried open the new gallon of mocha-colored latex paint I'd originally bought for Dorothy's room, but as I stirred, my attention dropping deeper and deeper into the swirling eddies of the thick paint, it dawned on me that the walls would never dry in time. And that the entire house would, in fact, stink. I was alone—Dorothy was still quiet, inside her room—and I sank: *Perhaps all of this is too much? Too late?* I shuddered to imagine how pointless it would feel, hearing someone recount a moment like this at a memorial: *I'll never forget that day I painted the dining room while she was holed up in her room with her headphones on.* I sat like that until the paint acquired a thin skin. I had forgotten it was another chemo day. Once again, sadness seeped in from under her door on a line of drab light.

When Dorothy came shuffling out for more tea, her dour silence reminded me just how much she'd invested in feeling her best for the big dinner. She'd scheduled that day's cycle for the earliest slot available; it would be a more potent drip than the last, and she wanted to give herself plenty of time to get home and rest. She understood this would leave her in bad shape Saturday, but it should be worth it because by Sunday, when she could take her steroids that morning before the dinner, she'd be most likely to feel the full benefit.

I covered the paint, to accompany her to the clinic.

When you're caring closely for someone with a deadly disease, you repeatedly run up against how insignificant your own daily trials are, relative to theirs. Few people can manage living at such a high, existential pitch with any grace. Dorothy was doing beautifully so far. Each time I went in with her, I was humbled to see how comfortably she could chat with her doctor about such extraordinary topics as the size and density of her tumor. Clinicians, nurses, orderlies, even counselors—when had I ever really watched and taken in what these people do? They're bigger than I am. The first time I ever witnessed a woman's wide hands give Dorothy a neck rub one moment, and then glove-up, grab her arm, and slap and puncture a vein in the next,

I gasped out loud. I've dealt with my share of medical professionals before, but until then, I must not have looked any deeper than their game face. No matter how tiny and wrinkled Dorothy looks as we drive in to each appointment, as soon as her name's called in the waiting room she always stands like someone who owns the place—the bandaged commander reentering the battlefield where she, alone, knows the odds of victory. I once fought an urge to applaud. Honest. Every clinician meets her eyes with true respect, and there's one who hails her with an admiration that borders on envy. As she strides in, with her chin out and her arms back, I see the small points of bone in her shoulders, under her T-shirt, and the thinning skin at her elbows where it frowns out of shape. Her narrow neck has become darkly freckled from our beach walks, but even that tan looks unwholesome and artificial in the clinic's light. Her eyebrows have vanished. I can always feel it in advance: the approach of someone dropping their impersonal veneer to "become present" and "get real" with Dorothy. First, their brows flatten as they gaze into each other's eyes for that confirmation that it's okay to let your guard down. Depending on how strong Dorothy feels that day, or how articulate her pain is and how willing she is to describe it with me in the room, the more her and the nurse's eyes will dilate as they talk around it. Their shoulders and voices drop: They make little quips while needles and tubes are unwrapped. *Okay? Couldn't be better.* They reach out to hold hands and wrists sometimes, soothing each other with a closeness that says: *We're doing this—you and me.*

That Friday's treatment felt interminable. She had to ask to have the flow slowed, she was finding it so difficult. She sent me down to the cafeteria and encouraged me to walk outside: It was going to take a few hours. I did as she suggested, and when I returned and called back to her, I found the curtain in the corner drawn around her recliner. She didn't ordinarily use the curtain, and none of the other patients had theirs drawn—it's something of a social scene, usually—but she'd needed privacy. There was no way to knock, obviously, so I gently called her name and riffled the curtain rings. I found her reclining still, pressing a flap of gauze to her lowered arm with one twiggy finger. She looked pale and fatigued as always, but this time her eyes wouldn't meet mine, at first. It looked like she'd been crying.

Her hands were too weak to unroll her sleeve, but she tried feebly anyway, before allowing me to help. I had to guess at what she might need. She let me grip her firmly under one arm as we made our way to the elevator, and for the first time ever, she didn't shrug that help away. We walked at a shuffling pace, and as I supported her I tried to keep up a calm, easy patter to call her attention out and away—to the pigeons, the shafts of sunlight, the blowing leaves—and she seemed comforted by all of that, though she added no words of her own. I eased her up into the Jeep and helped stretch her seat belt, but when we strapped her in she groaned once at some pain inside. I begged her to simply sit, as long as she needed. More than ever I regretted not driving. I was ashamed, in fact. I don't know why she hadn't asked Gerald to join us that day, but I guessed she was saving him for later.

After several deep breaths, she started the Jeep and drove us up the underground spiral and into the light.

At home, she heaved chipped ice for an hour. And then, thank God, she slept.

I knocked on her door later that afternoon, but there was no answer.

Cautiously, I cracked the door. She was lying on her back on her bed. My heart leapt at seeing her with her arms crossed over her chest, but they also rose rhythmically: She was breathing, and asleep. She'd taken off her baseball cap, and I crept in closer to watch the veins pulse gently at her temples. They were lavender, like a baby's. I was again free to take in how drawn her face had become in just the past week—*of course: she hasn't cleaned her plate in days, she who's requested a big family dinner for everyone else.* Her lashless eyelids winced faintly. The bones of her hands looked brittle, with skin too thin to be her own. She looked like someone older, and I felt I was the kid, sneaking around her room. She didn't stir when I pulled the blankets up to her shoulders, or when I pulled down the shade.

And what if she *had* been awake when I first peered in? What could I have said to make that interruption worth more to her than my leaving her to work in peace, alone, while I peeled potatoes? *I love you?* Would that be enough for one of our remaining afternoons at home together? In truth, all I'd hoped for, peeking in just then, was a smile, some reassurance from her that she was as well as could be. But instead, as she breathed shallowly in the shadows with all her video equipment powered down and her chest rising and falling like some fragile mechanism, her lips thin, Dorothy looked like someone who would not be pleased to wake up. Not just yet.

Against my will and best efforts, the bitterness welled up in me again. I worried I'd infect the space around her with it. I picked up the mug and empty water glasses from her workspace, checked that her trash can was empty, and left the room.

I filled the teapot in the kitchen, for when she woke up, and put out the tin of multigrain biscuits she sometimes found easy to keep down. I knew there was nothing more I could do, and that there might be even less to do in the future. I searched for something to write a note on, but all I found in the drawer was a pad Jackie'd left behind, with kittens on it. Dorothy hated cute stuff—daisy magnets, bunny cards—so I searched deeper. I found nothing. Soon the only thing that kept me from dumping the entire drawer in the sink was knowing it would wake her. I ripped a blank page from a cookbook and wrote big enough to fill the whole sheet: *Gone to Safeway. Be back soon.*

But it was no relief to be back in the fog, retracing my steps on another of the paths I've walked for decades. It felt wrong to leave Dorothy behind, asleep. It was unsettling that the world should look the same as it does every other gray day—that while Dorothy lay at home with her arms folded, nothing outside our house resonated her presence.

I walked twenty blocks through the dripping park, then up the hill. I felt quick and thin. I too had been losing weight.

I broke into a sweat by the time I reached Saint Thomas's. It's the church we used to bring the kids to on Christmas and Easter. It's where Dorothy had started elementary school. I sprinted up the steps to go inside. The big doors were locked.

In the paved yard beside it, a summer-school group was playing. There were a few dozen children screaming and bouncing around the asphalt in white shirts and plaid pants and skirts—little kids who would go home that night and eat supper with their families and do homework at the kitchen table, brush their teeth, and go to bed, just like mine used to. A lumpy teacher in a hoodie strained her eyes so as not to appear to be watching me as warily as she truly was, and then I realized I had my fingers curled through the chain-link fence, watching back. But what could I, a damp old man, shout to her over the kids' cries that might help her understand the significance of the silence I'd just run from at home?

"Why are all the doors locked?"

I hadn't meant to yell. She shook her head and turned sharply away from me, stomping her feet to pretend she had shuddered because of the wind. Inside her pockets she rolled her fists, feeling around for a tissue, or a phone.

I marched off a dozen more blocks, to the Russian cathedral. I had faith I could get inside there and light all the candles I wanted. *Probably Xenia had been setting me up earlier for this very moment.* So what? Why not buy some visible hope for a miracle? Didn't someone wager that you can't lose by living as if you believed in God, even if you don't entirely, because living in a godless world is so much emptier? And if, in the end, you find out God *does* exist, then you win all the more? I'd never liked the calculation in that. I don't know what it means to "live as if God exists." Does it simply raise the stakes in your life? Isn't pretending hypocrisy? I realized I'd never taken a strong stand: I've been constitutionally incapable of true atheism, too full of second-guesses, and unable to act on partial beliefs. *People should settle such questions for themselves before retiring, you'd think.* Or before their kids get cancer.

Did Dorothy believe in Carol's "higher power"—about which I've asked nothing? Gerald once joked that he believes because he keeps getting Higher Power Bills. Did she find that funny? Maybe that was part of why I felt so exposed in front of Sharon: Because the first time

I'd ever asked my daughter if she believed in God was in a doctor's office—and even that was after prompting from a paid professional. It felt like I'd failed her—something necessary we should have given our kids along with warm meals and clean clothes.

One clear thought surfaced: *To live as if you believe in God, do as Xenia does.*

It was no surprise to find one of the tall bronze cathedral doors wide open to the swirling fog. I bounded up the steps, as if chased, into the sweetly fragrant darkness.

A heavy-lidded woman with a bandanna over her white hair tried to mask her alarm at my sudden entrance. She gave me a tiny, grim nod in welcome; I walked up to her as if summoned. A green banker's lamp glowed on the counter before her. She pressed a little book flat against her chest in her surprisingly round, veined hand, with a knotted prayer rope wound around her wrist. The print on her book was Cyrillic. I finally let my eyes drift up to meet hers, and then, without moving, her expression opened, and deepened.

"I need candles," I said, looking anxiously over her shoulder, inside to Saint John's shrine.

She pursed her lips as if to work something out of her teeth, but instead pointed down to boxes on the counter, between us.

The beeswax tapers—some plump, some slender—smelled like light and warmth itself. I pulled out two, just as Xenia had. There was no price tag on anything. In fact, as my eyes scanned the counter, I saw nothing was marked—the little icons, the tchotchkes, the incomprehensible books and boxes of powdered incense. I didn't know what anything cost.

I looked up at the woman, who all the time had been watching me.

"What do I owe you?" I said, trying to sound as if I'd merely forgotten. How absurd: trying to mask the fact that you don't know the answer while asking a question.

She smiled a little and tipped her head a bit to one side, hunching her shoulder forward. Her expression could have meant *Nothing* or *Everything*, but it also directed my eyes to the square, worn wooden box with a slot on top, next to the candles. I stuffed in a few bills.

I put my palm up to peer through the smoked glass that separated us from the nave. The candles, floating in clusters here and there in the darkness, flickered like stars. I would need to go in and walk past these stands to get to Saint John in repose.

"May I go in?" I asked.

Again, she looked at me with puzzled concern.

She tightened her scarf and stepped out unevenly from behind her station. She was surprisingly tall; the hem of her rusty smock seemed to float above her feet with every other step. I couldn't tell by her chapped-looking cheeks if she were put out by my interruption, impatient, or pressed by more urgent cares. Maybe she worried that, unless she hurried, I might turn and run back out to the street—which just then was a strong impulse of mine, I confess. But when she stopped huffing and pushed on the glass with one flattened hand, she cupped my shoulder, warmly, with the other and said "Come," speaking to me for the first time. She even gave me a little nudge.

As I entered that perfumed space I felt her near, but I was surprised, when I glanced back, that she hadn't actually followed me in.

My eyes adjusted to the new light. I was the only visitor.

It stunned me how familiar the place smelled, as if I'd already spent many days there, over years, rather than just one visit weeks ago with Xenia. Once again I felt the wonder I had on that prior trip—that this entirely other world had existed right alongside my everyday life, a life that now seemed to fade into the distance with each additional moment I stood still here. It was also amazing that such a dark, dense space could feel so delicate and light—an airiness that seeped into me. But my heart beat faster at the same time, as if I were trespassing: an intruder.

I glanced back to reassure myself by the woman's silhouette, behind the glass. She had indeed been watching me. She pointed me toward the shrine, as if I still didn't know: *Go.*

I tried to wave back convincingly, but the sight of the shrine, with its casket and flowers, sobered me fast. I recalled how Xenia continually crossed herself as she approached the saint. I tried to do the same, facing east, as I took a step forward. I fought the impulse to reach all the way down to the parquet floor and graze it with my fingertips, as she had done. That gesture was too foreign to me. It only would have reinforced my creeping fear that I was a fraud.

Behind me the glass door closed snugly, with a sigh. I was alone.

I had my own candles this time; I knew how to begin. At the brass stands on either side of the shrine, I held each of my trembling tapers in the lamp in the middle of the tray until they took light, and then planted them deep in the sand to stand upright. I stood back and crossed myself as I'd been taught by nuns, growing up. But then, once done, my doubts redoubled. One of my candles slowly tipped to drip wax over the rim and onto the floor. I leaped forward and instantly set it right, and in that sudden, unthinking act, I found my place. I was present—wholly there. My candles burned straight.

This is good.

I took the final step up to the sepulcher and stopped to stare at last.

I must have expected that the incorrupt hands of a saint should appear as white and warm as ivory, elegantly folded, and somehow aglow, but the desiccated skin and bird-thin bones that curled around the crucifix Saint John held to his heart were disturbing to see. They betrayed suffering more than otherworldliness. His face, which must have been equally wan, was covered by an ornate gold brocade cloth. For that I was glad. His body was child-sized, but I'd already learned that from Xenia's booklet: He'd been arthritic, and small from birth. He never slept more than a few hours, nor on a bed, for the entirety of his career. Instead he stayed up all night writing, reading, and praying in his small office off the kitchen of the orphanage he'd established nearby, catching naps as he sat. He's nicknamed "the Wonderworker." One picture shows him hunched over his desk, like Dorothy before her monitors, and he looks miserably uncomfortable, with his neck crooked as he peers through big-rimmed glasses at his old Royal typewriter, but he often slept in that same posture. Sometimes they found him asleep on the floor, prostrate before his icons. Perhaps even more uncomfortably.

I crossed myself and descended slowly to my knees, on the cushion.

Xenia had made three prostrations when she approached Saint John, coming closer with each step. Recalling that, I felt an urge to rise, walk back, and begin again. To do it right.

That's enough, was the stronger, overriding thought. *You're here now.*

I began to whisper an "Our Father" as I would at a wake, but the words came out indistinctly and soon were muffled by a rising surge of traffic noise outside. I took a breath and, just as quickly, the street noise receded. Perhaps someone had come in, opening the big doors. Maybe my time would be up soon.

I leaned in closer to him.

"I've come for Dorothy," I whispered.

How foolish you look, begging this man's corpse that the daughter you left behind at home—alone—not pass away like he has. And like you will too.

This five-foot body did not allow me to take anything lightly, however.

A dread flooded my heart at the possibility that what I'd really hoped to accomplish in visiting Saint John was simply to make myself feel better—as if, once finished, I might feel reassured I'd covered my bases and done all I could, as a father.

Once finished?

"I'm sorry."

Of course I wanted Dorothy to get better. Could a prayer, or any wonderworking saint's intercession, do that? Truly, I do not know. Not the way I know other things. The way I live every day attests to how much I trust the words of doctors, and caregivers, and books, and to how I believe research and statistics far more than anything else, even myself. I bet most people admit the same when forced by similar, extreme circumstances to take a stand. But what a sting I got, hearing it said outside myself—that lack of faith. Nothing kills a hope like your declaring it impossible. Up till then, a little part of you must still remain open, even if the odds of winning the lottery look better. But in that instant, kneeling in the shrine before Saint John, I knew a big part of me would feel like a hypocrite if I'd prayed: *Please save my daughter.*

But I would also have felt a profound shame—a fear, even—to *not* pray that. Not praying would be even more selfish, as if I valued my own wobbly integrity over her life. As if her well-being weren't worth my pride.

I recoiled, lifting my fingers from the glass as if my flaws might taint what I touched. My gaze dropped. I studied the sooty scuff marks and blobs of wax on the parquet floor, the grit-filled gaps between wood tiles and the pilled edge of the carpet runner. I began to count the soiled, folded petitions that believers had tucked beneath the edge of the glass for Saint John to read, and marveled at how just seconds before I myself had considered writing one with the pencil nubs and cards stacked by the icon. A tissue was wadded beneath one corner: Damp with tears of contrition? Some broken pilgrim's sweat? The trail of lint-stuck lamp oil that dripped where people dip their fingertips to bless themselves with it—I saw how unmiraculously it stains the floor and dulls the base of the brass lamp stand like splatter from a gutter.

That bitterness sickened me—as it should—but I couldn't think it away.

Was it really fear of being a hypocrite that made me think of running when, at the same time, a similar fear kept me there? Had I come that far to please Xenia because I was worried of falling further out of my son's world too? Did I remain kneeling because the matron guarding the doors was likely still watching me? I bet she had little surveillance cameras and black screens she monitored under her counter, next to the phone and light switch. Wouldn't it be more respectful and reverent for me to simply stand up and walk out? Or was it something more than a cowardly self-regard that kept me from boldly pleading with this little man?

I drew closer again to stare at his humble figure to prove I wasn't troubled by the sight of it. But I was. I watched his grayed veins for a pulse; I held my breath, searching for signs of life in this body that had stopped living more than thirty years ago. But the longer I stayed by his side, the more pity and dread I felt. And with that, awe.

The darkness swirled open and deepened around me. Each authentic wisp of reverence that rose in me, for him, fluttered in the reminder that every hope I'd brought for Dorothy was just as thin as all the other dreams I'd never dared to imagine I could make real. Like the one where Jackie comes back and, without any need to say *I'm sorry*, looks into my eyes once more with that big-eyed joyful laugh. Or where my brother shaves his face again, suits up, starts chewing gum, and throws me a curve ball.

I held those dreams long enough for them to die. That my daughter will outlive me: That's the dream to act on. Now.

"Forgive me. I'm praying on my knees to one day believe. Not because I do."

My fingers clutched the smudged glass like the edge of a cliff. They slipped. So I let go. There was nowhere to slide but facedown, forehead to the carpet. In someone else's context, this would have been a prostration, but I was gasping for breath like a man spit free from a wave. The pile of the carpet was deep, and as I gripped it my thoughts leached away.

Even if I were a hypocrite, at that moment I was also someone who'd been drawn close to this small man who'd guided thousands of exiles through revolution and outside their language, who'd shepherded hundreds of orphans across the globe, and who never rested until all those he loved were flourishing in their new home. I was not being called upon to do anywhere near as much—just to face up to some bad possibilities.

A cool gentleness, long hidden from me, surfaced. It pooled like a spring, suffusing the moment with more sweetness than any prayer I uttered on my own. And slowly, with that humility, came hope.

CHAPTER 13

Sunday morning's weather was perfect—damp and dark—as wintry a San Francisco day as you could hope for in early August. My kids, as natives, always see wet, overcast days as holiday weather, the same way I did snowstorms when I was a boy. That day's fog was a gift. I opened the front drapes, lit a fire log, turned on a few lamps, and everything glowed golden, ready for company.

Again, I'd woken up too early. I sat out front with my morning coffee—with two, actually—and watched the passersby: some dog-walkers, a hooded mother with a stroller. A surfer waved. I was grateful for the everyday good fortune to be in this place, which had been home for half my life, and for all of our kids' lives. We were doing right to wring yet another day's living and memory from it, come what may.

Dorothy shuffled out to me as if on cue. She wore sheepskin slippers and some red woolen socks she must have put aside for the day. She'd swaddled herself like a doll in the crocheted coverlet I'd pulled up to her chin the night before. Her eyes were red but sparkling. Clearly she was feeling better and happier to be awake and afoot than she had for weeks, especially the week we'd just finished. Smiling, she glanced at the blazing hearth. She felt the same fleeting holiday magic too.

"Happy Thanksgiving!" I said as she gathered us tightly in her wrap to hug. She still felt frail, but she smelled so much more like a warm, drowsy Dorothy than she had the day before. It's an animal thing, knowing the scent of your kids, and that everyday familiarity was something I'd been missing, without knowing it, due to her chemo and occasional smoking. It was comforting to hold her close and to remember how she'd felt when she was a small, soft girl.

She curled into the couch to face the fire. I rolled an old leather hassock, which Carol had somehow revived, closer to her. I offered to make tea. Jokingly, she wagged a languid finger in the air: *Yes, dear—please do.* At last, she was ready to accept the royal treatment—to embrace, finally, all the pampering attention we'd hoped to give her for so long. For a day, at least.

When I returned, the fire was crackling with multicolored flames, as advertised. Dorothy thumbed through the orange crate of worn LPs I'd brought up from the garage. For old time's sake, we loaded a stack on the record changer in the console and together watched, in silence, as it teetered and clicked through its gears, dropping a single album to the platter. She even clapped a little in delight.

She tucked back into the couch with her tea to read liner notes. Warm and well wrapped, she looked like the embodiment of coziness, so I slipped back to the kitchen. I wanted to spare her the mounting anxiety that always precedes roast turkey. It's a panic I fight each Thanksgiving, no matter how well I prepare and how many times I've done it—the daymare of an oven belching smoke, a withered bird. It usually goes away once I get busy, and there were sausage and onions to fry, and sage to chop for cornbread stuffing, and once that sauté was sizzling in a cast-iron pot, laying the foundation for Dorothy's Big Day, we could all breathe easier. That was my hope, anyway.

This gathering was going to be the largest we'd hosted in a decade. I did not expect to like Dick. I surely didn't look forward to meeting him, nor could I imagine digesting anything well while facing him and Jackie across the table, should he sit next to her—which he would, of course, and which is why I'd asked Carol to make place cards to keep them off to my side, out of my direct sight lines. Carol was dreading this mixer too, and she couldn't hide it from me. Last Thursday, in the final hours she'd joined us, she'd worked harder and quieter than either Dorothy or I had ever seen. She'd probably spent all of Saturday chain-smoking at home, in preparation. Dorothy was the only one of us who seemed confident people could work out for themselves where to sit, and what to say and do. I'd done everything I could to let go, even though I did bring the Scrabble set in from the garage, in case we needed a mixer. (I'd pulled the Twister set out too, but Carol helped me think better of that.)

My kitchen timer rang for the first of what would be a dozen times that day. I'd been walking in a small circle, sink to counter to fridge to stove to sink. The pipes shuddered deep within the house as Dorothy shut off the shower. I peered out at the empty living room. Coltrane's "Central Park West" wafted through—a three-minute gem I once re-played for an hour without tiring: It's bottomless. *We can play that again tomorrow, after company leaves.*

Carol arrived as early as she'd promised. She had her own key to the front, so when she pushed into the kitchen holding out some droopy sunflowers in her fist, she'd startled me as I stood at the sink, staring out the window. She looked different. She'd had her hair done. It was the same natural salt-and-pepper as before, but shorter, cut just above her shoulders, and her curls looked looser. They bounced. They also hid her face a bit, so you had to look deeper in to find her eyes, and when I did, it was unclear if she was happy with it. Although she didn't often use makeup, that morning her lips were shiny, and she wore a tweed jacket and a russet turtleneck the color of an autumn buckeye. She looked professional but, behind her eyes, she appeared to be just as wound-up as I had begun to feel.

No peck on the cheek that day: She scoped me up and down slowly, like a stranger, until her eyes stopped, smarting, at my chest.

"What are you *wearing*?" she said.

It was the turkey apron. I'd forgotten. For Dorothy, each year I wear this thing the kids gave me for Christmas, with tie-straps like tail feathers. The chest pocket is a beak. You can guess the rest.

She wasn't smiling. She swept past to hang her jacket on the porch.

"I'm on painkillers," she announced flatly. "Just telling you."

"Was it from gardening last week?"

Holding back, she again scanned my clothes warily.

"It's everything." She knotted her apron too tightly, cinching her waist. "I got no sleep last night either. All Chuck has in his cabinet is Vicodin. So I'm numb and dumb now, instead of sore and tense."

She uncovered the pie we'd made. That stopped her a moment. She inhaled deeply and held it up to admire, turning it around and around for at least half a minute before putting it down to turn aside and sneeze. She tucked a fresh tissue into my apron pocket too. Then, holding her flowers high like an axe, she sallied out the swinging door—which we'd recently regreased, for the first time in years—to the dining room. Her crepey skirt swirled behind her. She'd never worn a skirt before, that I had noticed. But then, I recalled, we'd known each other for less than two months.

Before the door shut snugly behind her, I heard the honeyed-sounding stereo play Vivaldi—a turkey-prep favorite in our house. Dorothy must have snuck that one into the stack. It made me long to sit down with a drink. It also sounded like it was skipping—it's difficult to tell when Vivaldi skips—so I peeked out to make sure I'd heard right.

Carol stood above the console with its heavy lid in her fingertips. She peered inside almost fearfully.

"This turntable *works*?" she said, watching the platter revolve.

"It did for Dorothy."

Wow, she said distantly. Then she smacked the side of the cabinet hard with her palm, sending the skipping tone arm back into its groove.

At the sound of her name, Dorothy returned to the room. She too had dressed for the occasion. *And why not?* After weeks of wearing T-shirts and sneakers and jeans, she'd put on a white blouse, gray slacks, a short tux-like jacket with padding for her shoulders, and something like a satin jockey's cap with a small bill on it. She had extra energy—she must have taken her steroids that morning. She'd drawn her brows in a little, and her eyes were bright with drops. In fact, she looked so disconcertingly well put-together it nearly sent me back to the kitchen to overstir something. Instead, Carol and I simply froze.

Without a word, Dorothy posed, pivoted, and stopped wide-legged on her red platform sneakers with her hands at her waist, swiveling her head over her shoulder to face us. The effort she made was evident, but she lifted her palms exultantly to the ceiling.

"Send me off in *this!*" she said, cackling unnaturally.

Carol cocked back like she'd been slapped. "*Dorothy!*" she shouted, in shock.

I too must have gasped.

Our suppressed grief registered slowly for her. She dropped her hands, then shrank like a kid.

"Sorry about that," she said. She didn't sound like herself—like she'd fully meant it. She tried harder. "Really—just joking. I must be working alone too much."

It appeared that the big day ahead—the day *she* was directing—made her feel a little disoriented too.

She stepped up to us, but Carol walked off to find something else to do.

"It's too early for jokes like that," I whispered. "Please be nice."

She nodded. She gave me one of the thumbs-up, toothy *Yes we can!* smiles we'd been mocking ever since working with Sharon. But that was just as annoying: not funny.

Behind me, Carol unfurled the tablecloth and bits of lavender filled the air and sprinkled across the floor. She paid no attention. Instead, she frowned and pressed her palms on the table, as if the linen were creeping away.

Dorothy watched from a distance.

"What can I do?" she said to me.

"Well, since you're all gussied up," I said, "go pick out something you want me to wear."

She brightened and rushed back to my room.

Carol and I set the table as if in slow motion, cautious and silent until it sparkled with silver and crystal. When the record changer began chugging through its paces to drop another album, we halted like guards on alert, but soon Paul Desmond played sweet as always, after all these years. Dorothy returned suddenly to catch us with her camera. We tried to busy ourselves as she buzzed around taking photos of everything else—the table, the spinning vinyl, my apron.

She grabbed Carol by the hand and forced her to sit by her on the couch to look at the photo albums I'd pulled up from the garage. Carol was quickly stilled by our old snapshots. She relaxed, looking up now and then to compare us to the people she'd never met—me as a new teacher or father of toddlers, Dorothy with her first earring or her oversize bass in her punk band. Carol seemed to wag her head in wonder at how little of our family's lives she knew, and it made me think how much less we knew of hers. When she pulled the book tighter to inspect pictures of Jackie, I realized today would be their first meeting. After she tapped her finger on one page, marveling at how much Gerald resembled her own son at that age, she rummaged in her purse for a photo of her own. But before she found it, Dorothy had blithely flipped ahead without waiting for her. It was surprising to see these jarring little discourtesies creep into Dorothy's behavior that morning, and as much as Carol tried to overlook it while she held her wallet open to show her own picture—which Dorothy ignored—it was clear her fuse was shortening too.

The table trembled as Gerald and Xenia tromped up the front steps, announcing themselves even before we heard his hearty knock.

Ho, ho, ho! he shouted, ducking into the doorway with a red bag full of gifts wrapped for Christmas. He and Xenia donned their usual boots and leather but also wore garish holiday sweaters that were so ugly they elevated my apron to the realm of haute couture. Xenia's fit tightly.

Gerald stood grinning, wet-eyed and pink from the cold. He slowed and scanned the room, looking for a tree or other Christmas props. He took in my apron, noted the squash on the table. Then, in dismay, his smile fell: He'd thought Dorothy wished to celebrate Christmas, not Thanksgiving, in August. He looked embarrassed at first. But as he stared, finally seeing her diminished self for the first time in a few weeks, his even deeper worry became clear to us all: *The cancer's so bad you can't even wait three months to do Thanksgiving in November, like always?*

Gerald doesn't hide his feelings well. As his shoulders drooped, even Xenia watched him in alarm. It's difficult for anyone to remain upbeat around cancer, and Gerald, despite his constant wisecracking, has never been able to con anyone effectively, but he couldn't even start to hide this surge of sadness. I feel such affection for him at times like these, when he's brave but overwhelmed: He's the young man my brother might have been if he'd been surrounded by less death, a loving mother, and a city full of smart people to hang with, with no one easy to fool, like me, to make him feel tougher than he really was.

"Well, *well* then!" Gerald said, exaggerating as he pushed his hair back, unable to focus. He stepped in front of his bag of gifts, as if to hide them. He looked like a prom-band crooner who'd misplaced the lyrics, trying to buy time.

Dorothy rushed up to him. Xenia, somewhat alarmed, released the arm she'd been clutching and stepped aside to make way.

"Um, actually," he mumbled, struggling for a story to hide in. "X and I weren't so sure we'd be around this Christmas. And you know how Dad is when you store gifts early in the garage—I didn't want him thinking one night that all these presents were for *him*—"

Dorothy tugged his collar. She too enjoyed getting him flustered.

"Really, Gerald?" she said, batting her lashless eyes. "And where do we think we *will* be this Christmas?"

She spoke far too brightly. It stung him anew to look at her up close—but she was oblivious. He swallowed hard and reshifted his weight.

"Oh, I thought, we—"

She pulled him down by his ear for a kiss, but as she did, he stooped and grabbed her in both arms, as if she'd fallen back, and hugged her to his heart. Lifting her, he buried his face in her neck and held her so tightly her feet dangled, limp, as he shuddered back a dry sob.

She waved helplessly behind him until she could wrap her free arm around his neck.

It took him a moment to become aware of the size of his emotions, compared to what anyone else in the room was willing to expose.

Gently, he lowered her back to her feet. He wiped his eyes with his fist, sniffed once, breathed hard, and again looked up.

Carol shot back to the kitchen.

Dorothy readjusted her cap. She was not teary. If anything, she looked a bit harder than she had before. Coolly, she kissed Xenia on both cheeks, like old friends—clearly, they'd met before—and as they clutched elbows, Xenia shook her too, with a deep, reverential gaze before letting go.

"At least I make no Christmas blini," Xenia said, smiling despite seeing that she was not understood. She proffered the foreign-looking vodka she'd been clutching in her painted, bitten fingers. "For table."

Dorothy palmed the bottle back to me. She pulled Xenia—with her brother, reattached—to the fire. The flames had grown higher from the cold air rushing in the door, and the log had broken down to spread red, smoldering lumps upon the hearth.

We all got busy making festive again. Gerald slammed back one of the ales he'd brought and squatted to mess with the fire. Xenia accepted some bubbly. Carol ferried out dishes of cheese and nuts and olives, making multiple trips with unnecessarily small loads. Dorothy continued taking pictures of everyone and everything, without a word, as if deliberately clinging to her standard family role. Once Gerald shucked off his sweater and helped X out of hers, I left the young people to themselves.

I returned to the kitchen to drag Carol back, and found her stabbing at the frost in the freezer with a chopstick. She was digging a tunnel in the ice.

"Ain't no spring chicken, is she?" she said without turning to me. "He's what—twenty-six?"

It was such an unusually catty thing for her to say that it took me a moment to hear.

"She's only thirty-three," I said. "You remember how young thirty-three used to feel."

"Not at *twenty-six* it didn't," she said. She stopped. "Twenty-six to thirty-three is like a quarter of your life."

She thrust again at the frost.

"I like her," I said. "She cares for him. She appreciates things. She thinks more than the other girls of his I've met."

"So *you* know her that well?"

"I ran into her once. At the library, in fact. Why, what's your read?"

"Well, we just met for the first time—today, of all days. So I don't really know *anything*."

Again—the sharp tone.

"If it's the vodka," I said, "I doubt she knows you don't drink."

And? She stared back at me, incredulous. *So?*

"You know it's not that," she said. "Although, who *does* bring a fifth of booze to brunch?"

"It's cultural. She doesn't know better. And it's a turkey dinner, not brunch."

She shook her head.

"You really want my 'read'?" she said. "If I'd met her for the first time—which I just did—and if I didn't know any more about her than that she's Russian—"

"Ukrainian."

She made a face—*Just like I said!*—brandishing her chopstick.

"And if I didn't know anything else, I would still tell you she wants a husband. And a baby. *Fast.* She knows what she's got her hands on there: Your Gerald, that boy, he's–a–a *dumpling*."

That was a new one to me. Must be women's jargon for something, I thought. To move on, I assumed she meant "a simple, good thing."

Another timer went off.

"But even if you are right about her," I said, "is that all so bad?"

"I just wonder," Carol said, "what he'd think if he ever took a day off for himself? If he could stop running around patting everything down and catch his breath for once?"

We heard music and talk just faintly through the door.

Carol turned and stabbed harder, with the beat of the music.

"Her bag's Gucci," she said. "That emerald looks real too. I know he's making good money for a kid his age, but you've got to wonder when a boy like him falls so hard for an older woman of the world like Xanadu . . ."

"Xenia," I said.

Her chopstick snapped in the ice. She extracted it and shoved the bottle, neck-first, into the hole she'd made. She'd broken a sweat, so she splashed her face with water at the sink before hopping back to the table to snap green beans. It felt like she was playing *Beat the Clock*.

I waited.

"All I'm saying," Carol said, "is maybe he could use some advice." She pitched her beans hard at the colander. "*You* should notice these things. Of all people."

Even if that remark were not anything approaching an assessment of me and my same-age ex, Jackie—who, I again recalled, she would meet in minutes, also for the first time—I still couldn't understand why she'd say such a thing. Carol had always been direct with me—clear as a bell. So these hasty little digs, with the kids in the next room—they weren't like her, and they threatened to sour the whole day. We had both promised to keep things waltzing along for Dorothy. We'd tacitly agreed to that. And I finally understood I couldn't do it alone.

"She's religious," I said.

"*So?*"

"So there's probably more motivating her than what you see. Maybe she does want a family. Maybe she does like nice things, or—I bet—maybe the bag's a fake. So what if her life's taken detours. Yours did too, right, when you were young?"

Her eyes locked on mine. She looked stricken. Her hands groped carelessly at the tabletop for stray beans, as if they might run away from her like the tablecloth had threatened to earlier.

"You surprise me, Carol. Why not give her a chance?"

She pushed back into a chair, her hair bouncing. She took a long, cleansing breath, as we'd been trained to do.

"Why *not*?" Her lips quivered. "Because I am *a wreck*, okay? Today's my Quit Day. My *third one* this month. That was going to be my gift to Dorothy—it's all she wanted from me. I promised her weeks ago. I wanted to give her that one little hope."

She stared down, rubbing her sore, shaking palms, and getting teary.

I sat next to her.

"As far as I'm concerned," I said, "if we're all still talking to each other by the end of the day, we've made it. Objective achieved. I don't think Dorothy could ask for more than that. To tell you the truth, I don't really think she has a right to."

That helped Carol, hearing that. She nodded.

"That scene—by the door?" she said, puffing her cheeks. "Your *poor* son. I can't take any more of that, you know? I was actually getting *pissed* at her—at Dorothy! Like, what the hell is she doing this for, forcing everybody together like this? Who needs more drama? I didn't sign up for this stuff. This ain't *my* family."

"You're every bit as much a part of this family as you want to be," I said.

"*That* you *are* right about," she said.

Finally, she sighed.

"Look," I said. "I plan to have a shot with dinner."

She didn't care.

"So maybe you can smoke today too?" I said.

She wagged her head.

"No, no, *no*! I've already got this damn nicotine thing on me," she cried, yanking in frustration at the cuff of her sweater. Like a junkie, she bared her arm and showed me the patch.

Xenia burst through the door. She blinked in the bright lights, holding Gerald's empties. Her cheeks shone. If she were mystified by what Carol and I and Carol's forearm were doing at the table, then her undaunted, sparkling eyes told us that mystery was part of the everyday for her.

She looked first to Carol—"Excuse!"—and then, to me, she said: "Jim—you have ashtray?"

With a terrible shredding sound, Carol tore the adhesive from her arm. She stood, took Xenia by the wrist, and led her out the back door, where they wiped down two lawn chairs. Outside, while I cooked, they huddled together in the fog, puffing and, soon, laughing like old friends. Through the porch window I saw Xenia talking more and more, making her big gestures and faces. Carol, with a mug on her knee and a smoke in hand, leaned in, enrapt: my favorite person to talk to. I longed to join in. *Later.*

In the living room, Dorothy and Gerald sat together, facing the fire with the photo album between them. He had his arm around the back of the couch, his hand dwarfing and lazily rubbing his sister's shoulder as she leaned over the book. I had to hold back to catch my breath. When I was a young parent and the kids were small, I used to daydream that one day I'd stumble upon a moment such as this, where I found our moist little bundles all grown up, well groomed, and witty, talking warmly with each other on their own. *Imagine how proud you'll feel.*

Now I know.

I wanted to sit with them too, but it wasn't time yet. I looked over their shoulders.

They had the book open to a series of photos I remember well: Jackie pushing Dorothy's stroller up a very steep incline of Russian Hill. Dorothy was strapped in, and she'd repeatedly spilled over like a slinky to touch her toes, dangling her bunny's ears into the stroller's wheels, which had jammed and frustrated her mother. I'd shot a full 35 mm roll that day, taking pictures first from the front (facing them, aiming downhill as they trudged up toward me), from behind, and then from the opposite sidewalk, across the street, documenting the event from every angle. Looking over the kids' shoulders, I noticed for the first time how Jackie had been gritting her teeth in every shot except those taken from the front, when she could see me facing her. She must have felt compelled to force a smile for posterity. Until that moment, my long-standing memory of the day had been what Jackie always said it was—a crisp day in autumn when we took Dorothy for a walk under the yellow ginkgoes to our neighborhood park. But now, seeing the objective record, I could better guess what Jackie might have truly felt that day.

I might have an entire life to re-remember.

Dorothy smiled back up at me.

"You know I confused the camera with you, right? My first word?"

She grabbed the book and thumbed back to an earlier page, full of Jackie's loopy handwriting. I'd never seen those notes either.

"Look here—Mom wrote that every time I saw a camera, I'd say: *Dada*."

This tickled Gerald.

"Even *then*," he shouted, shaking his fist in the air. "An artistic genius!" He lifted his beer to toast her. He'd spoken too loudly for just us, but at last he was enjoying himself.

The doorbell sputtered.

The sound was all the more alarming for how swiftly Dorothy slammed the book shut. She leaped to reshelve it by the fireplace. Gerald too jumped up and drained his beer in two athletic gulps.

It was Jackie, obviously. She began knocking before I could answer the bell. We were all as ready as could be, so I opened up.

Having just studied photos of her in distress, time and distance suddenly melted at seeing her again at our front door, in the flesh. She forced a smile and stood tall. Beneath her damp scarf, her wet eyes bulged in anticipation of every possible scenario she might encounter at such a heavily freighted get-together as Dorothy's dinner now threatened to become. But she too looked ready as could be. *Let's go.* Jackie is capable of carrying every feeling in her at full volume, wearing her heart on her sleeve and dragging a wagon to catch the overflow. But that day, staring back at me, she looked perfectly in place for the first time since she'd left. It was even reassuring—a relief—to see her. Her presence fit the scale of the day. I realized then I'd even been looking forward to it.

Most evident in Jackie's eyes was her pained, tender love for Dorothy. Again, her fierce, needy gaze aimed past me to find her inside. And when she did see her, even though they'd gone out together just last weekend, Jackie's wincing confirmed just how great a toll the week's chemo had taken on our daughter, in her eyes. It hurt to watch her assess Dorothy, because I knew how she felt. I almost wanted to hold her and tell her something comforting, but it was best she got that from Dorothy, and Gerald too.

"It's good you're here," I said, making way for her. She quickly pressed a cheek to mine, perhaps as a holiday courtesy. She put a bottle and an envelope in my hands and charged for the kids, where they stood limp by the fire, looking like we'd caught them sticking things through the screen. As I watched, it took seconds more to sense the dapper, silver-haired man who'd stepped up behind her, to stand watching us all.

Dick was just enough outside the door to offer me his hand without stretching, with a wordless cool that would remain his most welcome trait that day. Like Jackie, he was taller than me, and better put-together, all corduroy and suede. He looked a bit vain—one of those men who, despite wearing a full beard, overtrims it in a way that bespeaks more fuss than a regular, daily shave would. He had a stare that would have felt midwestern if I hadn't recalled that he was from the Central Valley—an eyes-wide-apart look that placed his attention far ahead of his aviator frames, instead of up front and present. His straight smile seemed a bit off too. He looked like a game show host sitting in on a news broadcast.

I thumbed back inside and may have said: "See these fine young people she and I have raised?"

He remained in the doorway, conveying nothing but patience and respect for the occasion. Which I appreciated. Either he had good manners or—and this was equally likely, given the smile—he'd arrived half lit. But I smelled no booze on him. Either way, Dick seemed to understand that he'd been invited at Dorothy's request, and that he should be little more than an observer at our table that day—that it would be presumptuous of him to act as if any piece of himself he'd brought along could be as meaningful to our family as we ourselves would be. The very fact that Jackie had just left him there behind her, on the doorstep, said it all, I thought.

I slowly snapped to attention. I stuffed the wine and envelope under my arm and shook his hand. It was bigger and warmer than mine.

"You must be Steve," I said.

Dick chuckled and stepped up. He accepted my offer to take his jacket. And then he gave me a wider smirk that, in turn, reminded me that I was still in my apron.

In the living room, Jackie was tugging at Gerald's sleeve at the same time she swayed Dorothy back and forth, cooing in a wobbly embrace. She'd half shed her coat on the way in—it hung off one arm—and wore a drab, long smock. Still, despite all that gray, or perhaps because of it, she'd become the first person you'd see if you didn't know it was Dorothy's day, or if Gerald weren't speechless, or if you didn't know Xenia and Carol were hiding, pretending to be busy in the kitchen.

Dorothy's chin jutted out over Jackie's shoulder, again giving me her caught-bird look. I couldn't tell if her glassy eyes said *Help?* or not, but it *was* her party—she could do what she wanted. It was easiest just to let Jackie have her moment. Dick seemed to know that too, holding back on the mat with his thumbs hooked on his belt.

Then, as Jackie slowed, I helped her with her coat. That's when I noticed how large the envelope was that she'd given me.

Instantly she turned, the tears still in her eyes.

"Jim, you've *got* to read that soon." She pointed. "It's your copy. They're selling the house."

"*Mom!*" Dorothy shouted, recoiling at the sight of the papers.

Gerald too spun around, angry. "What the *fuck*?!"

"You *stop* that, *both* of you!" Jackie shouted over everyone. "I can't *pretend* this all day. Jim—Old Man Lewis died. His kids are getting this place. They're going to sell it. I think."

They all froze and stared at me.

To everyone's amazement, including my own, my first response was to take a deep, cleansing breath. When I did, I was equally surprised to discover I felt relatively calm. After all, I'd listened to lots of bad news recently, from both Jackie and Dorothy, with the worst of that coming in the past few weeks. And in truth, this didn't feel too shocking—it was "in scope," as Gerald says. More stunning to me was how absurdly relieved Jackie looked at having finally unburdened herself, because this had always been her personal, epic fear for all of us: That we'd one day lose the house and become street people, or have to live off the land somewhere. It was a wonder, in fact, that she'd managed to wait as long as she had, given that (I later learned) she'd known since before her trip, in June. I knew her well enough to understand that her delivering the bad news that day wasn't mean-spirited; she wasn't doing this for effect. She simply felt too exhausted and vulnerable—too old—to hide it anymore. Especially today.

She exhaled, trained her eyes down to the floor, straightened her arms, and waited. Our kids, however, practically vibrated with anxiety as their eyes darted between Jackie and me.

Softly, Dorothy said to me: "That's not totally for sure, Dad."

"How fast could they do this?" I said.

Jackie slowly, woefully, shook her head.

"But what about you?" I said to Dorothy. "You live here now too." She came closer.

"We're looking at every scenario," she said. "If they sell, by law they've got to give you good notice and moving expenses. Sometimes buyers just want investments, so maybe they won't move in at all, or even resell it. Who knows what they'll do? And it's not like the Lewis kids are evil. They're old—I mean, they're like you and Mom. Maybe they just want to hold it and see if the market goes higher."

"Oh, it's going higher," Gerald said, popping open another beer with his key ring. He sounded pissed. "This boom won't bust until Y2K shuts everything down or someone bombs Wall Street."

Dick readjusted himself, by the door. "It's busted already," he said.

Jackie shot him a wary look. He raised an eyebrow at her but kept his mouth square and shut.

"We lost some money," she said, turning to me.

Carol and Xenia slipped out from the kitchen—Carol was holding a single salt shaker while X carried toothpicks. They sensed the gravity of the moment and held back.

Jackie didn't notice. "*Everything's* falling apart," she sputtered. "*Everyone's* grabbing everything. They'll sell as fast as they can—that's what I think."

Dorothy came even closer to me, to block out the others' faces.

"We're talking with them now, Dad, but it's difficult," she said. "Old Man Lewis called and gave Mom an early warning himself, when he was still sick, but his kids didn't know that, so when she contacted them first about this, with a lawyer—it spooked them. They're both in Colorado. They just don't get how crazy things are here."

"I didn't know *what to do*, Jim," Jackie said. "I *didn't*." She sank down to the couch in true remorse.

I admit: I wouldn't have known what to do with that information either.

Jackie said, "I wanted to tell you, but everyone made me wait."

Dorothy kept her eyes on me. She pointed her thumbs back at herself and frowned to show me who "everyone" was. But I didn't regret not having learned all of this sooner.

As everyone stood dumbfounded, watching Dorothy, she looked pleadingly for me to stay calm.

To me, she *was* the only person in the room. Her stare let me know she felt the same. To us, this conversation might have been just another of our morning chats about life, death, or Jeep trips. I slowly recalled how she'd been dropping hints about this, for weeks.

"But—how soon could it be sold?" I asked her again.

"The kids seem overwhelmed—maybe fighting. He owned a lot of properties. They still don't have an executor," Dorothy said. "So there'll be delays. Could take six months or more. And even after the estate settles, given your age, it would be three months minimum before we'd actually need to move, after the new owners tell us."

I very much liked the sound of that—*we*.

What no one else in the room knew, and what I perhaps had not been admitting to even myself before that moment, was that I'd never truly believed this rotting house would outlast us. In my heart, I've been saying goodbye to this place, piece by piece, a little crumbling bit each day for not just the three years since Jackie left it, but perhaps my whole life here. It felt good to admit that. There's a compensation that comes when you finally see your outside circumstance align with what you feel in your heart, even when that something is worrisome. It makes it easier to trust.

Dorothy waited patiently.

"If you look at it one way," I said to her, "one can do a lot in three months."

She smiled. *That's right.*

Carol and Xenia slipped out again. My ex-wife and kids stood apart, watching me, a triptych of worried care. But the four of us were together again, at home, and still talking. In our kitchen, the squeaking door of the oven—a range so old we can't find a replacement hinge—reminded us that we had a fine meal awaiting us, just around the corner. My head filled with all of that. Each line in the room led to Dorothy's eyes, where she stood before me with her hands on her hips, looking stronger by the minute, and better than she had all month. It was easy to move on.

Another, little tremor came up through the floor. It was Dick, still standing just inside the Lewises' doorway, tapping his foot lightly in beat with Brubeck. I pulled him farther in, by the shoulder.

I had Gerald fetch drinks for the others.

Then, I walked back to my room to change.

CHAPTER 14

My bedroom is at the end of the hall, on the back corner of the house opposite the porch. There's a wide window that looks out onto the yard, shaded by a bushy toyon. I keep a smaller chair near that window too, for moments just like this.

I sat. I told myself: If I keep it short, there's no reason to feel guilty for stealing a few minutes to myself, to catch my breath. After all, I'll never again feel so settled in this house.

I left the door cracked. From down the hall, I heard Dorothy share some quick, short words with her mother, but there was no fight. Gerald used his big supervisor voice to offer Dick a drink, as if they were old colleagues or he was mocking him, but soon they too spoke genially—discussing computer things. An unusually hushed Xenia introduced herself and Carol to the room, but Jackie's nose-blowing drowned out most of the quiet courtesies that followed. I didn't need to listen for more: Everyone was acting as they should.

I tossed Jackie's and Dick's coats on my bed. They were made of matching golden leather. They smelled alike and were similarly, smartly tailored. It pleased me to cover his with hers, then both with my apron.

On my pillow lay the shirt and tie Dorothy had chosen for me to wear. I hadn't seen the tie in a very long time. It was a gift she'd given me for Father's Day, when she was fifteen—the same year we visited City Lights together. She'd saved her babysitting money for weeks and mailed off to an ad she'd seen in the back of one of our magazines.

The tie is silk, too wide, and bright yellow, with dozens of multicolored signatures printed on it. The overall effect is of graffiti—all but illegible. Years ago, when I first saw it, she'd interrupted me on the porch to make me open it, and I had no chance to think through the moment well enough in advance; my first impulse then had been to hold it closer, for inspection, and see what the hell was scribbled all over the thing. I couldn't tell, really. I have no talent for receiving gifts, particularly those I don't know what to do with. But once I'd begun poring over the names, I recognized Hemingway's surprisingly curvaceous script, and then I got it: *These are all American authors.*

In that moment, back then, I'd forgotten that teenaged Dorothy was standing just beside me, holding her breath to see my reaction to this treasure she'd discovered for me, and into which she'd put so much time and thought—her first grown-up gift. But by the time I'd finally sensed her there and turned back to say thank you, she was withering in disappointment. She'd been watching me closely all that time, and she could tell I found it ugly (it is), and she was already guessing I'd never wear it unless she forced me to. Her hand was just inches from mine, ready to whisk the tie away in a fury. She would return it, she said. I didn't deserve it. I had taken far too long.

In all the years since then, nothing I've said or done could make her talk about that day or listen to my apologies, despite the fact that I've dutifully kept the tie hanging, and ready, at the top of the rack inside my closet. But now the time had come for me to put it on—the moment she'd interrupted me for so long ago.

Conversations brightened down the hall. Glasses clinked as Gerald made a toast. Little hiccups of talk bubbled up around whatever Dorothy, and occasionally Jackie, was saying.

I have not knotted a necktie in years, so it took me a few tries. I did understand that the thing was too wide to tie without a dimple, so I did it again. And as I folded and twisted it over itself, I noticed something I must have missed years before: Very subtly, near the bottom and drawn artfully with a marker in such a way that it fits in with all the others, I found a forgery of a signature I've spent a lifetime looking at from every possible angle: *Jim Finley.*

I let it drop from my hand, and stared instead into the mirror, to finish before my eyes filled with tears.

Where can you run from that? Not even to your room.

I looked at my crooked, puffed-up knot. How lucky I was to have this second chance to do things right for Dorothy—things I'd neglected. At last, for her, I could walk back out and play my part. But before I did, I knew it would be easier for everyone outside if I shut my door that final inch, for just a moment. My heart was too full. My head wouldn't clear until I wept. So I did.

Finally I made a decent knot. I secured the tie with a big paper clip, for thematic effect—Dorothy would like that—and walked out to my family.

Everyone but Dorothy had their back to me. She stood before the fire, bowing over her camera, which she cradled like some talisman that could keep us alive and together forever. She was happy. At long last, she'd allowed herself to become the center of our attention. Somehow, she'd managed to get everyone on and around the couch, to pose for a group photo.

As I stepped in, her camera, and then her eyes, focused on my tie. She lit up with a joy I could have looked back on all these years, had I not been reading someone else the first time she'd offered her gift.

"Nice knot," she said softly.

She walked across the room to straighten it.

"I just saw this, down here," I whispered, pointing to my name when she drew close. No one else could see or hear.

"I put that there," she whispered back. "Just now."

I struggled to say thank you, and she helped with a quick kiss, nodding me to the couch.

Behind her, the largest of her monitors, her speakers, and other equipment sat at the ready on a utility cart. Just as I'd suspected.

She saw me notice.

"I've made a rough-cut short," she said.

"I've got an uncarved turkey," I said.

"Oh, Carol's got that." She pulled me in. "Come see."

I joined the others.

Dorothy took the floor. She looked briefly at each of us, channeling everything into her wringing fists until her cool returned. Of course she would be anxious—we were her first audience, and this her masterpiece. No doubt she wouldn't have used that term herself, but that's what her project had to be. Because why would she aim for anything less than her best work—her best hope for a full-length feature? The thought made me worry for her until she spoke up, with a voice that came from the deepest part of her, commanding attention.

First, like a gracious director, she thanked us for coming.

"But of course I made you," she said.

We took our cue to chuckle.

"This won't be long. I just want to show you this before we sit down at the table together. Sort of an icebreaker. I understand this dinner was a strange request—especially with three of you so new to the family. I know that."

She gave a little wave out to Carol, who'd just slipped in from the kitchen to stand by the door, holding a serving spoon. Her eyes were wet; she held her free hand to her mouth.

"But you're *all* part of this," Dorothy continued. "Like it or not. And I needed your feedback as soon as I could get it. What, with the bum odds I may be facing—"

Jackie cried out.

"What *odds*, Dotty?"

Dorothy took a deep breath and clasped her hands even tighter, as if to pack that atrocity into the smallest possible package.

"If they decide to go ahead with surgery, and if that goes well, I have a fifteen-to-seventeen percent chance of living more than five years," she said.

Jackie swooned. "*Dotty!?* Why didn't you *tell* me!?" she said, struggling to get up from the couch.

Dick braced her waist with his hand as if she were a falling tree.

"Mom, *please*—can we let Dorothy *do this*?" Gerald said, leaning in to pull her back down to the couch. He looked doe-eyed himself, as if those numbers were news to him too. "Just *let* her—okay?"

For a second, Dorothy's eyes slipped back into the weird, ironic space she'd first entered that morning. But once more she breathed herself back into the room.

"I feel strongest when I'm honest," she said. "And right now feeling strong, here with you, means a whole lot more than any upbeat number they can give me. So."

Quickly she turned and flicked switches on her machines. The screen sucked static into its center. Our collective relief at seeing a few small lights power up was palpable. We were grateful for a place to focus.

"This is just my start," she said, talking to the blank screen. "You're my make-believe audience. It's short—promise."

She pushed one last button before walking over to close the drapes, darkening the room.

The screen remained black. Soon, an orchestra shattered the silence through the big speakers on the floor. A two-word title in bold, block script slapped up on the screen, one word at a time in rhythm with the music: *Where's Dorothy?*

The pounding discord was loud and attention-grabbing, and sounded familiar—*Stravinsky?*—but it was much, much too big-feeling to me. I twisted in my seat, immediately anxious for her, and then embarrassed for feeling that way. *What if it's no good?* What if she'd lost control and this was something dreadful, with an operatic, body-strewn finale and a huge *Finis* covering the screen at the end?

Dorothy deliberately stood at a distance behind us, so I couldn't turn entirely away from the screen to read her face. I panicked that she might fall headlong into the same sort of grandiosity I'd always come face-to-face with the few times I'd tried writing poetry of my own. She should not suffer that isolating humiliation of standing to one side to watch all your imagined grandeur shrivel in the daylight—of discovering yourself to be less of a living quantity than those around you just because they weren't foolish enough to waste their time attempting something too high.

Please—I prayed, on impulse—*let this be magnificent.*

On-screen, the white letters fade slowly. A picture comes up behind them: a close-up of seagrass in a breeze. We pull away to see dunes, the beach stretching out beneath them, and the surf whitening into recognition as we pan up the shore, where joggers and strollers come into focus. By the time the title's vanished, we stop in front of a lumpy golden retriever, digging in the sand. The dog faces us, working with all her cross-eyed might as if she's trying to find water in a desert. There's something ludicrous about the dog's earnest brow and the way her fat body rocks as she digs, burrowing so deeply into the hole with both paws at once that she drops halfway in as her hind end seesaws up—as if this time, at long last, she'll dive right through to the other side. We zoom in slowly to the dog's droopy brow as waves and seabirds fade in volume behind her. A cool, clear voice—Dorothy's, closely miked—speaks.

"One day after I turned thirty—after I caught my boyfriend in our bed with someone else, after I was passed up again for a permanent job, and after a golf ball cracked my windshield as I drove through the park—I found a lump in my gut. I had a sonogram, a scan, and a biopsy. I was given a guess of how long I might live."

The dog freezes, on-screen, and stares down the hole, tongue hanging.

"So now," the voice-over says, "I overlook the small stuff. Now I focus on one big question: 'What's next?'"

The dog cocks back and barks once down the hole. Her tail swats, stiff and slow, to one side, and she barks again. Nothing emerges.

Dorothy leaned in close behind me, and to my profound relief, she was chuckling.

"You cannot buy a shot like this dog," she whispered. "Perfect."

Everyone heard her. Gerald turned to shoot her a twisted, public grin, and we all breathed easier: *Whew. We can laugh at the goofy dog.*

The dog stands still, hunched, her eyebrows rising as we zoom slowly past to a broadening shot of the beach. The ocean shimmers with sunlight that dances along the tops of waves, then shrinks as the screen darkens and Dorothy's voice continues:

"To find answers," it says, "I must stop asking questions. If I don't, I just keep digging. When I dig, all I see is the hole."

The screen fades to black.

"So," her voice-over says, "here's what I've found so far."

On-screen, we see the front of our house slowly brighten into focus, seen from across the street. Like a day dawning. At first it looks like a still shot, but a crow lands on the Jeep parked out front, stops long enough to shit on the hood, and hops off to scratch the sidewalk. A breeze stirs our shrub, our neighbor's bamboo flutters at the side of the picture, and, in black and white, our house looks cleaner and squarer than it should. It's also unusual to see the front drapes open, and, through the window, the sun striking the very furniture we were sitting on as we watched the film.

Dorothy's voice-over returns:

"A card I received once said: 'To see where you are, know where you're from.'"

On-screen, we zoom close enough to the front door to read our last name, in capital letters, drawn with a black marker on the rusty mailbox I keep meaning to repaint. The camera stops there a moment before fading to the next shot: me, at the kitchen sink in my bathrobe. I come into focus slowly; I'm making coffee. It's a shot Dorothy could have taken any day after she'd moved in. My hair shines in the overhead lights, and we hear muted kitchen noises—water running as I rinse the carafe, the cupboards shutting. I make a muffled grunt as I bend over to dump grounds in the compost bin beneath the sink, and miss. In that brief moment, with my head ducked, we catch Dorothy's reflection mirrored in the grayed window, like a ghost holding a camera.

On-screen, as I make coffee in gradually slower motion, a smoky voice lifts over the fading kitchen sounds. It's Jackie's. She sounds closer and warmer than I'd heard in years.

"One of the *first* things?" Jackie's voice-over says as I wipe up my compost mess. "It was his way with words. A kind of weightiness I loved. That was new to me. My folks had to sell the ranch, and I wanted to run away from all those ticky-tacky houses they were throwing up, and to me, back then, anything 'back East' felt old-world—exciting, but scary too, you know, for a cowgirl. New York? *Scary.* Chicago? Well I figured that's just next door to New York, right?!" Her laugh is beautiful. "But Oxford, Ohio—that sounded just right. I got a full ride for my math scores and my folks were broke. And then I met this handsome boy who talks like a professor and holds doors open for me? That was *it.* He talked like he put more value on things, even though he doesn't hang on to much. I think that's why he's happy with so little."

In her voice-over, Jackie laughs to herself. On-screen I scoop coffee into the grinder in silence, spilling a few beans on the counter, watching them roll away, and stop.

"But our biggest fight?" Jackie's voice says, shifting gears to grow serious. "He'd never told me he had mild seizures before he fell in the library. It was a late night, we were studying for finals, and he just glazed over, dropped, and stared up from the floor and began to—it was a shock, no warning—and then it was over. He told me later he'd stopped taking his medication since he met me; he promised he'd go back on it. And he did. But I could never forget that constant threat. It scared me to death, the thought of him dropping you babies. And when he brought you to the Prop 13 protest, he swore he'd be safe, but then the next week I saw you in the paper, riding high on his shoulders—and I went berserk. That one lasted a few days. But I couldn't stay mad: You were so adorable, Dotty, sitting there, pumping your little fist in the air. You—"

Jackie's voice chokes with emotion.

Throughout this, the camera follows me and my coffee slowly to the porch. Muted, I sit, put my mug on the windowsill, pull a book from the stack, and press it flat to my knee. The camera zooms closer to my profile, and as my eyes blink and read, some background noise—a restaurant—rises in the background. Within that, Jackie's voice-over continues:

"That night," she says, "you were too excited to sleep. You wanted to go to 'work with Dad' again, the next morning. And I said, 'No— *you* are going to school; that's the job girls do.' But you argued with

me for half an hour, like a little lawyer. It kind of spooked me. I remember thinking: She sounds just like her father—these are the sort
of things he says."

As the shot of me reading on the porch fades to black, Jackie's
voice-over concludes:

"You got that from him," it says, darker. "That look too—that flat
way of looking over people. Sometimes it makes me feel gone."

But as Jackie's voice says this, her face comes up on-screen. She's
no longer laughing. She leans forward, over her plate, in a low-
buttoned blouse, her earrings swaying and eyes and lips dark in the
black and white. She's beautiful. And even more so for being unconscious of it—as always. She sits at the table she shared with Dorothy
at The Spinnaker. Her eyes, heavy-lidded from their long night, still
sparkle with reflected candles, while behind her, in the dark window, San Francisco shimmers like a picture of what a city skyline
should look like on a starry night. Compared to the hazy grays of
the scenes with me, the contrasts in Jackie's shot are sharp—everything's vivid. She's glamorously disheveled, with a strap escap-
ing one shoulder of her blouse as she gazes past her long, folded
hands up to our daughter—and us—watching Dorothy with such
unblushing affection it took everything in me to not reach out for
her as we watched.

Her voice-over fades out, taking the noisy restaurant background
with it.

Her face continues to fill the screen as the scene returns to slow
motion, with a new voice-over: a man's deep voice.

"Close enough?" he says. "That good?" There's a muffled affirma-
tion made off-mic.

On-screen, we see velvety vignettes of Jackie at the table, fading
in and out of all the emotions she'd felt that night: her half-buzzed
giggles, her surprised, big eyes when at a loss for words, her delight at
the taste of her food, a passing cloud of remorse, and the toothy smile
she makes to push sadness off. A little lipstick stains a front tooth. In
one shot, her hand reaches across the table for Dorothy, so close to
the camera it's clear she's forgotten it's there.

As this montage plays, the man's voice is stolid in contrast. It's Dick, sounding much less self-assured than he had minutes before, at the front door.

"Our shared history had been founded not so much on the things we said," he says, trying to hit his stride, "but on the things we both knew we would never say. Years ago, one unusually warm fall morning after one of the frequent nights she couldn't sleep, I'd come out early to this back room with my coffee and found her in the garden . . . in shorts, barefoot, her slender knees dimpled with pebbles as she weeded a row of radishes. The weeds were still wet with dew and lay limp in the paths between rows, and to one side sat a basket with a few green onions and three perfect, oversized lemons from the tree we'd planted when we first moved here. They glowed from within. I watched, quietly, because I'd so rarely seen her as I had just then, apart, as she was before I began to draw her inside. To speak at such moments means leaving them."

Dick's voice pauses. A page turns noisily.

On-screen, we see Jackie slowly push back from her plate, giddy with laughter; she stops short a moment and turns, behind her, to a white-haired woman who'd been scowling at her the whole time, at the next table, unnoticed until then. She laughs again, muted.

"Three years now after she left," says Dick's voice-over, "and what I miss most . . . is the chance to sit out here one last time and say: *I see what you're showing me—I'm alone now too.* I used to think it was something I could say to no one else—that it was a private understanding only she could share. Now I know that's not true."

It honestly took some time for me to realize: These are my words. Dorothy must have transcribed them from our conversation on the porch, after some night she sat out with me. She simply replaced Jackie with a pronoun. How it changed me, being read out loud by someone else; I felt disembodied and intact at once. It didn't sound like Dick knew the script wasn't written by Dorothy; for all he knew she'd simply pulled a page from a book for his screen test. Which, in a way, she had. But now, sitting in our dark living room, we all understood.

As we watched the film, Dorothy remained standing behind our seats. Gerald shot her another anxious look, his profile blue-lit by the screen—*You're really doing this?*—but he turned back just as quickly so as not to miss a word. His mother sat immobile at his side, a tissue pressed to her nose.

On-screen, Jackie's face fades as the camera zooms deeper into the city skyline behind her. It focuses tightly on a few lights, which refract and widen like headlights on a wet window. The screen briefly goes dark.

The next scene we four knew well: It's a clip from our Super 8 home movies, from when Dorothy first began making videos in third grade. For this, she'd hidden herself with the camera in her closet, leaving the door ajar, waiting to scare Gerald when he opened it. Our family has replayed this clip so many times that we all know Dorothy is hiding, standing on a stool in an overcoat amid her hanging clothes, wearing a red devil mask from Halloween. She is nine years old, and Gerald barely five. Because the original Super 8 was smaller than her new film's format, in converting it she put the slightly grainy image inside a rounded frame, like an old television screen, so that, watching it, we all felt nostalgic from the first frame.

On-screen, shot through the narrow opening of the closet door, we see Gerald enter. He's just a little guy but his eyes are huge—his fear is obvious the second he enters her darkened bedroom. He steps only one foot in at first, flicking on the light and yelling back over his shoulder for reassurance. *Dad? Mom? Where's Dorothy?* he cries in a tiny voice that's all the more vulnerable for sounding like it's coming through an old telephone, long-distance.

Dorothy always loved playing practical jokes on him. For the first time, I saw how cruel that had been, and how isolated he must have felt, hearing us laugh at him all these years.

On-screen, through the crack in the closet door, we see Gerald retreat: He slowly backs up, withdrawing his foot from the room, into the hall behind him. Then he hears something and stops. The view shudders—Dorothy correcting her balance as she wobbles on the stool inside the closet—and his eyes widen at the creaking sound.

He pokes his foot back into the room, and with a smirk takes another step, toward the bed.

Oh, Dorothy? he says.

But then his audio goes silent as we hear Xenia in voice-over, with a bright echo, as if she were recorded in a glassed-in studio:

"My ex-husband—his mother is spiritual. She died when he was boy."

On-screen, we see Gerald drop fast to his knees by the bed. He gets down on his hands to peek underneath.

Xenia's voice says: "He goes to prison, and one night she comes to him. He was not spiritual; he is amazed. Dream or real? They mix up, in times of suffering."

On-screen, Gerald passes his hand deep under the bed. Finding nothing, he shoots back up to his feet. The screen shakes once again as young Dorothy's grip on the zoom choppily refocuses from the dark on his anxious, wet-nosed face as he notices the closet door ajar.

Xenia's voice says: "He tells me: He sees her holding candles. And she tells him: Pray with me. Pray, and I am with you. Here, now. And you are with me too."

Gerald's silly little smile grows as he tiptoes closer. He's sure he'll be the one to surprise her, where she's hiding.

Xenia's voice says: "So it is good you come and see."

His fingertips curl around the closet door.

"Go in," Xenia says.

Gerald yanks the door wide open and there's a sucking *whoosh*— the sound from the smoked glass entrance to the cathedral nave. In a brief flare of overexposed light, he freezes in terror facing Dorothy's mask. He gapes and screams, in silence, bug-eyed. He gulps and screams again, halting in slow motion, as his gummy, gap-toothed mouth becomes a tunnel we zoom down until the full screen fades to black.

None of us moved.

On-screen, a distant, haloed sun slowly descends from outside the frame. The soft sound of waves comes up as we're gently returned to the beach where we started, to face the golden retriever again. She's still digging, but the second she's back in focus she stops, perks up her ears at some distant call, and bounds away, leaving behind the sloppy hole she's dug as if she finally sees what she wants off-screen. Our view widens farther to include the shore, the surf, and, soon, the headlands and mountain beyond. As the horizon broadens, we hear more—the cries of kids and gulls, the waves bubbling and fizzing like the sound of sunshine itself as we pull back slowly to stand, at last, in the wind-bent grass.

"Where's Dorothy?" her voice-over says as the screen brightens to white. "Stop looking. I'm right here."

And so she was. With her hand on my shoulder.

I gazed at her until she knew how beautiful I'd found it all, and how clear everything had become. I watched the square blue light in her eyes, and in those frames I saw the world fast-forward. I saw how, tomorrow, she'll be approved for the procedure that will remove her pancreas, but which will also take the tumor—intact. I saw how we'll stay in this place for months, because we work so well here, and there's no longer any pressing distraction demanding our attention. Not now. And soon, when the economy topples and rents begin to fall, we'll look at new places together, for fun, once it's certain her operation was a near-miraculous, but not unheard-of, success. Because, to be healthy, you begin by living as if you already are. And because fifteen-to-seventeen percent is a one-in-six chance—not the worst odds. Not if you're lucky. And later still, when Dorothy one day finds someone new and she repacks her tapes and equipment and moves out on me again, I will still feel so very lucky. Because I will be.

ACKNOWLEDGMENTS

Many people have lit up the thirty years it took to tell this story, which I began in the son's seat and finished older than Jim Finley himself.

My parents, George and Peggy, never drew a line between what they dreamed and how they lived. Dad: Here's the log home you designed and built at seventy-five. Mom: I miss and hear you still.

My sister-in-law, Michele Hamilton, and her caregiver, my brother-in-law Chris Fricke, showed us all what bravery means in the face of cancer. May this honor them.

English teachers are my heroes, especially Barbara Spear in Southwick, Massachusetts. I'm also indebted to my tutors and classmates at St. John's College in Annapolis, and to the writers at San Francisco State, where Michelle Carter taught me to hear my voice. I'm thankful to the *Chicago Tribune* for publishing the story that evolved into a first chapter; to Annie Proulx and Liz Darhansoff for stunning, early encouragement; to Dave Blum for renewing that hope decades later; and finally, to Farley Chase and Jim McCoy, my intrepid agent and publisher who, along with the good people at University of Iowa Press, made a dream real.

There isn't room enough here to thank all the friends and colleagues who've been encouraging and helpful, but I must call out Julie Glass and Eric Bagan. I might not have gotten to this page without you.

Finally, deepest thanks go to my best friend and wife, Kee Fricke-Pothier. "Being there together" with you all these years has been so very much more than "enough," and always will be.